For Janet and Mark

THE LAKE

25 — xii — 1980.

G000017446

BY THE SAME AUTHOR

(from this publisher)

The Untilled Field
Hail and Farewell
Drama in Muslin

THE LAKE

by
George Moore

With an Afterword by Richard Allen Cave

COLIN SMYTHE
Gerrards Cross, 1980

Copyright 1905, 1921 by George Moore
This edition copyright © 1980 by Richard Cave
First edition 1905, 2nd edition 1905, 3rd edition 1921.

This edition first published by Colin Smythe Ltd.
P.O. Box 6, Gerrards Cross, Buckinghamshire
in 1980

British Library Cataloguing in Publication Data

Moore, George, *b. 1852*
The lake. – 3rd ed.
I. Title
823′.8   PR5042.L/

ISBN 0–900675–75–6
ISBN 0–901072–82–6 Pbk

Set by Inforum Ltd., Portsmouth
and printed and bound by Billing & Sons Ltd.
Guildford, London & Worcester

CONTENTS

Epître dédicatoire (1905)   vii

Preface to the New Edition of 1921   ix

The Lake   1

Afterword by Richard Allen Cave   181

Appendices

A.   Chapter IX of the first edition of 1905   241

B.   Gogarty's dinner party, from the second
1905 edition   259

C.   'King and Hermit' and 'The Monk And His Pet'
translated by Kuno Meyer   269

ÉPÎTRE DÉDICATOIRE

17 Août, 1905.

MON CHER DUJARDIN,

Il se trouve que je suis à Paris en train de corriger mes épreuves au moment où vous donnez les dernières retouches au manuscrit de 'La Source du Fleuve Chrétien,' un beau titre — si beau que je n'ai pu m'empêcher de le 'chipper' pour le livre de Ralph Elles, un personnage de mon roman qui ne paraît pas, mais dont on entend beaucoup parler. Pour vous dédommager de mon larcin, je me propose de vous dédier 'Le Lac'. Il y a bien des raisons pour que je désire voir votre nom sur la première page d'un livre de moi; la meilleure est, peut-être, parceque vous êtes mon ami depuis 'Les Confessions d'un Jeune Anglais' qui ont paru dans votre jolie *Revue Indépendante;* et, depuis cette bienheureuse année, nous avons causé littérature et musique, combien de fois! Combien d'heures nous avons passées ensemble, causant, toujours causant, dans votre belle maison de Fontainebleau, si française avec sa terrasse en pierre et son jardin avec ses gazons maigres et ses allées sablonneuses qui serpentent parmi les grands arbres forestiers. C'est dans ce jardin à l'orée de la forêt et dans la forêt même, parmi la mélancolie de la nature primitive, et à Valvins où demeurait notre vieil ami Mallarmé, triste et charmant bonhomme, comme le pays du reste (n'est-ce-pas que cette tristesse croît depuis qu'il s'en est allé?) que vous m'avez entendu raconter 'Le Lac.'

A Valvins, la Seine coule silencieusement tout le long des berges plates et graciles, avec des peupliers alignés; comme ils sont tristes au printemps, ces peupliers, surtout avant qu'ils ne deviennent verts, quand ils sont rougeâtres, posés contre un ciel gris, des ombres immobiles et ternes dans les eaux, dix fois tristes quand les hirondelles volent bas! Pour expliquer la tristesse de ce beau pays parsemé de châteaux vides, hanté par le souvenir des fêtes d'autrefois, il faudrait tout un orchestre. Je l'entends d'abord sur les violons; plus tard on ajouterait d'autres instruments, des cors sans doute; mais pour rendre la tristesse de mon pauvre pays là bas il ne faudrait pas tout cela. Je l'entends très bien sur une seule flute placée dans une île entourée des eaux d'un lac, le joueur assis sur les vagues ruines d'un réduit gallois ou bien Normand. Mais, cher ami, vous êtes Normand et peut-être bien que ce sont vos ancêtres qui ont pillé mon pays; c'est une raison de plus pour que je vous offre ce roman. Acceptez-le sans le connaître davantage et n'essayez pas de le lire; ne vous donnez pas la peine d'apprendre l'anglais pour lire 'Le Lac'; que le lac ne soit jamais traversé par vous! Et parce que vous allez rester fatalement sur le bord de 'mon lac' j'ai un double plaisir à vous le dédier. Lorsqu'on dédie un livre, on prévoit l'heure où l'ami le prend, jette un coup d'oeil et dit: 'Pourquoi m'a-t-il dédié une niaiserie pareille?' Toutes les choses de l'esprit, sauf les plus grandes, deviennent niaiseries tôt ou tard. Votre ignorance de ma langue m'épargne cette heure fatale. Pour vous, mon livre sera toujours une belle et noble chose. Il ne peut jamais devenir pour vous banal comme une épouse. Il sera pour vous une vierge, mieux qu'une vierge, il sera pour vous une demi-vierge. Chaque fois que vous l'ouvrirez, vous penserez à des années écoulées, au jardin où les rossignols chantent, à la forêt où rien ne se passe sauf la chute des feuilles, à nos promenades à Valvins pour voir le cher bonhomme; vous penserez à votre jeunesse et peut-être un peu à la mienne. Mais je veux que vous lisiez cette dédicace, et c'est pour cela que je l'ai écrite en français, dans un français qui vous est très familier, le mien. Si je l'écrivais en anglais et le faisais traduire dans le langage à la dernière mode de Paris, vous ne retrouveriez pas les accents barbares de votre vieil ami. Ils sont barbares, je le conçois, mais il y a des chiens qui sont laids et que l'on finit par aimer.

Une poignée de mains,
GEORGES MOORE.

PREFACE

The concern of this preface is with the mistake that was made when 'The Lake' was excluded from the volume entitled 'The Untilled Field', reducing it to too slight dimensions, for bulk counts; and 'The Lake', too, in being published in a separate volume lost a great deal in range and power, and criticism was baffled by the division of stories written at the same time and coming out of the same happy inspiration, one that could hardly fail to beget stories in the mind of anybody prone to narrative — the return of a man to his native land, to its people, to memories hidden for years, forgotten, but which rose suddenly out of the darkness, like water out of the earth when a spring is tapped.

Some chance words passing between John Eglinton and me as we returned home one evening from Professor Dowden's were enough. He spoke, or I spoke, of a volume of Irish stories; Tourguéniev's name was mentioned, and next morning — if not the next morning, certainly not later than a few mornings after — I was writing 'Homesickness', while the story of 'The Exile' was taking shape in my mind. 'The Exile' was followed by a series of four stories, a sort of village odyssey. 'A Letter to Rome' is as good as these and as typical of my country. 'So on He Fares' is the one that, perhaps, out of the whole volume I like the best, always excepting 'The Lake', which, alas, was not included, but which belongs so strictly to the aforesaid stories that my memory includes it in the volume.

In expressing preferences I am transgressing an established rule of literary conduct, which ordains that an author must always speak of his own work with downcast eyes, excusing its existence on the ground of his own incapacity. All the same an author's preferences interest his readers, and having transgressed by telling that these Irish stories lie very near to my heart, I will proceed a little further into literary sin, confessing that my reason for liking 'The Lake' is related to the very great difficulty of the telling, for the one vital event in the priest's life befell him before the story opens, and to keep the story in the key in which it was conceived, it was necessary to recount the priest's life during the course of his walk by the shores of a lake, weaving his memories continually, without losing sight, however, of the long, winding, mere-like lake, wooded to its shores, with hills appearing and disappearing into mist and distance. The difficulty overcome is a joy to the artist, for in his conquest over the material he draws nigh to his idea, and in this book mine was the essential rather than the daily life of the priest, and as I read for this edition I seemed to hear it. The drama passes within the priest's soul; it is tied and untied by the flux and reflux of sentiments, inherent in and proper to his nature, and the weaving of a story out of the soul substance without ever seeking the aid of external circumstance seems to me a little triumph. It may be that I heard what none other will hear, not through his own fault but through mine, and it may be that all ears are not tuned, or are too indifferent or indolent to listen; it is easier to hear 'Esther Waters' and to watch her struggles for her child's life than to hear the mysterious warble, soft as lake water, that abides in the heart. But I think there will be a few who will agree with me that there is as much life in 'The Lake', as there is in 'Esther Waters' — a different kind of life, not so wide a life, perhaps, but what counts in art is not width but depth.

Artists, it is said, are not good judges of their own works, and for that reason, and other reasons, maybe, it is considered to be unbecoming for a writer to praise himself. So to make atonement for the sins I have committed in this preface, I will confess to very little admiration for 'Evelyn Innes' and 'Sister Teresa'. The writing of 'Evelyn Innes' and 'Sister Teresa' was useful to me inasmuch that if I had not written them I could not have written 'The Lake' or 'The Brook Kerith'. It seems ungrateful, therefore, to refuse to allow two of my most successful books into the canon merely because they do not correspond with my aestheticism. But a writer's aestheticism is his all; he cannot surrender it, for his art

x

is dependent upon it, and the single concession he can make is that if an overwhelming demand should arise for these books when he is among the gone — a storm before which the reed must bend — the publisher shall be permitted to print 'Evelyn Innes' and 'Sister Teresa' from the original editions, it being, however, clearly understood that they are offered to the public only as apocrypha. But this permission must not be understood to extend to certain books on which my name appears — viz., 'Mike Fletcher', 'Vain Fortune', 'Parnell and His Island'; to some plays, 'Martin Luther', 'The Strike at Arlingford', 'The Bending of the Boughs'; to a couple of volumes of verse entitled 'Pagan Poems' and 'Flowers of Passion' — all these books, if they are ever reprinted again, should be issued as the work of a disciple — Amico Moorini I put forward as a suggestion.

G.M.

I

It was one of those enticing days at the beginning of May when
white clouds are drawn about the earth like curtains. The lake lay
like a mirror that somebody had breathed upon, the brown
islands showing through the mist faintly, with gray shadows falling into the water, blurred at the edges. The ducks were talking
in the reeds, the reeds themselves were talking, and the water
lapping softly about the smooth limestone shingle. But there was
an impulse in the gentle day, and, turning from the sandy spit,
Father Oliver walked to and fro along the disused cart-track
about the edge of the wood, asking himself if he were going
home, knowing very well that he could not bring himself to
interview his parishioners that morning.

On a sudden resolve to escape from anyone that might be
seeking him, he went into the wood and lay down on the warm
grass, and admired the thickly-tasselled branches of the tall
larches swinging above him. At a little distance among the
juniper-bushes, between the lake and the wood, a bird uttered a
cry like two stones clinked sharply together, and getting up he
followed the bird, trying to catch sight of it, but always failing to
do so; it seemed to range in a circle about certain trees, and he
hadn't gone very far when he heard it behind him. A stonechat he
was sure it must be, and he wandered on till he came to a great
silver fir, and thought that he spied a pigeon's nest among the
multitudinous branches. The nest, if it were one, was about sixty
feet from the ground, perhaps more than that; and, remembering that the great fir had grown out of a single seed, it seemed
to him not at all wonderful that people had once worshipped

trees, so mysterious is their life, so remote from ours. And he stood a long time looking up, hardly able to resist the temptation to climb the tree—not to rob the nest like a boy, but to admire the two gray eggs which he would find lying on some bare twigs.

At the edge of the wood there were some chestnuts and sycamores. He noticed that the large-patterned leaf of the sycamores, hanging out from a longer stem, was darker than the chestnut leaf. There were some elms close by, and their half-opened leaves, dainty and frail, reminded him of clouds of butterflies. He could think of nothing else. White, cotton-like clouds unfolded above the blossoming trees; patches of blue appeared and disappeared; and he wandered on again, beguiled this time by many errant scents and wilful little breezes.

Very soon he came upon some fields, and as he walked through the ferns the young rabbits ran from under his feet, and he thought of the delicious meals that the fox would snap up. He had to pick his way, for thorn-bushes and hazels were springing up everywhere. Derrinrush, the great headland stretching nearly a mile into the lake, said to be one of the original forests, was extending inland. He remembered it as a deep, religious wood, with its own particular smell of reeds and rushes. It went further back than the island castles, further back than the Druids; and was among Father Oliver's earliest recollections. Himself and his brother James used to go there when they were boys to cut hazel stems, to make fishing-rods; and one had only to turn over the dead leaves to discover the chips scattered circlewise in the open spaces where the coopers sat in the days gone by making hoops for barrels. But iron hoops were now used instead of hazel, and the coopers worked there no more. In the old days he and his brother James used to follow the wood-ranger, asking him questions about the wild creatures of the wood — badgers, marten cats, and otters. And one day they took home a nest of young hawks. He did not neglect to feed them, but they had eaten each other, nevertheless. He forgot what became of the last one.

A thick yellow smell hung on the still air. 'A fox', he said, and he trailed the animal through the hazel-bushes till he came to a rough shore, covered with juniper-bushes and tussocked grass, the extreme point of the headland, whence he could see the mountains — the pale southern mountains mingling with the white sky, and the western mountains, much nearer, showing in bold relief. The beautiful motion and variety of the hills delighted him, and there was as much various colour as there were many dips and curves, for the hills were not far enough away to dwindle to one blue tint; they were blue, but the pink heather showed through the blue, and the clouds continued to fold and unfold, so that neither the colour nor the lines were ever the same. The retreating and advancing of the great masses and the delicate illumination of the crests could be watched without weariness. It was like listening to music. Slieve Cairn showing straight as a bull's back against the white sky, a cloud filling the gap between Slieve Cairn and Slieve Louan, a quaint little hill like a hunchback going down a road. Slieve Louan was followed by a great boulder-like hill turned sideways, the top indented like a crater, and the priest likened the long, low profile of the next hill to a reptile raising itself on its forepaws.

He stood at gaze, bewitched by the play of light and shadow among the slopes; and when he turned towards the lake again, he was surprised to see a yacht by Castle Island. A random breeze just sprung up had borne her so far, and now she lay becalmed, carrying, without doubt, a pleasure-party, inspired by some vague interest in ruins, and a very real interest in lunch; or the yacht's destination might be Kilronan Abbey, and the priest wondered if there were water enough in the strait to let her through in this season of the year. The sails flapped in the puffing breeze, and he began to calculate her tonnage, certain that if he had such a boat he would not be sailing her on a lake, but on the bright sea, out of sight of land, in the middle of a great circle of water. As if stung by a sudden sense of sea, of its perfume and its freedom, he imagined the filling of the sails and the rattle of the ropes, and how a fair wind would carry him as far as the cove of Cork before morning. The run from Cork to Liverpool would be slower, but the wind might veer a little, and in four-and-twenty hours the Welsh mountains would begin to show above the horizon. But he would not land anywhere on the Welsh coast. There was nothing to see in Wales but castles, and he was weary of castles, and longed to see the cathedrals of York and Salisbury; for he had often seen them in pictures, and had more than once thought of a walking tour through England. Better still if the yacht were to land him somewhere on the French coast. England was, after all, only an island like Ireland — a little larger, but still an island — and he thought he would like a continent to roam in. The French cathedrals were more beautiful than the English, and it would be pleasant to wander in the French country in happy-go-lucky fashion, resting when he was tired, walking when it pleased him, taking an interest in whatever might strike his fancy.

It seemed to him that his desire was to be freed for a while from everything he had ever seen, and from everything he had ever heard. He merely wanted to wander, admiring everything there was to admire as he went. He didn't want to learn anything, only to admire. He was weary of argument, religious and political. It wasn't that he was indifferent to his country's welfare, but every mind requires rest, and he wished himself away in a foreign country, distracted every moment by new things, learning the language out of a volume of songs, and hearing music, any music, French or German — any music but Irish music. He sighed, and wondered why he sighed. Was it because he feared that if he once went away he might never come back?

This lake was beautiful, but he was tired of its low gray shores; he was tired of those mountains, melancholy as Irish melodies, and as beautiful. He felt suddenly that he didn't want to see a lake or a mountain for two months at least, and that his longing for a change was legitimate and most natural. It pleased him to remember that everyone likes to get out of his native country for a while, and he had only been out of sight of this lake in the years he spent in Maynooth. On leaving he had pleaded that he might be sent to live among the mountains by Kilronan Abbey, at the north end of the lake, but when Father Conway died he was moved round to the western shore; and every day since he walked by the lake, for there was nowhere else to walk, unless up and down the lawn under the sycamores, imitating Father Peter whose wont it was to walk there, reading his breviary, stopping from time to time to speak to a parishioner in the road below; he too used to read his breviary under the sycamores; but for one reason or another he walked there no longer, and every afternoon now found him standing at the end of this sandy spit, looking across the lake towards Tinnick, where he was born, and where his sisters lived.

He couldn't see the walls of the convent to-day, there was too much mist about; and he liked to see them; for whenever he saw them he began to think of his sister Eliza, and he liked to think of her — she was his favourite sister. They were nearly the same age, and had played together; and his eyes dwelt in memory on the dark corner under the stairs where they used to play. He could even see their toys through the years, and the tall clock which used to tell them that it was time to put them aside. Eliza was only eighteen months older than he; they were the red-haired ones, and though they were as different in mind as it was possible to be, he seemed nearer Eliza than anyone else. In what this affinity consisted he couldn't say, but he had always felt himself of the same flesh and blood. Neither his father nor mother had inspired this sense of affinity; and his sister Mary and his brothers seemed to him merely people whom he had known always — not more than that; whereas Eliza was quite different, and perhaps it was this very mutuality, which he could not define, that had decided their vocations.

No doubt there is a moment in every man's life when something happens to turn him into the road which he is destined to follow; for all that it would be superficial to think that the fate of one's life is dependent upon accident. The accident that turns one into the road is only the means which Providence takes to procure the working out of certain ends. Accidents are many: life is as full of accidents as a fire is full of sparks, and any spark is enough to set fire to the train. The train escapes a thousand, but at last a spark lights it, and this spark always seems to use the only one that could have done it. We cannot imagine how the same result could have been obtained otherwise. But other ways would have been found; for Nature is full of resource, and if Eliza had not been by to fire the idea hidden in him, something else would. She was the means, but only the means, for no man escapes his vocation, and the priesthood was his. A vocation always finds a way out. But was he sure if it hadn't been for Eliza that he wouldn't have married Annie McGrath? He didn't think he would have married Annie, but he might have married another. All the same, Annie was a good, comfortable girl, a girl that everybody was sure would make a good wife for any man, and at that time many people were thinking that he should marry Annie. On looking back he couldn't honestly say that a stray thought of Annie hadn't found its way into his mind; but not into his heart — there is a difference.

At that time he was what is known as a growing lad; he was seventeen. His father was then dead two years, and his mother looked to him, he being the eldest, to take charge of the shop, for at that time it was almost settled that James was to go to America. They had two or three nice grass farms just beyond the town: Patsy was going to have them; and his sisters' fortunes were in the bank, and very good fortunes they were. They had a hundred pounds apiece and should have married well. Eliza could have married whomever she pleased. Mary could have married too, and to this day he couldn't tell why she hadn't married.

The chances his sister Mary had missed rose up in his mind — why, he did not know; and a little bored by these memories, he suddenly became absorbed in the little bleat of a blackcap perched on a bush, the only one amid a bed of flags and rushes; 'an alder-bush', he said. 'His mate is sitting on her eggs, and there are some wood-gatherers about; that's what's worrying the little fellow.' The bird continued to utter its troubled bleat, and the priest walked on, thinking how different was its evensong. He meditated an excursion to hear it, and then, without his being aware of any transition, his thoughts returned to his sister Mary, and to the time when he had once indulged in hopes that the mills along the river-side might be rebuilt and Tinnick restored to its former commercial prosperity. He was not certain if he had ever really believed that he might set these mills going, or if he had, he encouraged an illusion, knowing it to be one. He was only certain of this, that when he was a boy and saw no life ahead of him except that of a Tinnick shopman, he used to feel that if he remained at home he must have the excitement of adventure. The beautiful river, with its lime-trees, appealed to his imagination; the rebuilding of the mills and the reorganization of trade, if he succeeded in reorganizing trade, would mean spending his mornings on the wharves by the river-side, and in those days his one desire was to escape from the shop. He looked upon the shop as a prison. In those days he liked dreaming, and it was pleasant to dream of giving back to Tinnick its trade of former days; but when his mother asked him what steps he intended to take to get the necessary capital, he lost his temper with her. He must have known that he could never make enough money in the shop to set the mills working! He must have known that he would never take his father's place at the desk by the dusty window! But if he shrank from an avowal it was because he had no other proposal to make. His mother understood him, though the others didn't, and seeing his inability to say what kind of work he would put his hand to, she had spoken of Annie McGrath. She didn't say he should marry Annie — she was a clever woman in her way — she merely said that Annie's relations in America could afford to supply sufficient capital to start one of the mills. But he never wanted to marry Annie, and couldn't do else but snap when the subject was mentioned, and many's the time he told his mother that if the mills were to pay it would be necessary to start business on a large scale. He was an impracticable lad and even now he couldn't help smiling when he thought of the abruptness with which he would go down to the river-side to seek a new argument wherewith to confute his mother, to return happy when he had found one, and sit watching for an opportunity to raise the question again.

No, it wasn't because Annie's relations weren't rich enough that he hadn't wanted to marry her. And to account for his prejudice against marriage, he must suppose that some notion of the priesthood was stirring in him at the time, for one day, as he sat looking at Annie across the tea-table, he couldn't help thinking that it would be hard to live alongside of her year in and year out. Although a good and a pleasant girl, Annie was a bit tiresome to listen to, and she wasn't one of those who improve with age. As he sat looking at her, he seemed to understand, as he had never understood before, that if he married her all that had happened in the years back would happen again — more children scrambling about the counter, with a shopman (himself) by the dusty window putting his pen behind his ear, just as his father did when he came forward to serve some country woman with half a pound of tea or a hank of onions.

And as these thoughts were passing through his mind, he remembered hearing his mother say that Annie's sister was thinking of starting dressmaking in the High Street. 'It would be nice if Eliza were to join her,' his mother added casually. Eliza laid aside the skirt she was turning, raised her eyes and stared at mother, as if she were surprised mother could say anything so stupid. 'I'm going to be a nun,' she said, and, just as if she didn't wish to answer any questions, went on sewing. Well might they be surprised, for not one of them suspected Eliza of religious inclinations. She wasn't more pious than another, and when they asked her if she were joking, she looked at them as if she thought the question very stupid, and they didn't ask her any more.

She wasn't more than fifteen at the time, yet she spoke out of her own mind. At the time they thought she had been thinking on the matter — considering her future. A child of fifteen doesn't consider, but a child of fifteen may *know*, and after he had seen the look which greeted his mother's remarks, and heard Eliza's simple answer, 'I've decided to be a nun,' he never doubted that what she said was true. From that day she became for him a different being; and when she told him, feeling, perhaps, that he sympathized with her more than the others did, that one day she would be Reverend Mother of the Tinnick Convent, he felt convinced that she knew what she was saying — how she knew he could not say.

His childhood had been a slumber, with occasional awakenings or half awakenings, and Eliza's announcement that she intended to enter the religious life was the first real awakening; and this awakening first took the form of an acute interest in Eliza's character, and, persuaded that she or her prototype had already existed, he searched the lives of the saints for an account of her, finding many partial portraits of her; certain typical traits in the lives of three or four saints reminded him of Eliza, but there was no complete portrait. The strangest part of the business was that he traced his vocation to his search for Eliza in the lives of the saints. Everything that happened afterwards was the emotional sequence of taking down the books from the shelf. He didn't exaggerate; it was possible his life might have taken a different turn, for up to that time he had only read books of adventure — stories about robbers and pirates. As if by magic, his interest in such stories passed clean out of his mind, or was exchanged for an extraordinary enthusiasm for saints, who by renouncement of animal life had contrived to steal up to the last bounds, whence they could see into the eternal life that lies beyond the grave. Once this power was admitted, what interest could we find in the feeble ambitions of temporal life, whose scope is limited to three score and ten years? And who could doubt that saints attained the eternal life, which is God, while still living in the temporal flesh? For did not the miracles of the saints prove that they were no longer subject to natural laws? Ancient Ireland, perhaps, more than any other country, understood the supremacy of spirit over matter, and strove to escape through mortifications from the prison of the flesh. Without doubt great numbers in Ireland had fled from the torment of actual life into the wilderness. If the shore and the islands on this lake were dotted with fortress castles, it was the Welsh and the Normans who built them, and the priest remembered how his mind took fire when he first heard of the hermit who lived in Church Island, and how disappointed he was when he heard that Church Island was ten miles away, at the other end of the lake.

For he could not row himself so far; distance and danger compelled him to consider the islands facing Tinnick — two large islands covered with brushwood, ugly brown patches — ugly as their names, Horse Island and Hog Island, whereas Castle Island had always seemed to him a suitable island for a hermitage, far more so than Castle Hag. Castle Hag was too small and bleak to engage the attention of a sixth-century hermit. But there were trees on Castle Island, and out of the ruins of the castle a comfortable sheiling could be built, and the ground thus freed from the ruins of the Welshman's castle might be cultivated. He remembered commandeering the fisherman's boat, and rowing himself out, taking a tape to measure, and how, after much application of the tape, he had satisfied himself that there was enough arable land in the island for a garden; he had walked down the island certain that a quarter of an acre could grow enough vegetables to support a hermit, and that a goat would be able to pick a living among the bushes and the tussocked grass: even a hermit might have a goat, and he didn't think he could live without milk. He must have been a long time measuring out his garden, for when he returned to his boat the appearance of the lake frightened him; it was full of blustering waves, and it wasn't likely he'd ever forget his struggle to get the boat back to Tinnick. He left it where he had found it, at the mouth of the river by the fisherman's hut, and returning home thinking how he would have to import a little hay occasionally for the goat. Nor would this be all; he would have to go on shore every Sunday to hear Mass, unless he built a chapel. The hermit of Church Island had an oratory in which he said Mass! But if he left his island every Sunday his hermitage would be a mockery. For the moment he couldn't see how he was to build a chapel — a sheiling, perhaps; a chapel was out of the question, he feared.

He would have to have vestments and a chalice, and, immersed in the difficulty of obtaining these, he walked home, taking the path along the river from habit, not because he wished to consider afresh the problems of the ruined mills. The dream of restoring Tinnick to its commerce of former days was forgotten, and he walked on, thinking of his chalice, until he heard somebody call him. It was Eliza, and as they leaned over the parapet of the bridge, he could not keep himself from telling her that he had rowed out to Castle Island, never thinking that she would reprove him, and sternly, for taking the fisherman's boat without asking leave. It was no use to argue with Eliza that the fisherman didn't want his boat, the day being too rough for fishing. What did she know about fishing? She had asked very sharply what brought him out to Castle Island on such a day. There was no use saying he didn't know; he never was able to keep a secret from Eliza, and feeling that he must confide in somebody, he told her he was tired of living at home, and was thinking of building a sheiling on the island.

Eliza didn't understand, and she understood still less when he spoke of a beehive hut, such as the ancient hermits of Ireland lived in. She was entirely without imagination; but what surprised him still more than her lack of sympathy with his dream-project was her inability to understand an idea so inherent in Christianity as the hermitage, for at that time Eliza's mind was made up to enter the religious life. He waited a long time for her answer, but the only answer she made was that in the early centuries a man was either a bandit or a hermit. This wasn't true: life was peaceful in Ireland in the sixth and seventh centuries; even if it weren't, she ought to have understood that change of circumstance cannot alter an idea so inherent in man as the hermitage, and when he asked her if she intended to found a new Order, or to go out to Patagonia to teach the Indians, she laughed, saying she was much more interested in a laundry than in the Indians. Her plea that the Tinnick Convent was always in straits for money did not appeal to him then any more than it did to-day.

'The officers in Tinnick have to send their washing to Dublin. A fine reason for entering a convent,' he answered.

But quite unmoved by the sarcasm, she replied that a woman can do nothing unless she be a member of a congregation. He shrank from Eliza's mind as from the touch of something coarse, and his suggestion that the object of the religious life is meditation did not embarrass her in the very least, and he remembered well how she had said:

'Putting aside for the moment the important question whether there may or may not be hermits in the twentieth century, tell me, Oliver, are you thinking of marrying Annie McGrath? You know she has rich relations in America, and you might get them to supply the capital to set the mills going. The mills would be a great advantage. Annie has a good head-piece, and would be able to take the shop off your hands, leaving you free to look after the mills.'

'The mills, Eliza! there are other things in the world beside those mills!'

'A hermitage on Castle Island?

Eliza could be very impertinent when she liked. If she had no concern in what was being said, she looked round, displaying an irritating curiosity in every passer-by, and true to herself she had drawn his attention to the ducks on the river while he was telling her of the great change that had come over him. He had felt like boxing her ears. But the moment he began to speak of taking Orders she forgot all about the ducks; her eyes were fixed upon him, she listened to his every word, and when he finished speaking, she reminded him there had always been a priest in the family. All her wits were awake. He was the one of the family who had shown most aptitutde for learning, and their cousin the Bishop would be able to help him. What she would like would be to see him parish priest of Tinnick. The parish was one of the best in the diocese. Not a doubt of it, she was thinking at that moment of the advantage this arrangement would be to her when she was directing the affairs of the convent.

If there was no other, there was at least one woman in Ireland who was interested in things. He had never met anybody less interested in opinions or in ideas than Eliza. They had walked home together in silence, at all events not saying much, and that very evening she left the room immediately after supper. And soon after they heard the sounds of trunks being dragged along the passage; furniture was being moved, and when she came downstairs she just said she was going to sleep with Mary.

'Oliver is going to have my room. He must have a room to himself on account of his studies.'

On that she gathered up her sewing, and left him to explain. He felt that it was rather sly of her to go away like that, leaving all the explanation to him. She wanted him to be a priest, and was full of little tricks. There was no time for thinking it over. There was only just time to prepare for the examination. He worked hard, for his work interested him, especially the Latin language; but what interested him far more than his aptitude for learning whatever he made up his mind to learn was the discovery of a religious vocation in himself. Eliza feared that his interest in hermits sprang from a boyish taste for adventure rather than from religious feeling, but no sooner had he begun his studies for the priesthood, than he found himself overtaken and over-powered by an extraordinary religious fervour and by a desire for prayer and discipline. Never had a boy left home more zealous, more desirous to excel in piety and to strive for the honour and glory of the Church.

An expression of anger, almost of hatred, passed over Father Oliver's face, and he turned from the lake and walked a few yards rapidly, hoping to escape from memories of his folly; for he had made a great fool of himself, no doubt. But, after all, he preferred his enthusiasms, however exaggerated they might seem to him now, to the commonplace— he could not call it wisdom— of those whom he had taken into his confidence. It was foolish of him, no doubt, to have told how he used to go out in a boat and measure the ground about Castle Island, thinking to build himself a bee-hive hut out of the ruins. He knew too little of the world at that time; he had no idea how incapable the students were of under-standing anything outside the narrow interests of an ecclesiastical career. Anyhow, he had had the satisfaction of having beaten them in all the examinations; and if he had cared to go in for advancement, he could have easily got ahead of them all, for he had better brains and better interest than any of them. When he last saw that ignorant brute Peter Fahy, Fahy asked him if he still put pebbles in his shoes. It was to Fahy he had confided the cause of his lameness, and Fahy had told on him; he was ridiculously innocent in those days, and he could still see them gathered about him, pretending not to believe that he kept a cat-o'-nine-tails in his room, and scourged himself at night. It was Tom Bryan who said that he wouldn't mind betting a couple of shillings that Gogarty's whip wouldn't draw a squeal from a pig on the road-side. The answer to that was: 'A touch will make a pig squeal: you should have said an ass!' But at the moment he couldn't think of an answer.

No doubt everyone looked on him as a ninny, and they persuaded him to prove to them that his whip was a real whip by letting Tom Bryan do the whipping for him. Tom Bryan was a rough fellow, who ought to have been driving a plough; a ploughman's life was too peaceful an occupation for him — a drover's life would have suited him best, prodding his cattle along the road with a goad; it was said that was how he maintained his authority in the parish. The remembrance of the day he bared his back to that fellow was still a bitter one. With a gentle smile he had handed the whip to Tom Bryan, the very smile which he imagined the hermits of old times used to wear. The first blow had so stunned him that he couldn't cry out, and this blow was followed by a second which sent the blood flaming through his veins, and then by another which brought all the blood into one point in his body. He seemed to lose consciousness of everything but three inches of back. Nine blows he bore without wincing; the tenth overcame his fortitude, and he had reeled away from Tom Bryan.

Tom had exchanged the whip he had given him for a great leather belt; that was why he had been hurt so grievously — hurt till the pain seemed to reach his very heart. Tom had belted him with all his strength; and half a dozen of Tom's pals were waiting outside the door, and they came into the room, their wide mouths agrin, asking him how he liked it. But they were unready for the pain his face expressed, and in the midst of his agony he noticed that already they foresaw consequences, and he heard them reprove Tom Bryan, their intention being to dissociate themselves from him. Cowards! cowards! cowards!

They tried to help him on with his shirt, but he had been too badly beaten, and Tom Bryan came up in the evening to ask him not to tell on him. He promised, and he wouldn't have told if he could have helped it. But some explanation had to be forthcoming — he couldn't lie on his back. The doctor was sent for. . . .

And next day he was told the President wished to see him. The President was Eliza over again; hermits and hermitages were all very well in the early centuries, but religion had advanced, and nowadays a steadfast piety was more suited to modern requirements than pebbles in the shoes. If it had been possible to leave for America that day he thought he would have gone. But he couldn't leave Maynooth because he had been fool enough to bare his back to Tom Bryan. He couldn't return home to tell such a story as that. All Tinnick would be laughing at him, and Eliza, what would she think of him? He wasn't such a fool as the Maynooth students thought him, and he realized at once that he must stay in Maynooth and live down remembrance of his folly. So, as the saying goes, he took the bit between his teeth.

The necessity of living down his first folly, of creating a new idea of himself in the minds of the students, forced him to apply all his intelligence to his studies, and he made extraordinary progress in the first years. The recollection of the ease with which he out-distanced his fellow-students was as pleasant as the breezes about the lake, and his thoughts dwelt on the opinion which he knew was entertained, that for many years no one at Maynooth had shown such aptitude for scholarship. He only had to look at a book to know more about it than his fellow-students would know if they were to spend days over it. He won honours. He could have won greater honours, but his conscience reminded him that the gifts he received from God were not bestowed upon him for the mere purpose of humiliating his fellow-students. He often felt then that if certain talents had been given to him, they were given to him to use for the greater glory of God rather than for his own glorification; and his feeling was that there was nothing more hateful in God's sight than intellectual, unless perhaps spiritual, pride, and his object during his last years at Maynooth was to exhibit himself to the least advantage.

It is strange how an idea enters the soul and remakes it, and when he left Maynooth he used his influence with his cousin, the Bishop, to get himself appointed to the poorest parish in Connaught. Eliza had to dissemble, but he knew that in her heart she was furious with him. We are all extraordinarily different one from another, and if we seem most different from those whom we are most like, it is because we know nothing at all about strangers. He had gone to Kilronan in spite of Eliza, in spite of everyone, their cousin the Bishop included. He had been very happy in Bridget Clery's cottage, so happy that he didn't know himself why he ever consented to leave Kilronan.

No, it was not because he was too happy there. He had to a certain extent outgrown his very delicate conscience.

II

A BREEZE rose, the forest murmured, a bird sang, and the sails of
the yacht filled. The priest stood watching her pass behind a
rocky headland, knowing now that her destination was Kilronan
Abbey. But was there water enough in the strait at this season of
the year? Hardly enough to float a boat of her size. If she stuck,
the picnic-party would get into the small boat, and, thus light-
ened, the yacht might be floated into the other arm of the lake. 'A
pleasant day indeed for a sail', and in imagination he followed the
yacht down the lake, past its different castles, Castle Carra and
Castle Burke and Church Island, the island on which Marban —
Marban, the famous hermit poet, had lived.

It seemed to him strange that he had never thought of visiting
the ruined church when he lived close by at the northern end of
the lake. His time used to be entirely taken up with attending to
the wants of his poor people, and the first year he spent in
Garranard he had thought only of the possibility of inducing the
Goverment to build a bridge across the strait. That bridge was
badly wanted. All the western side of the lake was cut off from
railway communication. Tinnick was the terminus, but to get to
Tinnick one had to go round the lake, either by the northern or
the southern end, and it was always a question which was the
longer road — round by Kilronan Abbey or by the Bridge of Keel.
Many people said the southern road was shorter, but the difference wasn't more than a mile, if that, and Father Oliver preferred
the northern road; for it took him by his curate's house, and he
could always stop there and give his horse a feed and a rest; and
he liked to revisit the abbey in which he had said Mass for so long,

and in which Mass had always been said for a thousand years, even since Cromwell had unroofed it, the celebrant sheltered by an arch, the congregation kneeling under the open sky, whether it rained or snowed.

The roofing of the abbey and the bridging of the strait were the two things that the parish was really interested in. He tried when he was in Kilronan to obtain the Archbishop's consent and collaboration; Moran was trying now: he did not know that he was succeeding any better; and Father Oliver reflected a while on the peculiar temperament of their diocesan, and jumping down from the rock on which he had been sitting, he wandered along the sunny shore, thinking of the many letters he had addressed to the Board of Works on the subject of the bridge. The Board believed, or pretended to believe, that the parish could not afford the bridge; as well might it be urged that a cripple could not afford crutches. Without doubt a public meeting should be held; and in some little indignation Father Oliver began to think that public opinion should be roused and organized. It was for him to do this: he was the people's natural leader; but for many months he had done nothing in the matter. Why, he didn't know himself. Perhaps he needed a holiday; perhaps he no longer believed the Government susceptible to public opinion; perhaps he had lost faith in the people themselves! The people were the same always; the people never change, only individuals change.

And at the end of the sandy spit, where some pines had grown and seeded, he stood looking across the silvery lake wondering if his parishioners had begun to notice the change that had come over him since Nora Glynn left the parish, and as her name came into his mind he was startled out of his reverie by the sound of voices, and turning from the lake, he saw two wood-gatherers coming down a little path through the juniper-bushes. He often hid himself in the woods when he saw somebody coming, but he couldn't do so now without betraying his intention, and he stayed where he was. The women passed on, bent under their loads. Whether they saw him or not he couldn't tell; they passed near enough for him to recognize them, and he remembered that they were in church the day he alluded to Nora in his sermon. A hundred yards further on the women unburdened and sat down to rest a while, and Father Oliver began to consider what their conversation might be. His habit of wandering away by himself had no doubt been noticed, and once it was noticed it would become a topic of conversation. 'And what they do be saying now is, "That he has never been the same man since he preached against the schoolmistress, for what should he be doing by the lake if he wasn't afraid that she made away with herself?" And perhaps they are right,' he said, and walked up the shore, hoping that as soon as he was out of sight the women would forget to tell when they returned home that they had seen him walking by the lake.

All the morning he had been trying to keep Nora Glynn out of his mind, but now, as he rambled, he could not put back the memory of the day he met her for the first time, nearly two years ago, for to-day was the fifteenth of May; it was about that time a little later in the year; it must have been in June, for the day was very hot, and he had been riding fast, not wishing to keep Catherine's dinner waiting, and as he pushed his bicycle through the gate, he saw the great cheery man, Father Peter, with a face like an apple, walking up and down the sycamores reading his breviary. It must have been in June, for the mowers were in the field opposite, in the field known as the priest's field, though Father Peter had never rented it. There had never been such weather in Ireland before, and the day he rode his bicycle over to see Father Peter seemed to him the hottest day of all. But he had heard of the new schoolmistress's musical talents, and despite the heat of the day had ridden over, so anxious was he to hear if Father Peter were satisfied with her in all other respects. 'We shall be able to talk better in the shade of the sycamores,' Father Peter said, and on this they crossed the lawn, but not many steps were taken back and forth before Father Peter began to throw out hints that he didn't think Miss Glynn was altogether suited to the parish.

'But if you're satisfied with her discipline,' Father Oliver jerked out, and it was all he could do to check himself from further snaps at the parish priest, a great burly man who could not tell a minor from a major chord, yet was venting the opinion that good singing distracted the attention of the congregation at their prayers. He would have liked to ask him if he was to understand that bad singing tended to a devotional mood, but wishing to remain on good terms with his superior, he said nothing and waited for Father Peter to state his case against the new schoolmistress, which he seemed to think could be done by speaking of the danger of young unmarried women in the parish. It was when they came to the break in the trees that Father Peter nudged him and said under his breath:

'Here is the young woman herself coming across the fields.'

He looked that way and saw a small, thin girl coming towards the stile. She hopped over it as if she enjoyed the little jump into the road. Father Peter called to her and engaged her in conversation; and he continued to talk to her of indifferent things, no doubt with the view to giving him an opportunity of observing her. But they saw her with different eyes: whereas Father Peter descried in her one that might become a mischief in the parish, he could discover no dangerous beauty in her, merely a crumpled little face that nobody would notice were it not for the eyes and forehead. The forehead was broad and well shapen and promised an intelligence that the eyes were quick to confirm; round, gray, intelligent eyes, smiling, welcoming eyes. Her accent caressed the ear, it was a very sweet one, only faintly Irish, and she talked easily and correctly, like one who enjoyed talking, laughing gaily, taking, he was afraid, undue pleasure in Father Peter's rough sallies, without heeding that he was trying to entrap her into some slight indiscretion of speech that he could make use of afterwards, for he must needs justify himself to himself if he decided to dismiss her.

As he had been asked to notice her he remarked her shining brown hair. It frizzled like a furze-bush about her tiny face, and curled over her forehead. Her white even teeth showed prettily between her lips. She was not without points, but notwithstanding these it could not be said that she deserved the adjective pretty; and he was already convinced that it was not good looks that prejudiced her in Father Peter's eyes. Nor was the excuse that her singing attracted too much attention an honest one. What Father Peter did not like about the girl was her independent mind, which displayed itself in every gesture, in the way she hopped over the stile, and the manner with which she toyed with her parasol — a parasol that seemed a little out of keeping with her position, it is true. A very fine parasol it was; a blue silk parasol. Her independence betrayed itself in her voice: she talked to the parish priest with due respect, but her independent mind informed every sentence, even the smallest, and that was why she was going to be dismissed from her post. It was shameful that a grave injustice should be done to a girl who was admittedly competent in the fulfilment of all her duties, and he had not tried to conceal his opinion from Father Peter during dinner and after dinner, leaving him somewhat earlier than usual, for nothing affronted him more than injustice, especially ecclesiastical injustice.

As he rode his bicycle down the lonely road to Bridget's cottage, the thought passed through his mind that if Nora Glynn were a stupid, intelligent woman no objection would have been raised against her. 'An independent mind is very objectionable to the ecclesiastic,' he said to himself as he leaped off his bicycle . . . 'Nora Glynn. How well suited the name is to her. There is a smack in the name. Glynn, Nora Glynn,' he repeated, and it seemed to him that the name belonged exclusively to her.

A few days after this first meeting he met her about two miles from Garranard; he was on his bicycle, she was on hers, and they both leaped instinctively from their machines. What impressed him this time far more than her looks was her happy, original mind. While walking beside her he caught himself thinking that he had never seen a really happy face before. But she was going to be sent away because she was happy and wore her soul in her face.

They had seemed unable to get away from each other, so much had they to say. He mentioned his brother James, who was doing well in America and would perhaps one day send them the price of a harmonium. She told him she couldn't play on the wheezy old thing at Garranard, and at the moment he clean forgot that the new harmonium would avail her little, since Father Peter was going to get rid of her; he only remembered it as he got on his bicycle, and he returned home ready to espouse her cause against anybody.

She must write to the Archbishop, and if he wouldn't do anything she must write to the papers. Influence must be brought to bear, and Father Peter must be prevented from perpetrating a gross injustice. He felt that it would be impossible for him to remain Father Peter's curate if the schoolmistress were sent away for no fault of hers, merely because she wore a happy face. What Father Peter would have done if he had lived no one would ever know. He might have dismissed her; even so the injustice would have been slight compared with what had happened to her; and the memory of the wrong that had been done to her put such a

pain into his heart that he seemed to lose sight of everything, till a
fish leaping in the languid lake awoke him, and he walked on,
absorbed in the memory of his mistake, his thoughts swinging
back to the day he had met her on the roadside, and to the events
that succeeded their meeting. Father Peter was taken ill, two days
after he was dead, before the end of the week he was in his coffin;
and it was left to him to turn Nora Glynn out of the parish. No
doubt other men had committed faults as grave as his; but they
had the strength to leave the matter in the hands of God, to say: 'I
can do nothing, I must put myself in the hands of God; let him
judge. He is all wise.' He hadn't their force of character. He
believed as firmly as they did, but, for some reason which he
couldn't explain to himself, he was unable to leave the matter in
God's hands, and was always thinking how he could get news of
her.

If it hadn't been for that woman, for that detestable Mrs.
O'Mara, who was the cause of so much evil-speaking in the parish!
. . . And with his heart full of hatred so black that it surprised him,
he asked himself if he could forgive that woman. God might, he
couldn't. And he fell to thinking how Mrs. O'Mara had long been
a curse upon the parish. Father Peter was more than once compelled to speak about her from the altar, and to make plain that the
stories she set going were untrue. Father Peter had warned him,
but warnings are no good; he had listened to her convinced at the
time that it was wrong and foolish to listen to scandalmongers, but
unable to resist that beguiling tongue, for Mrs. O'Mara had a
beguiling tongue — fool that he was, that he had been. There was
no use going over the wretched story again; he was weary of going
over it, and he tried to put it out of his mind. But it wouldn't be
put out of his mind, and in spite of himself he began to recall the
events of the fatal day. He had been out all the morning, walking
about with an engineer who was sent down by the Board of Works
to consider the possibility of building the bridge, and had just
come in to rest. Catherine had brought him a cup of tea; he was
sitting by the window, almost too tired to drink it. The door was
flung open. If Catherine had only asked him if he were at home to
visitors, he would have said he wasn't at home to Mrs. O'Mara, but
he wasn't asked; the door was flung open, and he found himself
face to face with the parish magpie. And before he could bless

himself she began to talk to him about the bridge, saying that she knew all about the engineer, how he had gotten his appointment, and what his qualifications were. It is easy to say one shouldn't listen to such gossips, but it is hard to shut one's ears or to let what one hears with one ear out the other ear, for she might be bringing him information that might be of use to him. So he listened, and when the bridge, and the advantage of it, had been discussed, she told him she had been staying at the convent. She had tales to tell about all the nuns and about all the pupils. She told him that half the Catholic families in Ireland had promised to send their daughters to Tinnick if Eliza succeeded in finding somebody who could teach music and singing. But Eliza didn't think there was anyone in the country qualified for the post but Nora Glynn. If Mrs. O'Mara could be believed, Eliza said that she could offer Nora Glynn more money than she was earning in Garranard. Until then he had only half listened to Mrs. O'Mara's chatter, for he disliked the woman — her chatter amused him only as the chatter of a bird might; but when he heard that his sister was trying to get his schoolmistress away from him he had flared up. 'Oh, but I don't think that your schoolmistress would suit a convent school. I shouldn't like my daughter — ' 'What do you mean?' Her face changed expression, and in her nasty mincing manner she began to throw out hints that Nora Glynn would not suit the nuns. He could see that she was concealing something — there was something at the back of her mind. Women of her sort want to be persuaded; their bits of scandal must be dragged from them by force; they are the unwilling victims who would say nothing if they could help it. She had said enough to oblige him to ask her to speak out, and she began to throw out hints about a man whom Nora used to meet on the hillside (she wouldn't give the man's name, she was too clever for that). She would only say that Nora had been seen on the hillside walking in lonely places with a man. Truly a detestable woman! His thoughts strayed from her for a moment, for it gave him pleasure to recollect that he had defended his schoolmistress. Didn't he say: 'Now, then, Mrs. O'Mara, if you have anything definite to say, say it, but I won't listen to vague charges.' 'Charges — who is making charges?' she asked, and he had unfortunately called her a liar. In the middle of the row she dropped a phrase: 'Anyhow, her appearance is against her.' And it was true that Nora Glynn's appearance had changed in the last few months. Seeing that her words had a certain effect, Mrs. O'Mara quieted down; and while he stood wondering if it could possibly be true that Nora had deceived them, that she had been living in sin all these months he suddenly heard Mrs. O'Mara saying that he was lacking in experience — which was quite true, but her way of saying it had roused the devil in him. Who was she that she should come telling him that he lacked experience? To be sure, he wasn't an old midwife, and that's what Mrs. O'Mara looked like, sitting before him.

He had lost control of himself, saying, 'Now, will you get out of this house, you old scandalmonger, or I'll take you by the shoulders and put you out!' And he had thrown the front-door open. What a look she gave him as she passed out! At that moment the clock struck three and he remembered suddenly that the children were coming out of school at that moment. It would have been better if he had waited. But he couldn't wait: he'd have gone mad if he'd waited; and he recalled how he had jumped into the road, squeezed through the stile, and run across the field. 'Why all this hurry?' he had asked himself.

She was locking up the desks; the children went by him, curt-seying, and he had to wait till the last one was past the door. Nora must have guessed his errand, for her face noticeably hardened. 'I've seen Mrs. O'Mara,' he blurted out, 'and she tells me that you've been walking with some man on the hillside in lonely places . . . Don't deny it if it is true.' 'I'm not going to deny anything that is true.' How brave she was! Her courage attracted him and softened his heart. But everything was true, alas! Everything. She told him that her plans were to steal out of the parish without saying a word to anyone, for she was determined not to disgrace him or the parish. She was thinking of him in all her trouble, and everything might have ended well if he had not asked her who the man was. She would not say, nor give any reasons why she wouldn't do so. Only this, that if the man had deserted her she didn't want anybody to bring him back, if he could be brought back; if the man were dead it were better to say nothing about him. 'But if it were his fault?' 'I don't see that that would make any difference.'

They went out of the school-house talking in quite a friendly way. There was a little drizzle in the air, and, opening her umbrella, she said, 'I'm afraid you'll get wet.' 'Get wet, get wet!

what matter?' he had answered impatiently, for the remark
annoyed him. By the hawthorn-bush he began to tell her again
that it would relieve his mind to know who the man was. She tried
to get away from him, but he wouldn't let her go; and catching her
by the arm he besought her, saying that it would relieve his mind.
How many times had he said that? But he wasn't able to persuade
her, notwithstanding his insistence that as a priest of the parish he
had a right to know. No doubt she had some very deep reason for
keeping her secret, or perhaps his authoritative manner was the
cause of her silence. However this might be, any words would
have been better than 'it would relieve my mind to know who the
man was.' 'Stupid, stupid, stupid!' he muttered to himself, and he
wandered from the cart-track into the wood.

It was impossible to say now why he had wished to press her
secret from her. It would be unpleasant for him, as priest of the
parish, to know that the man was living in the parish; but it would
be still more unpleasant if he knew who the man was. Nora's
seducer could be none other than one of the young soldiers who
had taken the fishing-lodge at the head of the lake. Mrs. O'Mara
had hinted that Nora had been seen with one of them on the hill,
and he thought how on a day like this she might have been led
away among the ferns. At that moment there came out of the
thicket a floating ball of thistle-down. 'It bloweth where it listeth,'
he said. 'Soldier or shepherd, what matter now she is gone?' and
rising to his feet and coming down the sloping lawn, overflowing
with the shade of the larches, he climbed through the hawthorns
growing out of a crumbled wall, and once at the edge of the lake,
he stood waiting for nothing seemingly but to hear the tiresome
clanking call of the stonechat, and he compared its reiterated call
with the words 'atonement', 'forgiveness', 'death', 'calamity',
words always clanking in his heart, for she might be lying at the
bottom of the lake, and some day a white phantom would rise
from the water and claim him.

His thoughts broke away, and he re-lived in memory the very
agony of mind he had endured when he went home after her
admission that she was with child. All that night, all next day, and
for how many days? Would the time ever come when he could
think of her without a pain in his heart? It is said that time brings
forgetfulness. Does it? On Saturday morning he had sat at his
window, asking himself if he should go down to see her or if he

should send for her. There were confessions in the afternoon, and expecting that she would come to confess to him, he had not sent for her. One never knows; perhaps it was her absence from confession that had angered him. His temper took a different turn that evening. All night he had lain awake; he must have been a little mad that night, for he could only think of the loss of a soul to God, and of God's love of chastity. All night long he had repeated with variations that it were better that all which our eyes see — this earth and the stars that are in being — should perish utterly, be crushed into dust, rather than a mortal sin should be committed; in an extraordinary lucidity of mind he continued to ponder on God's anger and his own responsibility towards God, and feeling all the while that there are times when we lose control of our minds, when we are a little mad. He foresaw his danger, but he could not do else than rise from his bed and begin to prepare his sermon, for he had to preach, and he could only preach on chastity and the displeasure sins against chastity cause to God. He could think but of this one thing, the displeasure God must feel against Nora and the seducer who had robbed her of the virtue God prized most in her. He must have said things that he would not have said at any other time. His brain was on fire that morning, and words rose to his lips — he knew not whence nor how they came, and he had no idea now of what he had said. He only knew that she left the church during his sermon; at what moment he did not know, nor did he know that she had left the parish till next day, when the children came up to tell him there was no schoolmistress. And from that day to this no news of her, nor any way of getting news of her.

His thoughts went to the hawthorn-trees, for he could not think of her any more for the moment, and it relieved his mind to examine the green pips that were beginning to appear among the leaves. 'The hawthorns will be in flower in another week,' he said; and he began to wonder at the beautiful order of the spring. The pear and the cherry were the first; these were followed by the apple, and after the apple came the lilac, the chestnut, and the laburnum. The forest trees, too, had their order. The ash was still leafless, but it was shedding its catkins, and in another fifteen days its light foliage would be dancing in the breeze. The oak was last of all. At that moment a swallow flitted from stone to stone, too tired to fly far, and he wondered whence it had come. A cuckoo called from a distant hill; it, too, had been away and had come back.

His eyes dwelt on the lake, refined and wistful, with reflections of islands and reeds, mysteriously still. Rose-coloured clouds descended, revealing many new and beautiful mountain forms, every pass and every crest distinguishable. It was the hour when the cormorants come home to roost, and he saw three black specks flying low about the glittering surface; rising from the water, they alighted with a flutter of wings on the corner wall of what remained of Castle Hag, 'and they will sleep there till morning,' he said, as he toiled up a little path, twisting through ferns and thorn-bushes. At the top of the hill was his house, the house Father Peter had built. Its appearance displeased him, and he stood for a long time watching the evening darkening, and the yacht being towed home, her sails lowered, the sailors in the rowing-boat.

'They will be well tired before they get her back to Tinnick;' and he turned and entered his house abruptly.

III

CATHERINE'S curiosity was a worry. As if he knew why he hadn't come home to his dinner! If she'd just finish putting the plates on the table and leave him. Of course, there had been callers. One man, the man he especially wished to see, had driven ten miles to see him. It was most unfortunate, but it couldn't be helped; he had felt that morning that he couldn't stay indoors — the business of the parish had somehow got upon his nerves, but not because he had been working hard. He had done but little work since she left the parish. Now was that story going to begin again? If it did, he should go out of his mind; and he looked round the room, thinking how a lonely evening breeds thoughts of discontent.

Most of the furniture in the room was Father Peter's. Father Peter had left his curate his furniture, but the pretty mahogany bookcase and the engravings upon the walls were Father Oliver's own taste; he had bought them at an auction, and there were times when these purchases pleased him. But now he was thinking that Father Peter must have known to whom the parish would go at his death, for he could not have meant all his furniture to be taken out of the house — 'there would be no room for it in Bridget Clery's cottage;' and Father Oliver sat thinking of the evenings he used to spend with Father Peter. How often during those evenings Father Peter must have said to himself, 'One day, Gogarty, you will be sitting in my chair and sleeping in my bed.' And Father Oliver pondered on his affection for the dead man. There were no differences of opinion, only one — the neglected garden at the back of the house; and, smiling sadly, Father Oliver remembered how he used to reprove the parish priest.

'I'm afraid I'm too big and too fat and too fond of my pipe and my glass of whisky to care much about carnations. But if you get the parish when I'm gone, I'm sure you'll grow some beauties, and you'll put a bunch on my grave sometimes, Gogarty.' The very ring of the dead man's voice seemed to sound through the lonely room, and, sitting in Father Peter's chair with the light of Father Peter's lamp shining on his face and hand, Father Oliver's thoughts flowed on. It seemed to him that he had not understood and appreciated Father Peter's kindliness, and he recalled his perfect good nature. 'Death reveals many things to us,' he said; and he lifted his head to listen, for the silence in the house and about the house reminded him of the silence of the dead, and he began to consider what his own span of life might be. He might live as long as Father Peter (Father Peter was fifty-five when he died); if so, twenty-one years of existence by the lake's side await-ed him, and these years seemed to him empty like a desert — yes, and as sterile. 'Twenty-one years wondering what became of her, and every evening like this evening — the same loneliness.'

He sat watching the hands of his clock, and a peaceful medita-tion about a certain carnation that unfortunately burst its calyx was interrupted by a sudden thought. Whence the thought came he could not tell, nor what had put it into his head, but it had occurred to him suddenly that 'if Father Peter had lived a few weeks longer he would have found means of exchanging Nora Glynn for another schoolmistress, more suitable to the requirements of the parish. If Father Peter had lived he would have done her a grievous wrong. He wouldn't have allowed her to suffer, but he would have done her a wrong all the same.' And it were better that a man should meet his death than he should do wrong to another. But he wasn't contemplating his own death nor Nora's when this end to the difficulty occurred to him. Our inherent hypocrisy is so great that it is difficult to know what one does think. He surely did not think it well that Father Peter had died, his friend, his benefactor, the man in whose house he was living? Of course not. Then it was strange he could not keep the thought out of his mind that Father Peter's death had saved the parish from a great scandal, for if Nora had been dismissed he might have found himself obliged to leave the parish.

Again he turned on himself and asked how such thoughts could come into his mind. True, the coming of a thought into the consciousness is often unexpected, but if the thought were not latent in the mind, it would not arise out of the mind; and if Father Peter knew the base thoughts he indulged in — yes, indulged in, for he could not put them quite out of his mind — he feared very much that the gift of all this furniture might— No, he was judging Father Peter ill: Father Peter was incapable of a mean regret.

But who was he, he'd like to be told, that he should set himself up as Father Peter's judge? The evil he had foreseen had happened. If Father Peter felt that Nora Glynn was not the kind of schoolmistress the parish required, should he not send her away? The need of the parish, of the many, before the one. Moreover, Father Peter was under no obligation whatsoever to Nora Glynn. She had been sent down by the School Board subject to his approval. 'But my case is quite different. I chose her; I decided that she was to remain.' And he asked himself if his decision had come about gradually. No, he had never hesitated, but dismissed Father Peter's prejudices as unworthy. . . . The church needed some good music. But did he think of the church? Hardly at all. His first consideration was his personal pleasure, and he wished that the best choir in the diocese should be in his church, and Nora Glynn enabled him to gratify his vanity. He made her his friend, taking pleasure in her smiles, and in the fact that he had only to express a desire for it to be fulfilled. After school, tired though she might be, she was always willing to meet him in the church for choir practice. She would herself propose to decorate the altar for feast-days. How many times had they walked round the garden together gathering flowers for the altar! And it was strange that she could decorate so well without knowing much about flowers or having much natural taste for flowers.

Feeling he was doing her an injustice, he admitted that she had made much progress under his guidance in her knowledge of flowers.

'But how did he treat her in the end, despite all her kindness? Shamefully, shamefully, shamefully!' and getting up from his chair Father Oliver walked across the room, and when he turned he drew his hand across his eyes. The clock struck twelve. 'I shall be awake at dawn,' he said, 'with all this story running in my head,' and he stopped on the threshold of his bedroom, frightened at the sight of his bed. But he had reached the stint of his sufferings, and that morning lay awake, hardly annoyed at all by the black-birds' whistling, contentedly going over the mistakes he had made — a little surprised, however, that the remembrance of them did not cause him more pain. At last he fell asleep, and when his housekeeper knocked at his door and he heard her saying that it was past eight, he leaped out of bed cheerily, and sang a stave of song as he shaved himself, gashing his chin, however, for he could not keep his attention fixed on his chin, but must peep over the top of the glass, whence he could see his garden, and think how next year he would contrive a better arrangement of colour. It was difficult to stop the bleeding, and he knew Catherine would grumble at the state he left the towels in (he should not have used his bath-towel); but these were minor matters. He was happier than he had been for many a day.

The sight of strawberries on his breakfast-table pleased him; the man who drove ten miles to see him yesterday called, and he shared his strawberries with him in abundant spirit. The sunlight was exciting, the lake called him, and it was pleasant to stride along, talking of the bridge (at last there seemed some prospect of getting one). The intelligence of this new inspector filled him with hope, and he expatiated in the advantages of the bridge and many other things. Nor did his humour seem to depend entirely on the companionship of his visitor. It endured long after his visitor had left him, and very soon he began to think that his desire to go away for a long holiday was a passing indisposition of mind rather than a need. His holiday could be postponed to the end of the year; there would be more leisure then, and he would be better able to enjoy his holiday than he would be now.

His changing mind interested him, and he watched it like a vane, unable to understand how it was that, notwithstanding his restlessness, he could not bring himself to go away. Something seemed to keep him back, and he was not certain that the reason he stayed was because the Government had not yet sent a formal promise to build the bridge. He could think of no other reason for delaying in Garranard; he certainly wanted change. And then Nora's name came into his mind, and he meditated for a moment, seeing the colour of her hair and the vanishing expression of her eyes. Sometimes he could see her hand, the very texture of its skin, and the line of the thumb and the forefinger. A cat had once scratched her hand, and she had told him about it. That was about

two months before Mrs. O'Mara had come to tell him that shocking story, two months before he had gone down to his church and
spoken about Nora in such a way that she had gone out of the
parish. But was he going to begin the story over again? He picked
up a book, but did not read many sentences before he was once
more asking himself if she had gone down to the lake, and if it
were her spell that kept him in Garranard. 'The wretchedness of
it all,' he cried, and fell to thinking that Nora's spirit haunted the
lake, and that his punishment was to be kept a prisoner always.
His imagination ran riot. Perhaps he would have to seek her out,
follow her all over the world, a sort of Wandering Jew, trying to
make atonement, and would never get any rest until this atonement was made. And the wrong that he had done her seemed the
only reality. It was his elbow companion in the evening as he sat
smoking his pipe, and every morning he stood at the end of a
sandy spit seeing nothing, hearing nothing but her. One day he
was startled by a footstep, and turned expecting to see Nora. But
it was only Christy, the boy who worked in his garden.

'Your reverence, the postman overlooked this letter in the morning. It was stuck at the bottom of the bag. He hopes the delay
won't make any difference.'

From Father O'Grady to Father Oliver Gogarty.

'June 1, 19—.

DEAR FATHER GOGARTY,

'I am writing to ask if you know anything about a young
woman called Nora Glynn. She tells me that she was schoolmistress in your parish and organist in your church, and that you
thought very highly of her until one day a tale-bearer, Mrs.
O'Mara by name, went to your house and told you that your
schoolmistress was going to have a baby. It appears that at first
you refused to believe her, and that you ran down to the school
to ask Miss Glynn herself if the story you had heard about her was
a true one. She admitted it, but on her refusal to tell you who was
the father of the child you lost your temper; and the following
Sunday you alluded to her so plainly in your sermon about
chastity that there was nothing for her but to leave the parish.

'There is no reason why I should disbelieve Miss Glynn's story;
I am an Irish priest like yourself, sir. I have worked in London
among the poor for forty years, and Miss Glynn's story is, to my

certain knowledge, not an uncommon one; it is, I am sorry to say, most probable; it is what would happen to any schoolmistress in Ireland in similar circumstances. The ordinary course is to find out the man and force him to marry the girl; if this fails, to drive the woman out of the parish, it being better to sacrifice one affected sheep than that the whole flock should be contaminated. I am an old man; Miss Glynn tells me that you are a young man. I can therefore speak quite frankly. I believe the practice to which I have alluded is inhuman and unchristian, and has brought about the ruin of many an Irish girl. I have been able to rescue some from the streets, and, touched by their stories, I have written frequently to the priest of the parish pointing out to him that his responsibility is not merely local, and does not end as soon as the woman has passed the boundary of his parish. I would ask you what you think your feelings would be if I were writing to you now to tell you that, after some months of degraded life, Miss Glynn had thrown herself from one of the bridges into the river? That might very well have been the story I had to write to you; fortunately for you, it is another story.

'Miss Glynn is a woman of strong character, and does not give way easily; her strength of will has enabled her to succeed where another woman might have failed. She is now living with one of my parishioners, a Mrs. Dent, of 24, Harold Street, who has taken a great liking to her, and helped her through her most trying time, when she had very little money and was alone and friendless in London. Mrs. Dent recommended her to some people in the country who would look after her child. She allowed her to pay her rent by giving lessons to her daughter on the piano. One thing led to another; the lady who lived on the drawing-room floor took lessons, and Miss Glynn is earning now, on an average, thirty shillings per week, which little income will be increased if I can appoint her to the post of organist in my church, my organist having been obliged to leave me on account of her health. It was while talking to Mrs. Dent on this very subject that I first heard Miss Glynn's name mentioned.

'Mrs. Dent was enthusiastic about her, but I could see that she knew little about her lodger's antecedents, except that she came from Ireland. She was anxious that I should engage her at once, declaring that I could find no one like her, and she asked me to see her that evening. I went, and the young woman impressed me very favourably. She came to my church and played for me. I could see that she was an excellent musician, and there seemed to be no reason why I should not engage her. I should probably have done so without asking any further questions — for I do not care to inquire too closely into a woman's past, once I am satisfied that she wishes to lead an honourable life — but Miss Glynn volunteered to tell me what her past had been, saying it was better I should hear it from her than from another. When she had told me her sad story, I reminded her of the anxiety that her disappearance from the parish would cause you. She shook her head, saying you did not care what might happen to her. I assured her that such a thing was not the case, and begged of her to allow me to write to you; but I did not obtain her consent until she began to see that if she withheld it any longer we might think she was concealing some important fact. Moreover, I impressed upon her that it was right that I should hear your story, not because I disbelieved hers — I take it for granted the facts are correctly stated — but in the event of your being able to say something which would put a different complexion upon them.

"Yours very sincerely,
'MICHAEL O'GRADY.'

IV

AFTER reading Father O'Grady's letter he looked round, fearing lest someone should speak to him. Christy was already some distance away; there was nobody else in sight; and feeling he was safe from interruption, he went towards the wood, thinking of the good priest who had saved her (in saving her Father O'Grady had saved him), and of the waste of despair into which he would have drifted certainly if the news had been that she had killed herself. He stood appalled, looking into the green wood, aware of the mysterious life in the branches; and then lay down to watch the insect life among the grass — a beetle pursuing its little or great destiny. But he was too exalted to remain lying down; the wood seemed to beckon him, and he asked if the madness of the woods had overtaken him. Further on he came upon a chorus of finches singing in some hawthorn-trees, and in Derrinrush he stopped to listen to the silence that had suddenly fallen. A shadow floated by; he looked up: a hawk was passing overhead, ready to attack rat or mouse moving among the young birches and firs that were springing up in the clearance. The light was violent, and the priest shaded his eyes. His feet sank in sand, he tripped over tufts of rough grass, and was glad to get out of this part of the wood into the shade of large trees.

Trees always interested him, and he began to think of their great roots seeking the darkness, and of their branches lifting themselves in love towards the light. He and these trees were one, for there is but one life, one mother, one elemental substance out of which all has come. That was it, and his thoughts paused. Only in union is there happiness, and for many weary months he had

been isolated, thrown out; but to-day he had been drawn suddenly into the general life, he had become again part of the
general harmony, and that was why he was so happy. No better
explanation was forthcoming, and he did not think that a better
one was required — at least, not to-day.

He noticed with pleasure that he no longer tried to pass behind
a thicket nor into one when he met poor wood-gatherers bent
under their heavy loads. He even stopped to speak to a woman
out with her children; the three were breaking sticks across their
knees, and he encouraged them to talk to him. But without his
being aware of it, his thoughts hearkened back, and when it came
to his turn to answer he could not answer. He had been thinking
of Nora, and, ashamed of his absentmindedness, he left them
tying up their bundles and went towards the shore, stopping
many times to admire the pale arch of evening sky with never a
wind in it, nor any sound but the cries of swallows in full pursuit.
'A rememberable evening', he said, and there was such a lightness
in his feet that he believed, or very nearly, that there were wings
on his shoulders which he only had to open to float away whither
he might wish to go.

His brain overflowed with thankfulness and dreams of her
forgiveness, and at midnight he sat in his study still thinking, still
immersed in his happiness; and hearing moths flying about the
burning lamp he rescued one for sheer love of her, and later in
the evening the illusion of her presence was so intense that he
started up from his chair and looked round for her. Had he not
felt her breath upon his cheek? Her very perfume had floated
past! There . . . it had gone by again! Not, it was not she — only the
syringa breathing in the window.

From Father Oliver Gogarty to Father O'Grady.

'GARRANARD, BOHOLA,
'JUNE 2, 19—.

'DEAR FATHER O'GRADY,
'Miss Glynn's disappearance caused me, as you rightly sur-
mise, the gravest anxiety, and it is no exaggeration to say that
whenever her name was mentioned, my tongue seemed to
thicken and I could not speak.

'I wish I could find words to thank you for what you have done.
I am still under the influence of the emotion that your letter

caused me, and can only say that Miss Glynn has told her story truthfully. As to your reproofs, I accept them, they are merited; and I thank you for your kind advice. I am glad that it comes from an Irishman, and I would give much to take you by the hand to thank you again and again.'

Getting up, he walked out of the room, feeling in a way that a calmer and more judicious letter would be preferable. But he must answer Father O'Grady, and at once; the letter would have to go. And in this resolve he walked out of his house into his garden, and stood there wondering at the flower-life growing so peacefully, free from pain.

The tall Madonna lilies flourished like sculpture about the porch, and he admired their tall stems and leaves and carven blossoms, thinking how they would die without strife, without complaint. The briar filled the air with a sweet, apple-like smell; and far away the lake shone in the moonlight, just as it had a thousand years ago when the raiders returned to their fortresses pursued by enemies. He could just distinguish Castle Island, and he wondered what this lake reminded him of: it wound in and out of gray shores and headlands, fading into dim pearl-coloured distance, and he compared it to a shroud, and then to a ghost, but neither comparison pleased him. It was like something, but the image he sought eluded him. At last he remembered how in a dream he had seen Nora carried from the lake; and now, standing among the scent of the flowers, he said: 'She has always been associated with the lake in my thoughts, yet she escaped the lake. Every man,' he continued, 'has a lake in his heart.' He had not sought the phrase, it had come suddenly into his mind. Yes, 'Every man has a lake in his heart,' he repeated, and returned to the house like one dazed, to sit stupefied until his thoughts took fire again, and going to his writing-table he drew a sheet of paper towards him, feeling that he must write to Nora. At last he picked up the pen.

From Father Oliver Gogarty to Miss Nora Glynn.

'GARRANARD, BOHOLA,
'JUNE 2, 19—.

'DEAR MISS GLYNN,
    'I must write to thank you for your kindness in asking Father

O'Grady to send me a letter. It appears that you were afraid I might be anxious about you, and I have been very anxious. I have suffered a great deal since you left, and it is a great relief to my mind to hear that you are safe and well. I can understand how loath you were to allow Father O'Grady to write to me; he doesn't say in his letter that you have forgiven me, but I hope that your permission to him to relieve my anxiety by a letter implies your forgiveness. Father O'Grady writes very kindly; it appears that everybody is kind except me. But I am thinking of myself again, of the ruin that it would have been if any of the terrible things that have happened to others had happened to you. But I cannot think of these things now; I am happy in thinking that you are safe.'

The evening post was lost, but if he were to walk to Bohola he would catch the morning mail, and his letter would be in her hands the day after tomorrow. It was just three miles to Bohola, and the walk there, he thought, would calm the extraordinary spiritual elation that news of Nora had kindled in his brain. The darkness of the night and the almost round moon high in the southern horizon suited his mood. Once he was startled by a faint sigh coming from a horse looking over a hedge, and the hedgerows were full of mysterious little cracklings. Something white ran across the road. 'The white belly of a stoat', he thought; and he walked on, wondering what its quest might be.

The road led him through a heavy wood, and when he came out at the other end he stopped to gaze at the stars, for already a grayness seemed to have come into the night. The road dipped and turned, twisting through gray fields full of furze-bushes, leading to a great hill, on the other side of which was Bohola. When he entered the village he wondered at the stillness of its street. 'The dawn is like white ashes,' he said, as he dropped his letters into the box; and he was glad to get away from the shadowy houses into the country road. The daisies and the dandelions were still tightly shut, and in the hedgerow a half-awakened chaffinch hopped from twig to twig, too sleepy to chirrup. A streak of green appeared in the east, and the death-like stillness was broken by cock-crows. He could hear them far away in the country and close by, and when he entered his village a little bantam walked up the road shrilling and clapping his wings, advancing to the fight. The priest admired his courage, and

allowed him to peck at his knees. Close by Tom Mulhare's dor-
king was crowing hoarsely, 'A hoarse bass,' said the priest, and at
the end of the village he heard a bird crowing an octave higher,
and from the direction he guessed it must be Catherine Murphy's
bird. Another cock, and then another. He listened, judging their
voices to range over nearly three octaves.

The morning was so pure, the air so delicious, and its touch so
exquisite on the cheek, that he could not bear even to think of a
close bedroom and the heat of a feather bed. He went into his
garden, and walking up and down he appreciated the beauty of
every flower, none seeming to him as beautiful as the anemones,
and he thought of Nora Glynn living in a grimy London lodging,
whereas he was here amid many flowers — anemones blue, scarlet, and purple, their heads bent down on their stalks. New ones
were pushing up to replace the ones that had blown and scattered
the evening before. The gentians were not yet open, and he
thought how they would look in a few hours — bluer than the
mid-day sky. He passed through the wicket, and stood on the
hill-top watching the mists sinking lower. The dawn light strengthened — the sky filled with pale tints of emerald, mauve, and
rose. A cormorant opened his wings and flew down the lake, his
fellows followed soon after; but Father Oliver stood on the hilltop waiting for daybreak. At last a red ball appeared behind a
reddish cloud; its colour changed to the colour of flame, paled
again, and at four flared up like a rose-coloured balloon.

The day had begun, and he turned towards his house. But he
couldn't sleep; the house was repellent, and he waited among the
thorn-bushes and ferns. Of what use to lie in one's bed when sleep
is far and will not be beckoned? and his brain being clear as day he
went away to the woods and watersides, saying: 'Life is orientated
like a temple; there are in every existence days when life streams
down the nave, striking the forehead of the God.' And during his
long life Father Oliver always looked back upon the morning
when he invaded the pantry and cut large slices of bread, taking
the butter out of the old red crock, with a little happy sadness in
his heart. He wrapped the slices in paper and wandered without
thought for whither he was going, watching the birds in the
branches, interested in everything. He was fortunate enough to
catch sight of an otter asleep on a rock, and towards evening he
came upon a wild-duck's nest in the sedge; many of the ducklings

had broken their shells; these struggled after the duck; but there were two prisoners, two that could not escape from their shells, and, seeing their lives would be lost if he did not come to their aid, he picked the shells away and took them to the water's edge, for he had heard Catherine say that one could almost see little ducks growing when they had had a drop of water. The old duck swam about uttering a whistling sound, her cry that her ducklings were to join her. And thinking of the lives he had saved, he felt a sudden regret that he had not come upon the nest earlier, when Christy brought him Father O'Grady's letter.

The yacht appeared between the islands, her sails filled with wind, and he began to dream how she might cast anchor outside the reeds. A sailor might draw a pinnace alongside, and he imagined a woman being helped into it and rowed to the landing-place. But the yacht did not cast anchor; her helm was put up, her boom went over, and she went away on another tack. He was glad of his dream, though it lasted but a moment, and when he looked up a great gull was watching him. The bird had come so near the he could see the small round head and the black eyes; as soon as he stirred it wheeled and floated away. Many other little adventures happened before the day ended. A rabbit crawled by him screaming, for he could run no longer, and lay waiting for the weasel that appeared out of the furze. What was to be done? Save it and let the weasel go supperless? At eight the moon rose over Tinnick, and it was a great sight to see the yellow mass rising above the faint shores; and while he stood watching the moon an idea occurred to him that held him breathless. His sister had written to him some days ago asking if he could recommend a music-mistress to her. It was through his sister that he might get Nora back to her country, and it was through his sister that he might make atonement for the wrong he had done. The letter must be carefully worded, for nuns understood so little, so estranged were they from the world. As for his sister Mary, she would not understand at all — she would oppose him; but Eliza was a practical woman, and he had confidence in her good sense.

He entered the house, and, waving Catherine aside, who reminded him that he had had nothing to eat since his dinner the day before, he went to his writing-table and began his letter.

From Father Oliver Gogarty to the Mother Abbess, Tinnick Convent.

'GARRANARD, BOHOLA,
'*JUNE 3, 19—*.

'MY DEAR ELIZA,

'I hope you will forgive me for having delayed so long to answer your letter, but I could not think at the moment of anybody whom I could recommend as music-mistress, and I laid the letter aside, hoping that an idea would come to me. Well, an idea has come to me. I do not think you will find——'

The priest stopped, and after thinking a while he laid down his pen and got up. The sentence he had been about to write was, 'I do not think you will find anyone better than Miss Glynn.' But he would have to send Father O'Grady's letter to his sister, and even with Father O'Grady's letter and all that he might add of an explanation, she would hardly be able to understand; and Eliza might show the letter to Mary, who was prejudiced. Father Oliver walked up and down the room thinking. . . . A personal interview would be better than the letter, for in a personal interview he would be able to answer his sister's objections, instead of the long letter he had intended to write he wrote a short note, adding that he had not seen them for a long time, and would drive over to-morrow afternoon.

V

THE southern road was the shorter, but he wanted to see Moran and to hear when he proposed to begin to roof the abbey. Father Oliver thought, moreover, that he would like to see the abbey for a last time in its green mantle of centuries. The distance was much the same — a couple of miles shorter by the southern road, no doubt, but what are a couple of miles to an old roadster? Moreover, the horse would rest in Jimmy Maguire's stable whilst he and Moran rambled about the ruin. An hour's rest would compensate the horse for the two extra miles.

He tapped the glass; there was no danger of rain. For thirty days there had been no change — only a few showers, just enough to keep the country going; and he fell asleep thinking of the drive round the lake from Garranard to Tinnick in the sunlight and from Tinnick to Garranard in the moonlight.

He was out of bed an hour before his usual time, calling to Catherine for hot water. His shaving, always disagreeable, sometimes painful, was a joyous little labour on this day. Stropping his razor, he sang from sheer joy of living. Catherine had never seen him spring on the car with so light a step. And away went the old gray pulling at the bridle, little thinking of the twenty-five Irish miles that lay before him.

The day was the same as yesterday, the meadows drying up for the want of rain; and there was a thirsty chirruping of small birds in the hedgerows. Everywhere he saw rooks gaping on the low walls that divided the fields. The farmers were complaining; but they were always complaining — everyone was complaining. He had complained of the dilatoriness of the Board of Works, and now for the first time in his life he sympathized a little with the Board. If it had built the bridge he would not be enjoying this long drive; it would be built by-and-by; he couldn't feel as if he wished to be robbed of one half-hour of the long day in front of him; and he liked to think it would not end for him till nine o'clock.

'These summer days are endless,' he said.

After passing the strait the lake widened out. On the side the priest was driving the shore was empty and barren. On the other side there were pleasant woods and interspaces and castles. Castle Carra appeared, a great ivy-grown ruin showing among thorn-bushes and ash-trees, at the end of a headland. In bygone times the castle must have extended to the water's edge, for on every side fragments of arches and old walls were discovered hidden away in the thickets. Father Oliver knew the headland well and every part of the old fortress. Many a time he had climbed up the bare wall of the banqueting-hall to where a breach revealed a secret staircase built between the walls, and followed the staircase to a long straight passage, and down another staircase, in the hope of finding matchlock pistols. Many a time he had wandered in the dungeons, and listened to old stories of oubliettes.

The moat which once cut the neck of land was now dry and overgrown; the gateway remained, but it was sinking — the earth claimed it. There were the ruins of a great house a little way inland, to which no doubt the descendants of the chieftain retired on the decline of brigandage; and the rough hunting life of its semi-chieftains was figured by the gigantic stone fox on a pillar in the middle of the courtyard and the great hounds on either side of the gateway.

Castle Carra must have been the strongest castle in the district of Tyrawley, and it was built maybe by the Welsh who invaded Ireland in the thirteenth century, perhaps by William Barrett himself, who built certainly the castle on the island opposite to Father Oliver's house.

William Fion (*i.e.*, the Fair) Barrett landed somewhere on the west coast, and no doubt came up through the great gaps between Slieve Cairn and Slieve Louan — it was not likely that he landed on the east coast; he could hardly have marched his horde across Ireland — and Father Oliver imagined the Welshmen standing on the very hill on which his house now stood, and Fion telling his followers to build a castle on each island. Patsy Murphy, who knew more about the history of the country than anybody, thought that Castle Carra was of later date, and spoke of the Stantons, a fierce tribe. Over yonder was the famous causeway, and the gross tragedy that was enacted there he yesterday heard from the wood-cutter.

William's party of Welshmen were followed by other Welsh-men— the Cusacks, the Petits, and the Brownes; and these in time fell out with the Barretts, and a great battle fought, the Battle of Moyne, in 1281, in which William Barrett was killed. But in spite of their defeat, the Barretts held the upper hand of the country for many a long year, and the priest began to smile, thinking of the odd story the old woodman had told him about the Barretts' steward, Sgnorach bhuid bhearrtha, 'saving your reverence's presence,' the old man said, and, unable to translate the words into English fit for the priest's ears, he explained that they meant a glutton and a lewd fellow.

The Barretts sent Sgnorach bhuid bhearrtha to collect rents from the Lynotts, another group of Welshmen, but the Lynotts killed him and threw his body into a well, called ever afterwards Tobar na Sgornaighe (the Well of the Glutton), near the town-land of Moygawnagh, Barony of Tyrawley. To avenge the mur-der of their steward, the Barretts assembled an armed force, and, having defeated the Lynotts and captured many of them, they offered their prisoners two forms of mutilation: they were either to be blinded or castrated. After taking counsel with their wise men, the Lynotts chose blindness; for blind men could have sons, and these would doubtless one day revenge the humiliation that was being passed upon them. A horrible story it was, for when their eyes were thrust out with needles they were led to a cause-way, and those who crossed the stepping-stones without stumb-ling were taken back; and the priest thought of the assembled horde laughing as the poor blind men fell into the water.

The story rambled on, the Lynotts plotting how they could be revenged on the Barretts, telling lamely but telling how the Lynotts, in the course of generations, came into their revenge. 'A badly told story,' said the priest, 'with one good incident in it,' and, instead of trying to remember how victory came to the Lynotts, Father Oliver's eyes strayed over the landscape, taking pleasure in the play of light along sides and crests of the hills.

The road followed the shore of the lake, sometimes turning inland to avoid a hill or a bit of bog, but returning back again to the shore, finding its way through the fields, if they could be called fields — a little grass and some hazel-bushes growing here and there between the rocks. Under a rocky headland, lying within embaying shores, was Church Island, some seven or eight acres, a handsome wooded island, the largest in the lake, with the ruins of a church hidden among the tall trees, only an arch of it remaining, but the paved path leading from the church to the hermit's cell could be followed. The hermit who used this paved path fourteen hundred years ago was a poet; and Father Oliver knew that Marban loved 'the shieling that no one knew save his God, the ash-tree on the hither side, the hazel-bush beyond it, its lintel of honeysuckle, the wood shedding its mast upon fat swine;' and on this sweet day he found it pleasanter to think of Ireland's hermits than of Ireland's savage chieftains always at war, striving against each other along the shores of this lake, and from island to island.

His thoughts lingered in the seventh and eighth centuries, when the arts were fostered in monasteries — the arts of gold-work and illuminated missals— 'Ireland's halcyon days', he said; 'a deep peace brooded, and under the guidance of the monks Ireland was the centre of learning when England was in barbarism. The first renaissance was the Irish, centuries before a gleam showed in Italy or in France. But in the middle of the eighth century the Danes arrived to pillage the country, and no sooner were they driven out than the English came to continue the work of destruction, and never since has it ceased.' Father Oliver fell to thinking if God were reserving the bright destiny for Ireland which he withheld a thousand years ago, and looked out for the abbey that Roderick, King of Connaught, built in the twelfth century.

It stood on a knoll, and in the distance, almost hidden in bulrushes, was the last arm of the lake. 'How admirable! how admirable!' he said. Kilronan Abbey seemed to bid him remember the things that he could never forget; and, touched by the beauty of the legended ruins, his doubts returned to him regarding the right of the present to lay hands on these great wrecks of Ireland's past. He was no longer sure that he did not side with the Archbishop, who was against the restoration— for entirely insufficient reasons, it was true. 'Put a roof,' Father Oliver said, 'on the abbey, and it will look like any other church, and another link will be broken. "Which is the better — a great memory or some trifling comfort?" ' A few moments after the car turned the corner and he caught sight of Father Moran, 'out for his morning's walk,' he said; and compared Moran's walk up and down the highroad with his own rambles along the lake shores and through the pleasant woods of Carnecun.

For seven years Father Oliver had walked up and down that road, for there was nowhere else for him to walk; he walked that road till he hated it, but he did not think that he had suffered from the loneliness of the parish as much as Moran. He had been happier than Moran in Bridget Clery's cottage — a great idea enabled him to forget every discomfort; and 'we are never lonely as long as our idea is with us,' he ejaculated. 'But Moran is a plain man, without ideas, enthusiasms, or exaltations. He does not care for reading, or for a flower garden, only for drink. Drink gives him dreams, and man must dream,' he said.

He knew that his curate was pledged to cure himself, and believed he was succeeding; but, all the same, it was terrible to think that the temptation might over-power him at any moment, and that he might stagger helpless through the village — a very shocking example to everybody.

The people were prone enough in that direction, and for a priest to give scandal instead of setting a good example was about as bad as anything that could happen in the parish. But what was he to do? There was no hard-and-fast rule about anything, and Father Oliver felt that Moran must have his chance.

'I was beginning to think we were never going to see you again;' and Father Moran held out a long, hard hand to Father Oliver. 'You'll put up your horse? Christy, will you take his reverence's horse? You'll stay and have some dinner with me?'

'I can't stay more than half an hour. I'm on my way to Tinnick; I've business with my sister, and it will take me some time.'

'You have plenty of time.'

'No, I haven't. I ought to have taken the other road; I'm late as it is.'

'But you will come into the house, if only for a few minutes.'

Father Oliver had taught Bridget Clery cleanliness; at least, he had persuaded her to keep the fowls out of the kitchen, and he

had put a paling in front of the house and made a little garden—
an unassuming one, it is true, but a pleasant spot of colour in the
summer-time — and he wondered how it was that Father Moran
was not ashamed of its neglected state, nor of the widow's kitchen.
These things were, after all, immaterial. What was important was
that he should find no faintest trace of whisky in Moran's room. It
was a great relief to him not to notice any, and no doubt that was
why Moran insisted on bringing him into the house. The
specifications were a pretext. He had to glance at them, however.

'No doubt if the abbey is to be roofed at all the best roof is the
one you propose.'

'Then you side with the Archbishop?'

'Perhaps I do in a way, but for different reasons. I know very
well that the people won't kneel in the rain. Is it really true that he
opposes the roofing of the abbey on account of the legend? I have
heard the legend, but there are many variants. Let's go to the
abbey and you'll tell the story on the way.'

'You see, he'll only allow a portion of the abbey to be roofed.'

'You don't mean that he is so senile and superstitious as that?
Then the reason of his opposition really is that he believes his
death to be implicit in the roofing of Kilronan.'

'Yes; he thinks that;' and the priests turned out of the main
road.'

'How beautiful it looks!' and Father Oliver stopped to admire.

The abbey stood on one of the lower slopes, on a knoll overlooking rich water-meadows, formerly abbatial lands.

'The legend says that the abbey shall be roofed when a De
Stanton is Abbot, and the McEvillys were originally De Stantons;
they changed their name in the fifteenth century on account of a
violation of sanctuary committed by them. A roof shall be put on
those walls, the legend says, when a De Stanton is again Abbot of
Kilronan, and the Abbot shall be slain on the highroad.'

'And to save himself from a violent death, he will only allow you
to roof a part of the abbey. Now, what reason does he give for
such an extraordinary decision?'

'Are Bishops ever expected to have reasons?'

The priests laughed, and Father Oliver said: 'We might appeal
to Rome.'

'A lot of good that would do us. Haven't we all heard the
Archbishop say that any of his priests who appeals to Rome

against him will get the worst of it?'

'I wonder that he dares to defy popular opinion in this way.'

'What popular opinion is there to defy? Wasn't Patsy Donovan saying to me only yesterday that the Archbishop was a brave man to be letting any roof at all on the abbey? And Patsy is the best-educated man in this part of the country.'

'People will believe anything.'

'Yes, indeed.'

And the priests stopped at the grave of Seaghan na Soggarth, or 'John of the Priests', and Father Oliver told Father Moran how a young priest, who had lost his way in the mountains, had fallen in with Seaghan na Soggarth. Seaghan offered to put him into the right road, but instead of doing so he led him to his house, and closed the door on him, and left him there tied hand and foot. Seaghan's sister, who still clung to religion, loosed the priest, and he fled, passing Seaghan, who was on his way to fetch the soldiers. Seaghan followed after, and on they went like hare and hound till they got to the abbey. There the priest, who could run no further, turned on his foe, and they fought until the priest got hold of Seaghan's knife and killed him with it.

'But you know the story. Why am I telling it to you?'

'I only know that the priest killed Seaghan. Is there any more of it?'

'Yes there is more.'

And Father Oliver went on to tell it, though he did not feel that Father Moran would be interested in the legend; he would not believe that it had been prophesied that an ash-tree should grow out of the buried head, and that one of the branches should take root and pierce Seaghan's heart. And he was right in suspecting his curate's lack of sympathy. Father Moran at once objected that the ash-tree had not yet sent down a branch to pierce the priest-killer's heart.

'Not yet; but this branch nearly touches the ground, and there's no saying that it won't take root in a few years.'

'But his heart is there no longer.'

'Well, no,' said Father Oliver, 'it isn't; but if one is to argue that way, no one would listen to a story at all.'

Father Moran held his peace for a little while, and then he began talking about the penal times, telling how religion in Ireland was another form of love of country, and that, if Catholics

were intolerant to every form of heresy, it was because they
instinctively felt that the questioning of any dogma would mean
some slight subsidence from the idea of nationality that held the
people together. Like the ancient Jews, the Irish believed that the
faith of their forefathers could bring them into their ultimate
inheritance; this was why a proselytizer was hated so intensely.

'More opinions,' Father Oliver said to himself. 'I wonder he
can't admire that ash-tree, and be interested in the story, which is
quaint and interesting, without trying to draw an historical parallel between the Irish and the Jews. Anyhow, thinking is better
than drinking,' and he jumped on his car. The last thing he heard
was Moran's voice saying, 'He who betrays his religion betrays his
country.'

'Confound the fellow, bothering me with his preaching on this
fine summer's day! Much better if he did what he was told, and
made up his mind to put the small green slates on the abbey, and
not those coarse blue things which will make the abbey look like a
common barn.'

Then, shading his eyes with his hand, he peered through the
sun haze, following the shapes of the fields. The corn was six
inches high, and the potatoes were coming into blossom. True,
there had been a scarcity of water, but they had had a good
summer, thanks be to God, and he thought he had never seen the
country looking so beautiful. And he loved this country, this poor
Western plain with shapely mountains enclosing the horizon.
Ponies were feeding between the whins, and they raised their
shaggy heads to watch the car passing. In the distance cattle were
grazing, whisking the flies away. How beautiful was everything —
the white clouds hanging in the blue sky, and the trees! There
were some trees, but not many — only a few pines. He caught
glimpses of the lake through the stems; tears rose to his eyes, and
he attributed his happiness to his native land and to the thought
that he was living in it. Only a few days ago he wished to leave it —
no, not for ever, but for a time; and as his old car jogged through
the ruts he wondered how it was that he had ever wished to leave
Ireland, even for a single minute.

'Now, Christy, which do you reckon to be the shorter road?'

'The shorter road, your reverence, is the Joyce-town road, but I
doubt if we can get the car through it.'

'How is that?'

And the boy answered that since the Big House had been burnt the road hadn't been kept in repair.

'But,' said Father Oliver, 'the Big House was burnt seventy years ago.'

'Well, your reverence, you see, it was a good road then, but the last time I heard of a car going that way was last February.'

'And if a car got through in February, why can't we get through on the first of June?'

'Well, your reverence, there was the storm, and I do be hearing that the trees that fell across the road then haven't been removed yet.'

'I think we might try the road, for all that, for though if we have to walk the greater part of it, there will be a saving in the end.'

'That's true, your reverence, if we can get the car through; but if we can't we may have to come all the way back again.'

'Well, Christy, we'll have to risk that. Now, will you be turning the horse up the road? And I'll stop at the Big House — I've never been inside it. I'd like to see what it is like.'

Joycetown House was the last link between the present time and the past. In the beginning of the century a duellist lived there; the terror of the countryside he, for he was never known to miss his man. For the slightest offence, real or imaginary, he sent seconds demanding redress. No more than his ancestors, who had doubtless lived on the islands, in Castle Island and Castle Hag, could he live without fighting. But when he completed his round dozen, a priest said, 'If we don't put a stop to his fighting, there won't be a gentleman left in the country,' and wrote to him to that effect.

The story runs how Joyce, knowing the feeling of the country was against him, tried to keep the peace. But the blood fever came on him again, and he called out his nearest neighbour, Browne of the Neale, the only friend he had in the world. Browne lived at Neale House, just over the border, in County Galway, so the gentlemen arranged to fight in a certain field near the mearing. It was Browne of Neal who was the first to arrive. Joyce, having to come a dozen miles, was a few minutes late. As soon as his gig was seen, the people, who were in hiding, came out, and they put themselves between him and Browne, telling him up to his face there was to be no fighting that day! And the priest, who was at the head of them, said the same; but Joyce, who knew his countrymen, paid no heed, but stood up in the gig, and, looking round him, said, 'Now, boys, which is it to be? The Mayo cock or the Galway cock?' No sooner did he speak these words than they began to cheer him, and in spite of all the priest could say they carried him into the field in which he shot Browne of the Neale.

'A queer people, the queerest in the world,' Father Oliver thought, as he pulled a thorn-bush out of the doorway and stood looking round. There were some rough chimney-pieces high up on the grass-grown walls, but beyond these really nothing to be seen, and he wandered out seeking traces of terraces along the hillside.

On meeting a countryman out with his dogs he tried to inquire about the state of the road.

'I wouldn't be saying, your reverence, that you mightn't get the car through by keeping close to the wall; but Christy mustn't let the horse out of a walk.'

The countryman said he would go a piece of the road with them, and tell Christy the spots he'd have to look out for.

'But your work?'

'There's no work doing now to speak of, your reverence.'

The three of them together just managed to remove a fallen tree, which seemed the most serious obstacle, and the countryman said once they were over the top of the hill they would be all right; the road wasn't so bad after that.

Half a mile further on Father Oliver found himself in sight of the main road, and of the cottage that his sister Mary had lived in before she joined Eliza in the convent.

To have persuaded Mary to take this step proved Eliza's superiority more completely than anything else she had done, so Father Oliver often said, adding that he didn't know what mightn't have happened to poor Mary if she had remained in the world. For her life up to the time she entered the convent was little else than a series of failures. She was a shop-assistant, but standing behind the counter gave her varicose veins; and she went to Dublin as nursery-governess. Father Oliver had heard of musical studies: she used to play the guitar. But the instrument was not popular in Dublin, so she gave it up, and returned to Tinnick with the intention of starting a rabbit and poultry farm. Who put this idea into her head was her secret, and when he received Eliza's letter telling him of this last experiment, he remembered throwing up his hands. Of course, it could only end in failure, in a loss of money; and when he read that she was going to take the pretty cottage on the road to Tinnick, he had become suddenly sad.

'Why should she have selected that cottage, the only pretty one in the county? Wouldn't any other do just as well for her foolish experiment?'

VI

THE flowered cottage on the road to Tinnick stood in the midst of trees, on a knoll some few feet above the roadway, and Father Oliver, when he was a boy, often walked out by himself from Tinnick to see the hollyhocks and the sunflowers; they overtopped the palings, the sunflowers looking like saucy country girls and the hollyhocks like grand ladies, delicate and refined, in pink muslin dresses. He used to stand by the gate looking into the garden, delighted by its luxuriance, for there were clumps of sweet pea and beds of red carnations and roses everywhere, and he always remembered the violets and pansies he saw before he went away to Maynooth. He never remembered seeing the garden in bloom again. He was seven years at Maynooth, and when he came home for his vacations it was too late or too early in the season. He was interested in other things; and during his curacy at Kilronan he rarely went to Tinnick, and when he did, he took the other road, so that he might see Father Peter.

He was practically certain that the last time he saw the garden in bloom was just before he went to Maynooth. However, this might be, it was certain he would never see it in bloom again. Mary had left the cottage a ruin, and it was sad to think of the clean thick thatch and the whitewashed walls covered with creeper and China roses, for now the thatch was black and mouldy; and of all the flowers only a few stocks survived; the rose-trees were gone — the rabbits had eaten them. Weeds overtopped the currant and gooseberry bushes; here and there was a trace of box edging. 'But soon,' he said, 'all traces will be gone, the roof will fall in, and the garden will become part of the waste.' His eyes roved over the country into which he was going — almost a waste; a meagre black soil, with here and there a thorn-bush and a peasant's cabin. Father Oliver knew every potato field and every wood, and he waited for the elms that lined the roadway a mile ahead of him, a long pleasant avenue that he knew well, showing above the high wall that encircled a nobleman's domain. Somewhere in the middle of that park was a great white house with pillars, and the story he had heard from his mother, and that roused his childish imaginations, was that Lord Carra was hated by the town of Tinnick, for he cared nothing for Ireland and was said to be a man of loose living, in love with his friend's wife, who came to Tinnick for visits, sometimes with, sometimes without, her husband. It may have been his Lordship's absenteeism, as well as the scandal the lady gave, that prompted a priest to speak against Lord Carra from the altar, if not directly, indirectly. 'Both are among the gone,' Father Oliver said to himself. 'No one speaks of them now; myself hasn't given them a thought this many a year——' His memories broke off suddenly, for a tree had fallen, carrying a large portion of the wall with it, but without revealing the house, only a wooded prospect through which a river glided. 'The Lord's mistress must have walked many a time by the banks of that river,' he said. But why was he thinking of her again? Was it the ugly cottage that put thoughts of her into his mind? for she had done nothing to alleviate the lives of the poor, who lived without cleanliness and without light, like animals in a den. Or did his thoughts run on the woman, whom he had never seen, because Tinnick was against her and the priest had spoken slightingly of the friends that Lord Carra brought from England? The cause of his thoughts might be that he was going to offer Nora Glynn to his sister as music-mistress. But what connection between Nora Glynn and this dead woman? None. But he was going to propose Nora Glynn to Eliza, and the best line of argument would be that Nora would cost less than anyone as highly qualified as she. Nuns were always anxious to get things cheap, but he must not let them get Nora too cheap. But the question of price wouldn't arise between him and Eliza. Eliza would see that the wrong he did to Nora was preying on his conscience, and that he'd never be happy until he had made atonement — that was the light in which she would view the matter, so it would be better to let things take their natural course and to avoid making plans.

The more he thought of what he should say to Eliza, the less likely was he to speak effectively; and feeling that he had better rely on the inspiration of the moment, he sought distraction from his errand by noting the beauty of the hillside. He had always liked the way the road dipped and then ascended steeply to the principal street in the town. There were some pretty houses in the dip — houses with narrow doorways and long windows, built, no doubt, in the beginning of the nineteenth century — and his ambition was once to live in one of these houses.

The bridge was an eighteenth-century bridge, with a foaming weir on the left, and on the right there was a sentimental walk under linden-trees, and there were usually some boys seated on the parapet fishing. He would have liked to stop the car, so remote did the ruined mills seem — so like things of long ago that time had mercifully weaned from the stress and struggle of life.

At the corner of the main street was the house in which he was born. The business had passed into other hands, but the old name — 'Gogarty's Drapery Stores' — remained. Across the way were the butcher and the grocer, and a little higher up the inn at which the commercial travellers lodged. He recalled their numerous leather trunks, and for a moment stood a child again, seeing them drive away on post-cars. A few more shops had been added — very few — and then the town dwindled quickly, slated roofs giving way to thatched cottages, and of the same miserable kind that was wont to provoke his antipathy when he was a boy.

This sinful dislike of poverty he overcame in early manhood. A high religious enthusiasm enabled him to overcome it, but his instinctive dislike of the lowly life — intellectual lowliness as well as physical — gathered within these cottages, seemed to have returned again. He asked himself if he were wanting in natural compassion, and if all that he had of goodness in him were a debt he owed to the Church. It was in patience rather than in pity maybe that he was lacking; and pursuing this idea, he recalled the hopes he entertained when he railed off a strip of ground in front of Bridget Clery's house. But that strip of garden had inspired no spirit of emulation. Eliza was perhaps more patient than he, and he began to wonder if she had any definite aim in view, and if the spectacle of the convent, with its show of nuns walking under the trees, would eventually awaken some desire of refinement in the people, if the money their farms now yielded would produce some sort of improvement in their cottages, the removal of those dreadfully heavy smells, and a longing for colour that would find expression in the planting of flowers.

They gave their money willingly enough for the adornment of their chapel, for stained glass, incense, candles, and for music, and were it not for the services of the Church he didn't know into what barbarism the people mightn't have fallen: the tones of the organ sustaining clear voices of nuns singing a Mass by Mozart must sooner or later inspire belief in the friendliness of pure air and the beauty of flowers. Flowers are the only beautiful things within the reach of these poor people. Roses all may have, and it was pleasant to think that there is nothing more entirely natural or charming in the life of man than his love of flowers; it preceded his love of music; no doubt an appreciation of something better in the way of art than a jig played on the pipes would follow close on the purification of the home.

Nora Glynn was beautiful, and her personality was winning and charming, her playing delightful, and her singing might have inspired the people to cultivate beauty. But she was going to the convent. The convent had gotten her. It was a pity. Mrs. O'Mara's scandalous stories, insinuating lies, had angered him till he could bear with her no longer, and he had put her out the door. He didn't believe that Eliza had ever said she could give Nora more than she was earning in Garranard. It mattered very little if she had, for it had so fallen out that she was going to get her. He begrudged them Nora. But Eliza was going to get her, and he'd have to make the best terms he could.

But he could not constrain his thoughts to the present moment. They would go back to the fateful afternoon when he ran across the fields to ask Nora if what Mrs. O'Mara had said of her were true. If he had only waited! If she had come to him to confession on Saturday, as he expected she would! If something had prevented him from preaching on Sunday! A bad cold might have prevented him from speaking, and she might have gone away for a while, and, when her baby was born, she might have come back. It could have been easily arranged. But fate had ordered her life otherwise, and here he was in the Tinnick Convent, hoping to make her some poor amends for the wrong he had done her. Would Eliza help him? — that was the question he asked himself as he crossed the beeswaxed floor and stood looking at the late afternoon sunlight glancing through the trees, falling across the green sward.

'How do you do, Oiver?'

His face lighted up, but it changed expression and became gray again. He had expected to see Eliza, tall and thin, with yellow eyebrows and pale eyes. Hers was a good, clearly-cut face, like his own, whereas Mary's was quite different. Yet a family likeness stared through Mary's heavy white face. Her eyes were smaller than his, and she already began to raise them and lower them, and to look at him askance, in just the way he hated. Somehow or other she always contrived to make him feel uncomfortable, and the present occasion was no exception. She was already reproving him, hoping he was not disappointed at seeing her, and he had to explain that he expected to see Eliza, and that was why he looked surprised. She must not confuse surprise with disappointment. He was very glad to see her.

'I know I am not as interesting as Eliza,' she began, 'but I thought you might like to see me, and if I hadn't come at once I shouldn't have had an opportunity of seeing you alone.'

'She has something to confide,' Father Oliver said to himself, and he hoped that her confidences might be cut short by the timely arrival of Eliza.

'Eliza is engaged at present. She told Sister Agatha to tell you that she would be with you presently. I met Sister Agatha in the passage, and I said I would take the message myself. I suppose I oughtn't to have done so, but if I hadn't I shouldn't have had an opportunity of speaking with you.'

'Why is that?'

'I don't think she likes me to see you alone.'

'My dear Mary!'

'You don't know, Oliver, what it is to live in a convent, and your own sister the head of it.'

'I should have thought, Mary, that it was especially pleasant, and that you were especially fortunate. And as for thinking that Eliza is not wishing you to see me alone, I am sure——'

'You are sure I'm mistaken.'

'What reason could she have?'

'Eliza doesn't wish the affairs of the convent discussed. You know, I suppose, that the building of the new wing has put a burden of debt on the convent.'

'I know that; so why should Eliza——'

'Eliza tries to prevent my seeing any of the visitors. Now, do you think that quite right and fair towards one's sister?'

Father Oliver tried to prevent himself from smiling, but he sympathized so entirely with Eliza's efforts to prevent Mary from discussing the affairs of the convent that he could hardly keep down the smile that rose to his lips. He could see Eliza's annoyance on coming into the parlour and finding Mary detailing all the gossip and confiding her own special woes, for the most part imaginary, to a visitor. Nor would Mary refrain from touching on the Reverend Mother's shortcomings. He was so much amused that he might have smiled if it had not suddenly come to his mind that Mary might leave the convent and insist on living with him; and a little scared he began to think of what he could say to pacify her, remembering in the midst of his confusion and embarrassment that Mary was professed last year, and therefore could not leave the convent; and this knowledge filled him with such joy that he could not keep back the words, but must remind his sister that she had had ample opportunity of considering if she were suited to the religious life.

'You see, Mary, you should have thought of all this before you were professed.'

'I shan't take my final vows till next year.'

'But, my dear Mary, once a woman has taken the black veil . . . it is the same thing, you know.'

'Not quite, otherwise there would be no meaning in the delay.'

'You don't mean to say you're thinking of leaving the convent, Mary?'

'Not exactly, but it is very hard on me, Oliver. I was thinking of writing to you, but I hoped that you would come to see us. You have been a long time now without coming.'

'Well, Mary——'

'Eliza loves ruling everybody, and just because I am her sister she is harder on me than anyone else. Only the other day she was furious with me because I stopped at confession a few minutes longer than usual. "I think," she said, "you might spare Father Higgins your silly scruples." Now, how is one to stop in a convent if one's own sister interferes in one's confessions?'

'Well, Mary, what are you thinking of doing?'

'There are some French nuns who have just come over and

want to open a school, and are looking for Irish subjects. I was
thinking they'd like to have me. You see, I wouldn't have to go
through the novitiate again, for they want an experienced person
to teach them English and to mind the school for them. It is really
a mistake to be under one's own sister.'

At that moment the door opened and Eliza came in,
apologizing for having kept her brother so long waiting.

'You see, my dear Oliver, I've had two mothers here this morning, and you know what parents are. I suppose Mary has told
you about our difficulties. Now, do you mean to say that you have
found a person who will suit us? . . . It is really very kind of you.'

'I can't say for certain, Eliza. Of course, it is difficult for me to
know exactly what you want, but, so far as I know, I think the
person I have in my mind will suit you.'

'But has she a diploma from the Academy? We must have a
certificate.'

'I think she'll suit you, but we'll talk about her presently. Don't
you think we might go into the garden?'

'Yes, it will be pleasanter in the garden. And you, Mary— you've
had your little chat with Oliver.'

'I was just going, Eliza. If I'd known that Oliver wanted to speak
privately to you, I'd have gone sooner.'

'No, no, I assure you, Mary.'

'I suppose I shall not see you again, unless, perhaps, you're
stopping the night with Father Higgins. It would be nice if you
could do that. You could say Mass for us in the morning.'

Father Oliver shook his head.

'I'm afraid I must get back to-night.'

'Well, then, good-bye.' And Mary went out of the room regret-
fully, like one who knows that the moment her back is turned all
her faults will become the subject of conversation.

'I hear from Mary that some French nuns are coming over, and
want to open a school. I hope that won't interfere with yours,
Eliza; you spent a great deal of money upon the new wing.'

'It will interfere very much indeed; but I'm trying to get some
of the nuns to come here, and I hope the Bishop will not permit a
new foundation. It's very hard upon us Irish women if we are to
be eaten out of house and home by pious foreigners. I'm in
correspondence with the Bishop about it. As for Mary——'

'You surely don't think she's going to leave?'

'No, I don't suppose she'll leave; it would be easier for me if she did, but it would give rise to any amount of talk. And where would she go if she did leave, unless she lived with you?'

'My house is too small; besides, she didn't speak of leaving, only that she hadn't yet taken her final vows. I explained that no one will distinguish between the black veil and final vows. Am I not right?'

'I think those vows will take a great weight off your mind, Oliver. I wish I could say as much for myself.'

The Reverend Mother opened a glass door, and brother and sister stood for some time admiring the flower vases that lined the terrace.

'I can't get her to water the geraniums.'

'If you'll tell me where I can get a can——'

'You'll excuse me, Reverend Mother.'

It was the Sister in charge of the laundry, and, seeing her crippled arm, Father Oliver remembered that her dress had become entangled in the machinery. He didn't know, however, that the fault lay with Mary, who was told off to watch the machinery and stop it instantly in case of necessity.

'She can't keep her attention fixed on anything, not even on her prayers, and what she calls piety I should call idleness. It's terrible to have to do with stupid women, and the convent is so full of them that I often wonder what is the good of having a convent at all.'

'But, Eliza, you don't regret——'

'No, of course I don't regret. I should do just the same again. But don't let us waste our time talking about vocations. I hear enough of that here. I want you to tell me about the music-mistress; that's what interests me.'

And when Father Oliver had told her the whole story and showed her Father O'Grady's letter, she said:

'You know I always thought you were a little hard on Miss Glynn. Father O'Grady's letter convinces me that you were.'

'My dear Eliza, I don't want advice; I've suffered enough.'

'Oliver dear, forgive me.' And the nun put out her hand to detain him.

'Well, don't say again, Eliza, that you always thought. It's irritating, and it does no good.'

'Her story is known, but she could live in the convent; that would shelter her from any sort of criticism. I don't see why she shouldn't take the habit of one of the postulants, but——'

The priest waited for his sister to speak, and after waiting a little while he asked her what she was going to say.

'I was going to ask you,' said the nun, waking from her reverie, 'if you have written to Miss Glynn.'

'Yes, I wrote to her.'

'And she's willing to come back?'

'I haven't spoken to her about that. It didn't occur to me until afterwards, but I can write at once if you consent.'

'I may be wrong, Oliver, but I don't think she'll care to leave London and come back here, where she is known.'

'But, Eliza, a girl likes to live in her own country. Mind you, I am responsible. I drove her out of her country among strangers. She's living among Protestants.'

'I don't think that will trouble her very much.'

'I don't know why you say that, Eliza. Do you think that a woman cannot repent? that because she happens to have sinned once——'

'No; I suppose there are repentant sinners, but I think we most often go on as we begin. Now, you see, Father O'Grady says that she's getting on very well in London, and we like to live among those who appreciate us.'

'Well, Eliza, of course, if you start with the theory that no one can repent——'

'I didn't say that, Oliver. But she wouldn't tell you who the man was. She seems a person of character — I mean, she doesn't seem to be lacking in strength of character.'

'She's certainly a most excellent musician. You'll find no one like her, and you may be able to get her very cheap. And if your school doesn't pay——'

A shade passed across the Reverend Mother's face.

'There's no doubt that the new wing has cost us a great deal of money.'

'Then there are the French nuns——'

'My dear Oliver, if you wish me to engage Miss Glynn as music-mistress I'll do so. There's no use speaking to me about the French nuns. I'll engage her because you ask me, but I cannot pay her as much as those who have diplomas. How much do you think she'd come for?'

'I don't know what she's earning in London, but I suppose you can pay her an average wage. You could pay her according to results.' ˒

'What you say is quite true, Oliver.' The priest and the nun continued their walk up and down in front of the unfinished building. 'But you don't know, Oliver, if she's willing to leave London. You'll have to write and find out.'

'Very well, Eliza, I'll write. You'll be able to offer her as much as she was earning in my parish as schoolmistress. That's fifty pounds a year.'

'It's more than we can afford, Oliver, but if you wish it.'

'I do wish it, Eliza. Thank you. You've taken a great weight off my mind.'

They passed into the house, and, stopping in front of the writing-table, the nun looked to see if there were paper and envelopes in the blotter.

'You'll find everything you want, even sealing-wax,' she said. 'Now I'll leave you.'

From Father Oliver Gogarty to Miss Nora Glynn.

'TINNICK CONVENT,
June 4, 19—.

'DEAR MISS GLYNN,

'I take it for granted that you received the letter I sent you two days ago, telling you how much I appreciated your kindness in asking Father O'Grady to write to tell me that you were quite safe and getting on well. Since writing that letter I feel more keenly than ever that I owe you reparation, for it was through an error of judgment on my part that you are now an exile from your own country. Everyone is agreed that I have committed an error of judgment. My sister, the Mother Superior of this convent from where I am writing, is of that opinion. The moment I mentioned your name she began, "I always thought that——" and I begged of her to spare me advice on the subject, saying that it was not for advice that I came to her, but to ask her to help me to make atonement, which she could do by engaging you to teach music in her convent. You see, I had heard that my sister was in a difficulty. The new wing is nearly completed, and she could get the best families in Ireland to send their daughters to be educated in her convent if she could provide sufficient musical instruction. I thought you might like to live in your own country, now that your thoughts have again turned towards God, and I can imagine the unpleasantness it must be to a Catholic to live in a Protestant country. I told my sister this, and she answered that if you wish to come over here, and if Father O'Grady advises it, she will take you as music-mistress. You will live in the convent. You can enter it, if you wish, as a postulant, or if you should remain an extern teacher the salary they will give you will be fifty pounds a year. I know you can make more than that in London, but you can live more cheaply here, and you will be among friends.

'I shall be glad to hear from you on this subject.

'Very sincerely yours,
'OLIVER GOGARTY, P.P.'

When he looked up, the darkness under the trees surprised him, and the geraniums so faintly red on the terrace, and his sister passing up and down like a phantom.

'Eliza.'

He heard her beads drop, and out of a loose sleeve a slim hand took the letter. There was not enough light in the room to read by, and she remained outside, leaning against the glass door.

'You haven't written exactly the letter I should have written, but, then, we're quite different. I should have written a cold and more business-like letter.' His face changed expression, and she added: 'I'm sorry if I'm unsympathetic, Oliver.'

The touch of her hand and the look in her eyes surprised him, for Eliza was not demonstrative, and he wondered what had called forth this sudden betrayal of feeling. He expected her to ask him not to send the letter, but instead of doing so she said:

'If the letter were written otherwise it wouldn't be like yourself, Oliver. Send it, and if she leaves London and comes back here, I will think better of her. It will be proof that she has repented. I see you'll not have an easy mind until you make atonement. You exaggerate, I think; but everyone for himself in a matter like this.'

'Thank you, Eliza. You always understand.'

'Not always. I failed to understand when you wanted to set up a hermitage on Castle Island.'

'Yes, you did; you have better sense than I. Yet I feel we are more alike than others. You have counted for a great deal in my life, Eliza. Do you remember saying that you intended to be

Reverend Mother? And now you are Reverend Mother.'

'I don't think I said "I intended". But I felt that if I became a nun, one day or another I should be Reverend Mother; one knows most often than not what is going to happen — one's own fate, I mean.'

'I wonder if Mary knows?'

'If she does, I wish she'd tell us.'

'We'll have time to walk round the garden once more. You have no idea what a pleasure it is for me to see you — to talk with you like this.'

And, talking of Mary, they walked slowly, forgetful of everything but each other.

A bell rang.

'I must be going; it will be late before I get home.'

'Which way are you going? Round by Kilronan or across the Bridge of Keel?'

'I came by Kilronan. I think I'll take the other way. There will be a moon to-night.'

Brother and sister entered the convent.

'You'll enjoy the drive?'

'Yes.' And he fell to thinking of the drive home by the southern road, the mountains unfolding their many aspects in the gray moonlight, and melting away in misty perspectives.

VII

From Miss Nora Glynn to Father Oliver Gogarty.

'4, WILSON STREET,
LONDON,
June 8, 19—.

'FATHER GOGARTY,

'I did not answer your first letter because the letters that came into my mind to write, however they might begin, soon turned to bitterness, and I felt that writing bitter letters would not help me to forget the past. But your second letter with its proposal that I should return to Ireland to teach music in a convent school forces me to break silence, and it makes me regret that I gave Father O'Grady permission to write to you; he asked me so often, and his kindness is so winning, that I could not refuse him anything. He said you would certainly have begun to see that you had done me a wrong, and I often answered that I saw no reason why I should trouble to soothe your conscience. I do not wish to return to Ireland; I am, as Father O'Grady told you, earning my own living, my work interests me, and very soon I shall have forgotten Ireland. That is the best thing that can happen, that I should forget Ireland, and that you should forget the wrong you did me. Put the whole thing, and me, out of your mind; and now, good-bye, Father Gogarty.

'NORA GLYNN.'

'Good heavens! how she hates me, and she'll hate me till her dying day. She'll never forget. And this is the end of it, a bitter,

unforgiving letter.' He sat down to think, and it seemed to him
that she wouldn't have written this letter if she had known the
agony of mind he had been through. But of this he wasn't sure.
No, no; he could not believe her spiteful. And he walked up and
down the room, trying to quell the bitterness rising up within him.
No other priest would have taken the trouble; they would have
just forgotten all about it, and gone about congratulating themselves on their wise administration. But he had acted rightly,
Father O'Grady had approved of what he had done; and this was
his reward. She'll never come back, and will never forgive him;
and ever since writing to her he had indulged in dreams of her
return to Ireland, thinking how pleasant it would be to go down to
the lake in the mornings, and stand at the end of the sandy spit
looking across the lake towards Tinnick, full of the thought that
she was there with his sisters earning her living. She wouldn't be
in his parish, but they'd have been friends, neighbours, and he'd
have accepted the loss of his organist as his punishment. Eva
Maguire was no good; there would never be any music worth
listening to in his parish again. Such sternness as her letter betrayed was not characteristic of her; she didn't understand, and
never would. Catherine's step awoke him; the awakening was
painful, and he couldn't collect his thoughts enough to answer
Catherine; and feeling that he must appear to her daft, he tried to
speak, but his speech was only babble.

'You haven't read your other letter, your reverence.'
He recognized the handwriting; it was from Father O'Grady.

From Father O'Grady to Father Oliver Gogarty.

'June 8, 19—.

'MY DEAR FATHER GOGARTY,
    'I was very glad to hear that Miss Glynn told her story truth-
fully; for if she exaggerated or indulged in equivocation, it would
be a great disappointment to me and to her friends, and would
put me in a very difficult position, for I should have to tell certain
friends of mine, to whom I recommended her, that she was not all
that we imagined her to be. But all's well that ends well; and you
will be glad to hear that I have appointed her organist in my
church. It remains, therefore, only for me to thank you for your
manly letter, acknowledging the mistake you have made.
    'I can imagine the anxiety it must have caused you, and the

great relief it must have been to you to get my letter. Although Miss Glynn spoke with bitterness, she did not try to persuade me that you were naturally hard-hearted or cruel. The impression that her story left on my mind was that your allusions to her in your sermon were unpremeditated. Your letter is proof that I was not mistaken, and I am sure the lesson you have received will bear fruit. I trust that you will use your influence to restrain other priests from similar violence. It is only by gentleness and kindness that we can do good. I shall be glad to see you if you ever come to London.

'I am, sir,
'Very sincerely yours,
'MICHAEL O'GRADY.'

'All's well that ends well. So that's how he views it! A different point of view.' And feeling that he was betraying himself to Catherine, he put both letters into his pocket and went out of the house. But he had not gone many yards when he met a parishioner with a long story to tell, happily not a sick call, only a dispute about land. So he invented an excuse postponing his intervention until the morrow, and when he returned home tired with roaming, he stopped on his door-step. 'The matter is over now, her letter is final,' he said. But he awoke in a different mood next morning; everything appeared to him in a different light, and he wondered, surprised to find that he could forget so easily; and taking her letter out of his pocket, he read it again. 'It's a hard letter, but she's a wise woman. Much better for us both to forget each other. "Goodbye, Father Gogarty," she said; "Good-bye, Nora Glynn," say I.' And he walked about his garden tending his flowers, wondering at his light-heartedness.

She thought of her own interests, and would get on very well in London, and Father O'Grady had been lucky too. Nora was an excellent organist. But if he went to London he would meet her. A meeting could hardly be avoided — and after that letter! Perhaps it would be wiser if he didn't go to London. What excuse? O'Grady would write again. He had been so kind. In any case he must answer his letter, and that was vexatious. But was he obliged to answer it? O'Grady wouldn't misunderstand his silence. But there had been misunderstandings enough; and before he had walked the garden's length half a dozen conclusive reasons for

writing occurred to him. First of all Father O'Grady's kindness in
writing to ask him to stay with him, added to which the fact that
Nora would, of course, tell Father O'Grady she had been invited
to teach in the convent; her vanity would certainly urge her to do
this, and Heaven only knows what account she would give of his
proposal. There would be his letter, but she mightn't show it. So
perhaps on the whole it would be better that he should write
telling O'Grady what had happened. And after his dinner as he
sat thinking, a letter came into his mind; the first sentences
formulated themselves so suddenly that he was compelled to go to
his writing-table.

From Father Oliver Gogarty to Father O'Grady.

'GARRANARD, BOHOLA,
'June 12, 19—.

'DEAR FATHER O'GRADY,

'I enclose a letter which I received three days ago from Miss
Nora Glynn, and I think you will agree with me that the letter is a
harsh one, and that, all things considered, it would have been
better if she had stinted herself to saying that I had committed an
error of judgment which she forgave. She did not, however,
choose to do this. As regards my sister's invitation to her to come
over here to teach, she was, of course, quite right to consider her
own interests. She can make more money in London than she
could in Ireland. I forgot that she couldn't bring her baby with
her, remembering only that my eldest sister is Mother Abbess in
the Tinnick Convent— a very superior woman, if I may venture
to praise my own sister. The convent was very poor at one time,
but she has made the school a success, and, hearing that she
wanted someone who would teach music and singing, I proposed
to her that she should engage Miss Glynn, with whose story she
was already acquainted. She did not think Miss Glynn would
return to Ireland; and in this opinion she showed her good
judgment. She was always a wonderful judge of character. But
she could see that I was anxious to atone for any wrong that I
might have done Miss Glynn, and after some hesitation she consented, saying: "Well, Oliver, if you wish it."

'Miss Glynn did not accept the proposal, and I suppose that the
episode now ends so far as I am concerned. She has fallen into
good hands; she is making her living, thanks to your kindness.

But I dare not think what might not have happened if she had not met you. Perhaps when you have time you will write again; I shall be glad to hear if she succeeds in improving your choir. My conscience is now at rest; there is a term, though it may not be at the parish boundary, when our responsibility ceases.

'Thanking you again, and hoping one of these days to have the pleasure of making your acquaintance,

'I am very truly yours,

'OLIVER GOGARTY.'

From Father O'Grady to Father Oliver Gogarty.

'*June 18, 19—.*

'DEAR FATHER GOGARTY,

'Thank you for sending me Miss Glynn's letter, and I agree with you when you describe it as harsh; but I understand it in a way. Miss Glynn came over to London almost penniless, and expecting the birth of her illegitimate child. She suffered all that a woman suffers in such circumstances. I do not want to harass you unnecessarily by going over it all again, but I do wish you to forgive her somewhat intemperate letter. I'll speak to her about it, and I am sure she will write to you in a more kindly spirit later on; meanwhile, rest assured that she is doing well, and not forgetful of the past. I shall try to keep a watchful eye over her, seeing that she attends to her duties every month; there is no better safeguard. But in truth I have no fear for her, and am unable to understand how she could have been guilty of so grave a sin, especially in Ireland. She seems here most circumspect, even strict, in her manner. She is an excellent musician, and has improved my choir. I have been tempted to comply with her request and spend some more money upon the singing. . . .

'While writing these lines I was interrupted. My servant brought me a letter from Miss Glynn, telling me that a great chance had come her way. It appears that Mr. Walter Poole, the father of one of her pupils, has offered her the post of secretary-ship, and she would like to put into practice the shorthand and typewriting that she has been learning for the last six months. Her duties, she says, will be of a twofold nature: she will help Mr. Poole with his literary work and she will also give music lessons to his daughter Edith. Mr. Poole lives in Berkshire, and wants her to come down at once, which means she will have to leave me in the lurch. "You will be without an organist," she writes, "and will have to put up with Miss Ellen McGowan until you can get a better. She may improve — I hope and think she will; and I'm sorry to give trouble to one who has been so kind to me, but, you see, I have a child to look after, and it is difficult to make both ends meet on less than three pounds a week. More money I cannot hope to earn in my present circumstances; I am therefore going down to Berkshire to-morrow, so I shall not see you again for some time. Write and tell me you are not angry with me."

'On receiving this letter, I went round to Miss Glynn's lodgings, and found her in the midst of her packing. We talked a long while, and very often it seemed to me that I was going to persuade her, but when it came to the point she shook her head. Offer her more money I could not, but I promised to raise her wages to two pounds a week next year if it were possible to do so. I don't think it is the money; I think it is change that tempts her. Well, it tempts us all, and though I am much disappointed at losing her, I cannot be angry with her, for I cannot forget that I often want change myself, and the longing to get out of London is sometimes almost irresistible. I do not know your part of the country, but I do know what an Irish lake is like, and I often long to see one again. And very often, I suppose, you would wish to exchange the romantic solitude of your parish for the hurly-burly of a town, and for its thick, impure air you would be willing — for a time only, of course — to change the breezes of your mountain-tops.

> 'Very truly yours,
> 'MICHAEL O'GRADY.'

From Father Oliver Gogarty to Father O'Grady.

> 'GARRANARD, BOHOLA,
> *June 22, 19—.*

'DEAR FATHER O'GRADY,

'No sooner had I begun to feel easier in my conscience and to dream that my responsibilities were at an end than your letter comes, and I am thrown back into all my late anxieties regarding Nora Glynn's future, for which I am and shall always be responsible.

'It was my words that drove her out of Ireland into a great English city in which some dreadful fate of misery and death might have befallen her if you had not met her. But God is good, and he sent you to her, and everything seems to have happened for the best. She was in your hands, and I felt safe. But now she has taken her life into her own hands again, thinking she can manage it without anybody's help!

'The story you tell seems simple enough, but it doesn't sound all right. Why should she go away to Berkshire to help Mr. Walter Poole with his literature without giving you longer notice? It seems strange to write to one who has taken all the trouble you have to find her work — "I have discovered a post that suits me better and am going away to-morrow." Of course she has her child to think of. But have you made inquiries? I suppose you must have done. You would not let her go away to a man of whom you know nothing. She says that he is the father of one of her pupils. But she doesn't know him, yet she is going to live in his house to help him with his literature. Have you inquired, dear Father O'Grady, what this man's writings are, if he is a Catholic or a Protestant? I should not like Miss Nora Glynn to go into a Protestant household, where she would hear words of disrespect for the religion she has been brought up in.

'As I write I ask myself if there is a Catholic chapel within walking distance; and if there isn't, will he undertake to send her to Mass every Sunday? I hope you have made all these inquiries, and if you have not made them, will you make them at once and write to me and relieve my anxiety? You are aware of the responsibilities I have incurred and will appreciate the anxiety that I feel.

'Yours very sincerely,
'OLIVER GOGARTY.'

It seemed to Father Oliver so necessary that Father O'Grady should get his letter as soon as possible that he walked to Bohola; but soon after dropping the letter in the box he began to think that he might have written more judiciously, and on his way home he remembered that he had told Father O'Grady, and very explicitly, that he should have made inquiries regarding Mr. Walter Poole's literature before he allowed Nora Glynn to go down to Berkshire to help him with his literary work. Of course he hoped, and it was only natural that he should hope, that Father O'Grady had made all reasonable inquiries; but it seemed to him now that he had expressed himself somewhat peremptorily. Father O'Grady was an old man — how old he did not know — but

himself was a young man, and he did not know in what humour
Father O'Grady might read his letter. If the humour wasn't
propitious he might understand it as an impertinence. It vexed
him that he had shown so much agitation, and he stopped to
think. But it was so natural that he should be concerned about
Nora Glynn. All the same, his anxiety might strike Father
O'Grady as exaggerated. A temperate letter, he reflected, is
always better; and the evening was spent in writing another letter
to Father O'Grady, a much longer one, in which he thanked
Father O'Grady for asking him to come to see him if he should
ever find himself in London. 'Of course,' he wrote, 'I shall be only
too pleased to call on you, and no doubt we shall have a great deal
to talk about — two Irishmen always have; and when I feel the
need of change imminent, I will try to go to London, and do you,
Father O'Grady, when you need a change, come to Ireland. You
write: "I do not know your part of the country, but I know what an
Irish lake is like, and I often long to see one again." Well, come
and see my lake; it's very beautiful. Woods extend down to the
very shores with mountain peaks uplifting behind the woods, and
on many islands there are ruins of the castles of old time. Not far
from my house it narrows into a strait, and after passing this strait
it widens out into what might almost be called another lake. We
are trying to persuade the Government to build a bridge, but it is
difficult to get anything done. My predecessor and myself have
been in correspondence on this subject with the Board of Works;
it often seems as if success were about to come, but it slips away,
and everything has to be begun again. I should like to show you
Kilronan Abbey, an old abbey unroofed by Cromwell. The
people have gone there for centuries, kneeling in the snow and
rain. We are sadly in need of subscription. Perhaps one of these
days you will be able to help us; but I shall write again on this
subject, and as soon as I can get a photograph of the abbey I will
send it.

                    'Yours very sincerely,
                        'OLIVER GOGARTY.'

'Now, what will Father O'Grady answer to all this?' he said
under his breath as he folded up his letter. 'A worthy soul, an
excellent soul, there's no doubt about that.' And he began to feel
sorry for Father O'Grady. But his sorrow was suddenly suspen-

ded. If he went to London he wouldn't be likely to see her. 'Another change,' he said; 'things are never the same for long. A week ago I knew where she was; I could see her in her surroundings. Berkshire is not very far from London. But who is Mr. Poole?' And he sat thinking.

A few days after he picked up a letter from his table from Father O'Grady, a long garrulous letter, four pages about Kilronan Abbey, Irish London, convent schools — topics interesting enough in themselves, but lacking in immediate interest. The letter contained only three lines about her. That Mr. Poole explained everything to her, and that she liked her work. The letter dropped from his hand; the hand that had held the letter fell upon his knee, and Father Oliver sat looking through the room. Awaking suddenly, he tried to remember what he had been thinking about, for he had been thinking a long while; but he could not recall his thoughts, and went to his writing-table and began a long letter telling Father O'Grady about Kilronan Abbey and enclosing photographs. And then, feeling compelled to bring himself into as complete union as possible with his correspondent, he sat, pen in hand, uncertain if he should speak of Nora at all. The temptation was by him, and he found excuse in the thought that after all she was the link; without her he would not have known Father O'Grady. And so convinced was he of this that when he mentioned her he did so on account of a supposed obligation to sympathize once again with Father O'Grady's loss of his organist. His letter rambled on about the Masses Nora used to play best and the pieces she used to sing.

A few days after he caught sight of her handwriting on his breakfast-table, and he sat reading the letter, to Catherine's annoyance, who said the rashers were getting cold.

From Miss Nora Glynn to Father Oliver Gogarty.

'BEECHWOOD HALL,
'BERKSHIRE,
'*July 20, 19—*.

'DEAR FATHER GOGARTY,
'One is not always in a mood to give credit to others for good intentions, especially when one returns home at the close of day disappointed, and I wrote a hard, perhaps a cruel, letter; but I'm feeling differently now. The truth is that your letter arrived at an

unfortunate moment when things were going badly with me.'

'I'm forgiven,' Father Oliver cried— 'I'm forgiven;' and his joy was so great that the rest of the letter seemed unnecessary, but he continued to read:

'Father O'Grady has no doubt told you that I have given up my post of organist in his church, Mr. Poole having engaged me to teach his daughter music and to act as his secretary. In a little letter which I received about a fortnight ago from him he told me he had written to you, and it appears that you have recovered from your scruples of conscience, and have forgotten the wrong you did me; but if I know you at all, you are deceiving yourself. You will never forget the wrong you did me. But I shall forget. I am not sure that it has not already passed out of my mind. This will seem contradictory, for didn't I say that I couldn't forget your cruelty in my first letter? I wonder if I meant it when I wrote, "Put the whole thing and me out of your mind. . . ." I suppose I did at the time, and yet I doubt it. Does anyone want to be forgotten utterly?

'I should have written to you before, but we have been busy. Mr. Poole's book has been promised by the end of the year. It's all in type, but he is never satisfied. To-day he has gone to London to seek information about the altars of the early Israelites. It's a wonderful book, but I cannot write about it to-day; the sun is shining, the country is looking lovely, and my pupil is begging me to finish my letter and go out with her.
                    'Very sincerely yours,
                        'NORA GLYNN.'

'So forgiveness has come at last,' he said; and as he walked along the shore he fell to thinking that very soon all her life in Garranard would be forgotten. 'She seems interested in her work,' he muttered; and his mind wandered over the past, trying to arrive at a conclusion, if there was or was not a fundamental seriousness in her character, inclining on the whole to think there was, for if she was not serious fundamentally, she would not have been chosen by Mr. Poole for his secretary. 'My little schoolmistress, the secretary of a great scholar! How very extraordinary! But why is it extraordinary? When will she write again?' And every night he wished for the dawn, and every morning he asked if there were any letters for him. 'No, your reverence, no letters this morning;' and when Catherine handed him some envelopes they only contained bills or uninteresting letters from the parishioners or letters from the Board of Works about the bridge in which he could no longer feel any interest whatever.

At last he began to think he had said something to offend her, and to find out if this were so he would have to write to Father O'Grady telling him that Miss Glynn had written saying that she had forgiven him. Her forgiveness had brought great relief; but Miss Glynn said in her letter that she was alone in Berkshire, Mr. Poole having gone to London to seek information regarding the altars of the early Israelites.

From Father O'Grady to Father Oliver Gogarty.
'*August 1, 19—.*

'DEAR FATHER GOGARTY,
    'I am sorry I cannot give you the information you require regarding the nature of Mr. Poole's writings, and if I may venture to advise you, I will say that I do not think any good will come to her by your inquiry into the matter. She is one of those women who resent all control; and, if I may judge from a letter she wrote to me the other day, she is bent now on educating herself regardless of the conclusions to which her studies may lead her. I shall pray for her, and that God may watch over and guide her is my hope. I am sure it is yours too. She is in God's hands, and we can do nothing to help her. I am convinced of that, and it would be well for you to put her utterly out of your mind.
            'I am, very truly yours,
                'MICHAEL O'GRADY.'

'Put her utterly out of my mind,' Father Oliver cried aloud; 'now what does he mean by that?' And he asked himself if this piece of advice was Father O'Grady's attempt to get even with him for having told him that he should have informed himself regarding Mr. Poole's theological opinions before permitting her to go down to Berkshire.

It did not seem to him that Father O'Grady would stoop to such meanness, but there seemed to be no other explanation, and he fell to thinking of what manner of man was Father O'Grady — an old man he knew him to be, and from the tone of his letters he had judged him a clever man, experienced in the human weakness and conscience. But this last letter! In what light was he to read it? Did O'Grady fail to understand that there is no more intimate association than that of an author and his secretary. If we are to believe at all in spiritual influences — and who denies them? — can we minimize these? On his way to the writing-table he stopped. Mr. Poole's age — what was it? He imagined him about sixty. 'It is at that age,' he said, 'that men begin to think about the altars of the early Israelites,' and praying at intervals that he might be seventy, he wrote a short note thanking Father O'Grady for his advice and promising to bear it in mind. He did not expect to get an answer, nor did he wish for an answer; for he had begun to feel that he and Father O'Grady had drifted apart, and had no further need one for the other.

'Are there no letters this morning?' he asked Catherine.

'None, sir. You haven't had one from London for a long time.'

He turned away. 'An intolerable woman — intolerable! I shall be obliged to make a change soon,' he said, turning away so that Catherine should not see the annoyance that he felt on his face.

Father Oliver Gogarty to Miss Nora Glynn.

'GARRANARD, BOHOLA,
'*August 6, 19—.*

'DEAR MISS GLYNN,

'You said in your very kind letter, which I received a fortnight ago, and which I answered hastily, that on some future occasion you would perhaps tell me about the book Mr. Poole is writing. I wonder if this occasion will ever arise, and, if so, if it be near or far — near, I hope, for interested as I naturally am in your welfare, I have begun to feel some anxiety regarding this book. On the day that——'

'Father O'Grady, your reverence.' Father Oliver laid his letter aside, and then hid it in the blotter, regretting his haste and his fumbling hands, which perhaps had put the thought into O'Grady's mind that the letter was to Nora. And so he came forward faintly embarrassed to meet a small pale man, whom he judged to be seventy or thereabouts, coming forward nimbly, bent a little, with a long, thin arm and bony hand extended in a formal langour of welcome. A little disappointing was the first moment, but it passed away quickly, and when his visitor was seated Father Oliver noticed a large nose rising out of the pallor and on either side of it dim blue eyes and some long white locks.

'You're surprised to see me,' Father O'Grady said in a low, winning voice. 'Of course you're surprised — how could it be otherwise? but I hope you're glad.'

'Very glad,' Father Oliver answered. 'Glad, very glad,' he repeated; and begged his visitor to allow him to help him off with his overcoat.

'How pleasant,' Father O'Grady said, as soon as he was back in the armchair, as if he felt that the duty fell upon him to find a conversation that would help them across the first five minutes — 'how pleasant it is to see a turf fire again! The turf burns gently, mildly, a much pleasanter fire than coal; the two races express themselves in their fires.'

'Oh, we're fiery enough over here,' Father Oliver returned; and the priests laughed.

'I did not feel that I was really in Ireland,' Father O'Grady continued, 'till I saw the turf blazing and falling into white ash. You see I haven't been in Ireland for many years.'

Father Oliver threw some more sods of turf into the grate, saying: 'I'm glad, Father O'Grady, that you enjoy the fire, and I'm indeed glad to see you. I was just thinking——'

'Of me?' Father O'Grady asked, raising his Catholic eyes.

The interruption was a happy one, for Father Oliver would have found himself embarrassed to finish the sentence he had begun. For he would not have liked to have admitted that he had just begun a letter to Nora Glynn, to say, 'There it is on the table.' Father O'Grady's interruption gave him time to revise his sentence.

'Yes, I was thinking of you, Father O'Grady. Wondering if I might dare to write to you again.'

'But why should you be in doubt?' Father O'Grady asked; and then, remembering a certain asperity in Father Oliver's last letter, he thought it prudent to change the conversation. 'Well, here I am and unexpected, but, apparently, welcome.'

'Very welcome,' Father Oliver murmured.

'I'm glad of that,' the old man answered; 'and now to my story.' And he told how a variety of little incidents had come about, enabling him to spend his vacation in Ireland. 'A holiday is necessary for every man. And, after all, it is as easy to go from London to Ireland as it is to go to Margate, and much more agreeable. But I believe you are unacquainted with London, and Margate is doubtless unknown to you. Well, I don't know that you've missed much;' and he began to tell of the month he had spent wandering in the old country, and how full of memories he had found it — all sorts of ideas and associations new and old. 'Maybe it was you that beguiled me to Ireland; if so, I ought to thank you for a very pleasant month's holiday. Now I'm on my way home, and finding that I could fit in the railway journey I went to Tinnick, and I couldn't go to Tinnick without driving over to Garranard.'

'I should think not, indeed,' Father Oliver answered quickly. 'It was very good of you to think of me, to undertake the journey to Tinnick and the long drive from Tinnick over here.'

'One should never be praised for doing what is agreeable to one to do. I liked you from your letters; you're like your letters, Father Oliver — at least I think you are.'

'I'm certain you're like yours,' Father Oliver returned, 'only I imagined you to speak slower.'

'A mumbling old man,' Father O'Grady interjected.

'You know I don't mean that,' Father Oliver replied, and there was a trace of emotion in his voice. 'It was really very good of you to drive over from Tinnick. You say that you only undertook the journey because it pleased you to do so. If that philosophy were accepted, there would be no difference between a good and an evil action; all would be attributed to selfishness.' He was about to add: 'This visit is a kindness that I did not expect, and one which I certainly did not deserve;' but to speak these words would necessitate an apology for the rudeness he felt he was guilty of in his last letter, and the fact that he knew that Father O'Grady had come to talk to him about Nora increased his nervousness. But their talk continued in commonplace and it seemed impossible to lift it out of the rut. Father O'Grady complimented Father Oliver on his house and Oliver answered that it was Peter Conway that built it, and while praising its comfort, he enlarged on the improvements that had been made in the houses occupied by priests.

'Yes, indeed,' Father O'Grady answered, 'the average Irish priest lived in my time in a cottage not far removed from those the peasants lived in. All the same, there was many a fine scholar

among them. Virgil, Horace, Ovid, Catullus, Cicero in the book-
cases. Do you ever turn to these books? Do you like reading
Latin?'

And Father Oliver replied that sometimes he took down his
Virgil. 'I look into them all sometimes,' he added.

'And you still read Latin, classical Latin, easily?' Father
O'Grady inquired.

'Fairly,' Father Oliver replied; 'I read without turning to the
dictionary, though I often come to words I have never seen or
have forgotten the meaning of. I read on. The Latin poets are
more useful than the English to me.'

'More useful?' Father O'Grady repeated.

'More useful,' Father Oliver rejoined, 'if your object is a new
point of view, and one wants that sometimes, living alone in the
silent country. One sometimes feels frightened sitting by the fire
all alone listening to the wind. I said just now that I was thinking
of you. I often think of you, Father O'Grady, and envy you your
busy parish. If I ever find myself in London I shall go for long
tram drives, and however sordid the district I shall view the dim
congregation of houses with pleasure and rejoice in the hub of the
streets.'

'You would soon weary of London, I promise you that, Father
Oliver.'

'A promise for which it would be an affectation to thank you,'
Father Oliver answered. And Father O'Grady spoke of the miles
of docks.

'The great murky Thames,' he said, 'wearies, but it is very
wonderful. Ah, Landor's "Hellenics" in the original Latin: how
did that book come here?'

'A question I've often asked myself,'Father Oliver returned. 'A
most intellectual volume it is to find in the house of an Irish priest.
Books travel, and my predecessor, Father Peter, is the last man in
the world who would have cared to spend an hour on anything so
literary as Landor. He used to read the newspaper — all the
newspapers he could get hold of.'

Father Peter's personality did not detain them long, and feeling
somewhat ashamed of their inability to talk naturally, without
thinking of what they were to say next, Father O'Grady ventured
to doubt if Horace would approve of Landor's Latin and of the
works written in comparatively modern times. Buchanan, for

instance. At last the conversation became so trite and wearisome
that Father O'Grady began to feel unable to continue it any
longer.

'You've a nice garden, Father Oliver.'

'You'd like to see my garden?' Father Oliver asked, very much
relieved at having escaped from Buchanan so easily. And the two
priests went out, each hoping that the other would break the ice;
and to encourage Father Oliver to break it, Father O'Grady
mentioned that he was going back that evening to Tinnick — a
remark that was intended to remind Father Oliver that the time
was passing by. Father Oliver knew that the time for speaking of
her was passing by, but he could not bring himself to speak, and
instead he tried to persuade Father O'Grady to stay to dinner, but
he could not be persuaded; and they walked to and fro, talking
about their different parishes, Father O'Grady asking Father
Oliver questions about his school and his church. And when
Father Oliver had contributed a great deal of unnecessary
information, he questioned Father O'Grady about his parish, and
gained much information regarding the difficulties that a
Catholic priest met with in London, till religion became as wearisome as the Latin language. At last it suddenly struck Father
Oliver that if he allowed the talk to continue regarding the difficulties of the Catholic priest in London, Father O'Grady might
speak of girls that had been driven out of Ireland by the priests, to
become prostitutes in London. A talk on this subject would be too
painful, and to escape from it he spoke of the beauty of the trees
about the garden and the flowers in the garden, calling Father
O'Grady's attention to the chrysanthemums, and, not willing to
be outdone in horticulture, the London priest began to talk about
the Japanese mallow in his garden, Father Oliver listening indif-
ferently, saying, when it came to him to make a remark, that the
time had come to put in the bulbs.

'Miss Glynn was very fond of flowers,' he said suddenly, 'and
she helped me with my garden; it was she who told me to plant
roses in that corner, and to cover the wall with rambling robin.
Was it not a very pretty idea to cover that end of the garden with
rambling roses?'

'It was indeed. She is a woman of great taste in music and many
other things. She must have regretted your garden.'

'Why do you think she regretted my garden?' Father Oliver
asked.

'Because she always regretted that mine wasn't larger. She helped me with my garden;' and feeling that they had at last got into a conversation that was full of interest for them both, Father Oliver said:

'Shall we go into the house? We shall be able to talk more agreeably by the fireside.'

'I should like to get back to that turf fire; for it is the last that I shall probably see. Let us get back to it.'

'I'm quite agreeable to return to the fire. Catherine will bring in the tea presently.'

And as soon as they were back in the parlour, Father Oliver said:

'Father O'Grady, that is your chair. It was very good of you to take the trouble to drive over.'

'I wished to make my correspondent's acquaintance,' Father O'Grady murmured; 'and there is much that it is difficult to put down on paper without creating a wrong impression, whereas in talk one is present to rectify any mistakes one may drop into. I am thinking now of the last subject dealt with in our correspondence, that I should have informed myself regarding Mr. Poole's writing before I consented to allow Nora Glynn to accept the post of secretary.'

'You must forgive me, Father O'Grady,' Father Oliver cried.

'There is nothing to forgive, Father Oliver; but this criticism surprised me, for you have known Miss Nora Glynn longer than I have, and it seems strange that you should have forgotten already her steadfastness. Nothing that I could have said would have availed, and it seems to me that you were mistaken in asking me to urge Miss Glynn to decline the chance of improving her circumstances. I could not compel Miss Glynn even if I had wished to compel her. But we have discussed that question; let it pass.'

'All the same,' Father Oliver interjected, 'if one sees a woman going into danger, surely one may warn her. A word of warning dropped casually is sometimes effective.'

'But it is fatal to insist,' Father O'Grady remarked; 'and one should not try to bar the way — that is my experience at least.'

'Well, your experiences are longer than mine, Father O'Grady, I submit. The mistake I made will certainly not be repeated. But since hearing from you I've heard from Miss Glynn, and the remarks she makes in her letters about Mr. Poole's literary work, unless indeed he be a Catholic, alarm me.'

'Biblical criticism is not a Catholic characteristic,' Father O'Grady answered. 'So Miss Glynn has written to you?'

'Yes, but nothing definite about Mr. Poole's work — nothing definite. Do you know anything, Father O'Grady, about this man's writing? What is his reputation in the literary world?'

'I've heard a great deal about him,' Father O'Grady answered. 'I've made inquiries and have read some of Mr. Poole's books, and have seen them reviewed in the newspapers; I've heard his opinions discussed, and his opinions are anti-Christian, inasmuch as he denies the divinity of our Lord.'

'Could anybody be more anti-Christian than that?' Father Oliver asked.

'Yes, very much more,' Father O'Grady replied. 'There have always been people, and their number is increasing, who say that Christianity is not only untruthful but, what is worse, a great evil, having set men one against the other, creating wars innumerable. Millions have owed their deaths to tortures they have received because they differed regarding some trifling passage in Scripture. There can be no doubt of that, but it is equally true that Christianity has enabled many more millions to live as much from a practical point of view as from a spiritual. If Christianity had not been a necessity it would not have triumphed;' and Father O'Grady continued to speak of Mr. Poole's historical accounts of the history of the rise and influence of Christianity till Father Oliver interrupted him, crying out:

'And it is with that man her life will henceforth be passed, reading the books he reads and writes, and, what is worse, listening to his insidious conversation, to his subtle sophistries, for, no doubt, he is an eloquent and agreeable talker.'

'You think, then,' Father O'Grady said, 'that a Christian forfeits his faith if he inquires?'

'No, if I thought that I should cease to be a Christian. She is not inquiring the matter out of her own account; she is an enforced listener, and hears only one side. Every day a plausible account is being poured into her ears, and her circumstances are such as would tempt her to give a willing ear to Mr. Poole's beliefs that God has not revealed his existence, and that we are free to live as we please, nature being our only guide. I cannot imagine a young woman living in a more dangerous atmosphere than this.

'All you tell me, Father O'Grady, frightens me. I discovered my
suspicions to you in my letters, but I can express myself better in
talking than on paper — far better. It is only now that I realize
how wrongly I acted towards this young woman. I was frightened
in a measure before, but the reality of my guilt has never
appeared so distinctly to me till now. You have revealed it to me,
and I'm thinking now of what account I could give to God were I
to die to-morrow. "Thou has caused a soul to be lost," he would
say. "The sins of the flesh are transitory like the flesh, the sins of
the faith are deeper," may be God's judgment. Father O'Grady,
I'm frightened, frightened; my fear is great, and at this moment I
feel like a man on his deathbed. My agony is worse, for I'm in
good health and can see clearly, whereas the dying man understands little. The senses numb as death approaches.'

'Have you spoken of the mistake you made in confession,
Father Oliver?'

'No, why should I?' he answered, 'for none here would understand me. But I'll confess to you. You may have been sent to hear
me. Who knows? Who can say?' and he dropped on his knees
crying: 'Can I be forgiven if that soul be lost to God? Tell me if
such a sin can be forgiven?'

'We must not fall into the sin of despair,' Father O'Grady
answered. And he murmured the Latin formula *Absolve te,* etc.,
making the sign of the cross over the head of his penitent. For a
while after the priests knelt together in prayer, and it was with a
feeling that his burden had been lifted from him that Father
Oliver rose from his knees, and, subdued in body and mind, stood
looking through the room, conscious of the green grass showing
through his window, lighted by a last ray of the setting sun. It was
the wanness of this light that put the thought into his mind that it
would soon be time to send round to the stables for his visitor's
car. His visitor! That small, frail man sitting in his armchair would
soon be gone, carrying with him this, Father Oliver's, confession.
What had he confessed? Already he had forgotten, and both men
stood face to face thinking of words wherewith they might break
the silence.

'I do not know,' Father O'Grady said, 'that I altogether share
your fear that an anti-Christian atmosphere necessarily implies
that the Catholic who comes into it will lose her faith, else faith
would not be a pure gift from God. God doesn't overload his

creatures unbearably, nor does he put any stress upon them from which they cannot extricate themselves. I could cite many instances of men and women whose faith has been strengthened by hostile criticism; the very arguments that have been urged against their faith have forced them to discover other arguments, and in this way they have been strengthened in their Catholic convictions.' And to Father Oliver's question if he discerned any other influence except an intellectual influence in Mr. Poole, he answered that he had not considered this side of the question.

'I don't know what manner of man he is in his body,' said Father Oliver, 'but his mind is more dangerous. An intellectual influence is always more dangerous than a sensual influence, and the sins of faith are worse than the sins of the flesh. I have never thought of him as a possible seducer. But there may be that danger too. I still think, Father O'Grady, that you might have warned Nora of her danger. Forgive me; I'm sure you did all that was necessary. You do forgive me?'

The men's eyes met, and Father O'Grady said, as if he wished to change the subject:

'You were born at Tinnick, were you not?'

'Yes, I was born in Tinnick,' Father Oliver repeated mechanically, almost as if he had not heard the question.

'And your sisters are nuns?'

'Yes, yes.'

'Tell me how it all came about.'

'How all what came about?' Father Oliver asked, for he was a little dazed and troubled in his mind, and was, therefore, easily led to relate the story of the shop in Tinnick, his very early religious enthusiasms, and how he remembered himself always as a pious lad. On looking into the years gone by, he said that he saw himself more often than not by his bedside rapt in innocent little prayers. And afterwards at school he had been considered a pious lad. He rambled on, telling his story almost unconsciously, getting more thoughtful as he advanced into it, relating carefully the absurd episode of the hermitage in which, to emulate the piety of the old time, he chose Castle Island as a suitable spot for him to live in.

Father O'Grady listened, seriously moved by the story; and Father Oliver continued it, telling how Eliza, coming to see the priest in him, gave up her room to him as soon as their cousin the

Bishop was consulted. And it was at this point of the narrative that Father O'Grady put a question.

'Was no attempt,' he asked, 'made to marry you to some girl with a big fortune?'

And Father Oliver told of his liking for Annie McGrath and of his aversion for marriage, acquiescing that aversion might be too strong a word; indifference would more truthfully represent him.

'I wasn't interested in Annie McGrath nor in any woman as far as I can remember until this unfortunate conduct of mine awakened an interest in Nora Glynn. And it would be strange, indeed, if it hadn't awakened an interest in me,' he muttered to himself. Father O'Grady suppressed the words that rose up in his mind, 'Now I'm beginning to understand.' And Father Oliver continued, like one talking to himself: 'I'm thinking that I was singularly free from all temptations of the sensual life, especially those represented by womankind. I was ordained early, when I was twenty-two, and as soon as I began to hear confessions, the things that surprised me the most were the stories relating to those passionate attachments that men experience for women and women for men — attachments which sometimes are so intense that if the sufferer cannot obtain relief by the acquiescence of the object of their affections, he, if it be he, she, if it be she, cannot refrain from suicide. There have been cases of men and women going mad because their love was not reciprocated, and I used to listen to these stories wonderingly, unable to understand, bored by the relation.'

If Father Oliver had looked up at that moment, Father O'Grady's eyes would have told him that he had revealed himself, and that perhaps Father O'Grady now knew more about him than he knew himself. But without withdrawing his eyes from the fire he continued talking till Catherine's step was heard outside.

'She's coming to lay the cloth for our tea,' Father Oliver said. And Father O'Grady answered:

'I shall be glad of a cup of tea.'

'Must you really go after tea?' Father Oliver asked; and again he begged Father O'Grady to stay for dinner. But Father O'Grady, as if he felt that the object of his visit had been accomplished, spoke of the drive back to Tinnick and of the convenience of the branch line of railway. It was a convenience certainly, but it was also an inconvenience, owing to the fact that the trains run from Tinnick sometimes missed the mail train; and this led Father Oliver to speak of the work he was striving to accomplish, the roofing of Kilronan Abbey, and many other things, and the time passed without their feeling it till the car came round to take Father O'Grady away.

'He goes as a dream goes,' Father Oliver said, and a few minutes afterwards he was sitting alone by his turf fire, asking himself in what dreams differed from reality. For like a dream Father O'Grady had come and he had gone, never to return. 'But does anything return?' he asked himself, and he looked round his room, wondering why the chairs and table did not speak to him, and why life was not different from what it was. He could hear Catherine at work in the kitchen preparing his dinner, she would bring it to him as she had done yesterday, he would eat it, he would sit up smoking his pipe for a while, and about eleven o'clock go to his bed. He would lie down in it, and rise and say Mass and see his parishioners. All these things he had done many times before, and he would go on doing them till the day of his death — 'Until the day of my death,' he repeated, 'never seeing her again, never seeing him. Why did he come here?' And he was surprised that he could find no answer to any of the questions that he put to himself.

VIII

'NOTHING will happen again in my life — nothing of any interest. This is the end! And if I did go to London, of what should I speak to him? It will be better to try to forget it all, and return, if I can, to the man I was before I knew her;' and he stood stock still, thinking that without this memory he would not be himself.

Father O'Grady's coming had been a pleasure to him, for they had talked together; he had confessed to him; had been shriven. At that moment he caught sight of a newspaper upon his table. '*Illustrated England*,' he muttered, his thoughts half away; and he fell to wondering how it had come into the house. 'Father O'Grady must have left it,' he said, and began to unroll the paper. But while unrolling it he stopped. Half his mind was still away, and he sat for fully ten minutes lost in sad sensations, and it was the newspaper slipping from his hand that awoke him. The first thing that caught his eye on opening the paper was an interview with Mr. Walter Poole, enbellished with many photographs of Beechwood Hall.

'Did O'Grady leave this paper here for me to read,' he asked himself, 'or did he forget to take it away with him? We talked of so many things that he may have forgotten it, forgotten even to mention it. How very strange!'

The lodge gates and the long drive, winding between different woods, ascending gradually to the hilltop on which Beechwood Hall was placed by an early eighteenth-century architect, seemed to the priest to be described with too much unction by the representative of *Illustrated England*. To the journalist Beechwood Hall stood on its hill, a sign and symbol of the spacious leisure of the eighteenth century and the long tradition that it represented, one that had not even begun to drop into decadence till 1850, a tradition that still existed, despite the fact that democracy was finding its way into the agricultural parts of England. The journalist was impressed, perhaps unduly impressed, by the noble hall and the quiet passages that seemed to preserve a memory of the many generations that had passed through them on different errands, now all hushed in the family vault.

Father Oliver looked down the column rapidly, and it was not until the footman who admitted the journalist was dismissed by the butler, who himself conducted the journalist to the library, that Father Oliver said: 'We have at last arrived at the castle of learning in which the great Mr. Poole sits sharpening the pen which is to slay Christianity. But Christianity will escape Mr. Poole's pen. It has outlived many such attacks in the past. We shall see, however, what kind of nib he uses, fine or blunt?' The journalist followed the butler down the long library overlooking green sward to a quiet nook, if he might venture to speak of Mr. Walter Poole's study as a quiet nook. It seemed to surprise him that Mr. Walter Poole should rise from his writing-table and come forward to meet him, and he expressed his gratitude to Mr. Walter Poole, whose time was of great importance, for receiving him. And after all this unction came a flattering description of Mr. Walter Poole himself.

He was, in the interviewer's words, a young man, tall and clean-shaven, with a high nose which goes well with an eye-glass. The chin is long and drops straight; his hair is mustard-coloured and glossy, and it curls very prettily about the broad, well-shapen forehead. He is reserved at first, and this lends a charm to the promise, which is very soon granted you, of making the acquaintance with the thoughts and ideas which have interested Mr. Walter Poole since boyhood — in fine, which have given him his character. If he seems at first sight to conceal himself from you, it is from shyness, or because he is reluctant to throw open his mind to the casual curious. Why should he not keep his mind for his own enjoyment and for the enjoyment of his friends, treating it like his pleasure grounds or park? His books are not written for the many but for the few, and he does not desire a larger audience than those with whom he is in natural communion from the first, and this without any faintest appearance of affectation.

'I suppose it isn't fair,' the priest said, 'to judge a man through his interviewer; but if this interviewer doesn't misrepresent Mr. Walter Poole, Mr. Walter Poole is what is commonly known as a very superior person. He would appear from this paper,' the priest said, 'to be a man between thirty and forty, not many years older than myself.' The priest's thoughts floated away back into the past, and, returning suddenly with a little start to the present, he continued reading the interview, learning from it that Mr. Walter Poole's conversation was usually gentle, like a quiet river, and very often, like a quiet river, it rushed rapidly when Mr. Walter Poole became interested in his subject.

'How very superior all this is,' the priest said. 'The river of thought in him,' the interviewer continued, 'is deep or shallow, according to the need of the moment. If, for instance, Mr. Walter Poole is asked if he be altogether sure that it is wise to disturb people in their belief in the traditions and symbols that have held sway for centuries, he will answer quickly that if truth lies behind the symbols and traditions, it will be in the interest of the symbols and traditions to inquire out the truth, for blind belief— in other words, faith— is hardly a merit, or if it be a merit it is a merit that cannot be denied to the savages who adore idols. But the civilized man is interested in his history, and the Bible deserves scientific recognition, for it has a history certainly and is a history. "We are justified, therefore," Mr. Walter Poole pleaded, "in seeking out the facts, and the search is conducted as much in the interests of theology as of science; for though history owes nothing to theology, it cannot be denied that theology owes a great deal to history." '

'He must have thought himself very clever when he made that remark to the interviewer,' the priest muttered; and he walked up and down his room, thinking of Nora Glynn living in this unchristian atmosphere.

He picked up the paper again and continued reading, for he would have to write to Nora about Father O'Grady's visit and about the interview in *Illustrated England*.

The interviewer inquired if Mr. Walter Poole was returning to Palestine, and Mr. Walter Poole replied that there were many places that he would like to re-visit, Galilee, for instance, a country that St. Paul never seemed to have visited, which, to say the least, was strange. Whereupon a long talk began about Paul and Jesus,

Mr. Walter Poole maintaining that Paul's teaching was identical
with that of Jesus, and that Peter was a clown despised by Paul and
Jesus.

'How very superior,' Father Oliver muttered — 'how very
superior.' He read that Mr. Walter Poole was convinced that the
three Synoptic Gospels were written towards the close of the first
century; and one of the reasons he gave for this attribution was as
in Matthew, chapter xxvii., verse 7, 'And they took counsel, and
bought with them (the thirty pieces of silver) the potter's field, to
bury strangers in. Wherefore that field was called, The field of
blood, unto this day' — a passage which showed that the Gospel
could not have been written till fifty or sixty years after the death
of Jesus.

'England must be falling into atheism if newspapers dare to
print such interviews,' Father Oliver said; and he threw the paper
aside angrily. 'And it was I,' he continued, dropping into his
armchair, 'that drove her into this atheistical country. I am
responsible, I alone.'

From Father Oliver Gogarty to Miss Glynn.

'GARRANARD, BOHOLA,
'*August 10, 19—.*

'DEAR MISS GLYNN,

'I have a piece of news for you. Father O'Grady has been
here, and left me a few hours ago. Catherine threw open the
door, saying, "Father O'Grady, your reverence," and the small,
frail man whom you know so well walked into the room, surprising me, who was altogether taken aback by the unexpected-
ness of his visit.

'He was the last person in the world I expected at that moment
to meet, yet it was natural that an Irish priest, on the mission in
England, would like to spend his holidays in Ireland, and still
more natural that, finding himself in Ireland, Father O'Grady
should come to see me. He drove over from Tinnick, and we
talked about you. He did not seem on the whole as anxious for
your spiritual safety as I am, which is only what one might expect,
for it was not he that drove you out of a Catholic country into a
Protestant one. He tried to allay my fears, saying that I must not
let remorse of conscience get hold of me, and he encouraged me
to believe that my responsibility had long ago ended. It was

pleasant to hear these things said, and I believed him in a way; but he left by accident or design a copy of *Illustrated England* on my table. I am sufficiently broad-minded to believe that it is better to be a good Protestant than a bad Catholic; but Mr. Walter Poole is neither Catholic nor Protestant, but an agnostic, which is only a polite word for an atheist. Week in and week out you will hear every argument that may be used against our holy religion. It is true that you have the advantage of being born a Catholic, and were well instructed in your religion; and no doubt you will accept with caution his statements, particularly that very insidious statement that Jesus lays no claim to divinity in the three Synoptic Gospels, and that these were not written by the apostles themselves, but by Greeks sixty, seventy, or perhaps eighty years after his death. I do not say he will try to undermine your faith, but how can he do otherwise if he believe in what he writes? However careful he may be to avoid blasphemy in your presence, the fact remains that you are living in an essentially unchristian atmosphere, and little by little the poison which you are taking in will accumulate, and you will find that you have been influenced without knowing when or how.

'If you lose your faith, I am responsible for it; and I am not exaggerating when I say the thought that I may have lost a soul to God is always before me. I can imagine no greater responsibility than this, and there seems to be no way of escaping from it. Father O'Grady says that you have passed out of our care, that all we can do is to pray for you. But I would like to do something more, and if you happen upon some passages in the books you are reading that seem in contradiction to the doctrines taught by the Catholic Church, I hope you will not conclude that the Church is without an answer. The Church has an answer ready for every single thing that may be said against her doctrines. I am not qualified to undertake the defence of the Church against anyone. I quite recognize my own deficiency in this matter, but even I may be able to explain away some doubts that may arise. If so, I beg of you not to hesitate to write to me. If I cannot do so myself, I may be able to put you in the way of finding out the best Catholic opinion on matters of doctrine.

'Very sincerely yours,
'OLIVER GOGARTY.'

From Miss Nora Glynn to Father Oliver Gogarty.

'BEECHWOOD HALL,
BERKSHIRE,
'*August 15, 19—.*

'I am sorry indeed that I am causing you so much trouble of conscience. You must try to put it out of your mind that you are responsible for me. The idea is too absurd. When I was in your parish I was interested in you, and that was why I tried to improve the choir and took trouble to decorate the altar. Have you forgotten how anxious I was that you should write the history of the lake and its castles? Why don't you write it and send it to me? I shall be interested in it, though for the moment I have hardly time to think of anything but Jewish history. Within the next few weeks, for certain, the last chapter of Mr. Poole's book will be passed for press, and then we shall go abroad and shall visit all the great men in Europe. Some are in Amsterdam, some are in Paris, some live in Switzerland. I wish I understood French a little better. Isn't it all like a dream? Do you know, I can hardly believe I ever was in forlorn Garranard teaching little barefooted children their Catechism and their A, B, C.

'Good-bye, Father Gogarty. We go abroad next week. I lie awake thinking of this trip—the places I shall see and the people I shall meet.

'Very sincerely yours
'NORA GLYNN.'

It seemed to him that her letter gave very little idea of her. Some can express themselves on paper, and are more real in the words they write than in the words they speak. But hardly anything of his idea of her transpired in that letter — only in her desire of new ideas and new people. She was interested in everything—in his projected book about the raiders faring forth from the island castles, and now in the source of the Christian River; and he began to meditate a destructive criticism of Mr. Poole's ideas in a letter addressed to the editor of *Illustrated England*, losing heart suddenly, he knew not why, feeling the task to be beyond him. Perhaps it would be better not to write to Nora again.

From Father Oliver Gogarty to Miss Nora Glynn.

'GARRANARD, BOHOLA,
'August 22, 19—.

'DEAR MISS GLYNN,
   'I gather from your letter that religion has ceased to interest you, except as a subject for argument, and I will not begin to argue with you, but will put instead a simple question to you: In what faith do you intend to bring up your child? and what will be your answer when your child asks: "Who made me?" Mr. Poole may be a learned man, but all the learning in the world will not tell you what answer to make to your child's questions; only the Church can do that.
   'I have thought a great deal about the danger that your post of secretary to Mr. Poole involves and am not sure that the state of indifference is not the worst state of all. One day you will find that indifference has passed into unbelief, and you will write to me (if we continue to write to each other) in such a way that I shall understand that you have come to regard our holy religion as a tale fit only for childhood's ears. I write this to you, because I have been suddenly impelled to write, and it seems to me that in writing to you in this simple way I am doing better than if I spent hours in argument. You will not always think as you do now; the world will not always interest you as much as it does now. I will say no more on this point but will break off abruptly to tell you that I think you are right when you say that we all want change. I feel I have lived too long by the side of this lake, and I am thinking of going to London. . . .'

   The room darkened gradually, and, going to the window, he longed for something to break the silence, and was glad when the rain pattered among the leaves. The trees stood stark against the sky, in a green that seemed unnatural. The sheep moved as if in fear towards the sycamores, and from all sides came the lowing of cattle. A flash drove him back from the window. He thought he was blinded. The thunder rattled; it was as if a God had taken the mountains in his arms and was shaking them together. Crash followed crash; the rain came down; it was as if the rivers of heaven had been opened suddenly. Once he thought the storm was over; but the thunder crashed again, the rain began to thic-ken; there was another flash and another crash, and the pour began again. But all the while the storm was wearing itself out, and he began to wonder if a sullen day, ending in this apocalypse, would pass into a cheerful evening. It seemed as if it would, for some blue was showing between the clouds drifting westward, threatening every moment to blot out the blue, but the clouds continued to brighten at the edges. 'The beginning of the sunset,' the priest said; and he went out on his lawn and stood watching the swallows in the shining air, their dipping, swerving flight showing against a back-ground of dappled clouds. He had never known so extraordinary a change; and he walked to and fro in the freshened air, thinking that Nora's health might not have withstood the strain of trudging from street to street, teaching the piano at two shillings an hour, returning home late at night to a poky little lodging, eating any food a landlady might choose to give her. As a music teacher she would have had great difficulty in supporting herself and her baby, and it pleased him to imagine the child as very like her mother; and returning to the house, he added this paragraph:

'I was interrupted while writing this letter by a sudden darkening of the light, and when I went to the window the sky seemed to have sunk close to the earth, and there was a dreadful silence underneath it. I was driven back by a flash of lightning, and the thunder was terrifying. A most extraordinary storm lasting for no more than an hour, if that, and then dispersing into a fine evening. It was a pleasure to see the change — the lake shrouded in mist, with ducks talking softly in the reeds, and swallows high up, advancing in groups like dancers on a background of dappled clouds.

'I have come back to my letter to ask if you would like me to go to see your baby? Father O'Grady and I will go together if I go to London, and I will write to you about it. You will be glad, no doubt, to hear that the child is going on well.

'Very sincerely yours,
'OLIVER GOGARTY.'

From Father Oliver Gogarty to Miss Nora Glynn.

'GARRANARD, BOHOLA,
'*September 4, 19—*.

'Forgive me, my dear friend, but I am compelled to write to apologize for the introduction of my troubles of conscience and my anxiety for your spiritual welfare into my last letter. You found a way out of difficulties — difficulties into which I plunged you. But we will say no more on that point: enough has been said. You have created a life for yourself. You have shown yourself to be a strong woman in more ways than one, and are entitled to judge whether your work and the ideas you live among are likely to prove prejudicial to your faith and morals. By a virtue of forgiveness which I admire and thank you for, you write telling me of the literary work you are engaged upon. If I had thought before writing the letter I am now apologizing for, I could not have failed to see that you write to me because you would relieve my loneliness as far as you are able. But I did not think: I yielded to my mood, and see now that my letters are disgracefully egotistical, and very often absurd; for have I not begged of you to remember that since God will hold me responsible for your soul, it would be well that you should live a life of virtue and renunciation, so that I shall be saved the humiliation of looking down from above upon you in hell?

'Loneliness begets sleeplessness, and sleeplessness begets a sort of madness. I suffer from nightmare, and I cannot find words to tell you how terrible are the visions one sees at dawn. It is not so much that one sees unpleasant and ugly things — life is not always pretty or agreeable, that we know — but when one lies between sleeping and waking, life itself is shown in mean aspects, and it is whispered that one has been duped till now; that now, and for the first time, one knows the truth. You remember how the wind wails about the hilltop on which I live. The wailing of wind has something to do with my condition of mind; one cannot sit from eight o'clock in the evening till twelve at night staring at the lamp, hearing the wind, and remain perfectly sane.

'But why am I writing about myself? I want to escape from myself, and your letters enable me to do so. The names of the cities you are going to visit transport me in imagination, and last night I sat a long while wondering why I could not summon courage to go abroad. Something holds me back. I think if I once left Garranard, I should never return to the lake and its island. I hope you haven't forgotten Marban, the hermit who lived at the end of the lake in Church Island. I visited his island yesterday. I should have liked to have rowed myself through the strait and along the shores, seeing Castle Cara and Castle Burke as I passed;

but Church Island is nearly eight miles from here, and I don't know if I should have been man enough to pull the fisherman's boat so far, so I put the gray horse into the shafts and went round by road.

'Church Island lies in a bay under a rocky shore, and the farmer who cuts the grass there in the summer-time has a boat to bring away the hay. It was delightful to step into it, and as the oars chimed I said to myself, "I have Marban's poem in my pocket — and will read it walking up the little path leading from his cell to his church." The lake was like a sheet of blue glass, and the island lay yellow and red in it. As we rowed, seeking a landing-place under the tall trees that grow along the shores, the smell of autumn leaves mingled with the freshness of the water. We rowed up a beautiful little inlet overhung with bushes. The quay is at the end of it, and on getting out of the boat, I asked the boatman to point out to me what remained of Marban's Church. He led me across the island — a large one, the largest in the lake — not less than seven acres or nine, and no doubt some parts of it were once cultivated by Marban. Of his church, however, very little remains — only one piece of wall, and we had great difficulty in seeing it, for it is now surrounded by a dense thicket. The little pathway leading from his cell to the church still exists; it is almost the same as he left it — a little overgrown, that is all.

'Marban was no ordinary hermit; he was a sympathetic natural-ist, a true poet, and his brother who came to see him, and whose visit gave rise to the colloquy, was a king. I hope I am not wron-ging Marban, but the island is so beautiful that I cannot but think that he was attracted by its beauty and went there because he loved Nature as well as God. His poem is full of charming obser-vations of nature, of birds and beasts and trees, and it proves how very false the belief is that primitive man had no eyes to see the beauties of the forest and felt no interest in the habits of animals or of birds, but regarded them merely as food. It pleases me to think of the hermit sitting under the walls of his church or by his cell writing the poem which has given me so much pleasure, including in it all the little lives that came to visit him — the birds and the beasts — enumerating them as carefully as Wordsworth would, and loving them as tenderly. Marban! Could one find a more beautiful name for a hermit? Guaire is the brother's name. Marban and King Guaire. Now, imagine the two brothers meeting for a poetic disputation regarding the value of life, and each speaking from his different point of view! True that Guaire's point of view is only just indicated — he listens to his brother, for a hermit's view of life is more his own than a king's. It pleases me to think that the day the twain met to discourse of life and its mission was the counterpart of the day I spent on the island. My day was full of drifting cloud and sunshine, and the lake lay like a mirror reflecting the red shadow of the island. So you will understand that the reasons Marban gave for living there in preference to living the life of the world seemed valid, and I could not help peering into the bushes, trying to find a rowan-tree — for he speaks of one. The rowan is the mountain-ash. I found several. One tree was covered with red berries, and I broke off a branch and brought it home, thinking that perchance it might have come down to us from one planted by Marban's hand. Of blackthorns there are plenty. The adjective he uses is "dusky". Could he have chosen a more appropriate one? I thought, too, of "the clutch of eggs, the honey and the mast" that God sent him, of "the sweet apples and red whortleberries", and of his dish of "strawberries of good taste and colour".

'It is hard to give in an English translation an idea of the richness of the verse, heavily rhymed and winningly alliterated, but you will see that he enumerates the natural objects with skill. The eternal summer — the same in his day as in ours — he speaks of as "a coloured mantle," and he mentions "the fragrance of the woods". And seeing the crisp leaves — for the summer was waning — I repeated his phrase, "the summer's coloured mantle", and remembered:

> "Swarms of bees and chafers, the little musicians of the world —
> A gentle chorus."

"The wren", he says, "is an active songster among the hazel boughs. Beautifully hooded birds, wood-peckers, fair white birds, herons, sea-gulls, come to visit me". There is no mournful music in his island; and as for loneliness, there is no such thing in

> ' "My lowly little abode, hidden in a mane of green-barked yew-tree.
> Near is an apple-tree,

Big like a hostel;
A pretty bush thick as a fist of hazel-nuts, a choice spring and
    water fit for a Prince to drink.
Round it tame swine lie down,
A badger's brood,
A peaceful troop, a heavy host of denizens of the soil
A-trysting at my house.
To meet them foxes come.
How delightful!"

'The island is about a hundred yards from the shore, and I
wondered how the animals crossed from the mainland as I sat
under the porch of the ruined church. I suppose the water was
shallower than it is now. But why and how the foxes came to meet
the wild swine is a matter of little moment; suffice it that he lived
in this island aware of its loneliness, "without the din of strife,
grateful to the Prince who giveth every good to me in my bower."
To which Guaire answered:

"I would give my glorious kingship
  With my share of our father's heritage,—
  To the hour of my death let me forfeit it,
  So that I may be in thy company, O Marban."

There are many such beautiful poems in early Irish. I know of
another, and I'll send it to you one of these days. In it is a monk
who tells how he and his cat sit together, himself puzzling out
some literary or historical problem, the cat thinking of hunting
mice, and how the catching of each is difficult and requires much
patience.
'Ireland attained certainly to a high degree of civilization in the
seventh and eighth centuries, and if the Danes had not come,
Ireland might have anticipated Italy. The poems I have in mind
are the first written in Europe since classical times, and though
Italy and France be searched, none will be found to match them.
'I write these things to you because I wish you to remember
that, when religion is represented as hard and austere, it is the
fault of those who administer religion, and not of religion itself.
Religion in Ireland in the seventh and eighth centuries was clearly
a homely thing, full of tender joy and hope, and the inspiration
not only of poems, but of many churches and much ornament of

all kinds, illuminated missals, carven porches. If Ireland had been left to herself — if it had not been for the invasion of the Danes, and the still worse invasion of the English — there is no saying what high place she might not have taken in the history of the world. But I am afraid the halcyon light that paused and passed on in those centuries will never return. We have gotten the after-glow, and the past should incite us; and I am much obliged to you for reminding me that the history of the lake and its castles would make a book. I will try to write this book, and while writing will look forward to the day when I shall send you a copy of the work, if God gives me strength and patience to complete it. Little is ever completed in Ireland. . . . But I mustn't begin to doubt before I begin the work, and while you and Mr. Poole are studying dry texts, trying to prove that the things that men have believed and loved for centuries are false, I shall be engaged in writing a sympathetic history — the history of natural things and natural love.

'Very sincerely yours,
'OLIVER GOGARTY.'

From Miss Nora Glynn to Father Oliver Gogarty.

'ANTWERP,
'*September 3, 19—.*

'DEAR FATHER GOGARTY,
'You are a very human person after all, and it was very kind of you to think about my baby and kind of you to write to me about her. My baby is a little girl, and she has reddish hair like mine, and if ever you see her I think you will see me in her. The address of the woman who is looking after her is Mrs. Cust, 25, Henry Street, Guildford. Do go to see her and write me a long letter, telling me what you think of her. I am sure a trip to London will do you a great deal of good. Pack up your port-manteau, Father Gogarty, and go to London at once. Promise me that you will, and write to me about your impressions of London and Father O'Grady, and when you are tired of London come abroad. We are going on to Munich, that is all I know, but I will write again.

'Very sincerely yours,
'NORA GLYNN.'

Father Oliver sat wondering, and then, waking up suddenly, he went about his business, asking himself if she really meant all she said, for why should she wish him to go abroad, for his health or in the hope of meeting him — where? In Munich!

'A riddle, a riddle, which' — he reflected a moment — 'which my experience of life is not sufficient to solve.'

On his way to Derrinrush he was met by a man hurrying towards him. 'Sure it is I that am in luck this day, meeting your reverence on the road, for we shall be spared half a mile if you have the sacred elements about you.' So much the peasant blurted out between the gasps, and when his breath came easier the priest learnt that Catherine, the man's wife, was dying. 'Me brother's run for the doctor, but I, being the speedier, came for yourself, and if your reverence has the sacred elements about you, we'll go along together by a short cut over the hill.' 'I'm afraid I have not got the oil and there's nothing for it but to go back to the house.' 'The I'm afeard that Catherine will be too late to get the Sacrament. But she is a good woman, sorra better, and maybe don't need the oil,' which indeed proved to be a fact, for when they reached the cabin they found the doctor there before them, who rising from his chair by the bedside, said, 'The woman is out of danger, if she ever was in any.' 'All the same', cried the peasant, 'Catherine wouldn't refuse the Sacrament.' 'But if she be in no danger, of what use would the Sacrament be to her?' the doctor asked; the peasant answering, 'Faith, you must have been a Protestant before you were a Catholic to be talking like that,' and Father Oliver hesitated, and left the cabin sorrowed by the unseemliness of the wrangle. He was not, however, many yards down the road when the dispute regarding the efficacy of the Sacrament administered out of due time was wiped out by memory of something Nora had told him of herself: she had announced to the monitresses, who were discussing their ambitions, that hers was to be the secretary of a man of letters. 'So it would seem that she had an instinct of her destiny from the beginning, just as I had of mine. But had I? Her path took an odd turn round by Garranard. But she has reached her goal, or nearly. The end may be marriage — with whom? Poole most likely. Be that as it may, she will pass on to middle age; we shall grow older and seas and continents will divide our graves. Why did she come to Garranard?'

From Father Oliver Gogarty to Miss Nora Glynn

'*September 10, 19—.*

'DEAR MISS GLYNN,

'I received your letter this morning, written from Antwerp, and it has set me thinking that Mr. Poole's interests in scholarship must have procured for him many acquaintances among Dutch scholars, men with whom he has been in correspondence. You will meet them and hear them pour their vast erudition across dinner-tables. Rubens' great picture, "The Descent from the Cross," is in Antwerp; you will go to see it, and in Munich Mr. Poole will treat you to the works of Wagner and Mozart. You are very happy; everything has gone well with you, and it would ill befit me, who brought so much unhappiness upon you, to complain that you are too happy, too much intent on the things of this world. Yet, if you will allow me to speak candidly, I will tell you what I really think. You are changing; the woman I once knew hardly corresponds with the woman who writes to me. In reading the letters of the English Nora, I perceive many traces here and there of the Irish Nora, for the Irish Nora was not without a sense of duty, of kindness towards others, but the English Nora seems bent upon a life of pleasure, intellectual and worldly adventures. She delights in foreign travel, and no doubt places feelings above ideas, and regards our instincts as our sovereign guides. Now, when we find ourselves delighting to this extent in the visible, we may be sure that our lives have wandered far away from spiritual things. There is ever a divorce between the world of sense and the world of spirit, and the question of how much love we may expend upon external things will always arise, and will always be a cause of perplexity to those who do not choose to abandon themselves to the general drift of sensual life. This question is as difficult as the cognate question of what are our duties toward ourselves and our duties toward others. And your letters raise all these questions. I ponder them in my walks by the lake in the afternoon. In the evening in my house on the hilltop I sit thinking, seeing in imagination the country where I have been born and where I have always lived — the lake winding in and out of headlands, the highroad shaded by sycamores at one spot, a little further on wandering like a gray thread among barren lands, with here and there a village; and I make application of all the suggestions your letters contain to my own case. Every house in

Garranard I know, and I see each gable end and each doorway as I sit thinking, and all the faces of my parishioners. I see lights springing up far and near. Wherever there is a light there is a poor family.

'Upon these people I am dependent for my daily bread, and they are dependent upon me for spiritual consolation. I baptize them, I marry them, and I bury them. How they think of me, I know not. I suppose they hardly think at all. When they return home at night they have little time for thinking; their bodies are too fatigued with the labour of the fields. But as I sit thinking of them, I regret to say that my fear often is that I shall never see any human beings but them; and I dream of long rambles in the French country, resting at towns, reading in libraries. A voice whispers, "You could do very well with a little of her life, but you will never know any other life but your present one". A great bitterness comes up, a little madness gathers behind the eyes; I walk about the room and then I sit down, stunned by the sudden conviction that life is, after all, a very squalid thing — something that I would like to kick like an old hat down a road.

'The conflict going on within me goes on within every man, but without this conflict life would be superficial; we shouldn't know the deeper life. Duty has its rewards as well as its pain, and the knowledge that I am passing through a time of probationship sustains me. I know I shall come out of it all a stronger man.

'OLIVER GOGARTY.'

After posting his letter he walked home, congratulating himself that he made it plain to her that he was not a man she could dupe. Her letter was written plainly, and the more he thought of her letter the clearer did it seem that it was inspired by Poole. But what could Poole's reason be for wishing him to leave Ireland, to go abroad? It was certain that if Poole were in love with Nora he would do all in his power to keep a poor priest (was it thus they spoke of him?) in Ireland. Poole might wish to make a fool of him, but what was her reason for advising him to go abroad? Revenge was too strong a word.

In the course of the evening it suddenly struck him that, after all, she might have written her letter with a view of inducing him to come to Rome. She was so capricious that it was not impossible that she had written quite sincerely, and wished him out there with her. She was so many-sided, and he fell to thinking of her character without being able to arrive at any clear estimate of it, with this result, however — that he could not drive out the belief that she had written him an insincere letter. Or did she wish to revenge herself? The thought brought him to his feet, for he could never forget how deeply he had wronged her — it was through his fault that she had become Mr. Poole's secretary — maybe his mistress. If he had not preached that sermon, she would be teaching the choir in his parish. But, good heavens! what use was there in going over all that again? He walked to the window and stood there watching the still autumn weather — a dull leaden sky, without a ray of light upon the grass, or a wind in the trees — thinking that these gray days deprived him of all courage. And then he remembered suddenly how a villager's horse coming from market had tripped and fallen by the road-side. Would that he, too, might fall by the roadside, so weary was he. 'If I could only make known my suffering, she would take pity on me; but no one knows another's suffering.' He walked from his window sighing, and a moment after stopped in front of his writing-table. Perhaps it was the writing-table that put the thought into his mind that she might like to read a description of an Irish autumn.

From Father Oliver Gogarty to Miss Nora Glynn.

'GARRANARD, BOHOLA,
September.

'You know the wind is hardly ever at rest about the hilltop on which my house stands. Even in summer the wind sighs, a long, gentle little sigh, sometimes not unpleasant to hear. You used to speak of an Æolian harp, and say that I should place one on my window-sill. A doleful instrument it must be — a loud wailing sound in winter-time, and in the summer a little sigh. But in these autumn days an Æolian harp would be mute. There is not wind enough to-day on the hillside to cause the faintest vibration.

Yesterday I went for a long walk in the woods, and I can find no words that would convey an idea of the stillness. It is easy to speak of a tomb, but it was more than that. The dead are dead, and somnambulism is more mysterious than death. The season seemed to stand on the edge of a precipice, will-less, like a sleep-walker. Now and then the sound of a falling leaf caught my ear, and I shall always remember how a crow, flying high overhead towards the mountains, uttered an ominous "caw"; another crow answered, and there was silence again. The branches dropped and the leaves hung out at the end of long stems. One could not help pitying the trees, though one knew one's pity was vain.

'As I wandered in Derrinrush, I came suddenly upon some blood-red beech-trees, and the hollow was full of blood-red leaves. You have been to Derrinrush: you know how mystic and melancholy the wood is, full of hazels and Druid stones. After wandering a long while I turned into a path. It led me to a rough western shore, and in front of me stood a great Scotch fir. The trunk has divided, and the two crowns showed against the leaden sky. It has two birch-trees on either side, and their graceful stems and faint foliage, pale like gold, made me think of dancers with sequins in their hair and sleeves. There seemed to be nothing but silence in the wood, silence, and leaves ready to fall. I had not spoken to anyone for a fortnight — I mean I had no conversation with anyone — and my loneliness helped me to perceive the loneliness of the wood, and the absence of birds made me feel it. The lake is never without gulls, but I didn't see one yesterday. "The swallows are gone", I said; "the wild geese will soon be here", and I remembered their doleful cry as I scrambled under some blackthorn bushes, glad to get out of the wood into the fields. Though I knew the field I was in well, I didn't remember the young sycamores growing in one corner of it. Yesterday I could not but notice them, for they seemed to be like children dying of consumption in a hospital ward — girls of twelve or thirteen. You will think the comparison far-fetched and unheal-thy, one that could only come out of a morbidly excited imagin-ation. Well, I cannot help that; like you, I must write as I feel.

'Suddenly I heard the sound of an axe, and I can find no words to tell you how impressive its sound was in the still autumn day. "How soon will the tree fall?" I thought; and, desirous of seeing it fall, I walked on, guided by the sound, till I saw at the end of the glade— whom do you think? Do you remember an old man called Patsy Murphy? He had once been a very good carpenter, and had made and saved money. But he is now ninety-five, and I could hardly believe my eyes when I saw him trying to cut down a larch. What his object could be in felling the tree I could not tell, and, feeling some curiosity, I walked forward. He continued to chip away pieces of the bark till his strength failed him, and he had to sit down to rest. Seeing me, he took off his hat— you know the tall hat he wears — a hat given him twenty or thirty years ago by whom? Patsy Murphy's mind is beginning to wander. He tells stories as long as you will listen to him, and it appears now that his daughter-in-law turned him out of his house— the house he had built himself, and that he had lived in for half a century. This, however, is not the greatest wrong she had done him. He could forgive her this wrong, but he cannot forgive her stealing of his sword. "There never was a Murphy", he said, "who hadn't a sword". Whether this sword is an imagination of Patsy's fading brain, I cannot say; perhaps he had some old sword and lost it. The tale he tells to-day differs wholly from the tale he told yesterday and the tale he will tell to-morrow. He told me once he had been obliged to give up all his savings to his son. I went to interview the son, determined to sift the matter to the bottom, and discovered that Patsy had still one hundred and twenty pounds in the bank. Ten pounds had been taken out for — I needn't trouble you with further details. Sufficient has been said to enable you to understand how affecting it was to meet this old man in the red and yellow woods, at the end of a breathless autumn day, trying to fell a young larch. He talked so rapidly, and one story flowed so easily into another, that it was a long time before I could get in a word. At last I was able to get out of him that the Colonel had given him leave to build a house on the shore, where he would be out of everybody's way. "All my old friends are gone, the Colonel's father and his mother. God be merciful to her! she was a good woman, the very best. And all I want now is time to think of them that's gone. . . . Didn't I know the Colonel's grandfather and his grandmother? They're all buried in the cemetery yonder in Kiltoon, and on a fine evenin' I do like to be sittin' on a stone by the lake, thinking of them all."

'It was at once touching and impressive to see this old man, weak as a child, the only tembling thing in a moveless day, telling

these wonderings of an almost insane brain. You will say, "But
what matter? They may not be true in fact, but they are his truth,
they are himself, they are his age". His ninety-five years are
represented in his confused talk, half recollection, half complaints about the present. He knew my father and mother, too,
and, peering into my face, he caught sight of a gray hair, and I
heard him mutter:

' "Ah! they grow gray quicker now than they used to".

'As I walked home in the darkening light, I bethought myself of
the few years left to me to live, though I am still a young man, that
in a few years, which would pass like a dream, I should be as frail
as Patsy Murphy, who is ninety-five. "Why should I not live as
long?" I asked myself, losing my teeth one by one and my wits.'

'September.

'I was interrupted in my description of the melancholy season,
and I don't know how I should have finished that letter if I had
not been interrupted. The truth is that the season was but a
pretext. I did not dare to write asking you to forgive me for
having returned your letter. I do not do so now. I will merely say
that I returned the letter because it annoyed me, and, shameful as
the admission may be, I admit that I returned it because I wished
to annoy you. I said to myself, "If this be so — if, in return for kind
thought—— Why shouldn't she suffer? I suffer." One isn't— one
cannot be — held responsible for every base thought that enters
the mind. How long the mind shall entertain a thought before
responsibility is incurred I am not ready to say. One's mood
changes. A storm gathers, rages for a while, and disperses; but the
traces of the storm remain after the storm has passed away. I am
thinking now that perhaps, after all, you were sincere when you
asked me to leave Garranard and take my holiday in Rome, and
the baseness of which for a moment I deemed you capable was the
creation of my own soul. I don't mean that my mind, my soul, is
always base. At times we are more or less unworthy. Our tempers
are part of ourselves? I have been pondering this question lately.
Which self is the true self — the peaceful or the choleric? My
wretched temper aggravated my disappointment, and my failure
to write the history of the lake and its castles no doubt contributed
to produce the nervous depression from which I am suffering.

But this is not all; it seems to me that I may point out that your— I hardly know what word to use: "irrelevancy" does not express my meaning; "inconsequences" is nearer, yet it isn't the word I want — well, your inconsequences perplex and distract my thoughts. If you will look through the letter you sent me last you will find that you have written many things that might annoy a man living in the conditions in which I live. You follow the current of your mood, but the transitions you omit, and the reader is left hopelessly conjecturing. . . .'

She seemed so strange, so inconclusive. There seemed to be at least two, if not three, different women in the letters she had written to him, and he sat wondering how a woman with cheeks like hers, and a voice like hers, and laughter like hers, could take an interest in such arid studies. Her very name, Nora Glynn, seemed so unlike the woman who would accompany Mr. Poole into National Libraries, and sit by him surrounded by learned tomes. Moreover a mistress does not read Hebrew in a National Library with her paramour. But what did he know about such women? He had heard of them supping in fashionable restaurants covered with diamonds, and he thought of them with painted faces and dyed hair, and he was sure that Nora did not dye her hair or paint her face. No, she was not Poole's mistress. It was only his ignorance of life that could have led him to think of anything so absurd. . . . And then, weary of thinking and debating with himself, he took down a book that was lent some months ago, a monograph on a learned woman, a learned philosophical writer and translator of exegetical works from the German. Like Nora, she came from the middle classes, and, like Nora, she transgressed, how often he did not know, but with another woman's husband certainly. A critical writer and exponent of serious literature. Taste for learned studies did not preclude abstinence from those sins which in his ignorance of life he had associated with worldlings! Of course, St. Augustine was such a one. But is a man's truth also woman's truth? Apparently it is, and if he could believe the book he had been reading, Nora might very well be Poole's mistress. Therewith the question came up again, demanding answer: Why did she write declining any correspondence with him, and three weeks afterwards write another letter inveigling him, tempting him, bringing him to this last pitch of unhappiness? Was the letter he returned to her prompted by Mr. Poole and by a spirit of revenge? Three days after he took up his pen and added this paragraph to his unfinished letter:

'I laid aside my pen, fearing I should ask what are your relations with Mr. Poole. I have tried to keep myself from putting this question to you, but the torture of doubt overcomes me, and even if you should never write to me again, I must ask it. Remember that I am responsible to God for the life you lead. Had it not been for me, you would never have known Poole. You must grant to every man his point of view, and, as a Christian, I cannot put my responsibility out of mind. If you lose your soul, I am responsible for it. Should you write that your relations with Mr. Poole are not innocent, I shall not be relieved of my responsibility, but it will be a relief to me to know the truth. I shall pray for you, and you will repent your sins if you are living in sin. Forgive me the question I am putting to you. I have no right to do so whatever. Whatever right I had over you when you were in my parish has passed from me. I exceeded that right, but that is the old story. Maybe I am repeating my very fault again. It is not unlikely, for what do we do all through our lives but to repeat ourselves? You have forgiven me, and, having forgiven me once, maybe you will forgive me again. However this may be, do not delay writing, for every day will be an agony till I hear from you. At the end of an autumn day, when the dusk is sinking into the room, one lacks courage to live. Religion seems to desert one, and I am thinking of the leaves falling, falling in Derrinrush. All night long they will be falling, like my hopes. Forgive me this miserable letter. But if I didn't write it, I should not be able to get through the evening. Write to me. A letter from Italy will cheer me and help me to live. All my letters are not like this one. Not very long ago I wrote to you about a hermit who never wearied of life, though he lived upon an island in this lake. Did you receive that letter? I wonder. It is still following you about maybe. It was a pleasant letter, and I should be sorry if you did not get it. Write to me about Italy — about sunshine, about statues and pictures.

'Ever sincerely yours,
'OLIVER GOGARTY.'

From Father Oliver Gogarty to Miss Nora Glynn.

'GARRANARD, BOHOLA,
'*October 20, 19—.*

'DEAR MISS GLYNN,

'I wrote last week apologizing for troubling you again with a letter, pleading that the melancholy of autumn and the falling of the leaf forced me to write to someone. I wrote asking for a letter, saying that a letter about Italian sunshine would help me to live. I am afraid my letter must have seemed exaggerated. One writes out of a mood. The mood passes, but when it is with one, one is the victim of it. And this letter is written to say I have recovered somewhat from my depression of spirits. . . . I have found consolation in a book, and I feel that I must send it to you, for even you may one day feel depressed and lonely. Did you ever read "The Imitation of Christ"? There is no book more soothing to the spirit than it; and on the very first page I found some lines which apply marvellously well to your case:

' "If thou didst know the whole Bible outwardly, and the sayings of all the philosophers, what would it all profit thee without charity and the grace of God?"

'Over the page the saint says: "Every man naturally desireth to know; but what doth knowledge avail without the fear of God?"

' "Truly, a lowly rustic that serveth God is better than a proud philosopher who pondereth the course of the stars and neglecteth himself."

' "He that knoweth himself becometh vile to himself, and taketh no delight in the praises of men."

' "If I knew all things that are in the world, and were not in charity, what would it profit me in the sight of God, who will judge according to deeds?"

' "Cease from overweening desire of knowledge, because many distractions are found there, and much delusion."

'I might go on quoting till I reached the end, for on every page I note something that I would have you read. But why quote when I can send you the book? You have lost interest in the sentimental side of religion, but your loss is only momentary. You will never find anyone who will understand you better than this book. You are engaged now in the vain pursuit of knowledge, but some day, when you are weary of knowledge, you will turn to it. I do not ask you to read it now, but promise me that you will keep it. It will be a great consolation to me to know that it is by you.

'Very sincerely yours,
'OLIVER GOGARTY, P.P.'

From Father Oliver Gogarty to Miss Nora Glynn.

'GARRANARD, BOHOLA,
'*November 3, 19—.*

'DEAR MISS GLYNN,

'I sent you — I think it must be a fortnight ago — a copy of "The Imitation of Christ". The copy I sent is one of the original Elizabethan edition, a somewhat rare book and difficult to obtain. I sent you this copy in order to make sure that you would keep it; the English is better than the English of our modern translations. You must not think that I feel hurt because you did not write to thank me at once for having sent you the book. My reason for writing is merely because I should like to know if it reached you. If you have not received it, I think it would be better to make inquiries at once in the post. It would be a pity that a copy of the original Elizabethan edition should be lost. Just write a little short note saying that you have received it.

'Very sincerely yours,
'OLIVER GOGARTY, P.P.'

IX

'The Imitation' dropped on his knees, and he wondered if the spiritual impulse it had awakened in him was exhausted, or if the continual splashing of the rain on the pane had got upon his nerves.

'But it isn't raining in Italy,' he said, getting up from his chair; 'and I am weary of the rain, of myself — I am weary of everything.' And going to the window, he tried to take an interest in the weather, asking himself if it would clear up about 3 o'clock. It cleared usually late in the afternoon for a short while, and he would be able to go out for half an hour. But where should he go? He foresaw his walk from end to end before he began it: the descent of the hill, the cart-track and the old ruts full of water, the dead reeds on the shore soaking, the dripping trees. But he knew that about 3 o'clock the clouds would lift, and the sunset begin in the gaps in the mountains. He might go as far as the little fields between Derrinrush and the plantations, and from there he could watch the sunset. But the sunset would soon be over, and he would have to return home, for a long evening without a book. Terrible! And he began to feel that he must have an occupation — his book! To write the story of the island castles would pass the time, and wondering how he might write it, whether from oral tradition or from the books and manuscripts which he might find in national libraries, he went out about 3 o'clock and wandered down the old cart-track, getting his feet very wet, till he came to the pine-wood, into which he went, and stood looking across the lake, wondering if he should go out to Castle Island in a boat — there was no boat, but he might borrow one somewhere — and examine what remained of the castle. But he knew every heap of old stones, every brown bush, and the thick ivy that twined round the last corner wall. Castle Hag had an interest Castle Island had not. The cormorants roosted there; and they must be hungry, for the lake had been too windy for fishing this long while. A great gust whirled past, and he stood watching the clouds drifting overhead — the same thick vapour drifting and going out. For nearly a month he was waiting for a space of blue sky, and a great sadness fell upon him, a sick longing for a change; but if he yielded to this longing he would never return to Garranard. There seemed to be no way out of the difficulty — at least, he could see none.

A last ray lit up a distant hillside, his shadow floated on the wet sand. The evening darkened rapidly, and he walked in a vague diffused light, inexpressibly sad to find Moran waiting for him at the end of an old cart-track, where the hawthorns grew out of a tumbled wall. He would keep Moran for supper. Moran was a human being, and——

'I've come to see you, Gogarty; I don't know if I'm welcome.'

'It's joking you are. You'll stay and have some supper with me?'

'Indeed I will, if you give me some drink, for it's drink that I'm after, and not eating. I'd better get the truth out at once and have done with it. I've felt the craving coming on me for the last few days— you know what I mean— and now it's got me by the throat. I must have a drink. Come along, Gogarty, and give me some, and then I'll say good-bye to you for ever.'

'Now what are you saying?'

'Don't stand arguing with me, for you can't understand, Gogarty— no one can; I can't myself. But it doesn't matter what anybody understands — I'm done for.'

'We'll have a bit of supper together. It will pass from you.'

'Ah, you little know;' and the priests walked up the hill in silence.

'Gogarty, there's no use talking; I'm done for. Let me go.'

'Come in, will you?' and he took him by the arm. 'Come in. I'm a bigger man than you, Moran; come in!'

'I'm done for,' Father Moran said again.

Father Oliver made a sign of silence, and when they were in the parlour, and the door shut behind them, he said:

'You mustn't talk like that, and Catherine within a step of you.'

'I've told you, Gogarty, I'm done for, and I've just come here to bid you good-bye; but before we part I'd like to hear you say that I haven't been wanting in my duties — that in all the rest, as far as you know, I've been as good a man as another.'

'In all but one thing I know no better man, and I'll not hear that there's no hope.'

'Better waste no time talking. Just let me hear you say again that I've been a good man in everything but one thing.'

'Yes, indeed;' and the priests grasped hands.

And Catherine came into the room to ask if Father Moran was stopping to supper. Father Oliver answered hurriedly: 'Yes, yes, he's staying. Bring in supper as soon as you can;' and she went away, to come back soon after with the cloth. And while she laid it the priests sat looking at each other, not daring to speak, hoping that Catherine did not suspect from their silence and manner that anything was wrong. She seemed to be a long while laying the cloth and bringing in the food; it seemed to them as if she was delaying on purpose. At last the door was closed, and they were alone.

'Now, Moran, sit down and eat a bit, won't you?'

'I can't eat anything. Give me some whisky; that is what I want. Give me some whisky, and I will go away and you'll never see me again. Just a glass to keep me going, and I will go straight out of your parish, so that none of the disgrace will fall upon you; or — what do you think? You could put me up here; no one need know I'm here. All I want are a few bottles of whisky.'

'You mean that I should put you up here and let you get drunk?'

'You know what I mean well enough. I'm like that. And it's well for you who don't want whisky. But if it hadn't been for whisky I should have been in a mad-house long ago. Now, just tell me if you'll give me a drink. If you will, I'll stay and talk with you, for I know you're lonely; if not, I'll just be off with myself.'

'Moran, you'll be better when you've had something to eat. It will pass from you. I will give you a glass of beer.'

'A glass of beer! Ah, if I could tell you the truth! We've all our troubles, Gogarty — trouble that none knows but God. I haven't been watching you — I've been too tormented about myself to think much of anyone else — but now and then I've caught sight of a thought passing across your mind. We all suffer, you like another, and when the ache becomes too great to be borne we drink. Whisky is the remedy; there's none better. We drink and forget, and that is the great thing. There are times, Gogarty, when one doesn't want to think, when one's afraid, aren't there? — when one wants to forget that one's alive. You've had that feeling, Gogarty. We all have it. And now I must be off. I must forget everything. I want to drink and to feel the miles passing under my feet.'

And on that he got up from the fire.

'Come, Moran, I won't hear you speak like that.'

'Let me go. It's no use; I'm done for;' and Father Oliver saw his eyes light up.

'I'll not keep you against your will, but I'll go a piece of the road with you.'

'I'd sooner you didn't come, Gogarty.'

Without answering, Father Oliver caught up his hat and followed Father Moran out of the house. They walked without speaking, and when they got to the gate Father Oliver began to wonder which way his unhappy curate would choose for escape. 'Now why does he take the southern road?' And a moment after he guessed that Moran was making for Michael Garvey's public-house, 'and after drinking there,' he said to himself, 'he'll go on to Tinnick.' After a couple of miles, however, Moran turned into a by-road leading through the mountains, and they walked on without saying a word.

And they walked mile after mile through the worn mountain road.

'You've come far enough, Gogarty; go back. Regan's public-house is outside of your parish.'

'If it's outside my parish, it's only the other side of the boundary; and you said, Moran, that you wouldn't touch whisky till to-morrow morning.'

The priests walked on again, and Father Oliver fell to thinking now what might be the end of this adventure. He could see there was no hope of persuading Father Moran from the bottle of whisky.

'What time do you be making it, Gogarty?'

'It isn't ten o'clock yet.'

'Then I'll walk up and down till the stroke of twelve. . . . I'll keep my promise to you.'

'But they'll all be in bed by twelve. What will you do then?'

Father Moran didn't give Father Gogarty an answer, but started off again, and this time he was walking very fast; and when they got as far as Regan's public-house Father Oliver took his friend by the arm, reminding him again of his promise.

'You promised not to disgrace the parish.'

'I said that. . . . Well, if it's walking your heart is set upon, you shall have your bellyful of it.'

And he was off again like a man walking for a wager. But Father Oliver, who wouldn't be out-walked, kept pace with him, and they went striding along, walking without speaking.

Full of ruts and broken stones, the road straggled through the hills, and Father Oliver wondered what would happen when they got to the top of the hill. For the sea lay beyond the hill. The road bent round a shoulder of the hill, and when Father Oliver saw the long road before him his heart began to fail him, and a cry of despair rose to his lips; but at that moment Moran stopped.

'You've saved me, Gogarty.'

He did not notice that Father Gogarty was breathless, almost fainting, and he began talking hurriedly, telling Father Oliver how he had committed himself to the resolution of breaking into a run as soon as they got to the top of the hill.

'My throat was on fire then, but now all the fire is out of it; your prayer has been answered. But what's the matter, Gogarty? You're not speaking.'

'What you say is wonderful indeed, Moran, for I was praying for you. I prayed as long as I had breath; one can't pray without breath or speak. We'll talk of this presently.'

The priests turned back, walking very slowly.

'I feel no more wish to drink whisky than I do to drink bog-water. But I'm a bit hot, and I think I'd like a drink, and a drink of water will do me first-rate. Now look here, Gogarty: a miracle has happened, and we should thank God for it. Shall we kneel down?'

The road was very wet, and they thought it would do as well if they leant over the little wall and said some prayers together.

'I've conquered the devil; I know it. But I've been through a terrible time, Gogarty. It's all lifted from me now. I'm sorry I've brought you out for such a walk as this.'

'Never mind the walk, Moran, so long as the temptation has passed from you — that's the principal thing.'

To speak of ordinary things was impossible, for they believed in the miracle, and, thanking God for this act of grace, they walked on until they reached Father Oliver's gate.

'I believe you're right, Moran; I believe that a miracle has happened. You'll go home straight, won't you?'

Father Moran grasped Father Oliver's hand.

'Indeed I will.'

And Father Oliver stood by his gate looking down the road, and he didn't open it and go through until Father Moran had passed out of sight. Pushing it open, he walked up the gravel path, saying to himself, 'A miracle, without doubt. Moran called it a miracle and it seems like one, but will it last? Moran believes himself cured, that is certain;' and Father Oliver thought how his curate had gripped his hand, and felt sure that the grip meant, 'You've done me a great service, one I can never repay.'

It was a pleasure to think that Moran would always think well of him. 'Yes, Moran will always think well of me,' he repeated as he groped his way into the dark and lonely house in search of a box of matches. When his lamp was lighted he threw himself into his armchair so that he might ponder better on what had happened. 'I've been a good friend to him, and it's a great support to a man to think that he's been a good friend to another, that he kept him in the straight path, saved him from himself. Saved himself from himself,' he repeated; 'can anybody be saved from himself?' and he began to wonder if Moran would conquer in the end and take pride in his conquest over himself.

There was no sound, only an occasional spit of the lamp, and in the silence Father Oliver asked if it were the end of man's life to trample upon self or to encourage self. 'Nora,' he said, 'would answer that self is all we have, and to destroy it and put in its place conventions and prejudices is to put man's work above God's. But Nora would not answer in these words till she had spoken with Mr. Walter Poole.' The name brought a tightening about his heart, and when Father Oliver stumbled to his feet — he had walked many miles, and was tired — he began to think he must tell Nora of the miracle that had happened about a mile — he thought it was just a mile — beyond Patsy Regan's public-house. The miracle would impress her, and he looked round the room. It was then he caught sight of a letter — her letter. The envelope and foreign stamp told him that before he read the address — her writing! His hand trembled and his cheek paled, for she was telling him the very things he had longed to know. She was in love with Poole! she was not only in love with him — she was his mistress!

The room seemed to tumble about him, and he grasped the end of the chimney-piece. And then, feeling that he must get out into the open air, he thought of Moran. He began to feel he must speak to him. He couldn't remember exactly what he had to say to him, but there was something on his mind which he must speak to Moran about. It seemed to him that he must go away with Moran to some public-house far away and drink. Hadn't Moran said that there were times when we all wanted drink? He tried to collect his thoughts. . . . Something had gone wrong, but he couldn't remember what had gone wrong or where he was. It seemed to him that somebody had lost her soul. He must seek it. It was his duty. Being a priest, he must go forth and find the soul, and bring it back to God. He remembered no more until he found himself in the midst of a great wood, standing in an open space; about him were dripping trees, and a ghostly sky overhead, and no sound but that of falling leaves. Large leaves floated down, and each interested him till it reached the wet earth.

And then he began to wonder why he was in the wood at night, and why he should be waiting there, looking at the glimmering sky, seeing the oak-leaves falling, remembering suddenly that he was looking for her soul, for her lost soul, and that something had told him he would find the soul he was seeking in the wood; so he was drawn from glade to glade through the underwoods, and through places so thickly overgrown that it seemed impossible to pass through. And then the thorn-bushes gave way before him, for he was no longer alone. She had descended from the trees into his arms, white and cold, and every moment the wood grew dimmer; but when he expected it to disappear, when he thought he was going to escape for ever with her, an opening in the trees discovered the lake, and in fear he turned back into the wood, seeking out paths where there was little light.

Once he was within the wood, the mist seemed to incorporate again; she descended again into his arms, and this time he would have lifted the veil and looked into her face, but she seemed to forbid him to recognize her under penalty of loss. His desire overcame him, and he put out his hand to lift the veil. As he did so his eyes opened, he saw the wet wood, the shining sky, and she sitting by a stone waiting for him. A little later she came to meet him from behind the hawthorns that grew along the cart-track — a tall woman with a little bend in her walk.

He wondered why he was so foolish as to disobey her, and besought her to return to him, and they roamed again in the paths that led round the rocks overgrown with briars, by the great oak-tree where the leaves were falling. And wandering they went, smiling gently on each other, till she began to tell him that he must abide by the shores of the lake — why, he could not understand, for the wood was much more beautiful, and he was more alone with her in the wood than by the lake.

The sympathy was so complete that words were not needed, but they had begun in his ears. He strove to apprehend the dim words sounding in his ears. Not her words, surely, for there was a roughness in the voice, and presently he heard somebody asking him why he was about this time of night, and very slowly he began to understand that one of his parishioners was by him, asking him whither he was going.

'You'll be catching your death at this hour of the night, Father Oliver.'

And the man told Father Oliver he was on his way to a fair, and for a short-cut he had come through the wood. And Father Oliver listened, thinking all the while that he must have been dreaming, for he could remember nothing.

'Now, your reverence, we're at your own door, and the door is open. When you went out you forgot to close it.'

The priest didn't answer.

'I hope no harm will come to your reverence; and you'll be lucky if you haven't caught your death.'

X

HE stopped in his undressing to ponder how Moran had come to tell him that he was going away on a drinking-bout, and all their long walk together to within a mile of Regan's public-house returned to him bit by bit, how Moran knelt down by the roadside to drink bog-water, which he said would take the thirst from him as well as whisky; and after bidding Moran good-night he had fallen into his armchair. It was not till he rose to his feet to go to bed that he had caught sight of the letter. Nora wrote — he could not remember exactly what she wrote, and threw himself into bed. After sleeping for many hours, his eyes at last opened, and he awoke wondering, asking himself where he was. Even the familiar room surprised him. And once more he began the process of picking his way back, but he couldn't recall what had happened from the time he left his house in search of Moran till he was overtaken by Alec in the wood. In some semi-conscious state he must have wandered off to Derrinrush. He must have wandered a long while — two hours, maybe more — through the familiar paths, but unaware that he was choosing them. To escape from the effort of remembrance he was glad to listen to Catherine, who was telling him that Alec was at the door, come up from the village to inquire how the priest was.

She waited to hear Father Oliver's account of himself, but not having a story prepared, he pretended he was too tired to speak; and as he lay back in his chair he composed a little story, telling how he had been for a long walk with Father Moran, and, coming back in the dark, had missed his way on the outskirts of the wood. She began to raise some objections, but he said she was not to excite herself, and went out to see Alec, who, not being a quick-witted fellow, was easily persuaded into an acceptance of a very modified version of the incident, and Father Oliver lay back in his chair wondering if he had succeeded in deceiving Catherine. It would seem that he had, for when she came to visit him again from her kitchen she spoke of something quite different, which surprised him, for she was a very observant woman of inexhaustible curiosity. But this time, however, he had managed to keep his secret from her, and, dismissing her, he thought of Nora's letter.

From Miss Nora Glynn to Father Oliver Gogarty.

'RAPALLO, ITALY,
'*December 12, 19—.*

'DEAR FATHER GOGARTY,

'I received "The Imitation" today and your two letters, one asking me if I had got the book. We had left Munich without giving instructions about our letters, so please accept my apologies and my best thanks. The Elizabethan translation, as you point out, is beautiful English, and I am glad to have the book; it will remind me of you, and I will keep it by me even if I do not read it very often. I passed the book over to Mr. Poole; he read it for a few minutes, and then returned it to me. "A worthy man, no doubt," he said, "but prone to taking things for granted. 'The Imitation,' " he continued, "reminds me of a flower growing in the shade of a cloister, dying for lack of sun, and this is surely not the right kind of reading for you or your friend Father Oliver." I feel sure you want a change. Change of scene brings a change of mind. Why don't you come to Italy? Italy is the place for you. Italy is your proper mind. Mr. Poole says that Italy is every man's proper mind, and you're evidently thinking of Italy, for you ask for a description of where I am staying, saying that a ray of Italian sunlight will cheer you. Come to Italy. You can come here without any danger of meeting us. We are leaving at the end of the month.

'But I could go on chattering page after page, telling you about gardens and orange-trees (the orange-trees are the best part of the decoration; even now the great fruit hangs in the green leaves); and when I had described Italy, and you had described all the castles and the islands, we could turn back and discuss our religious differences. But I doubt if any good would come of this correspondence. You see, I have got my work to do, and you have got yours, and, notwithstanding all you say, I do not believe you to be unable to write the history of the lake and its castles. Your letters prove that you can, only your mind is unhinged by fears for my spiritual safety, and depressed by the Irish climate. It is very depressing, I know. I remember how you used to attribute the history of Ireland to the climate: a beautiful climate in a way, without extremes of heat and cold, as you said once, without an accent upon it. But you are not the ordinary Irishman; there is enough vitality in you to resist the langour of the climate. Your mood will pass away. . . . Your letter about the hermit that lived on Church Island is most beautiful. You have struck the right note — the wistful Irish note — and if you can write a book in that strain I am sure it will meet with great success. Go on with your book, and don't write to me any more — at least, not for the present. I have got too much to do, and cannot attend to a lengthy correspondence. We are going to Paris, and are looking forward to spending a great deal of time reading in the National Library. Some day we may meet, or take up this correspondence again. At present I feel that it is better for you and better for me that it should cease. But you will not think hardly of me because I write you this. I am writing in your own interests, dear Father Gogarty.

'Very sincerely yours,
'NORA GLYNN.'

He read the letter slowly, pondering every sentence and every word, and when he had finished it his hand dropped upon his knee; and when the letter fell upon the hearthrug he did not stoop to pick it up, but sat looking into the fire, convinced that everything was over and done. There was nothing to look forward to; his life would drag on from day to day, from week to week, month to month, year to year, till at last he would be taken away to the grave. The grave is dreamless! But there might be a long time before he reached it, living for years without seeing or even hearing from her, for she would weary of writing to him. He began to dream of a hunt, the quarry hearing with dying ears the horns calling to each other in the distance, and cast in his chair, his arms hanging like dead arms, his senses mercifully benumbed, he lay, how long he knew not, but it must have been a long time.

Catherine came into the room with some spoons in her hands, and asked him what was the matter, and, jumping up, he answered her rudely, for her curiosity annoyed him. It was irritating to have to wait for her to leave the room, but he did not dare to begin thinking while she was there. The door closed at last; he was alone again, and his thoughts fixed themselves at once on the end of her letter, on the words, 'Go on with your book, and don't write to me any more — at least, not for the present. I have too much to do, and cannot attend to a lengthy correspondence.' The evident cruelty of her words surprised him. There was nothing like this in any of her other letters. She intended these words as a *coup de grâce*. There was little mercy in them, for they left him living; he still lived — in a way.

There was no use trying to misunderstand her words. To do so would be foolish, even if it were possible for him to deceive himself, and the rest of her letter mattered nothing to him. The two little sentences with which she dismissed him were his sole concern; they were the keys to the whole of this correspondence which had beguiled him. Fool that he had been not to see it! Alas we see only what we want to see. He wandered about the lake, trying to bring himself to hate her. He even stopped in his walks to address insulting words to her. Words of common abuse came to his tongue readily, but there was an unconquerable tenderness in his heart always; and one day the thought went by that it was nobler of her to make him suffer than to have meekly forgiven him, as many women would have done, because he was a priest. He stopped affrighted, and began to wonder if this were the first time her easy forgiveness of his mistake had seemed suspicious. No, he felt sure that some sort of shadow of disappointment had passed at the back of his mind when he read her first letter, and after having lain for months at the back of his mind, this idea had come to the surface. An extraordinary perversion, truly, which he could only account for by the fact that he had always looked upon her as being more like what the primitive woman must have been than anybody else in the world; and the first instinct of the primitive woman would be to revenge any slight on her sexual pride. He had misread her character, and in this new reading he found a temporary consolation.

As he sat thinking of her he heard a mouse gnawing under the boards, and every night after the mouse came to gnaw. 'The teeth

of regret are the same; my life is being gnawed away. Never shall I
see her.' It seemed impossible that life would close on him without
his seeing her face or hearing her voice again, and he began to
think how it would be if they were to meet on the other side. For
he believed in heaven, and that was a good thing. Without such
belief there would be nothing for him to do but to go down to the
lake and make an end of himself. But believing as he did in
heaven and the holy Catholic Church to be the surest way of
getting there, he had a great deal to be thankful for. Poole's
possession of her was but temporary, a few years at most, whereas
his possession of her, if he were so fortunate as to gain heaven,
and by his prayers to bring her back to the true fold, would
endure for ever and ever. The wisest thing, therefore, for him to
do would be to enter a Trappist monastery. But our Lord says
that in heaven there is neither marriage nor giving in marriage,
and what would heaven be to him without Nora? No more than a
union of souls, and he wanted her body as well as her soul. He
must pray. He knew the feeling well— a sort of mental giddiness,
a delirium in the brain; and it increased rapidly, urging him to fall
on his knees. If he resisted, it was because he was ashamed and
feared to pray to God to reserve Nora for him. But the whirl in his
brain soon deprived him of all power of resistance, and, looking
round the room hurriedly to assure himself he was not watched,
he fell on his knees and burst into extemporary prayer: *'O my God,
whatever punishment there is to be borne, let me bear it. She sinned, no
doubt, and her sins must be atoned for. Let me bear the punishment that
thou, in thine infinite wisdom, must adjudge to her, poor sinful woman
that she is, poor woman persecuted by men, persecuted by me. O my God,
remember that I lent a willing ear to scandalmongers, that I went down
that day to the school and lost my temper with her, that I spoke against her
in my church. All the sins that have been committed are my sins; let me bear
the punishment. O my Lord Jesus Christ, do thou intercede with thy Father
and ask him to heap all the punishment on my head. Oh, dear Lord Jesus, if
I had only thought of thee when I went down to the school, if I had
remembered thy words, "Let him who is without sin cast the first stone," I
should have been spared this anguish. If I had remembered thy words, she
might have gone to Dublin and had her baby there, and come back to the
parish. O my God, the fault is mine; all the faults that have been committed
can be traced back to me, therefore I beseech of thee, I call upon thee, to let
me bear all the punishment that she has earned by her sins, poor erring*

*creature that she is. O my God, do this for me; remember that I served thee
well for many years when I lived among the poor folk in the mountains.
For all these years I ask this thing of thee, that thou wilt let me bear her
punishment. Is it too much I am asking of thee, O my God, is it too much?'*

When he rose from his knees, bells seemed to be ringing in his
head, and he began to wonder if another miracle had befallen
him, for it was as if someone had laid hands on him and forced
him on his knees. But to ask the Almighty to extend his protection
to him rather than to Mr. Poole, who was a Protestant, seemed not
a little gross. Father Oliver experienced a shyness that he had
never known before, and he hoped the Almighty would not be
offended at the familiarity of the language, or the intimate nature
of the request, for to ask for Nora's body as well as her soul did not
seem altogether seemly.

It was queer to think like that. Perhaps his brain was giving way.
And he pushed the plates aside; he could not eat any dinner, nor
could he take any interest in his garden.

The dahlias were over, the chrysanthemums were beginning.
Never had the country seemed so still: dead birds in the woods,
and the sounds of leaves, and the fitful December sunlight on the
strands — these were his distractions when he went out for a walk,
and when he came in he often thought it would be well if he did
not live to see another day, so heavy did the days seem, so un-
eventful, and in these languid autumn days the desire to write to
Nora crept nearer, until it always seemed about him like some
familiar animal.

From Father Oliver Gogarty to Miss Nora Glynn.

'GARRANARD, BOHOLA,
'December 30, 19—.

'DEAR MISS GLYNN,

'I should have written to you before, but I lacked courage. Do
you remember saying that the loneliness of the country sometimes forced you to kneel down to pray that you might die? I think
the loneliness that overcame you was the loneliness that comes at
the end of an autumn day when the dusk gathers in the room. It
seems to steal all one's courage away, and one looks up from one's
work in despair, asking of what value is one's life. The world goes
on just the same, grinding our souls away. Nobody seems to care;
nothing seems to make any difference.

'Human life is a very lonely thing, and for that it is perhaps religious. But there are days when religion fails us, when we lack courage, lonesomeness being our national failing. We were always lonesome, hundreds of years ago as much as to-day. You know it, you have been through it and will sympathize. A caged bird simply beats its wings and dies, but a human being does not die of loneliness, even when he prays for death. You have experienced it all, and you will know what I feel when I tell you that I spend my time watching the rain, thinking of sunshine, picture-galleries, and libraries.

'But you were right to bid me go on with the book I spoke to you about. If I had gone away, as you first suggested, I should have been unhappy; I should have thought continually of the poor people I left behind; my abandonment of them would have preyed on my mind, for the conviction is dead in me that I should have been able to return to them; we mayn't return to places where we have been unhappy. I might have been able to get a parish in England or a chaplaincy, but I should have always looked upon the desertion of my poor people as a moral delinquency. A quiet conscience is, after all, a great possession, and for the sake of a quiet conscience I will remain here, and you will be able to understand my scruple when you think how helpless my people are, and how essential is the kindly guidance of the priest.

'Without a leader, the people are helpless; they wander like sheep on a mountain-side, falling over rocks or dying amid snow-drifts. Sometimes the shepherd grows weary of watching, and the question comes, Has a man no duty towards himself? And then one begins to wonder what is one's duty and what is duty — if duty is something more than the opinions of others, something more than a convention which we would not like to hear called into question, because we feel instinctively that it is well for everyone to continue in the rut, for, after all, a rut means a road, and roads are necessary. If one lets one's self go on thinking, one very soon finds that wrong and right are indistinguishable, so perhaps it is better to follow the rut if one can. But the rut is beset with difficulties; there are big holes on either side. Sometimes the road ends nowhere, and one gets lost in spite of one's self. But why am I writing all these things to you?'

Why, indeed? If he were to send this letter she would show it to

Mr. Poole, and they would laugh over it together. 'Poor priesty!' they would say, and the paper was crumpled and thrown into the fire. 'My life is unendurable, and it will grow worse,' he said, and fell to thinking how he would grow old, getting every day more like an old stereotyped plate, the Mass and the rosary at the end of his tongue, and nothing in his heart. He had seen many priests like this. Could he fall into such miserable decadence? Could such obedience to rule be any man's duty? But where should he go? It mattered little whither he went, for he would never see her any more, and she was, after all, the only real thing in the world for him.

So did he continue to suffer like an animal, mutely, instinctively, mourning his life away, forgetful of everything but his grief; unmindful of his food, and unable to sleep when he lay down, or to distinguish between familiar things— the birds about his house, the boys and girls he had baptized. Very often he had to think a moment before he knew which was Mary and which was Bridget, which was Patsy and which was Mike, and very often Catherine was in the parlour many minutes before he noticed her presence. She stood watching him, wondering of what he was thinking, for he sat in his chair, getting weaker and thinner; and soon he began to look haggard as an old man or one about to die. He seemed to grow feebler in mind; his attention wandered away every few minutes from the book he was reading. Catherine noticed the change, and, thinking that a little chat would be of help, she often came up from her kitchen to tell him the gossip of the parish; but he could not listen to her, her garrulousness seemed to him more than ever tiresome, and he kept a book by him, an old copy of 'Ivanhoe,' which he pretended he was reading when he heard her step.

Father Moran came to discuss the business of the parish with him and insisted on relieving Father Oliver of a great deal of it, saying that he wanted a rest, and he often urged Father Oliver to go away for a holiday. He was kind, but his talk was wearisome, and Father Oliver thought he would prefer to read about the fabulous Rowena than to hear any more about the Archbishop. But when Father Moran left Rowena bored him, and so completely that he could not remember at what point he had left off reading, and his thoughts wandered from the tournament to some phrase he had made use of in writing to Nora, or, it might be, some phrase of hers that would suddenly spring into his mind. He sought no longer to discover her character from her letters, nor did he criticize the many contradictions which had perplexed him: it seemed to him that he accepted her now, as the phrase goes, 'as she was', thinking of her as he might of some super-natural being whom he had offended, and who had revenged herself. Her wickedness became in his eyes an added grace, and from the rack on which he lay he admired his executioner. Even her liking for Mr. Poole became submerged in a tide of suffering, and of longing, and weakness of spirit. He no longer had any strength to question her liking for the minor prophets: there were discrepancies in everyone, and no doubt there were in him as well as in her. He had once been very different from what he was today. Once he was an ardent student in Maynooth, he had been an energetic curate; and now what was he? Worse still, what was he becoming? And he allowed his thoughts to dwell on the fact that every day she was receding from him. He, too, was receding. All things were receding — becoming dimmer.

He piled the grate up with turf, and when the blaze came leaned over it, warming his hands, asking himself why she liked Mr. Poole rather than him. For he no longer tried to conceal from himself the fact that he loved her. He had played the hypocrite long enough; he had spoken about her soul, but it was herself that he wanted. This admission brought some little relief, but he felt that the relief would only be temporary. Alas! it was surrender. It was worse than surrender — it was abandonment. He could sink no deeper. But he could; we can all sink deeper. Now what would the end be? There is an end to everything; there must be an end even to humiliation, to self-abasement. It was Moran over again. Moran was ashamed of his vice, but he had to accept it, and Father Oliver thought how much it must have cost his curate to come to tell him that he wanted to lie drunk for some days in an outhouse in order to escape for a few days from the agony of living. 'That is what he called it, and I, too, would escape from it.'

His thoughts turned suddenly to a poem written by a peasant in County Cork a hundred years ago to a woman who inspired a passion that wrecked his mind altogether in the end. And he wondered if madness would be the end of his suffering, or if he would go down to the lake and find rest in it.

'Oh, succour me, dear one, give me a kiss from thy mouth,
　And lift me up to thee from death,
Or bid them make for me a narrow bed, a coffin of boards,
　In the dark neighbourhood of the worm and his friends.
My life is not life but death, my voice is no voice but a wind,
　There is no colour in me, nor life, nor richness, nor health;
But in tears and sorrow and weakness, without music, without sport,
　　without power,
I go into captivity and woe, and in the pain of my love of thee.'

XI

From Father Oliver Gogarty to Miss Nora Glynn.

'GARRANARD, BOHOLA,
'March 12, 19—.

'A LONG time has passed without your hearing from me, and I am
sure you must have said more than once: "Well, that priest has
more sense than I gave him credit for. He took the hint. He
understood that it would be useless for us to continue to write
long letters to each other about remorse of conscience and Mr.
Poole's criticism of the Bible." But the sight of my handwriting
will call into question the opinion you have formed of my good
sense, and you will say: "Here he is, beginning it all over again."
No, I am not. I am a little ashamed of my former letters, and am
writing to tell you so. My letters, if I write any, will be quite
different in the future, thanks to your candour. Your letter from
Rapallo cured me; like a surgeon's knife, it took out the ulcer that
was eating my life away. The expression will seem exaggerated, I
know; but let it remain. You no doubt felt that I was in ignorance
of my own state of feelings regarding you, and you wrote just such
a letter as would force me to look into my heart and to discover
who I really was. You felt that you could help me to some knowledge of myself by telling me about yourself.

'The shock on reading your confession — for I look upon your
Rapallo letter as one — was very great, for on reading it I felt that
a good deal that I had written to you about the salvation of your
soul was inspired, not by any pure fear that I had done anything
that might lose a soul to God, but by pure selfishness. I did not

dare to write boldly that I loved yourself, and would always love you; I wore a mask and a disguise, and in order to come to terms with myself I feel it necessary to confess to you; otherwise all the suffering I have endured would be wasted.

'But this is not all my confession; worse still remains. I have discovered that when I spoke against you in church, and said things that caused you to leave the parish, I did not do so, as I thought, because I believed that the morality of my parish must be maintained at any cost. I know now that jealousy— yes, sensual jealousy — prompted me. And when I went to my sisters to ask them to appoint you to the post of music-teacher in their school, I did not do so for their sake, but for my own, because I wished to have you back in the parish. But I do not wish you to think that when I wrote about atonement I wrote what I knew to be untrue. I did not; the truth was hidden from me. Nor did I wish to get you back to the parish in order that I might gratify my passion. All these things were very vague, and I didn't understand myself until now. I never had any experience of life till I met you. And is it not curious that one should know so little of one's self, for I might have gone down to my grave without knowing how false I was at heart, if I had not been stricken down with a great illness.

'One day, Catherine told me that the lake was frozen over, and, as I had been within doors a long while, she advised me to go out and see the boys sliding on the ice. Her advice put an idea into my head, that I might take out my skates and skate recklessly without trying to avoid the deeper portions where the ice was likely to be thin, for I was weary of life, and knowing that I could not go back upon the past, and that no one would ever love me, I wished to bring my suffering to an end. You will wonder why I did not think of the sufferings that I might have earned for myself in the next world. I had suffered so much that I could think of nothing but the present moment. God was good, and he saved me, for as I stood irresolute before a piece of ice which I knew wouldn't bear me, I felt a great sickness creeping over me. I returned home, and for several days the doctor could not say whether I would live or die. You remember Catherine, my servant? She told me that the only answer the doctor would give her was that if I were not better within a certain time there would be no hope of my recovery. At the end of the week he came into my room. Catherine was waiting outside, and I hear that she fell on her knees to thank God when the doctor said: "Yes, he is a little better; if there's no relapse he'll live."

'After a severe illness one is alone with one's self, the whole of one's life sings in one's head like a song, and listening to it, I learned that it was jealousy that prompted me to speak against you, and not any real care for the morality of my parish. I discovered, too, that my moral ideas were not my own. They were borrowed from others, and badly assimilated. I remembered, too, how at Maynooth the tradition was always to despise women, and in order to convince myself I used to exaggerate this view, and say things that made my fellow-students look at me askance, if not with suspicion. But while dozing through long convalescent hours many things hitherto obscure to me became clear, and it seems now to me to be clearly wrong to withhold our sympathy from any side of life. It seems to me that it is only by our sympathy we can do any good at all. God gave us our human nature; we may misuse and degrade our nature, but we must never forget that it came originally from God.

'What I am saying may not be in accordance with current theology, but I am not thinking of theology, but of the things that were revealed to me during my sickness. It was through my fault that you met Mr. Walter Poole, and I must pray to God that he will bring you back to the fold. I shall pray for you both. I wish you all happiness, and I thank you for the many kind things you have said, for the good advice you have given me. You are quite right: I want a change. You advise me to go to Italy, and you are right to advise me to go there, for my heart yearns for Italy. But I dare not go; for I still feel that if I left my parish I should never return to it; and if I were to go away and not return a great scandal would be caused, and I am more than ever resolved not to do anything to grieve the poor people, who have been very good to me, and whose interests I have neglected this long while.

'I send this letter to Beechwood Hall, where you will find it on your return. As I have already said, you need not answer it; no good will come by answering it. In years to come, perhaps, when we are both different, we may meet again.

'OLIVER GOGARTY.'

From Miss Nora Glynn to Father Oliver Gogarty.

'IMPERIAL HOTEL, CAIRO,
'EGYPT,
May 5, 19—.

'DEAR FATHER GOGARTY,

'By the address on the top of this sheet of paper you will see that I have travelled a long way since you last heard from me, and ever since your letter has been following me about from hotel to hotel. It is lucky that it has caught me up in Egypt, for we are going East to visit countries where the postal service has not yet been introduced. We leave here tomorrow. If your letter had been a day later it would have missed me; it would have remained here unclaimed— unless, indeed, we come back this way, which is not likely. You see what a near thing it was; and as I have much to say to you, I should be sorry not to have had an opportunity of writing.

'Your last letter put many thoughts into my head, and made me anxious to explain many things which I feel sure you do not know about my conduct since I left London, and the letters I have written to you. Has it not often seemed strange to you that we go through life without ever being able to reveal the soul that is in us? Is it because we are ashamed, or is it that we do not know ourselves? It is certainly a hard task to learn the truth about ourselves, and I appreciate the courage your last letter shows; you have faced the truth, and having learned it, you write it to me in all simplicity. I like you better now, Oliver Gogarty, than I ever did before, and I always liked you. But it seems to me that to allow you to confess yourself without confessing myself, without revealing the woman's soul in me as you have revealed the man's soul in yourself, would be unworthy.

Our destinies got somehow entangled, there was a wrench, the knot was broken, and the thread was wound upon another spool. The unravelling of the piece must have perplexed you, and you must have wondered why the shape and the pattern should have passed suddenly away into thread again, and then, after a lapse of time, why the weaving should have begun again.

'You must have wondered why I wrote to you, and you must have wondered why I forgave you for the wrong you did me. I guessed that our friendship when I was in the parish was a little more than the platonic friendship that you thought it was, so when you turned against me, and were unkind, I found an excuse for you. When my hatred was bitterest, I knew somehow, at the back of my mind — for I only allowed myself to think of it occasionally — that you acted from — there is but one word — jealousy (not a pretty word from your point of view); and it must have shocked you, as a man and as a priest, to find that the woman whom you thought so much of, and whose society gave you so much pleasure (I know the times we passed together were as pleasant to you as they were to me), should suddenly without warning appear in a totally different light, and in a light which must have seemed to you mean and sordid. The discovery that I was going to have a baby threw me suddenly down from the pedestal on which you had placed me; your idol was broken, and your feelings — for you are one of those men who feel deeply — got the better of you, and you indulged in a few incautious words in your church.

'I thought of these things sometimes, not often, I admit, in the little London lodging where I lived till my baby was born, seeing my gown in front getting shorter, and telling lies to good Mrs. Dent about the husband whom I said was abroad, whom I was expecting to return. That was a miserable time, but we won't talk of it any more. When Father O'Grady showed me the letter that you wrote him, I forgave you in a way. A woman forgives a man the wrongs he does when these wrongs are prompted by jealousy, for, after all, a woman is never really satisfied if a man is not a little jealous. His jealousy may prove inconvenient, and she may learn to hate it and think it an ugly thing and a crooked thing, but, from her point of view, love would not be complete without it.

'I smiled, of course, when I got your letter telling me that you had been to your sisters to ask them if they would take me as a schoolmistress in the convent, and I walked about smiling, thinking of your long innocent drive round the lake. I can see it all, dear man that you are, thinking you could settle everything, and that I would return to Ireland to teach barefooted little children their Catechism and their A, B, C. How often has the phrase been used in our letters! It was a pretty idea of yours to go to your sisters; you did not know then that you cared for me — you only thought of atonement. I suppose we must always be deceived. Mr. Poole says self-deception is the very law of life. We live enveloped in self-deception as in a film; now and again the film breaks like a cloud and the light shines through. We veil our eyes, for we do not like the light. It is really very difficult to tell the truth, Father Gogarty; I find it difficult now to tell you why I wrote all these letters. Because I liked you? Yes, and a little bit because I wished you to suffer; I don't think I shall ever get nearer the truth than that. But when I asked you to meet us abroad, I did so in good faith, for you are a clever man, and Mr. Poole's studies would please you. At the back of my mind I suppose I thought to meet him would do you good; I thought perhaps, that he might redeem you from some conventions and prejudices. I don't like priests; the priest was the only thing about you I never liked. Was it in some vain, proselytizing idea that I invited you? Candidly, I don't know, and I don't think I ever shall. We know so very little about this world that it seems to me waste of time to think about the next. My notion is that the wisest plan is to follow the mood of the moment, with an object more or less definite in view. . . . Nothing is worth more than that. I am at the present moment genuinely interested in culture, and therefore I did not like at all the book you sent me, "The Imitation", and I wrote to tell you to put it by, to come abroad and see pictures and statues in a beautiful country where people do not drink horrid porter, but nice wine, and where Sacraments are left to the old people who have nothing else to interest them. I suppose it was a cruel, callous letter, but I did not mean it so; I merely wanted to give you a glimpse of my new life and my new point of view. As for this letter, Heaven knows how you will take it— whether you will hate me for it or like me; but since you wrote quite frankly to me, confessing yourself from end to end, I feel bound to tell you everything I know about myself — and since I left Ireland I have learned a great deal about myself and about life. Perhaps I should have gone on writing to you if Mr. Poole had not one day said that no good would come of this long correspondence; he suspected I was a disturbing influence, and, as you were determined to live in Ireland, he said it were better that you should live in conventions and prejudices, without them your life would be impossible.

'Then came your last letter, and it showed me how right Mr. Poole was. Nothing remains now but to beg your forgiveness for having disturbed your life. The disturbance is, perhaps, only a passing one. You may recover your ideas — the ideas that are necessary to you— or you may go on discovering the truth, and in the end may perhaps find a way whereby you may leave your parish without causing scandal. To be quite truthful, that is what I hope will happen. However this may be, I hope if we ever meet again it will not be till you have ceased to be a priest. But all this is a long way ahead. We are going East, and shall not be back for many months; we are going to visit the buried cities in Turkestan. I do not know if you have ever heard about these cities. They were buried in sand somewhere about a thousand years ago, and some parts have been disinterred lately. Vaults were broken into in search of treasure. Gold and precious stones were discovered, but far more valuable than the gold and silver, so says Mr. Poole, are certain papyri now being deciphered by the learned professors of Berlin.

'You know the name of Mr. Poole's book, "The Source of the Christian River"? He had not suspected that its source went further back than Palestine, but now he says that some papyri may be found that will take it back into Central Asia.

'I am going with him on this quest. It sounds a little absurd, doesn't it? my going in quest of the Christian river? But if one thinks for a moment, one thing is as absurd as another. Do you know, I find it difficult to take life seriously, and I walk about the streets thinking of you, Father Gogarty, and the smile that will come over your face, half angry, half pleased, when you read that your schoolmistress is going to Central Asia in quest of the Christian river. What will you be doing all this time? You say that you cannot leave your parish because you fear to give scandal; you fear to pain the poor people, who have been good to you and who have given you money, and your scruple is a noble one; I appreciate and respect it. But we must not think entirely of our duties to others; we must think of our duties to ourselves. Each one must try to realize himself — I mean that we must try to bring the gifts that Nature gave us to fruition. Nature has given you many gifts: I wonder what will become of you?

'Very sincerely yours,
'NORA GLYNN.'

'Good God, how I love that woman!' the priest said, awaking from his reverie, for the clock told him that he had sat for nearly three-quarters of an hour, her letter in his hand, having read it. And lying back in his armchair, his hands clasped, his eyes fixed on the window, listening to the birds singing in the vine — it was already in leaf, and the shadows of the leaves danced across the carpet— he sought to define that sense of delight— he could find no other words for it — which she exhaled unconsciously as a flower exhales its perfume, that joy of life which she scattered with as little premeditation as the birds scattered their songs. But though he was constantly seeking some new form of expression of her charm, he always came back to the words 'sense of delight'. Sometimes he added that sense of delight which we experience when we go out of the house on an April morning and find everything growing about us, the sky wilful and blue, and the clouds going by, saying, 'Be happy, as we are.'

She was so different from every other woman. All other women were plain instincts, come into the world for the accomplishment of things that women had accomplished for thousands of years. Other women think as their mothers thought, and as their daughters will think, expressing the thoughts of the countless generations behind and in front of them. But this woman was moved merely by impulses; and what is more inexplicable than an impulse? What is the spring but an impulse? and this woman was mysterious, evanescent as its breath, with the same irresponsible seduction. He was certain that she was at last clear to him, though she might become dark to him again. One day she had come to gather flowers, and while arranging her posy she said casually: 'You are a ruler in this parish; you direct it, the administration of the parish is your business, and I am the little amusement that you turn to when your business is done.' He had not known how to answer her. In this way her remarks often covered him with confusion. She just thought as she pleased, and spoke as she pleased, and he returned to his idea that she was more like the primitive woman than anybody else.

Pondering on her words for the hundredth time, they seemed to him stranger than ever. That any human being should admit that she was but the delight of another's life seemed at first only extraordinary, but if one considered her words, it seemed to signify knowledge— latent, no doubt— that her beauty was part of the great agency. Her words implied that she was aware of her mission. It was her unconscious self that spoke, and it was that which gave significance to her words.

His thoughts melted into nothingness, and when he awoke

from his reverie he was thinking that Nora Glynn had come into his life like a fountain, shedding living water upon it, awakening it. And taking pleasure in the simile, he said, 'A fountain better than anything else expresses this natural woman', controlled, no doubt, by a law, but one hidden from him. 'A fountain springs out of earth into air; it sings a tune that cannot be caught and written down in notes; the rising and falling water is full of iridescent colour, and to the wilting roses the fountain must seem not a natural thing, but a spirit, and I too think of her as a spirit.' And his thoughts falling away again he became vaguely but intensely conscious of all the beauty and grace and the enchantment of the senses that appeared to him in the name of Nora Glynn.

At that moment Catherine came into the room. 'No, not now,' he said; and he went into the garden and through the wicket at the other end, thinking tenderly how he had gone out last year on a day just like the present day, trying to keep thoughts of her out of his mind.

The same fifteenth of May! But last year the sky was low and full of cotton-like clouds; and he remembered how the lake warbled about the smooth limestone shingle, and how the ducks talked in the reeds, how the reeds themselves seemed to be talking. This year the clouds lifted; there was more blue in the sky, less mist upon the water, and it was this day last year that sorrow began to lap about his heart like soft lake-water. He thought then that he was grieving deeply, but since last year he had learned all that a man could know of grief. For last year he was able to take an interest in the spring, to watch for the hawthorn-bloom; but this year he did not trouble to look their way. What matter whether they bloomed a week earlier or a week later? As a matter of fact they were late, the frost having thrown them back, and there would be no flowers till June. How beautifully the tasselled branches of the larches swayed, throwing shadows on the long May grass! 'And they are not less beautiful this year, though they are less interesting to me,' he said.

He wandered through the woods, over the country, noting the different signs of spring, for, in spite of his sorrow, he could not but admire the slender spring. He could not tell why, perhaps because he had always associated Nora with the gaiety of the spring-time. She was thin like the spring, and her laughter was blithe like the spring. She seemed to him like a spirit, and isn't the

spring like a spirit? She was there in the cow-parsley just coming
up, and the sight of the campions between the white spangles
reminded him of the pink flowers she wore in her hat. The
underwood was full of bluebells, but her eyes were not blue. The
aspens were still brown, but in a month the dull green leaves,
silvery underneath, would be fluttering at the end of their long
stems. And the continual agitation of the aspen-leaf seemed to
him rather foolish, reminding him of a weak-minded woman
clamouring for sympathy always. The aspen was an untidy tree;
he was not sure that he liked the tree, and if one is in doubt
whether one likes or dislikes, the chances are that one dislikes.
Who would think of asking himself if he liked beech-trees, or
larches, or willows? A little later he stood lost in admiration of a
line of willows all a-row in front of a stream; they seemed to him
like girls curtseying, and the delicacy of the green and yellow buds
induced him to meditate on the mysteries that common things
disclose.

Seeing a bird disappear into a hole in the wall, he climbed up.
The bird pecked at him, for she was hatching. 'A starling,' he said.
In the field behind his house, under the old hawthorn-tree, an
amiable-looking donkey had given birth to a foal, and he watched
the little thing, no bigger than a sheep, covered with long gray
hair. . . . There were some parishioners he would be sorry to part
with, and there was Catherine. If he went away he would never
see her again, nor those who lived in the village. All this present
reality would fade, his old church, surrounded with gravestones
and stunted Scotch firs, would become like a dream, every year
losing a little in colour and outline. He was going, he did not know
when, but he was going. For a long time the feeling had been
gathering in him that he was going, and her letter increased that
feeling. He would go just as soon as a reputable way of leaving his
parish was revealed to him.

By the help of his reason he could not hope to find out the way.
Nothing seemed more impossible than that a way should be
found for him to leave his parish without giving scandal; but
however impossible things may seem to us, nothing is impossible
to Nature. He must put his confidence in Nature; he must listen
to her. She would tell him. And he lay all the afternoon listening
to the reeds and the ducks talking together in the lake. Very often
the wood was like a harp; a breeze touched the strings, and every

now and then the murmur seemed about to break into a little tune, and as if in emulation, or because he remembered his part in the music, a blackbird, perched near to his mate, whose nest was in the hawthorns growing out of the tumbled wall, began to sing a joyful lay in a rich round contralto, soft and deep as velvet. 'All nature', he said, 'is talking or singing. This is talking and singing time. But my heart can speak to no one, and I seek places where no one will come.' And he began to ask if God would answer his prayer if he prayed that he might die.

The sunlit grass, already long and almost ready for the scythe, was swept by shadows of the larches, those long, shelving boughs hung with green tassels, moving mysteriously above him. Birds came and went, each on its special errand. Never was Nature more inveigling, more restful. He shut his eyes, shapes passed, dreams filled the interspaces. Little thoughts began. Why had he never brought her here? A memory of her walking under these larches would be delightful. The murmur of the boughs dissipated his dreams or changed them, or brought new ones; his consciousness grew fainter, and he could not remember what his last thoughts were when he opened his eyes.

And then he wandered out of the wood, into the sunlit country, along the dusty road, trying to take an interest in everyone whom he met. It was fair-day. He met drovers and chatted to them about the cattle; he heard a wonderful story about a heifer that one of them had sold, and that found her way back home again, twenty-five miles, and a little further on a man came across the fields towards him with a sheep-dog at his heels, a beautiful bitch who showed her teeth prettily when she was spoken to; she had long gold hair, and it was easy to see that she liked to be admired.

'They're all alike, the feminine sex,' the priest thought. 'She's as pretty as Nora, and acts very much the same.'

He walked on again, stopping to speak with everybody, glad to listen to every story. One was of a man who lived by poaching. He hadn't slept in a bed for years, but lay down in the mountains and the woods. He trapped rabbits and beat people; sometimes he enticed boys far away, and then turned upon them savagely. Well, the police had caught him again, and this time he wouldn't get off with less than five years. Listening to Mike Mulroy's talk, Father Oliver forgot his own grief. A little further on they came upon a cart filled with pigs. The cart broke down suddenly, and the pigs escaped in all directions, and the efforts of a great number of country people were directed to collecting them. Father Oliver joined in the chase, and it proved a difficult one, owing to the density of the wood that the pigs had taken refuge in. At last he saw them driven along the road, for it had been found impossible to mend the cart, and at this moment Father Oliver began to think that he would like to be a pig-driver, or better still, a poacher like Carmody. A wandering mood was upon him. Anything were better than to return to his parish, and the thought of the confessions he would have to hear on Saturday night and of the Mass he would have to say on Sunday was bitter indeed, for he had ceased to believe in these things. To say Mass, believing the Mass to be but a mummery, was detestable. To remain in his parish meant a constant degradation of himself. When a parishioner sent to ask him to attend a sick call, he could barely bring himself to anoint the dying man. Some way out of the dilemma must be found, and stopping suddenly so that he might think more clearly, he asked himself why he did not wander out of the parish instead of following the path which led him back to the lake? thinking that it was because it is hard to break with habits, convictions, prejudices. The beautiful evening did not engage his thoughts, and he barely listened to the cuckoo, and altogether forgot to notice the bluebells, campions, and cow-parsley; and it was not till he stood on the hilltop overlooking the lake that he began to recover self-possession.

'The hills,' he said, 'are turned hither and thither, not all seen in profile, and that is why they are so beautiful.'

The sunlit crests and the shadow-filled valleys roused him. In the sky a lake was forming, the very image and likeness of the lake under the hill. One glittered like silver, the other like gold, and so wonderful was this celestial lake that he began to think of immortals, of an assembly of goddesses waiting for their gods, or a goddess waiting on an island for some mortal, sending bird messengers to him. A sort of pagan enchantment was put upon him, and he rose up from the ferns to see an evening as fair as Nora and as fragrant. He tried to think of the colour of her eyes, which were fervid and oracular, and of her hands, which were long and curved, with fragile fingers, of her breath, which was sweet, and her white, even teeth. The evening was like her, as subtle and as persuasive, and the sensation of her presence became so clear that he shut his eyes, feeling her about him — as near to him as if she lay in his arms, just as he had felt her that night in the wood, but then she was colder and more remote. He walked along the foreshore feeling like an instrument that had been tuned. His perception seemed to have been indefinitely increased, and it seemed to him as if he were in communion with the stones in the earth and the clouds in heaven; it seemed to him as if the past and the future had become one.

The moment was one of extraordinary sweetness; never might such a moment happen in his life again. And he watched the earth and sky enfolded in one tender harmony of rose and blue — blue fading to gray, and the lake afloat amid vague shores, receding like a dream through sleep.

XII

From Father Oliver Gogarty to Miss Nora Glynn.

'GARRANARD, BOHOLA,
June 18, 19—.

'THOUGHTS are rising up in my mind, and I am eager to write them down quickly, and with as little consideration as possible. Perhaps my thoughts will seem trivial when I have written them, but the emotion that inspired them was very wonderful and over-powering. I am, as it were, propelled to my writing-table. I must write: my emotion must find expression. Even if I were sure you would not get this letter for months, I should write it. I believe if I knew you would never get it, I should write. But if I send it to Beechwood Hall it will be forwarded, I suppose, for you will not remain whole months without hearing from Europe. . . . In any case, you will get this letter on your return, and it will ease my heart to write it. Above all things, I would have you know that the report that I was drowned while bathing is not true, for a report to this effect will certainly find its way into the local papers, and in these days, once a piece of news gets reported, it flies along from newspaper to newspaper, and newspapers have a knack of straying into our hands when they contain a disagreeable item of news.

'You will remember how the interview with Mr. Poole, published in *Illustrated England*, came into my hands. That was the first number of *Illustrated England* I had seen. Father O'Grady brought it here and left it upon the table, and only the fate that is

over us knows why. In the same way, a paper containing a report
of my supposed drowning may reach you when you return to
England, and, as I do not want you to think that I have gone out of
this life, I am writing to tell you that the report of my death is
untrue, or, to speak more exactly, it will not be true, if my arms
and legs can make it a false report. These lines will set you
wondering if I have taken leave of my senses. Read on, and my
sanity will become manifest. Some day next month I intend to
swim across the lake, and you will, I think, appreciate this adventure. You praised my decision not to leave my parish because of
the pain it would give the poor people. You said that you liked me
better for it, and it is just because my resolve has not wavered that
I have decided to swim across the lake. Only in this way can I quit
my parish without leaving a scandalous name behind me.
Moreover, the means whereby I was enlightened are so strange
that I find it difficult to believe that Providence is not on my side.

'Have not men always believed in bird augury from the beginning of time? and have not prognostications a knack of coming
true? I feel sure that you would think as I do if what had happened to me happened to you. Yet when you read this letter you
will say, "No sooner has he disentangled himself from one
superstition than he drops into another!" However this may be, I
cannot get it out of my head that the strangely ill-fated bird that
came out of the wood last February was sent for a purpose. But I
have not told you about that bird. In my last letter my mind was
occupied by other things, and there was no reason why I should
have mentioned it, for it seemed at the time merely a curious
accident — no more curious than the hundred and one accidents
that happen every day. I believe these things are called coincidences. But to the story. The day I went out skating there was a
shooting-party in Derrinrush, and at the close of day, in the dusk,
a bird got up from the sedge, and one of the shooters, mistaking it
for a woodcock, fired, wounding the bird.

'We watched it till we saw it fall on the shore of Castle Island,
and, thinking that it would linger there for days, dying by inches,
I started off with the intention of saving it from a lingering death,
but a shot had done that. One pellet would have been enough, for
the bird was but a heap of skin and feathers, not to be wondered
at, its legs being tied together with a piece of stout string, twisted
and tied so that it would last for years. And this strangely ill-fated

curlew set me thinking if it were a tame bird escaped from captivity, but tame birds lose quickly their instinct of finding food. "It must have been freed yesterday or the day before," I said to myself, and in pondering how far a bird might fly in the night, this curlew came to occupy a sort of symbolic relation towards my past and my future life, and it was in thinking of it that the idea occurred to me that, if I could cross the lake on the ice, I might swim it in the summer-time when the weather was warm, having, of course, hidden a bundle of clothes amid the rocks on the Joycetown side. My clerical clothes will be found on this side, and the assumption will be, of course, that I swam out too far.

'This way of escape seemed at first fantastic and unreal, but it has come to seem to me the only practical way out of my difficulty. In no other way can I leave the parish without giving pain to the poor people, who have been very good to me. And you, who appreciated my scruples on this point, will, I am sure, understand the great pain it would give my sisters if I were to leave the Church. It would give them so much pain that I shrink from trying to imagine it. They would look upon themselves as disgraced, and the whole family. My disappearance from the parish would ever do them harm— Eliza's school would suffer for sure. This may seem an exaggeration, but certainly Eliza would never quite get over it. If this way of escape had not been revealed to me, I don't think I ever should have found courage to leave, and if I didn't leave I should die. Life is so ordered that a trace remains of every act, but the trace is not always discovered, and I trust you implicitly. You will never show this letter to anyone; you will never tell anyone.

'The Church would allow me, no doubt, to pick up a living as best I could, and would not interfere with me till I said something or wrote something that the Church thought would lessen its power; then the cry of unfrocked priest would be raised against me, and calumny, the great ecclesiastical weapon, would be used. I do not know what my future life will be: my past has been so beset with misfortune that, once I reach the other side, I shall never look back. I cannot find words to tell you of the impatience with which I wait the summer-time, the fifteenth of July, when the moon will be full. I cannot think what would have happened to me if I had stayed at home the afternoon that the curlew was shot; something would have happened, for we cannot go on always sacrificing ourselves. We can sacrifice ourselves for a time, but we cannot sacrifice ourselves all our life long, unless we begin to take pleasure in the immolation of self, and then it is no longer sacrifice. Something must have happened, or I should have gone mad.

'I had suffered so much in the parish. I think the places in which we have suffered become distasteful to us, and the instinct to wander takes us. A migratory bird goes, or dies of home-sickness; home is not always where we are born — it is among ideas that are dear to us: and it is exile to live among people who do not share our ideas. Something must have happened to me. I can think of nothing except suicide or what did happen, for I could never have made up my mind to give pain to the poor people and to leave a scandalous name behind; still less could I continue to administer Sacraments that I ceased to believe in. I can imagine nothing more shameful than the life of a man who continues his administrations after he has ceased to believe in them, especially a Catholic priest, so precise and explicit are the Roman Sacraments. A very abject life it is to murmur *Absolve te* over the heads of parishioners, and to place wafers on their tongues, when we have ceased to believe that we have power to forgive sins and to turn biscuits into God. A layman may have doubts, and continue to live his life as before, without troubling to take the world into his confidence, but a priest may not. The priest is a paid agent and the money an unbelieving priest receives, if he be not inconceivably hardened in sin, must be hateful to him, and his conscience can leave him no rest.

'At first I used to suspect my conversion, and began to think it unseemly that a man should cease to believe that we must renounce this life in order to gain another, without much pre-liminary study of the Scriptures; I began to look upon myself as a somewhat superficial person whose religious beliefs yielded before the charm of a pretty face and winsome personality, but this view of the question no longer seems superficial. I believe now that the superficial ones are those who think that it is only in the Scriptures that we may discover whether we have a right to live. Our belief in books rather than in Nature is one of human-ity's most curious characteristics, and a very irreligious one, it seems to me; and I am glad to think that it was your sunny face that raised up my crushed instincts, that brought me back to life, and ever since you have been associated in my mind with the sun and the spring-tide.

'One day in the beginning of March, coming back from a long walk on the hills, I heard the bleat of the lamb and the impatient cawing of the rook that could not put its nest together in the windy branches, and as I stopped to listen it seemed to me that something passed by in the dusk: the spring-tide itself seemed to be fleeting across the tillage towards the scant fields. As the spring-tide advanced I discovered a new likeness to you in the daffodil; it is so shapely a flower. I should be puzzled to give a reason, but it reminds me of antiquity, and you were always a thing divorced from the Christian ideal. While mourning you, my poor instincts discovered you in the wind-shaken trees, and in the gaiety of the sun, and the flowers that May gives us. I shall be gone at the end of July, when the carnations are in bloom, but were I here I am certain many of them would remind me of you. There have been saints who have loved Nature, but I always wondered how it was so, for Nature is like a woman. I might have read the Scriptures again and again, and all the arguments that Mr. Poole can put forward, without my faith being in the least shaken. When the brain alone thinks, the thinking is very thin and impoverished. It seems to me that the best thinking is done when the whole man thinks, the flesh and the brain together, and for the whole man to think the whole man must live; and the life I have lived hitherto has been a thin life, for my body lived only. And not even all my body. My mind and body were separated: neither were of any use to me. I owe everything to you. My case cannot be defined merely as that of a priest who gave up his religion because a pretty woman came by. He who says that does not try to understand; he merely contents himself with uttering facile common-place. What he has to learn is the great oneness in Nature. There is but one element, and we but one of its many manifestations. If this were not so, why should your whiteness and colour and gaiety remind me always of the spring-time?

'My pen is running fast, I hardly know what I am writing, but it seems to me that I am beginning to see much clearer. The mists are dissolving, and life emerges like the world at daybreak. I am thinking now of an old decrepit house with sagging roof and lichen-covered walls, and all the doors and windows nailed up. Every generation nailed up a door or a window till all were nailed up. In the dusty twilight creatures wilt and pray. About the house the sound of shutters creaking on rusty hinges never ceases. Your hand touched one, and the shutters fell, and I found myself looking upon the splendid sun shining on hills and fields, wooded prospects with rivers winding through the great green expanses. At first I dared not look, and withdrew into the shadow trem- blingly; but the light drew me forth again, and now I look upon the world without fear. I am going to leave that decrepit dusty house and mix with my fellows, and maybe blow a horn on the hillside to call comrades together. My hands and eyes are eager to know what I have become possessed of. I owe to you my liberation from prejudices and conventions. Ideas are passed on. We learn more from each other than from books. I was unconsciously affected by your example. You dared to stretch out both hands to life and grasp it; you accepted the spontaneous natural living wisdom of your instincts when I was rolled up like a dormouse in the dead wisdom of codes and formulas, dogmas and opinions. I never told you how I became a priest. I did not know until quite lately. I think I began to suspect my vocation when you left the parish.

'I remember walking by the lake just this time last year, with the story of my life singing in my head, and you in the background beating the time. You know, we had a shop in Tinnick, and I had seen my father standing before a high desk by a dusty window year after year, selling half-pounds of tea, hanks of onions, and farm implements, and felt that if I married my cousin, Annie McGrath, our lives would reproduce those of my father and mother in every detail. I couldn't undertake the job, and for that began to believe I had a vocation for the priesthood; but I can see now that it was not piety that sent me to Maynooth, but a certain spirit of adventure, a dislike of the commonplace, of the prosaic — that is to say, of the repetition of the same things. I was interested in myself, in my own soul, and I did not want to accept something that was outside of myself, such as the life of a shop- man behind a counter, or that of a clerk of the petty sessions, or the habit of a policeman. These were the careers that were open to me, and when I was hesitating, wondering if I should be able to buy up the old mills and revive the trade in Tinnick, my sister Eliza reminded me that there had always been a priest in the family. The priesthood seemed to offer opportunities of realizing myself, of preserving the spirit within me. It offered no such opportunities to me. I might as well have become a policeman, and all that I have learned since is that everyone must try to cling to his own soul; that is the only binding law. If we are here for anything, it is surely for that.

'But one does not free one's self from habits and ideas, that have grown almost inveterate, without much pain and struggle; one falls back many times, and there are always good reasons for following the rut. We believe that the rutted way leads us some-where: it leads us nowhere, the rutted way is only a seeming; for each man received his truth in the womb. You say in your letter that our destinies got entangled, and that the piece that was being woven ran out into thread, and was rewound upon another spool. It seemed to you and it seemed to me that there is no pattern; we think there is none because Nature's pattern is undistinguishable to our eyes, her looms are so vast, but sometimes even our little sight can follow a design here and there. And does it not seem to you that, after all, there was some design in what has happened? You came and released me from conventions, just as the spring releases the world from winter rust.

'A strange idea has come into my mind, and I cannot help smiling at the topsyturvydom of Nature, or what seems to be topsyturvydom. You, who began by living in your instincts, are now wandering beyond Palestine in search of scrolls; and I, who began my life in scrolls, am now going to try to pick up the lost thread of my instincts in some great commercial town, in London or New York. My life for a long time will be that of some poor clerk or some hack journalist, picking up thirty shillings a week when he is in luck. I imagine myself in a threadbare suit of clothes edging my way along the pavement, nearing a great building, and making my way to my desk, and, when the day's work is done, returning home along the same pavement to a room high up among the rafters, close to the sky, in some cheap quarter.

'I do not doubt my ability to pick up a living — it will be a shameful thing indeed if I cannot; for the poor curlew with its legs tied together managed to live somehow, and cannot I do as much? And I have taken care that no fetters shall be placed upon my legs or chain about my neck. Anything may happen — life is full of possibilities — but my first concern must be how I may earn my living. To earn one's living is an obligation that can only be

dispensed with at one's own great risk. What may happen afterwards, Heaven knows! I may meet you, or I may meet another
woman, or I may remain unmarried. I do not intend to allow
myself to think of these things; my thoughts are set on one thing
only — how to get to New York, and how I shall pick up a living
when I get there. Again I thank you for what you have done for
me, for the liberation you have brought me of body and mind. I
need not have added the words "body and mind" for these are not
two things, but one thing. And that is the lesson I have learned.
Good-bye.

'OLIVER GOGARTY.'

XIII

IT would be a full moon on the fifteenth of July, and every night he went out on the hillside to watch the horned moon swelling to a disc.

And on the fifteenth, the day he had settled for his departure, as he sat thinking how he would go down to the lake in a few hours, a letter started to his mind which, as well as he could remember, was written in a foolish, vainglorious mood — a stupid letter that must have made him appear a fool in her eyes. Had he not said something about—— The thought eluded him; he could only remember the general tone of his letter, and in it he seemed to consider Nora as a sort of medicine — a cure for religion.

He should have written her a simple little letter, telling her that he was leaving Ireland because he had suffered a great deal, and would write to her from New York, whereas he had written her the letter of a booby. And feeling he must do something to rectify his mistake, he went to his writing-table, but he had hardly put the pen to the paper when he heard a step on the gravel outside his door.

'Father Moran, your reverence.'

'I see that I'm interrupting you. You're writing.'

'No, I assure you.'

'But you've got a pen in your hand.'

'It can wait — a matter of no importance. Sit down.'

'Now, you'll tell me if I'm in the way?'

'My good man, why are you talking like that? Why should you be in the way?'

'Well, if you're sure you've nothing to do, may I stay to supper?'

'To supper?'

'But I see that I'm in the way.'

'No; I tell you you're not in the way. And you're going to stay to supper.'

Father Oliver flung himself between Father Moran and the door; Father Moran allowed himself to be led back to the armchair. Father Oliver took the chair opposite him, for he couldn't send Moran away; he mustn't do anything that would give rise to suspicion.

'You're quite sure I'm not in the way — I'm not interfering with any plans?'

'Quite sure. I'm glad you have come this evening.'

'Are you? Well, I had to come.'

'You had to come!'

'Yes, I had to come; I had to come to see if anything had happened. You needn't look at me like that; I haven't been drinking, and I haven't gone out of my mind. I can only tell you that I had to come to see you this evening.'

'And you don't know why?'

'No, I don't; I can't tell you exactly why I've come. As I was reading my breviary, walking up and down the road in front of the house, I felt that I must see you. I never felt anything like it in my life before. I had to come.'

'And you didn't expect to find me?'

'Well, I didn't. How did you guess that?'

'You'd have hardly come all that way to find me sitting here in this armchair.'

'That's right. It wasn't sitting in that chair I expected to see you; I didn't expect to see you at all — at least, I don't think I did. You see, it was all very queer, for it was as if somebody had got me by the shoulders. It was as if I were being pushed every yard of the road. Something was running in my mind that I shouldn't see you again, or if I did see you that it would be for the last time. You seemed to me as if you were going away on a long journey.'

'Was it dying or dead you saw me?'

'That I can't say. If I said any more I shouldn't be telling the truth. No, it wasn't the same feeling when I came to tell you I couldn't put up with the loneliness any more — the night I came here roaring for drink. I was thinking of myself then, and that you might save me or do something for me — give me drink or cure me. I don't know which thought it was that was running in my head, but I had to come to you all the same, just as I had to come to you today. I say it was different, because then I was on my own business; but this time it seemed to me that I was on yours. One good turn deserves another, as they say; and something was beating in my head that I could help you, serve as a stay; so I had to come. Where should I be now if it were not for you? I can see you're thinking that it was only nonsense that was running in my head, but you won't be saying it was nonsense that brought me the night I came like a madman roaring for drink. If there was a miracle that night, why shouldn't there be a miracle tonight? And if a miracle ever happened in the world, it happened that night, I'm thinking. Do you remember the dark gray clouds tearing across the sky, and we walking side by side, I trying to get away from you? I was that mad that I might have thrown you into the bog-hole if the craving had not passed from me. And it was just lifted from me as one might take the cap off one's head. You remember the prayer we said, leaning over the bit of wall looking across the bog? There was no lonesomeness that night coming home, Gogarty, though a curlew might have felt a bit.'

'A curlew!'

'Well, there were curlews and plovers about, and a starving ass picking grass between the road and the bog-hole. That night will be ever in my mind. Where would I be now if it hadn't been that you kept on with me and brought me back, cured? It wouldn't be a cassock that would be on my back, but some old rag of a coat. There's nothing in this world, Gogarty, more unlucky than a suspended priest. I think I can see myself in the streets, hanging about some public-house, holding horses attached to a cab-rank.'

'Lord of Heaven, Moran! what are you coming here to talk to me in this way for? The night you're speaking of was bad enough, but your memory of it is worse. Nothing of what you're saying would have happened; a man like you would be always able to pick up a living.'

'And where would I be picking up a living if it weren't on a cab-rank, or you either?'

'Well, 'tis melancholy enough you are this evening.'

'And all for nothing, for there you are, sitting in your old chair. I see I've made a fool of myself.'

'That doesn't matter. You see, if one didn't do what one felt like doing, one would have remorse of conscience for ever after.'

'I suppose so. It was very kind of you, Moran, to come all this way.'

'What is it but a step? Three miles——'

'And a half.'

Moved by a febrile impatience, which he could not control, Father Oliver got up from his chair.

'Now, Moran, isn't it strange? I wonder how it was that you should have come to tell me that you were going off to drink somewhere. You said you were going to lie up in a public-house and drink for days, and yet you didn't think of giving up the priesthood.'

'What are you saying, Gogarty? Don't you know well enough I'd have been suspended? Didn't I tell you that drink had taken that power over me that, if roaring hell were open, and I sitting on the brink of it and a table beside me with whisky on it, I should fill myself a glass?'

'And knowing you were going down to hell?'

'Yes, that night nothing would have stopped me. But, talking of hell, I heard a good story yesterday. Pat Carabine was telling his flock last Sunday of the tortures of the damned, and having said all he could about devils and pitchforks and caldrons, he came to a sudden pause — a blank look came into his face, and, looking round the church and seeing the sunlight streaming through the door, his thoughts went off at a tangent. "Now, boys," he said, "if this fine weather continues, I hope you'll be all out in the bog next Tuesday bringing home my turf." '

Father Oliver laughed, but his laughter did not satisfy Father Moran, and he told how on another occasion Father Pat had finished his sermon on hell by telling his parishioners that the devil was the landlord of hell. 'And I leave yourself to imagine the groaning that was heard in the church that morning, for weren't they all small tenants? But I'm afraid my visit has upset you, Gogarty.'

'How is that?'

'You don't seem to enjoy a laugh like you used to.'

'Well, I was thinking at that moment that I've heard you say that, even though you gave way to drink, you never had any doubts about the reality of the hell that awaited you for your sins.'

'That's the way it is, Gogarty, one believes, but one doesn't act up to one's belief. Human nature is inconsistent. Nothing is queerer than human nature, and will you be surprised if I tell you that I believe I was a better priest when I was drinking than I am now that I'm sober? I was saying that human nature is very queer; and it used to seem queer to myself. I looked upon drink as a sort of blackmail I paid to the devil so that he might let me be a good priest in everything else. That's the way it was with me, and there was more sense in the idea than you'd be thinking, for when the drunken fit was over I used to pray as I have never prayed since. If there was not a bit of wickedness in the world, there would be no goodness. And as for faith, drink never does any harm to one's faith whatsoever; there's only one thing that takes a man's faith from him, and that is woman. You remember the expulsions at Maynooth, and you know what they were for. Well, that sin is a bad one, but I don't think it affects a man's faith any more than drink does. It is woman that kills the faith in men.'

'I think you're right: woman is the danger. The Church dreads her. Woman is life.'

'I don't quite understand you.'

Catherine came into the room to lay the cloth, and Father Oliver asked Father Moran to come out into the garden. It was now nearing its prime. In a few days more the carnations would be all in bloom, and Father Oliver pondered that very soon it would begin to look neglected. 'In a year or two it will have drifted back to the original wilderness, to briar and weed,' he said to himself; and he dwelt on his love of this tiny plot of ground, with a wide path running down the centre, flower borders on each side, and a narrow path round the garden beside the hedge. The potato ridges, and the runners, and the cabbages came in the middle. Gooseberry-bushes and currant-bushes grew thickly, there were little apple-trees here and there, and in one corner the two large apple-trees under which he sat and smoked his pipe in the evenings.

'You're very snug here, smoking your pipe under your apple-trees.'

'Yes, in a way; but I think I was happier where you are.'

'The past is always pleasant to look upon.'

'You think so?'

The priests walked to the end of the garden, and, leaning on the wicket, Father Moran said:

'We've had queer weather lately—dull heavy weather. See how low the swallows are flying. When I came up the drive, the gravel space in front of the house was covered with them, the old birds feeding the young ones.'

'And you were noticing these things, and believing that Providence had sent you here to bid me good-bye.'

'Isn't it when the nerves are on a stretch that we notice little things that don't concern us at all?'

'Yes, Moran; you are right. I've never known you as wise as you are this evening.'

Catherine appeared in the kitchen door. She had come to tell them their supper was ready. During the meal the conversation turned on the roofing of the abbey and the price of timber, and when the tablecloth had been removed the conversation swayed between the price of building materials and the Archbishop's fear lest he should meet a violent death, as it had been prophesied if he allowed a roof to be put upon Kilronan.

'You know I don't altogether blame him, and I don't think anyone does at the bottom of his heart, for what has been foretold generally comes to pass sooner or later.'

'The Archbishop is a good Catholic who believes in everything the Church teaches—in the Divinity of our Lord, the Immaculate Conception, and the Pope's indulgences. And why should he be disbelieving in that which has been prophesied for generations about the Abbot of Kilronan?'

'Don't you believe in these things?'

Does anyone know exactly what he believes? Does the Archbishop really believe every day of the year and every hour of every day that the Abbot of Kilronan will be slain on the highroad when a De Stanton is again Abbot?' Father Oliver was thinking of the slip of the tongue he had been guilty of before supper, when he said that the Church looks upon woman as the real danger, because she is the life of the world. He shouldn't have made that remark, for it might be remembered against him, and he fell to thinking of something to say that would explain it away.

'Well, Moran, we've had a pleasant evening; we've talked a good deal, and you've said many pleasant things and many wise ones. We've never had a talk that I enjoyed more, and I shall not forget it easily.'

'How is that?'

'Didn't you say that it isn't drink that destroys a man's faith, but woman? And you said rightly, for woman is life.'

'I was just about to ask you what you meant, when Catherine came in and interrupted us.'

'Love of woman means estrangement from the Church, because you have to protect her and her children.'

'Yes, that is so; that's how it works out. Now you won't be thinking me a fool for having come to see you this evening, Gogarty? One never knows when one's impulses are true and when they're false. If I hadn't come the night when the drink craving was upon me, I shouldn't have been here now.'

'You did quite right to come, Moran; we've talked of a great many things.'

'I've never talked so plainly to anyone before; I wonder what made me talk as I've been talking. We never talked like this before, did we, Gogarty? And I wouldn't have talked to another as I've talked to you. I shall never forget what I owe to you.'

'You said you were going to leave the parish.'

'I don't think I thought of anything except to burn myself up with drink. I wanted to forget, and I saw myself walking ahead day after day, drinking at every public-house.'

'And just because I saved you, you thought you would come to save me?'

'There was something of that in it. Gad! it's very queer; there's no saying where things will begin and end. Pass me the tobacco, will you?'

Father Moran began to fill his pipe, and when he had finished filling it, he said:

'Now I must be going, and don't be trying to keep me; I've stopped long enough. If I were sent for a purpose——'

'But you don't believe seriously, Moran, that you were sent for a purpose?' Moran didn't answer, and his silence irritated Father Oliver, and, determined to probe his curate's conscience, he said: 'Aren't you satisfied now that it was only an idea of your own? You thought to find me gone, and here I am sitting before you.' After waiting for some time for Moran to speak, he said: 'You haven't answered me.'

'What should I be answering?'

'Do you still think you were sent for a purpose?'

'Well, I do.'

'You do?'

The priests stood looking at each other for a while.

'Can't you give a reason?'

'No; I can give no reason. It's a feeling. I know I haven't reason on my side. There you are before me.'

'It's very queer.'

He would have liked to have called back Moran. It seemed a pity to let him go without having probed this matter to the bottom. He hadn't asked him if he had any idea in his mind about the future, as to what was going to happen; but it was too late now. 'Why did he come here disturbing me with his beliefs,' he cried out, 'poisoning my will?' for he had already begun to fear that Moran's visit might come between him and his project. The wind sighed a little louder, and Father Oliver said: 'I wouldn't be minding his coming here to warn me, though he did say that it wasn't of his own will that he came, but something from the outside that kept pushing him along the road — I wouldn't be minding all that if this wind hadn't risen. But the omen may be a double one.' At that moment the wind shook the trees about the house, and he fell to thinking that if he had started to swim the lake that night he would be now somewhere between Castle Island and the Joycetown shore, in the deepest and windiest part of the lake. 'And pretty well tired I'd be at the time. If I'd started tonight a corpse would be floating about now.' The wind grew louder. Father Oliver imagined the waves slapping in his face, and then he imagined them slapping about the face of a corpse drifting towards the Joycetown shore.

XIV

THERE was little sleep in him that night, and turning on his pillow, he sought sleep vainly, getting up at last when the dawn looked through the curtains. A wind was shaking the apple-trees, and he went back to bed, thinking that if it did not drop suddenly he would not be able to swim across the lake that evening. The hours passed between sleeping and waking, thinking of the newspaper articles he would write when he got to America, and dreaming of a fight between himself and an otter on the shore of Castle Island. Awaking with a cry, he sat up, afraid to seek sleep again lest he might dream of drowning men. 'A dream robs a man of all courage,' and then falling back on his pillow, he said, 'Whatever my dreams may be I shall go. Anything were better than to remain taking money from the poor people, playing the part of a hypocrite.'

And telling Catherine that he could not look through her accounts that morning, he went out of the house to see what the lake was like. 'Boisterous enough; it would take a good swimmer to get across to-day. Maybe the wind will drop in the afternoon.'

The wind continued to rise, and next day he could only see white waves, tossing trees, and clouds tumbling over the mountains. He sat alone in his study staring at the lamp, the wind often awaking him from his reverie; and one night he remembered suddenly that it was no longer possible for him to cross the lake that month, even if the wind should cease, for he required not only a calm, but a moonlight night. And going out of the house, he walked about the hilltop, about the old thorn-bush, his hands clasped behind his back. He stood watching the moon setting high above the south-western horizon. But the lake — where was it? Had he not known that a lake was there, he would hardly have been able to discover one. All faint traces of one had disappeared, every shape was lost in blue shadow, and he wondered if his desire to go had gone with the lake. 'The lake will return,' he said, and next night he was on the hillside waiting for the lake to reappear. And every night it emerged from the shadow, growing clearer, till he could follow its winding shores. 'In a few days, if this weather lasts, I shall be swimming out there.' The thoughts crossed his mind that if the wind should rise again about the time of the full moon he would not be able to cross that year, for in September the water would be too cold for so long a swim. 'But it isn't likely,' he said; 'the weather seems settled.'

And the same close, blue weather that had prevailed before the storm returned, the same diffused sunlight.

'There is nothing so depressing,' the priest said, 'as seeing swallows flying a few feet from the ground.'

It was about eight o'clock — the day had begun to droop in his garden — that he walked up and down the beds admiring his carnations. Every now and again the swallows collected into groups of some six or seven, and fled round the gables of his house shrieking. 'This is their dinner-hour; the moths are about.' He wondered on, thinking Nora lacking; for she had never appreciated that beautiful flower Miss Shifner. But her ear was finer than his; she found her delight in music.

A thought broke through his memories. He had forgotten to tell her he would write if he succeeded in crossing the lake, and if he didn't write she would never know whether he was living or dead. Perhaps it would be better so. After hesitating a moment, the desire to write to her took strong hold upon him, and he sought an excuse for writing. If he didn't write, she might think that he remained in Garranard. She knew nothing of Moran's visit, nor of the rising of the wind, nor of the waning of the moon; and he must write to her about these things, for if he were drowned she would think that God had willed it. But if he believed in God's intervention, he should stay in his parish and pray that grace might be given to him. 'God doesn't bother himself about such trifles as my staying or my going,' he muttered as he hastened towards his house, overcome by an immense joy. For he was happy only when he was thinking of her, or doing some-

thing connected with her, and to tell her of the fatality that
seemed to pursue him would occupy an evening.

From Father Oliver Gogarty to Miss Nora Glynn.

'GARRANARD, BOHOLA,
July 25, 19—.

'You will be surprised to hear from me so soon again, but I
forgot to say in my last letter that, if I succeeded in crossing the
lake, I would write to you from New York. And since then many
things have happened, strange and significant coincidences.'

And when he had related the circumstance of Father Moran's
visit and the storm, he sought to excuse his half-beliefs that these
were part of God's providence sent to warn him against leaving
his parish.

'Only time can rid us of ideas that have been implanted in us in
our youth, and that have grown up in our flesh and in our mind.
A sudden influence may impel us to tear them up and cast them
aside, but the seed is in us always, and it grows again. "One year's
seed, seven years' weed." And behind imported Palestinian
supernature, if I may be permitted to drop into Mr. Poole's style,
or what I imagine to be his style, there is the home belief in fairies,
spirits, and ghosts, and the reading of omens. Who amongst us
does not remember the old nurse who told him stories of magic
and witchcraft? Nor can it be denied that things happen that seem
in contradiction to all we know of Nature's laws. Moreover, these
unusual occurrences have a knack of happening to men at the
moment of their setting out on some irrevocable enterprise.
'You who are so sympathetic will understand how my will has
been affected by Father Moran's visit. Had you heard him tell
how he was propelled, as it were, out of his house towards me,
you, too, would believe that he was a messenger. He stopped on
his threshold to try to find a reason for coming to see me; he
couldn't find any, and he walked on, feeling that something had
happened. He must have thought himself a fool when he found
me sitting here in the thick flesh. But what he said did not seem
nonsense to me; it seemed like some immortal wisdom come from
another world. Remember that I was on the point of going. Nor is

this all. If nothing else had happened, I might have looked upon Father Moran's visit as a coincidence. But why should the wind rise? So far as I can make out, it began to rise between eleven and twelve, at the very time I should have been swimming between Castle Island and the Joycetown shore. I know that belief in signs and omens and prognostics can be laughed at; nothing is more ridiculous than the belief that man's fate is governed by the flight of birds, yet men have believed in bird augury from the beginning of the world.

'I wrote to you about a curlew (I can still see it in the air, its beautifully shapen body and wings, its long beak, and its trailing legs; it staggered a little in its flight when the shot was fired, but it had strength enough to reach Castle Island: it then toppled over, falling dead on the shore); and I ask you if it is wonderful that I should have been impressed? Such a thing was never heard of before — a wild bird with its legs tied together!

'At first I believed that this bird was sent to warn me from going, but it was that bird that put the idea into my head how I might escape from the parish without giving scandal. Life is so strange that one doesn't know what to think. Of what use are signs and omens if the interpretation is always obscure? They merely wring the will out of us; and well we may ask, Who would care for his life if he knew he was going to lose it on the morrow? And what mother would love her children if she were certain they would fall into evil ways, or if she believed the soothsayers who told her that her children would oppose her ideas? She might love them independent of their opposition, but how could she love them if she knew they were only born to do wrong? Volumes have been written on the subject of predestination and freewill, and the truth is that it is as impossible to believe in one as in the other. Nevertheless, prognostications have a knack of coming true, and if I am drowned crossing the lake you will be convinced of the truth of omens. Perhaps I should not write you these things, but the truth is, I cannot help myself; there is no power of resistance in me. I do not know if I am well or ill; my brain is on fire, and I go on thinking and thinking, trying to arrive at some rational belief, but never succeeding. Sometimes I think of myself as a fly on a window-pane, crawling and buzzing, and crawling and buzzing again, and so on and so on. . . .

'You are one of those who seem to have been born without much interest in religion or fear of the hereafter, and in a way I

am like you, but with a difference: I acquiesced in early childhood, and accepted traditional beliefs, and tried to find happiness in the familiar rather than in the unknown. Whether I
should have found the familiar enough if I hadn't met you, I shall
never know. I've thought a good deal on this subject, and it has
come to seem to me that we are too much in the habit of thinking
of the intellect and the flesh as separate things, whereas they are
but one thing. I could write a great deal on this subject, but I stop,
as it were, on the threshold of my thought, for this is no time for
philosophical writing. I am all a-tremble, and though my brain is
working quickly, my thoughts are not mature and deliberate. My
brain reminds me at times of the skies that followed Father
Moran's visit — skies restlessly flowing, always different and
always the same. These last days are merciless days, and I have to
write to you in order to get some respite from purposeless thinking. Sometimes I stop in my walk to ask myself who I am and what
I am, and where I am going. Will you be shocked to hear that,
when I awoke and heard the wind howling, I nearly got out of bed
to pray to God, to thank him for having sent Moran to warn me
from crossing the lake? I think I did say a prayer, thanking him
for his mercy. Then I felt that I should pray to him for grace that I
might remain at home and be a good priest always, but that
prayer I couldn't formulate, and I suffered a great deal. I know
that such vacillations between belief and unbelief are neither
profitable nor admirable; I know that to pray to God to thank him
for having saved me from death while in mortal sin, and yet to
find myself unable to pray to him to do his will, is illogical, and I
confess that my fear is now lest old beliefs will claim me before the
time comes. A poor, weak, tried mortal man am I, but being what
I am, I cannot be different. I am calm enough now, and it seems as
if my sufferings were at an end; but tomorrow some new fear will
rise up like mist, and I shall be enveloped. What an awful thing it
would be if I should find myself without will on the fifteenth, or
the sixteenth, or the seventeenth of August! If the wind should
rise again, and the lake be windy while the moon is full, my chance
for leaving here this summer will be at an end. The water will be
too cold in September.

   'And now you know all, and if you don't get a letter from New
York, understand that what appears in the newspapers is true —
that I was drowned whilst bathing. I needn't apologize for this

long letter; you will understand that the writing of it has taken me
out of myself, and that is a great gain. There is no one else to
whom I can write, and it pleases me to know this. I am sorry for
my sisters in the convent; they will believe me dead. I have a
brother in America, the one who sent the harmonium that you
used to play on so beautifully. He will believe in my death, unless
we meet in America, and that is not likely. I look forward to
writing to you from New York.

'OLIVER GOGARTY.'

Two evenings were passed pleasantly on the composition and
the copying of this letter, and, not daring to entrust it to the
postboy, he took it himself to Bohola; and he measured the time
carefully, so as to get there a few minutes before the postmistress
sealed up the bag. He delayed in the office till she sealed it, and
returned home, following the letter in imagination to Dublin,
across the Channel to Beechwood Hall. The servant in charge
would redirect it. His thoughts were at ramble, and they followed
the steamer down the Mediterranean. It would lie in the post-
office at Jerusalem or some frontier town, or maybe a dragoman
attached to some Turkish caravansary would take charge of it,
and it might reach Nora by caravan. She might read it in the
waste. Or maybe it would have been better if he had written 'Not
to be forwarded' on the envelope. But the servant at Beechwood
Hall would know what to do, and he returned home smiling,
unable to believe in himself or in anything else, so extraordinary
did it seem to him that he should be writing to Nora Glynn, who
was going in search of the Christian river, while he was planning a
journey westward.

A few days more, and the day of departure was almost at hand;
but it seemed a very long time coming. What he needed was a
material occupation, and he spent hours in his garden watering
and weeding, and at gaze in front of a bed of fiery-cross. Was its
scarlet not finer than Lady Hindlip? Lady Hindlip, like fiery-
cross, is scentless, and not so hardy. No white carnation compares
with Shiela; but her calyx often bursts, and he considered the
claims of an old pink-flaked clove carnation, striped like a French
brocade. But it straggled a little in growth, and he decided that for
hardiness he must give the verdict to Raby Castle. True that

everyone grows Raby Castle, but no carnation is so hardy or
flowers so freely. As he stood admiring her great trusses of bloom
among the tea-roses, he remembered suddenly that it was his love
of flowers that had brought him to Garranard, and if he hadn't
come to this parish, he wouldn't have known her. And if he hadn't
known her, he wouldn't have been himself. And which self did he
think the worthier, his present or his dead self?

His brain would not cease thinking; his bodily life seemed to
have dissipated, and he seemed to himself to be more than a
mind, and, glad to interest himself in the business of the parish,
he listened with greater attention than he had ever listened
before to the complaints that were brought to him — to the man
who had failed to give up a piece of land that he had promised to
include in his daughter's fortune, and to Patsy Murphy, who had
come to tell him that his house had been broken into while he was
away in Tinnick. The old man had spent the winter in Tinnick
with some relations, for the house that the Colonel had given him
permission to build at the edge of the lake proved too cold for a
winter residence.

Patsy seemed to have grown older since the autumn; he seemed
like a doll out of which the sawdust was running, a poor shaking
thing — a large head afloat on a weak neck. Tresses of white hair
hung on his shoulders, and his watery eyes were red and restless
like a ferret's. He opened his mouth, and there were two teeth on
either side like tusks. Gray stubble covered his face, and he wore a
brown suit, the trousers retained about his pot-belly — all that
remained of his body — by a scarf. There was some limp linen and
a red muffler about his throat. He spoke of his age — he was
ninety-five — and the priest said he was a fine-looking, hearty
man for his years. There wasn't a doubt but he'd pass the hundred. Patsy was inclined to believe he would go to one hundred
and one; for he had been told in a vision he would go as far as that.

'You see, living in the house alone, the brain empties and the
vision comes.'

That was how he explained his belief as he flopped along by the
priest's side, his head shaking and his tongue going, telling tales
of all kinds, half-remembered things: how the Gormleys and the
Actons had driven the Colonel out of the country, and dispersed
all his family with their goings-on. That was why they didn't want
him — he knew too much about them. One of his tales was how

they had frightened the Colonel's mother by tying a lame hare by a horsehair to the knocker of the hall door. Whenever the hare moved a rapping was heard at the front-door. But nobody could discover the horsehair, and the rapping was attributed to a family ghost.

He seemed to have forgotten his sword, and was now inclined to talk of his fists, and he stopped the priest in the middle of the road to tell a long tale how once, in Liverpool, someone had spoken against the Colonel, and, holding up his clenched fist, he said that no one ever escaped alive from the fist of Patsy Murphy.

It was a trial to Father Oliver to hear him, for he could not help thinking that to become like him it was only necessary to live as long as he. But it was difficult to get rid of the old fellow, who followed the priest as far as the village, and would have followed him further if Mrs. Egan were not standing there waiting for Father Oliver — a delicate-featured woman with a thin aquiline nose, who was still good-looking, though her age was apparent. She was forty-five, or perhaps fifty, and she held her daughter's baby in her coarse peasant hands. Since the birth of the child a dispute had been raging between the two mothers-in-law: the whole village was talking, and wondering what was going to happen next.

Mrs. Egan's daughter had married a soldier, a Protestant, some two years ago, a man called Rean. Father Oliver always found him a straightforward fellow, who, although he would not give up his own religion, never tried to interfere with his wife's; he always said that if Mary liked she could bring up her children Catholics. But hitherto they were not blessed with children, and Mary was jeered at more than once, the people saying that her barrenness was a punishment sent by God. At last a child was given them, and all would have gone well if Rean's mother had not come to Garranard for her daughter-in-law's confinement. Being a black Protestant, she wouldn't hear of the child being brought up a Catholic or even baptized in a Catholic Church. The child was now a week old and Rean was fairly distracted, for neither his own mother nor his mother-in-law would give way; each was trying to outdo the other. Mrs. Rean watched Mrs. Egan, and Mrs. Egan watched Mrs. Rean, and the poor mother lay all day with the baby at her breast, listening to the two of them quarrelling.

'She's gone behind the hedge for a minute, your reverence, so I whipped the child out of me daughter's bed; and if your reverence would only hurry up we could have the poor cratur baptized in the Holy Faith. Only there's no time to be lost; she do be watchin' every stir, your reverence.'

'Very well, Mrs. Egan: I'll be waiting for you up at the chapel.'

'A strange rusticity of mind,' he said to himself as he wended his way along the village street, and at the chapel gate a smile gathered about his lips, for he couldn't help thinking how Mrs. Rean the elder would rage when the child was brought back to her a Catholic. So this was going to be his last priestly act, the baptism of the child, the saving of the child to the Holy Faith. He told Mike to get the things ready, and turned into the sacristy to put on his surplice.

The familiar presses gave out a pleasant odour, and the vestments which he might never wear again interested him, and he stood seemingly lost in thought. 'But I mustn't keep the child waiting,' he said, waking up suddenly; and coming out of the sacristy, he found twenty villagers collected round the font, come up from the cottages to see the child baptized in the holy religion.

'Where's the child, Mrs. Egan?'

The group began talking suddenly, trying to make plain to him what had happened.

'Now, if you all talk together, I shall never understand.'

'Will you leave off pushing me?' said one.

'Wasn't it I that saw Patsy? Will your reverence listen to me?' said Mrs. Egan. 'It was just as I was telling your reverence, if they'd be letting me alone. Your reverence had only just turned in the chapel gate when Mrs. Rean ran from behind the hedge, and, getting in front of me who was going to the chapel with the baby in me arms, she said: "Now I'll be damned if I'll have that child christened a Catholic!" and didn't she snatch the child and run away taking a short-cut across the fields to the minister's.'

'Patsy Kivel has gone after her, and he'll catch up on her, surely, and she with six ditches forninst her.'

'If he doesn't itself, maybe the minister isn't there, and then she'll be bet.'

'All I'm hopin' is that the poor child won't come to any harm between them; but isn't she a fearful terrible woman, and may the curse of the Son of God be on her for stealin' away a poor child the like of that!'

'I'd cut the livers out of the likes of them.'

'Now will you mind what you're sayin', and the priest listenin' to you?'

'Your reverence, will the child be always a Protestant? Hasn't the holy water of the Church more power in it than the water they have? Don't they only throw it at the child?'

'Now, Mrs. Egan——'

'Ah, your reverence, you're going to say that I shouldn't have given the child to her, and I wouldn't if I hadn't trod on a stone and fallen against the wall, and got afeard the child might be hurt.'

'Well, well,' said Father Oliver, 'you see there's no child——'

'But you'll be waitin' a minute for the sake of the poor child, your reverence? Patsy will be comin' back in a minute.'

On that Mrs. Egan went to the chapel door and stood there, so that she might catch the first glimpse of him as he came across the fields. And it was about ten minutes after, when the priest and his parishioners were talking of other things, that Mrs. Egan began to wave her arm, crying out that somebody should hurry.

'Will you make haste, and his reverence waitin' here this half-hour to baptize the innocent child! He'll be here in less than a minute now, your reverence. Will you have patience, and the poor child will be safe?'

The child was snatched from Patsy, and so violently that the infant began to cry, and Mrs. Egan didn't know if it was a hurt it had received, for the panting Patsy was unable to answer her.

'The child's all right,' he blurted out at last. 'She said I might take it and welcome, now it was a Protestant.'

'Ah, sure, you great thickhead of a boy! weren't you quick enough for her?'

'Now, what are you talkin' about? Hadn't she half a mile start of me, and the minister at the door just as I was gettin' over the last bit of a wall!'

'And didn't you go in after them?'

'What would I be doin', going into a Protestant church?'

Patsy's sense of his responsibility was discussed violently until Father Oliver said:

'Now, I can't be waiting any longer. Do you want me to baptize the child or not?'

'It would be safer, wouldn't it?' said Mrs. Egan.

'It would,' said Father Oliver; 'the parson mightn't have said the words while he was pouring the water.'

And, going towards the font with the child, Father Oliver took a cup of water, but, having regard for the child's cries, he was a little sparing with it.

'Now don't be sparin' with the water, your reverence, and don't be a mindin' its noise; it's twicest the quantity of holy water it'll be wanting, and it half an hour a Protestant.'

It was at that moment Mrs. Rean appeared in the doorway, and Patsy Kivel, who didn't care to enter the Protestant church, rushed to put her out of his.

'You can do what you like now with the child; for it's a Protestant, for all your tricks.'

'Go along, you old heretic bitch!'

'Now, Patsy, will you behave yourself when you're standing in the Church of God! Be leaving the woman alone,' said Father Oliver; but before he got to the door to separate the two, Mrs. Rean was running down the chapel yard followed by the crowd of disputants, and he heard the quarrel growing fainter in the village street.

Rose-coloured clouds had just begun to appear mid-way in the pale sky — a beautiful sky, all gray and rose — and all this babble about baptism seemed strangely out of his mind. 'And to think that men are still seeking scrolls in Turkestan to prove——' The sentence did not finish itself in his mind; a ray of western light falling across the altar steps in the stillness of the church awakened a remembrance in him of the music that Nora's hands drew from the harmonium, and, leaning against the Communion-rails, he allowed the music to absorb him. He could hear it so distinctly in his mind that he refrained from going up into the gallery and playing it, for in his playing he would perceive how much he had forgotten, how imperfect was his memory. It were better to lose himself in the emotion of the memory of the music; it was in his blood, and he could see her hands playing it, and the music was coloured with the memory of her hair and her eyes. His teeth clenched a little as if in pain, and then he feared the enchantment would soon pass away; but the music preserved it longer than he had expected, and it might have lasted still longer if he had not become aware that someone was standing in the doorway.

The feeling suddenly came over him that he was not alone; it was borne in upon him — he knew not how, neither by sight nor sound — through some exceptional sense. And turning towards the sunlit doorway, he saw a poor man standing there, not daring to disturb the priest, thinking, no doubt, that he was engaged in prayer. The poor man was Pat Kearney. So the priest was a little overcome, for that Pat Kearney should come to him at such a time was portentous. 'It is strange, certainly, coincidence after coincidence,' he said; and he stood looking at Pat as if he didn't know him, till the poor man was frightened and began to wonder, for no one had ever looked at him with such interest, not even the neighbour whom he had asked to marry him three weeks ago. And this Pat Kearney, who was a short, thick-set man, sinking into years, began to wonder what new misfortune had tracked him down. His teeth were worn and yellow as Indian meal, and his rough, ill-shaven cheeks and pale eyes reminded the priest of the country in which Pat lived, and of the four acres of land at the end of the boreen that Pat was digging these many years.

He had come to ask Father Oliver if he would marry him for a pound, but, as Father Oliver didn't answer him, he fell to thinking that it was his clothes that the priest was admiring, 'for hadn't his reverence given him the clothes himself? And if it weren't for the self-same clothes, he wouldn't have the pound in his pocket to give the priest to marry him.'

'It was yourself, your reverence——'

'Yes, I remember very well.'

Pat had come to tell him that there was work to be had in Tinnick, but that he didn't dare to show himself in Tinnick for lack of clothes, and he stood humbly before the priest in a pair of corduroy trousers that hardly covered his nakedness.

And it was as Father Oliver stood examining and pitying his parishioner's poverty it had occurred to him that, if he were to buy two suits of clothes in Tinnick and give one to Pat Kearney, he might wrap the other one in a bundle, and place it on the rocks on the Joycetown side. It was not likely that the shopman in Tinnick would remember, after three months, that he had sold two suits to the priest; but should he remember this, the explanation would be that he had bought them for Pat Kearney. Now, looking at this poor man who had come to ask him if he would marry him for a pound, the priest was lost in wonder.

'So you're going to be married, Pat?'

And Pat, who hadn't spoken to anyone since the woman whose potatoes he was digging said she'd as soon marry him as another, began to chatter, and to ramble in his chatter. There was so much to tell that he did not know how to tell it. There was his rent and the woman's holding, for now they would have nine acres of land, money would be required to stock it, and he didn't know if the bank would lend him the money. Perhaps the priest would help him to get it.

'But why did you come to me to marry you? Aren't you two miles nearer to Father Moran than you are to me?'

Pat hesitated, not liking to say that he would be hard set to get round Father Moran. So he began to talk of the Egans and the Reans. For hadn't he heard, as he came up the street, that Mrs. Rean had stolen the child from Mrs. Egan, and had had it baptized by the minister? And he hoped to obtain the priest's sympathy by saying:

'What a terrible thing it was that the police should allow a black Protestant to steal a Catholic child, and its mother a Catholic and all her people before her!'

'When Mrs. Rean snatched the child, it hadn't been baptized, and was neither a Catholic nor a Protestant,' the priest said maliciously.

Pat Kearney, whose theological knowledge did not extend very far, remained silent, and the priest was glad of his silence, for he was thinking that in a few minutes he would catch sight of the square white-washed school-house on the hillside by the pine-wood, and the thought came into his mind that he would like to see again the place where he and Nora once stood talking together. But a long field lay between his house and the school-house, and what would it avail him to see the empty room? He looked, instead, for the hawthorn-bush by which he and Nora had lingered, and it was a sad pleasure to think how she had gone up the road after bidding him good-bye.

But Pat Kearney began to talk again of how he could get an advance from the bank.

'I can back no bill for you, Pat, but I'll give you a letter to Father Moran telling him that you can't afford to pay more than a pound.'

Nora's letters were in the drawer of his writing-table; he unlocked it, and put the packet into his pocket, and when he had scribbled a little note to Father Moran, he said:

'Now take this and be off with you; I've other business to attend to besides you;' and he called to Catherine for his towels.

'Now, is it out bathing you're going, your reverence? You won't be swimming out to Castle Island, and forgetting that you have confessions at seven?'

'I shall be back in time,' he answered testily, and soon after he began to regret his irritation; for he would never see Catherine again, saying to himself that it was a pity he had answered her testily. But he couldn't go back. Moran might call. Catherine might send Moran after him, saying his reverence had gone down to bathe, or any parishioner, however unwarranted his errand, might try to see him out. 'And all errands will be unwarranted today,' he said as he hurried along the shore, thinking of the different paths round the rocks and through the blackthorn-bushes.

His mind was on the big wood; there he could baffle anybody following him, for while his pursuer would be going round one way he would be coming back the other. But it would be lonely in the big wood; and as he hurried down the old cart-track he thought how he might while away an hour among the ferns in the little spare fields at the end of the plantation, watching the sunset, for hours would have to pass before the moon rose, and the time would pass slowly under the melancholy hazel-thickets into which the sun had not looked for thousands of years. A wood had always been there. The Welshmen had felled trees in it to build rafts and boats to reach their island castles. Bears and wolves had been slain in it; and thinking how it was still a refuge for foxes, martens and badgers and hawks, he made his way along the shore through the rough fields. He ran a little, and after waiting a while ran on again. On reaching the edge of the wood, he hid himself behind a bush, and did not dare to move, lest there might be somebody about. It was not till he made sure there was no one that he stopped under the blackthorns, and followed a trail, thinking the animal, probably a badger, had its den under the old stones; and to pass the time he sought for a den, but could find none.

A small bird, a wren, was picking among the moss; every now and then it fluttered a little way, stopped, and picked again. 'Now what instinct guided its search for worms?' he asked, and getting up, he followed the bird, but it escaped into a thicket. There were only hazel-stems in the interspace he had chosen to hide himself in, but there were thickets nearly all about it, and it took some time to find a path through these. After a time one was found, and by noticing everything he tried to pass the time away and make himself secure against being surprised.

The path soon came to an end, and he walked round to the other side of the wood, to see if the bushes were thick enough to prevent anyone from coming upon him suddenly from that side; and when all searches finished he came back, thinking of what his future life would be without Nora. But he must not think of her, he must learn to forget her; for the time being at least, his consideration must be of himself in his present circumstances, and he felt that if he did not fix his thoughts on external things, his courage— or should he say his will?— would desert him. It did not need much courage to swim across the lake, much more to leave the parish, and once on the other side he must go any whither, no whither, for he couldn't return to Catherine in a frieze coat and a pair of corduroy trousers. Her face when she saw him! But of what use thinking of these things? He was going; everything was settled. If he could only restrain his thoughts — they were as wild as bees.

Standing by a hazel-stem, his hands upon a bough, he fell to thinking what his life would be, and very soon becoming implicated in a dream, he lost consciousness of time and place, and was borne away as by a current; he floated down his future life, seeing his garret room more clearly than he had ever seen it — his bed, his washhand-stand, and the little table on which he did his writing. No doubt most of it would be done at home; and at nightfall he would descend from his garret like a bat from the eaves.

Journalists flutter like bats about newspaper offices. The bats haunt the same eaves, but the journalist drifts from city to city, from county to county, busying himself with ideas that were not his yesterday, and will not be his tomorrow. An interview with a statesman is followed by a review of a book, and the day after he may be thousands of miles away, describing a great flood or a railway accident. The journalist has no time to make friends, and he lives in no place long enough to know it intimately; passing acquaintance and exterior aspects of things are his share of the world. And it was in quest of such vagrancy of ideas and affections that he was going.

At that moment a sudden sound in the wood startled him from his reverie, and he peered, a scared expression on his face, certain that the noise he had heard was Father Moran's footstep. It was but a hare lolloping through the underwood, and wondering at the disappointment he felt, he asked if he were disappointed that Moran had not come again to stop him. He didn't think he was, only the course of his life had been so long dependent on a single act of will that a hope had begun in his mind that some outward event might decide his fate for him. Last month he was full of courage, his nerves were like iron; to-day he was a poor vacillating creature, walking in a hazel-wood, uncertain lest delay had taken the savour out of his adventure, his attention distracted by the sounds of the wood, by the snapping of a dry twig, by a leaf falling through the branches.

'Time is passing,' he said, 'and I must decide whether I go to America to write newspaper articles, or stay at home to say Mass — a simple matter, surely.'

The ordinary newspaper article he thought he could do as well as another — in fact, he knew he could. But could he hope that in time his mind would widen and deepen sufficiently to enable him to write something worth writing, something that might win her admiration? Perhaps, when he had shed all his opinions. Many had gone already, more would follow, and one day he would be as free as she was. She had been a great intellectual stimulus, and soon he began to wonder how it was that all the paraphernalia of religion interested him no longer, how he seemed to have suddenly outgrown the things belonging to the ages of faith, and the subtle question, if passion were essential to the growth of the mind, arose. For it seemed to him that his mind had grown, though he had not read the Scriptures, and he doubted if the reading of the Scriptures would have taught him as much as Nora's beauty. 'After all,' he said, 'woman's beauty is more important to the world than a scroll.' He had begun to love and to put his trust in what was natural, spontaneous, instinctive, and might succeed in New York better than he expected. But he would not like to think that it was hope of literary success that tempted him from Garranard. He would like to think that in leaving his poor people he was serving their best interests, and this was surely the case. For hadn't he begun to feel that what they needed was a really efficient priest, one who would look after their temporal interests? In Ireland the priest is a temporal as well as a spiritual need. Who else would take an interest in this forlorn Garranard and its people, the reeds and rushes of existence?

He had striven to get the Government to build a bridge, but had lost patience; he had wearied of the task. Certain priests he knew would not have wearied of it; they would have gone on heckling the Government and the different Boards until the building of the bridge could no longer be resisted. His failure to get this bridge was typical, and it proved beyond doubt that he was right in thinking he had no aptitude for the temporal direction of his parish.

But a curate had once lived in Bridget Clery's cottage who had served his people excellently well, had intrigued successfully, and forced the Government to build houses and advance money for drainage and other useful works. And this curate had served his people in many capacities — as scrivener, land-valuer, surveyor, and engineer. It was not till he came to Garranard that he seemed to get out of touch with practical affaris, and he began to wonder if it was the comfortable house he lived in, if it were the wine he drank, the cigars he smoked, that had produced this degeneracy, if it were degeneracy. Or was it that he had worn out a certain side of his nature in Bridget Clery's cottage? It might well be that. Many a man has mistaken a passing tendency for a vocation. We all write poetry in the beginning of our lives; but most of us leave off writing poetry after some years, unless the instinct is very deep or one is a fool. It might well be that his philanthropic instincts were exhausted; and it might well be that this was not the case, for one never gets at the root of one's nature.

The only thing he was sure of was that he had changed a great deal, and, he thought, for the better. He seemed to himself a much more real person than he was a year ago, being now in full possession of his soul, and surely the possession of one's soul is a great reality. By the soul he meant a special way of feeling and seeing. But the soul is more than that — it is a light; and this inner light, faint at first, had not been blown out. If he had blown it out, as many priests had done, he would not have experienced any qualms of conscience. The other priests in the diocese experienced none when they drove erring women out of their parishes, and the reason of this was that they followed a light from without, deliberately shutting out the light of the soul.

The question interested him, and he pondered it a long while, finding himself at last forced to conclude that there is no moral law except one's own conscience, and that the moral obligation of every man is to separate the personal conscience from the impersonal conscience. By the impersonal conscience he meant the opinions of others, traditional beliefs, and the rest; and thinking of these things he wandered round the Druid stones, and when his thoughts returned to Nora's special case he seemed to understand that if any other priest had acted as he had acted he would have acted rightly, for in driving a sinful woman out of the parish he would be giving expression to the moral law as he understood it and as Garranard understood it. This primitive code of morals was all Garranard could understand in its present civilization, and any code is better than no code. Of course, if the priest were a transgressor himself he could not administer the law. Happily, that was a circumstance that did not arise often. So it was said; but what did he know of the souls of the priests with whom he dined, smoked pipes, and played cards? And he stopped, surprised, for it had never occurred to him that all a man knows of his fellow is whether he be clean or dirty, short or tall, thin or stout. 'Even the soul of Moran is obscure to me,' he said — 'obscure as this wood;' and at that moment the mystery of the wood seemed to deepen, and he stood for a long while looking through the twilight of the hazels.

Very likely many of the priests he knew had been tempted by women: some had resisted temptation, and some had sinned and repented. There might be a priest who had sinned and lived for years in sin; even so if he didn't leave his parish, if he didn't become an apostate priest, faith would return to him in the end. But the apostate priest is anathema in the eyes of the Church; the doctrine always has been that a sin matters little if the sinner repent. Father Oliver suddenly saw himself years hence, still in Garranard, administering the Sacraments, and faith returning like an incoming tide, covering the weedy shore, lapping round the high rock of doubt. If he desired faith, all he had to do was to go on saying Mass, hearing confessions, baptizing the young, burying the old, and in twenty years — maybe it would take thirty — when his hair was white and his skin shrivelled, he would be again a good priest, beloved by his parishioners, and carried in the fulness of time by them to the green churchyard where Father Peter lay near the green pines.

Only the other day, coming home from his afternoon's walk, he stopped to admire his house. The long shadow of its familiar trees awakened an extraordinary love in him, and when he crossed the threshold and sat down in his armchair, his love for his house had surprised him, and he sat like one enchanted by his own fireside, lost in admiration of the old mahogany bookcase with the inlaid panels, that he had bought at an auction. How sombre and quaint it looked, furnished with his books that he had had bound in Dublin, and what pleasure it always was to him to see a ray lighting up the parchment bindings! He had hung some engravings on his walls, and these had become very dear to him; and there were some spoons, bought at an auction some time ago — old, worn Georgian spoons — that his hands were accustomed to the use of; there was an old tea-service, with flowers painted inside the cups, and he was leaving these things; why? He sought for a reason for his leaving them. If he were going away to join Nora in America he could understand his going. But he would never see her again — at least, it was not probable that he would. He was not following her, but an idea, an abstraction, an opinion; he was separating himself, and for ever, from his native land and his past life, and his quest was, alas! not her, but—— He was following what? Life? Yes; but what is life? Do we find life in adventure or by our own fireside? For all he knew he might be flying from the very thing he thought he was following. His thoughts zigzagged, and, almost unaware of his thoughts, he compared life to a flower — to a flower that yields up its perfume only after long cultivation— and then to a wine that gains its fragrance only after it has been lying in the same cellar for many years, and he started up convinced that he must return home at once. But he had not taken many steps before he stopped:

'No, no, I cannot stay here year after year! I cannot stay here till I die, seeing that lake always. I couldn't bear it. I am going. It matters little to me whether life is to be found at home or abroad, in adventure or in habits and customs. One thing matters — do I stay or go?'

He turned into the woods and walked aimlessly, trying to escape from his thoughts, and to do so he admired the pattern of the leaves, the flight of the birds, and he stopped by the old stones that may have been Druid altars; and he came back an hour after, walking slowly through the hazel-stems, thinking that the law of change is the law of life. At that moment the cormorants were coming down the glittering lake to their roost. With a flutter of wings they perched on the old castle, and his mind continued to formulate arguments, and the last always seemed the best.

At half-past seven he was thinking that life is gained by escaping from the past rather than by trying to retain it; he had begun to feel more and more sure that tradition is but dead flesh which we must cut off if we would live. . . . But just at this spot, an hour ago, he had acquiesced in the belief that if a priest continued to administer the Sacraments faith would return to him; and no doubt the Sacraments would bring about some sort of religious stupor, but not that sensible, passionate faith which he had once possessed, and which did not meet with the approval of his superiors at Maynooth. He had said that in flying from the monotony of tradition he would find only another monotony, and a worse one — that of adventure; and no doubt the journal-ist's life is made up of fugitive interests. But every man has, or should have, an intimate life as well as an external life; and in losing interest in religion he had lost the intimate life which the priesthood had once given him. The Mass was a mere Latin formula, and the vestments and the chalice, the Host itself, a sort of fetishism — that is to say, a symbolism from which life had departed, shells retaining hardly a murmur of the ancient ecstasy. It was therefore his fate to go in quest of — what? Not of adven-ture. He liked better to think that his quest was the personal life — that intimate exaltation that comes to him who has striven to be himself, and nothing but himself. The life he was going to might lead him even to a new faith. Religious forms arise and die. The Catholic Church had come to the end of its thread; the spool seemed pretty well empty, and he sat down so that he might think better what the new faith might be. What would be its first principle? he asked himself, and not finding any answer to this question, he began to think of his life in America. He would begin as a mere recorder of passing events. But why should he assume that he would not rise higher? And if he remained to the end of his day a humble reporter, he would still have the supreme satisfaction of knowing that he had not resigned himself body and soul to the life of the pool, to a frog-like acquiescence in the stagnant pool.

His hand held back a hazel-branch, and he stood staring at the lake. The wild ducks rose in great flocks out of the reeds and went away to feed in the fields, and their departure was followed by a long interval, during which no single thought crossed his mind — at least, none that he could remember. No doubt his tired mind had fallen into lethargy, from which a sudden fear had roughly awakened him. What if some countryman, seeking his goats among the rocks, had come upon the bundle and taken it home! And at once he imagined himself climbing up the rocks naked. Pat Kearney's cabin was close by, but Pat had no clothes except those on his back, and would have to go round the lake to Garranard; and the priest thought how he would sit naked in Kearney's cottage hour after hour.

'If anyone comes to the cabin I shall have to hold the door to. There is a comic side to every adventure,' he said, 'and a more absurd one it would be difficult to imagine.'

The day had begun in a ridiculous adventure — the baptism of the poor child, baptized first a Protestant, then a Catholic. And he laughed a little, and then he sighed.

'Is the whole thing a fairy-tale, a piece of mid-summer madness, I wonder? No matter, I can't stay here, so why should I trouble to discover a reason for my going? In America I shall be living a life in agreement with God's instincts. My quest is life.'

And, remembering some words in her last letter, his heart cried out that his love must bring her back to him eventually, though Poole were to take her to the end of the earth, and at once he was carried quickly beyond the light of common sense into a dim happy world where all things came and went or were transformed in obedience to his unexpressed will. Whether the sun were curtained by leafage or by silken folds he did not know — only this: that she was coming towards him, borne lightly as a ball of thistledown. He perceived the colour of her hair, and eyes, and hands, and of the pale dress she wore; but her presence seemed revealed to him through the exaltation of some sense latent or non-existent in him in his waking moods. His delight was of the understanding, for they neither touched hands nor spoke. A little surprise rose to the surface of his rapture — surprise at the fact that he experienced no pang of jealousy. She had said that true love could not exist without jealousy! But was she right in this? It seemed to him that we begin to love when we cease to judge. If she were different she wouldn't be herself, and it was herself he loved — the mystery of her sunny, singing nature. There is no judgment where there is perfect sympathy, and he understood that it would be as vain for him to lament that her eyebrows were fair as to lament or reprove her conduct.

Continuing the same train of thought, he remembered that, though she was young today, she would pass into middle, maybe old age; that the day would come when her hair would be less bright, her figure would lose its willowness; but these changes would not lessen his love for her. Should he not welcome change? Thinking that perhaps fruit-time is better than blossom-time, he foresaw a deeper love awaiting him, and a tenderness that he could not feel today might be his in years to come. Nor could habit blunt his perceptions or intimacy unravel the mystery of her sunny nature. So the bourne could never be reached; for when everything had been said, something would remain unspoken. The two rhythms out of which the music of life is made, intimacy and adventure, would meet, would merge, and become one; and she, who was today an adventure, would become in the end the home of his affections.

A great bird swooped out of the branches above him, startling him, and he cried out: 'An owl — only an owl!' The wood was quiet and dark, and in fear he groped his way to the old stones; for one thing still remained to be done before he left — he must burn her letters.

He burnt them one by one, shielding the flame with his hand lest it should attract some passer-by, and when the last was burnt he feared no longer anything. His wonder was why he had hesitated, why his mind had been torn by doubt. At the back of his mind he had always known he was going. Had he not written saying he was going, and wasn't that enough? And he thought for a moment of what her opinion of him would be if he stayed in Garranard. In a cowardly moment he hoped that something would happen to save him from the ultimate decision, and now doubt was overcome.

A yellow disc appeared, cutting the flat sky sharply, and he laid his priest's clothes in the middle of a patch of white sand where they could be easily seen. Placing the Roman collar upon the top, and, stepping from stone to stone, he stood on the last one as on a pedestal, tall and gray in the moonlight — buttocks hard as a faun's, and dimpled like a faun's when he draws himself up before plunging after a nymph.

When he emerged he was among the reeds, shaking the water from his face and hair. The night was so warm that it was like swimming in a bath, and when he had swum a quarter of a mile he turned over on his back to see the moon shining. Then he turned over to see how near he was to the island. 'Too near,' he thought, for he had started before his time. But he might delay a little on the island, and he walked up the shore, his blood in happy circulation, his flesh and brain a-tingle, a little captivated by the vigour of his muscles, and ready and anxious to plunge into the water on the other side, to tire himself if he could, in the mile and a half of gray lake that lay between him and shore.

There were lights in every cottage window; the villagers would be about the roads for an hour or more, and it would be well to delay on the island, and he chose a rock to sit upon. His hand ran the water off his hard thighs, and then off his long, thin arms, and he watched the laggard moon rising slowly in the dusky night, like a duck from the marshes. Supporting himself with one arm, he let himself down the rock and dabbled his foot in the water, and the splashing of the water reminded him of little Philip Rean, who had been baptized twice that morning notwithstanding his loud protest. And now one of his baptizers was baptized, and in a few minutes would plunge again into the beneficent flood.

The night was so still and warm that it was happiness to be naked, and he thought he could sit for hours on that rock without feeling cold, watching the red moon rolling up through the trees round Tinnick; and when the moon turned from red to gold he wondered how it was that the mere brightening of the moon could put such joy into a man's heart.

Derrinrush was the nearest shore, and far away in the wood he heard a fox bark. 'On the trail of some rabbit,' he thought, and again he admired the great gold moon rising heavily through the dusky sky, and the lake formless and spectral beneath it.

Catherine no doubt had begun to feel agitated; she would be walking about at midnight, too scared to go to sleep. He was sorry for her; perhaps she would be the only one who would prefer to hear he was in America and doing well than at the bottom of the lake. Eliza would regret in a way, as much as her administration of the convent would allow her; Mary would pray for him — so would Eliza, for the matter of that; and their prayers would come easily, thinking him dead. Poor women! if only for their peace of mind he would undertake the second half of the crossing.

A long mile of water lay between him and Joycetown, but there was a courage he had never felt before in his heart, and a strength he had never felt before in his limbs. Once he stood up in the water, sorry that the crossing was not longer. 'Perhaps I shall have had enough of it before I get there;' and he turned on his side and swam half a mile before changing his stroke. He changed it and got on his back because he was beginning to feel cold and tired, and soon after he began to think that it would be about as much as he could do to reach the shore. A little later he was swimming frog-fashion, but the change did not seem to rest him, and seeing the shore still a long way off he began to think that perhaps after all he would find his end in the lake. His mind set on it, however, that the lake should be foiled, he struggled on, and when the water shallowed he felt he had come to the end of his strength. 'Another hundred yards would have done for me,' he said, and he was so cold that he could not think, and sought his clothes vaguely, sitting down to rest from time to time among the rocks. He didn't know for certain if he would find them, and if he didn't he must die of cold. So the rough shirt was very welcome when he discovered it, and so were the woollen socks. As soon as he was dressed he thought that he felt nearly strong enough to climb up the rocks, but he was not as strong as he thought, and it took him a long time to get to the top. But at the top the sward was pleasant — it was the sward of the terrace of the old house; and lying at length, fearful lest sleep might overtake him, he looked across the lake. 'A queer dusky night,' he said, 'with hardly a star, and that great moon pouring silver down the lake.'

'I shall never see that lake again, but I shall never forget it,' and as he dozed in the train, in a corner of an empty carriage, the spectral light of the lake awoke him, and when he arrived at Cork it seemed to him that he was being engulfed in the deep pool by the Joycetown shore. On the deck of the steamer he heard the lake's warble above the violence of the waves. 'There is a lake in every man's heart,' he said, 'and he listens to its monotonous whisper year by year, more and more attentive till at last he ungirds.'

AFTERWORD
BY
RICHARD ALLEN CAVE

I

The Lake was the first of George Moore's novels to receive immediate critical acclaim as a masterpiece. While some reviewers expressed reservations about the handling of certain episodes in the novel, all praised the remarkable originality of its conception and method. *The Saturday Review*[1] noted that Moore 'has always been a breaker of ground' and that this 'dreamlike study of spiritual development' was his most unusual and challenging performance to date. With *The Lake* that reviewer believed Moore had reached a late maturity, achieving a rare, scrupulous artistry: 'It is a very subtle piece of work . . . very fine and elaborate, very delicate and profound'. *The Times Literary Supplement* considered its style made such unusual demands on the reader that 'one must class it with prose poems'.[2] This was an acutely perceptive judgment. Most of the reviewers wrote appreciatively and at length about the style of *The Lake* and Moore's 'beautiful, sensitive and musical language' and yet seemed unconscious of *why* they had been compelled to do so. The reviewer for *The Times Literary Supplement* probed more deeply:

> The characters are the embodiments of conflicting points of view. The interest is in the play of mind, and the charm in the poetical presentation of the picture. We have seldom seen Irish scenery better realised and rendered, nor do we know of any modern novelist better skilled than Mr. Moore in getting fresh harmonious effects out of the language.

[1] *The Saturday Review*. December 2, 1905. pp. 723–4.
[2] *The Times Literary Supplement*. November 10, 1905. pp. 382–3.

The method of *The Lake*, this reviewer argued, was different from traditional realism; the subject was exclusively psychological and the characterization wholly internal and this demanded a new mode of expression. Style, in that here it is dramatising states of mind, *is* the meaning. What is remarkable in Moore's achievement is that the style conveys so much while never losing immediacy, flow and an engaging simplicity. Compared with many of Moore's earlier novels, the expression is austere but rich in implication.

To turn to the opening chapter again after completing Moore's novel is to realise how much more it has accomplished for all its seeming directness than mere exposition. Above all the flowing rhythms of the prose have persuasively won the reader over, almost unconsciously, to a new way of reading. Moore took pride in being a prose stylist but in no modish Aesthetic sense of the term. *The Lake*, he tells us in his Preface to the revised edition of 1921 (which is the text reprinted here), was to be about 'the essential rather than the daily life of the priest' (p. x); his story was to be woven out of the substance of Father Oliver Gogarty's soul 'without ever seeking the aid of external circumstance' (p. x). Narrative incident is kept to a minimum and held at a distance, for what preoccupies Moore is how certain incidents and decisions compel his priest to explore the darkest reaches of his consciousness and so transform the nature of his existence. A subtly varying prose style is Moore's means of evoking the stages of Father Gogarty's confrontation with his soul's identity. Style defines his changing modes of perception which result from the moods induced in him by subliminal forces; frankly scrutinising these moods allows him slowly to articulate and accept the promptings of his instincts which he had long suppressed from conscious consideration. What Gogarty learns of himself is profoundly humiliating; it taxes the resources of his courage to find reasons to continue living, but his resilience earns its reward.

As in Virginia Woolf's novels, style in *The Lake* acts as a kind of metaphor inviting the reader to engage imaginatively with a character's private perceptions and through them to apprehend intuitively what Moore's calls the 'underlife' of the soul: 'that vague, undefinable yet intensely real life that lies beneath our consciousness, that life which knows, wills and perceives without help from us'.[3] To commend a novel as above all a triumph of

[3] George Moore: 'Since the Elizabethans', *Cosmopolis*. October, 1896. p. 57.

style — and *The Lake* is that certainly — is perhaps dangerous in that it might suggest to some readers a contrived and mannered performance where method is made to compensate for a want of real matter. To make such an assumption would be to miss the vitality and richness of the experience of reading *The Lake* and the exciting challenge Moore's method poses to one's powers of interpretation. We can perhaps best test these judgements by looking closely at that opening chapter.

We first encounter Father Gogarty walking by Lough Carra in Mayo, the lake that has been the setting and, oftentimes, the focus of his whole life's experience, except for the years of his training at Maynooth. He knows the lake with a profound intimacy; even the woods of Derrinrush in which he now walks were the place he always came to as a boy, despite their distance from his home, to search out the best hazel stems for making fishing rods; 'and one had only to turn over the dead leaves to discover the chips scattered circlewise in the open spaces where the coopers sat in the days gone by making hoops for barrells' (p. 2). Familiarity has not dulled Gogarty's delight in the place, for the lake, its shores and islands, the hamlets and small towns that surround it, the ruined castles and abbeys that dominate any vista of its waters, all hold a wealth of private associations for him or call forth his wide knowledge of the folklore and history of the area and the factual awareness too that comes only from a lifetime's sensitive observation of one's environment. Watching the varieties of trees spring into leaf in the order the local climate dictates brings him pleasure because it confirms the truth of previous years' attentiveness and reflection. Scents and sounds, however subtle, he identifies immediately he becomes aware of them and he knows unerringly where to direct his steps to discover their source. The lake is an index to Father Oliver's wide-ranging sensibility and the storehouse of his memories; and, because the Mayo setting is so quintessentially Irish, the sensibility and the memories are distinctly Irish too. Lough Carra is a correlative for the reaches of his consciousness, (although Gogarty himself is not at first aware of this) stimulating in him the flow of his mind's patterns of associations, and reflecting his moods. Today he is expansive with the onset of spring.

Yet the mood is not quite as pure as it at first appears. Seeing a yacht passing northwards in the direction of Kilronan Abbey,

Gogarty muses on the exuberance that would be his if he could
but pursue his fondness for walking in a new, preferably French,
environment where there would be the challenge of so much that
was fresh to admire and discover. To his surprise he finds himself
admitting to a certain tiredness with the familiar despite the
buoyancy induced in him by the warmth and clarity of the May
morning. His steps, less consciously directed now, have conveyed
him to a headland from which he can view the town of Tinnick on
the far shore where he was born; and he begins to review the
events which have brought him to be parish priest in a remote
backwater, as if by thinking through the past he might renew the
certainty of purpose he felt in formerly making his present state
his goal in life. His adolescence is recalled with peculiar vividness
— the shortlived infatuation for Annie McGrath that is more a
response to parental pressures than a genuine inclination; his
financial ambitions to make a going concern of the town's delap-
idated mills and, in quick recoil from his mother's dismissive
criticism of this project, the zealous enthusiasm for a life of piety
and isolation; his fantasies of living a hermit's existence of
medieval rigour and self-deprivation being channelled by the
promptings of his more clear-sighted sister Eliza into a sense of
vocation for the priesthood. What gives the memories their vividness is Moore's eye for the specific psychological details that
succinctly convey to us the quality of Father Oliver's relationships
with the members of his family, so that something larger than his
subjective appraisal of his own youth is intimated to us: his pacing
beside the river till he has found another good reason for refuting
his mother's sarcasm about his hope to revive the mill-industry
and his sitting self-importantly by the fire having thought of one
in wait for the apt moment to introduce it into the conversation;
or Eliza's quiet announcement that she intends to be a nun, her
very tone and look convincing the family of her sincerity and
compelling them into silence and respect, since she is so utterly
devoid of embarrassment at having thus made herself the focus
of their scrutiny; or again Father Oliver's special affection for
Eliza, bound up as it is with his admiration for her rectitude and
insight, which renders him embarrassed and makes it impossible
for him to sustain any of his adolescent poses in her company.
Looking back now he shares his mother's and sister's view of his
precociousness and is amused by his former silliness. Dramati-

cally that easy tolerance vanishes before the onset of violent
emotion as the subliminal forces of his mind, aware of the
chronological progression of his thoughts, anticipate that his
ensuing memories must be of his career at Maynooth. 'His childhood had been a slumber' (p. 8), he decides, because it was
without any serious challenge to his sense of his own identity.
College life quickly exposed every aspect of his scrupulous piety
as pretence; the physical humiliations he inflicted on himself
were considered barbarous by his teachers and ridiculous by his
contemporaries. His penitential exercises met the judgement
they deserved: not a visiting of Grace but the spiritually
humiliating awareness that he was to others nothing but a fool.
Only his intellectual brilliance was left him through which to
recover his self-esteem: even that proved troublesome since his
awakening to his spiritual pretentiousness had left him with a
finically delicate conscience that despaired lest any outstanding
achievement be essentially self-display. That conscience had insisted he return to Lake Carra and seek out its poorest parish. He
assures himself of his happiness in being there; he has indeed had
the compensation of being in close proximity to the lake which
means so much to him; appreciating its beauty has become a daily
part of his worship. Certainly it has the power to intrude upon
and ease the pain of his current reveries.

Yet how secure is that assertion of happiness? On reflection one
realises how even the equanimity of the chapter's opening
intimated a disturbing undertow. It is, we are told immediately,
'one of those *enticing* days at the beginning of May', so alluring in
fact that it has tempted Gogarty to neglect his duties to his
parishioners; the phrase, '*one* of those days' implies, and rightly as
we later discover, that it is one typical of many others. Odd
phrases on re-reading the first few paragraphs, that might initially have seemed inconsequential take on a special poignance. In
the midst of an account of Gogarty's close study of the patterning
on some sycamore leaves and the opening leaf buds of a neigh-
bouring elm which remind him of 'clouds of butterflies' occurs
the remark: 'He could think of nothing else' (p. 2). The significance of this is ambiguous. Is it that there is such a wealth of
elm-buds that Gogarty's consciousness is overwhelmed by this
imagistic impression of being surrounded by butterflies? Or is it
suggesting that his mind is in a state of torpor or exhaustion and

capable only of registering sensory perceptions? Or is there a hint
of obsessiveness about the experience of his mind willing itself to
concentrate on external stimuli? How quickly afterwards his
mind turns his perception of the yacht travelling up the lake into a
fantasy about travelling himself! The desire is commonplace
enough but it takes on a peculiar desperation here — '. . . his
desire was to be freed for a while from everything he had ever
seen, and from everything he had ever heard. He merely wanted
to wander . . .' (p. 4) — implying a longing for total freedom from
the pressures of consciousness, from the fact of selfhood, though
immediately the mind recoils and tries to cover its tracks by
stating that its need is really for refreshing aesthetic stimuli, music
especially, in preference for known natural ones. The play of
light and shadow over the distant mountains which Father Oliver
earlier asserted he could watch 'without weariness', he now
admits is tiresome in its melancholy, however beautiful the fluctuations continue to seem. Like Coleridge in his state of dejection,
Gogarty can see but cannot *feel* that beauty of the landscape about
him; and Moore's prose in the first few pages, when one compares it retrospectively with later passages describing the lakeside
landscape does have a tense, studied, self-conscious quality about
it that evokes a careful and deliberate scrutiny rather than a
relaxed apprehension.

The tone lightens with the priest's recollections of his youth in
Tinnick as a calm suffuses his surface mood with his easy acceptance of his teenage follies. The memories are lingered over with
a delighted attention to circumstantial detail till they are unexpectedly dispelled by the surge of venom directed against the
thought of Maynooth. The memories here are of briefer dura-
tion; circumstantial details now actualise emotional and physical
pain with considerable immediacy. The recollections of childhood are simply memories; these recollections have the acuteness
of vision or hallucination. Here is an experience where the fact of
selfhood is annihilated most brutally. Is that the reason why,
given Gogarty's earlier state of mind, the experience has surfaced
so forcefully in his consciousness? Is this in fact his mind's way of
checking an impulse towards sentimentality? The corrective
seems to work, for Gogarty, having relived his humiliations in
full, ends by finding reassurance in the fact that he did recover his
self-respect in time and has since known happiness in Garranard.

And yet why does memory of that moral and spiritual failure recur and provoke such lacerating anguish? Confession and absolution should have brought peace and, if the renewed appreciation of himself were wholehearted, the sense of self-betrayal should have been steadily appeased. Has perhaps the full extent of his failure still to be learnt? The remarkable clarity of the memories suggests they constitute an epiphany of which he has missed the meaning. The chapter ends with Gogarty confronting his present mood of lassitude; he briefly questions whether it is some penalty for having been so very contented when he was a curate living even more remotely than now away at Kilronan, but dismisses the thought forcefully as a ludicrous scruple: 'He had to a certain extent outgrown his very delicate conscience' (p. 14). The chapter has given us much factual information about Gogarty's past, but in a fashion that directs our attention all the time to the perplexingly turbulent state of his consciousness in the present. The subtly varying tones of Moore's style intimate to us the quality of Gogarty's instinctive life, his subliminal self, which seems dangerously at variance with the flow of his conscious thoughts.

The full density of the opening chapter is appreciated only with the start of the second. Gogarty resumes his ramble and encounters a group of women from his parish returning home from gathering wood; their passing him by startles him into guilty embarrassment since he should after all have been attending to his parish duties. He identifies them all and wonders whether his presence in the woods will be a subject of local gossip. His guilt seems out of all proportion to the offence. He imagines the drift of the women's conversation voicing their suspicions that he is drawn repeatedly to the lake out of dread that a woman he denounced from his pulpit — the village schoolmistress, Nora Glynn — has drowned herself out of shame. Though the idea occurs as a fanciful projection, Gogarty's mind seizes on it as a truth and relentlessly tells over the train of events that led to that public outburst against the woman. All the material that made up the opening chapter, we now realise, was a concerted effort by the forces of his conscious mind to keep that deep-rooted fear at bay. Now we can appreciate the motive behind the strained, self-conscious quality of the description, the attempt at total self-abandon through sensory pleasures, the protracting of those memories of childhood because they were recollections of a time free of emotional complexity; even the sharply defined horror of Maynooth now seems a less daunting and so a more tolerable theme for contemplation than this recent moral failure concerning Nora Glynn. Formerly he was the exclusive victim of his delusions; now the consequences affect a wider range of responsibilities and may have cost a life.

All that we have been offered, then, in the opening chapter is a consciously wrought fiction by a distraught mind seeking respite from a more insistent story that his conscience relentlessly compels him to listen to. It is a story he longs to be free of, but, tell it how he will, he cannot resolve it in a fashion that restores his opinion of himself or eases his conscience. For all his short-comings in sensitivity and judgement which his attack on Nora Glynn reveals him guilty of, a kind of integrity persists in his quintessential self that compels him to search and search the experience through so as not again to miss the meaning. Defining the nature of that impulse towards integrity is on one level the purpose of Moore's novel. Fundamentally Gogarty's failure springs from a lack of imagination: his conscious mind interferes with the retelling of the story in the hope that he can shape it in a manner that will afford some excuse for, or condone his own conduct. Each time the narrative resists such manipulation and forces him to begin the tale afresh, Gogarty's sense of inadequacy and dejection increases. Everywhere — his house, the garden, the village — carries associations with Nora that can set the story going again in his head, so that he feels driven to distraction. The tale becomes a haunting, until one morning Gogarty is surprised to discover that the pain which suffuses his being with each telling is losing its intensity (p. 29), and a mood of levity ensues. His ego has found a way of compromising with that impulse to integrity by making the retellings a habit. Regular, deliberate repetitions will steadily numb the anguish and suppress the urgency of the voice within. Like Beckett's character Joe (and many features of the narrative told in *Eh Joe* resemble Gogarty's relationship with Nora Glynn), Father Gogarty is in danger of subsiding into the sin of apathy by reducing the sense of his own worthlessness to a daily ritual of self-abasement, a quickly performed act of remorse that is quite devoid of serious commitment and thus is utterly meaningless. Father Oliver's exuberance is cut short by the arrival of a letter from a Father O'Grady in London telling that Nora has been received into his congregation and reproving Gogarty for his want of charity. The story now has an ending but it is one which, strengthened by O'Grady's criticism of him, will never again allow Gogarty freedom to justify himself. He stands condemned by more than his own intuitive conscience; if he would know peace, he must search behind the facts of Nora's story for its deeper implications. Blind, enervating remorse gives way to a quest for atonement. Telling the story aright now becomes a necessity of every nerve.

If Moore has made us scrupulously aware of style in his early chapters, that is quite deliberate: telling a story is an act of the imagination and *how* it is told carries moral and emotional implications that leave the identity of the teller ruthlessly exposed. Moore's method with *The Lake* in confining narrative events to a remembered past allows him to use devices of fiction, kinds of style, even at times the very rhythms of his prose, to give us access to the various strata of Gogarty's consciousness. The very processes of fiction are to be seen as emblematic of states of mind. Learning how to tell his and Nora's story truthfully brings to Gogarty 'a special way of feeling and seeing' (p. 172); 'his perception,' he asserts, 'seemed to have been indefinitely increased' (p. 139). Sharing the stages of his path to this illumination instils in us a special way of reading too.

II

His chosen method demands of Moore a virtuoso control of style. His own preference for the novel as one of his best, he tells us, 'is related to the very great difficulty of the telling', because 'difficulty overcome is a joy to the artist' (p. x); and what impresses one on re-reading the novel is the lack of strain in what Moore calls his conquest over his material and the effortlessness with which, through his first chapters, he induces as sensitive and scrupulous a response from his reader. By the end of Chapter III the pattern of the novel is established: the priest's self-communing alternates at random intervals with a series of letters as Gogarty establishes a correspondence first with Father

O'Grady and later with Nora Glynn. She, he realises, has the courage to pursue her life according to her own standards; her very self-assurance, her being self-contained but in no way self-centred, was her initial attraction for Gogarty, an attraction that unconsciously revealed how circumscribed his existence was by duties, dogma and ordained rules of conduct. He condemned her out of a confused sense of inferiority and dejection because she caused him to question his own worth. Neither absolution from O'Grady nor Nora's stated forgiveness can restore Gogarty's trust in himself; courageously he chooses to search out a way of defining what his warped version of Nora's story has indirectly revealed as his deficiencies. The letters to Nora allow him from time to time to formulate what have to be in large measure intuitive perceptions about himself that he has discovered by trying to recollect the past in its fullness. Nora's replies test his experience against her own understanding of events and encourage his further enquiry, while her accounts of her life in London and on the continent (she has found employment as an author's secretary) keep alive in his mind his delight in her open, generous nature which he seeks to emulate as an ideal.

What Gogarty has to learn through his reveries is how to make connections between his fluctuating moods, as revealed by the particular quality of his perceptions, and the drift of his thoughts and memories. The mind chooses to sift from the multiplicity of its sensory responses certain details to bring into consciousness as perceptions; the process of sifting is wholly subliminal, instinctive. Making the connections, Gogarty begins to perceive how his moods and perceptions can be interpreted as monitors of the conscious processes of his mind, their fluctuations revealing the accuracy of his mind's understanding of itself or its deceptions. Gogarty has always believed conscience to be acquired; it is embodied in the church's catechism as a set of objective criteria against which one's personal behaviour is rigorously measured; now equally rigorous self-communion teaches him that it is innate, rooted in instinct, and that the 'voice' of this conscience is one's mode of perception. This awareness undermines his calling as a Catholic priest but strengthens his faith; in freeing himself from the shame at his instincts that was so fastidiously instilled in him by his training at Maynooth he wins a profounder reverence. Perception is a veritable blessing.

But this is to reduce the theme of the novel to statement whereas Moore's triumph lies in the subtlety with which he renders the slow process whereby Gogarty's consciousness works to heal its wracked condition so that that theme becomes an experience. The difficulties Moore faced are numerous: the landscape description might lose its metaphorical status for the reader and the novel become an extended exercise in pathetic fallacy; the subjective orientation might encourage an indulgence in purple prose. More difficult than either of these matters must have been the question of pace: on the one hand the stages of Gogarty's development needed to be conducted at a rate which in naturalistic terms made them psychologically convincing since, given his status as a Catholic priest and the strictness of his training, his conversion to a new creed could not be rapid or without an ebb and flow of doubt, fear, scruple and shock. On the other hand there was a need to avoid monotony of method (the letters are an excellent device that allows the predominantly subjective experience to be judged periodically from a more critical perspective with no loss of conviction or of thematic unity).

The versatility of styles Moore commands for rendering Gogarty's moods with vivid impact is impressive. There is the exuberance of his ride round the lake to Tinnick after receiving news of Nora's safety to suggest to his sister Eliza that she invite Nora back to Ireland to teach music in her convent (Chapter V). Father Oliver's eye is alert for every detail that confirms his newly recovered satisfaction in living there; he relishes afresh the tales and legends about the localities he passes through. The familiar has become pristine again; but are the zest and the wonder really, as he says, the product of his discovering a way of atoning for his cruelty to Nora by finding her a position in the neighbourhood? Or are they the product of his impulsively seizing on any project that will restore Nora's presence to him? Given that at this point Gogarty has no knowledge of Nora's feelings about him, (they could well be vindictive since her last experience of him was his public defamation of her character and, even if she chose not to be spiteful, for her to return to a community where she had been stripped of her character after she had found security and acceptance elsewhere would be beyond the bounds of commonsense) the whole enterprise is preposterous. His vivacity though infectious is undercut for the reader by irony and pathos; Gogarty is absurdly innocent and the prose here exactly captures his child-like, total self-absorbtion in following his whim:

> Ponies were feeding between the whins, and they raised their shaggy heads to watch the car passing. In the distance cattle were grazing, whisking the flies away. How beautiful was everything — the white clouds hanging in the blue sky, and the trees! There were some trees, but not many — only a few pines. He caught glimpses of the lake through the stems; tears rose to his eyes, and he attributed his happiness to his native land and to the thought that he was living in it. Only a few days ago he wished to leave it — no, not for ever, but for a time; and as his old car jogged through the ruts he wondered how it was that he had ever wished to leave Ireland, even for a single minute. (p. 47)

Or consider Moore's evocation of the moment when Gogarty loses his sexual innocence and recognises how many of his actions have been covert expressions of desire for Nora. Passion has steadily taken control of his imagination in its most negative manifestations. Nora's refusal to return to Tinnick has aroused in him prurient suspicions of her relationship with her new employer, the author Walter Poole; he justifies his insistent questioning as a pastoral responsibility for her spiritual safety, but in truth he is goaded on by jealousy. Nora's wish to terminate the correspondence as unhealthy he interprets as an admission of guilt. Gogarty finds her letter while in a state of physical exhaustion (he has been walking for some hours on the hills with his curate, Moran) and his psyche seizes on this unusual freedom from carefully imposed restraints on its conscious activity. Certain of Gogarty's memories that we have shared have had the vividness of hallucinations; now actual hallucinations take possession of him. Through fantasy he learns the heart's truth:

> Once he was within the wood, the mist seemed to incorporate again; she descended again into his arms, and this time he would have lifted the veil and looked into her face, but she seemed to forbid him to recognize her under penalty of loss. His desire overcame him, and he put out his hand to lift the veil. As he did so his eyes opened, he saw the wet wood, the shining sky, and she sitting by a stone waiting for him. A little later she came to meet him from behind the hawthorns that grew along the cart-track — a tall woman with a little bend in her walk.
> He wondered why he was so foolish as to disobey her, and besought

her to return to him, and they roamed again in the paths that led
round the rocks overgrown with briars, by the great oak-tree where
the leaves were falling. And wandering they went, smiling gently on
each other ... (pp. 115—6)

The visions of Nora tantalisingly elude his grasp. Characteristically Moore gives a naturalistic basis for the experience: the
dream-figures are tricks of perception, a distraught mind's
impressions of patches of mist seen in the eerie light of the woods
by night. Yet it is the subjective view that catches our attention.
The words have a blunt matter-of-factness; they define circumstantial details but the specificity is offset by the rapid staccato
phrasing of the sentences, that brings to the experience an emotional undertow of panting, frenetic desperation. The longing
for sentimental indulgence is acute but repeatedly denied. The
style actualises the mind's experience with remarkable exactness.

As one final example, consider Moore's account of Gogarty's
last few days in Garranard. Having elected to follow his new
philosophy of living 'in accord with God's instincts', Gogarty
decides he cannot in conscience remain a Catholic priest. His
imagination working in harmony now with his instincts has pre-
sented him with a scheme for leaving the parish without causing
scandal or disturbing the faith of those of his parishioners who
find Catholicism fulfilling. Forced to wait for several weeks for a
second opportunity to follow his plan after the first attempt was
frustrated, he pursues his clerical duties assiduously; and Moore
gives us the events of his last day in Garranard in detail. There is a
comic baptism where the solemnity of the occasion is disrupted by
fisticuffs between the baby's grandmothers — one a Catholic, one
a Protestant — over which Church the child is to be christened in,
that ends only with the child's immersion in both fonts; there are
encounters with a tediously garrulous and ancient parishioner
and a destitute one who comes to bargain over the price of a
wedding ceremony. It is a time of great tension for Gogarty (and
for the reader too, held back in suspense in this way from a
conclusion that has been made to seem aesthetically inevitable for
a long time now) but the tone betrays no impatience or bad
temper on the priest's part. The delay is putting the courage of
Gogarty's new found convictions to the test; circumstances compel him to be engrossed with provincial Catholicism at a level
where its tendencies to encourage bigotry and materialism

appear ridiculous. Contempt would be an understandable reaction, especially from one who has renounced Catholicism in preference for 'the personal life — that intimate exaltation that comes to him who has striven to be himself and nothing but himself' (p. 175). But what Gogarty has rooted out of his psyche is the urge to dogmatise and he now experiences no feeling of superiority. Executing his parish duties elicits from him a genuine imaginative sympathy towards his congregation. The level tone of Moore's recounting of these episodes, beautifully poised between pathos and an amused comedy, is the perfect correlative for Gogarty's quiet, sustained assurance.

These examples reveal the density of implication that the changing styles convey in *The Lake* and Moore's precision of judgement in matching an appropriate style with fluctuating states of mind. Isolating particular episodes like this, however, may fail to indicate the further skill and strength of the novel in presenting Gogarty's growth to wholeness of being as a sustained continuum of feeling. It is the movement of the mind to health that excites Moore's interest: the ebb and flow of positive and negative emotions, the hesitant but courageous advances in awareness and the nervous retreat from too sudden or comprehensive an illumination of the self that leaves the conscious mind frantic at the possible consequences of such an understanding. Purging his guilt over Nora requires Gogarty to accept both his passional self, which the obligations of his calling have kept suppressed, and, to his horror, his capacity for lust which in the urgency of its release can incite him even to blasphemy. Training for the priesthood was a protracted ritual of self-denial, a rooting-out of all vestiges of a private self so as to be blameless in the performance of his public duty; the only permitted intimacy with self was in the searching of his consciousness for any lingering cause of shame. Writing to a friend, Lena Milman, who was disturbed by the psychological and moral implications of his novel *Esther Waters* which she had read in draft-form, Moore countered her assertion that nothing is 'more despicable than the following of one's inclinations' with the argument:

> If one does not follow one's inclinations the result seems to me to be complete sterilization. It is only those who are wanting in strength who do not follow them — will you allow me to substitute the word instincts? We must discriminate between what is mere inclination and

what is instinct. All my sympathies are with instincts and their development. Instinct alone may lead us aright.[4]

When Gogarty is impelled to let his inner, private self speak, its voice is aggressively egocentric; inclination and impulse demand attention; rebuked or challenged, the voice whines in self-pity. Learning to discriminate between inclination and instinct forces Gogarty to confront all the worst aspects of his individuality so as to recognise the value of imaginative sympathy and generosity as finer expressions of his identity. Only then can he share Nora's fearless joy and independence of mind; and only then with the climactic letters which occur in Chapters XI and XII can he tell his own and Nora's story accurately; the tone is no longer a complex one of confession or complaint but one of simple, wholehearted gratitude:

> Again I thank you for what you have done for me, for the liberation you have brought me of body and mind. I need not have added the words 'body and mind', for these are not two things but one thing. And that is the lesson I have learned. (p. 147)

If in reading we finally acquiesce in Gogarty's belief that this wholeness of being comes only through trusting in the 'spontaneous natural living wisdom' (p. 145) of his instincts, it is because Moore proves its value through the way his prose matches Father Gogarty's growing insight, the ironies and inconsistencies resolving finally into an even-tempered purity of statement. On the day Father Gogarty receives O'Grady's first letter telling of Nora's safety, he becomes suddenly aware of how in his joy and relief his mind has, almost unconsciously, formulated an image: 'Every man . . . has a lake in his heart' (p. 35). He repeats it with wondering curiosity, uncertain of its precise significance yet finding in it a strange, calming satisfaction that enables him to face the difficulty of writing to Nora. Lake Carra continues throughout the coming year to be the setting and in many ways the companion of his meditations, the source and focus of his perceptions, as we have seen, and the correlative of his moods; but the meaning of the image eludes him right until the moment when he leaves the confines of the lake forever, swimming across it by night in

---

[4] *George Moore in Transition: Letters to T. Fisher Unwin and Lena Milman 1894–1910.* Edited by H.E. Gerber. Detroit, 1968. p. 71.

order to disappear from Ireland to follow a new life in America. He has found a way of interpreting the 'underlife' of his mind; responding to the peace it brings he reverences it as God-given and he takes an irrevocable step in support of his new creed. With the final sentence of the novel, Gogarty's psychological quest, the logic of the narrative, Moore's stylistic method and the metaphorical structure come into total fusion as the image is rephrased and clarified in the light of Gogarty's experience:

> 'There is a lake in every man's heart,' he said, 'and he listens to its monotonous whisper year by year, more and more attentive till at last he ungirds.' (p. 179)

Metaphor has been transformed into illumination; with the weight of Moore's artistry throughout the novel behind it, it is the only possible ending. The reader's sense of aesthetic inevitability is perfect: we have had our vision.

III

Moore had originally designed *The Lake* to be the last of the short stories that make the collection entitled *The Untilled Field*, but during composition it became obvious that the subject demanded more extensive handling than the form of the short story would allow. The creative rigour Moore exercised over the drafting of the novel delayed its publication for two years after the appearance of *The Untilled Field* in 1903; but novel and tales grew out of the same inspirational impulse and to turn to the stories after reading *The Lake* is to be aware not only of how much the two publications have in common in themes and style but also how complete a stage they form together in Moore's development as a novelist. The stories show us Moore practising his scales, as it were, discovering and delighting in a new technical command that facilitated the extended virtuoso performance that is the novel. Moore's pride in *The Lake* ensured that *The Untilled Field* met with its fair share of reflected glory in his estimation: '. . . these Irish stories,' he tells us, 'lie very near to my heart' (p. x).

The Untilled Field was one of the few works Moore undertook (at least initially) in the spirit of a commission. Moore had tried to persuade the Gaelic League to publish a work of fiction as a textbook to foster students' engagement with the language. While the idea had appealed, his recommendation of *The Arabian Nights* for the purpose had caused a scandal since not only was it not the work of an Irishman but, worse still, its author did not appear to hold chastity in particularly high esteem. Father Tom Finlay S.J., a prominent member of the League and founder of *The New Ireland Review*, urged Moore to write some stories himself which could be translated into Gaelic for publication in his magazine; as a Commissioner of National Primary Education he would then get the collection accepted for reissue as a textbook by the Intermediate Board of Education. The first six stories translated by Padraic O'Sullivan found their way into print in this manner, appearing in one volume in 1902 as *An T-ūr-Gort, Sgéalta*.

In talking the project over with John Eglinton, Moore had decided to use Turgenev's *Tales of a Sportsman* as a model. It was an inspired choice: Turgenev had exerted a powerful influence over the composition of one of Moore's early novels, *A Drama in Muslin* (1886); it too was a tale of Irish life and one in which landscape description had featured extensively as a means of defining the heroine, Alice Barton's slowly maturing conviction that she must resist her parents' pressures to conform to their effetely cultured existence. Though in writing about Turgenev shortly after completing this novel Moore had stated that for him the Russian master's great theme is 'obey nature's laws; be simple and obey; it is the best that you can do',[5] it was an injunction he himself chose to ignore for the next twelve years or more. With the notable exception of *Esther Waters*, the style of Moore's fiction in the 'Nineties is anything but simple or natural, as it came under the influence of Huysmans' ornate mannerisms and the theories of Symbolism. His inspiration seemed trapped in cloying Aestheticisms; purple seemed to be the only tone his prose could render and a certain repetitiveness and predictability set in with his narratives.

In the spring of 1901 Moore returned to his native Ireland, setting up house in Ely Place, Dublin — a change of scene motivated according to his autobiography, *Hail and Farewell*, by the overwhelming disgust with matters British that he experienced on seeing Londoners' reactions to the Boer War. But what in physical terms was an emigration was spiritually a release.

[5] George Moore: 'Turgueneff', *The Fortnightly Review*. 1888. p. 240.

Assiduously he helped Yeats, Martyn and Lady Gregory with the affairs and repertoire of the newly formed Irish National Theatre Society and campaigned for the Gaelic Revival. Writing plays in collaboration with Yeats and Martyn meant thinking seriously about other authors' creative principles; the new challenge of public debates and lectures for the Gaelic League revitalised Moore's energy, enthusiasm and confidence; the slower pace of Dublin life released him from the need to be intense. Within weeks of his arrival in Ireland, as the final chapters of *Sister Teresa* (1901) that were composed there demonstrate, his writing had acquired a relaxed and mellow tone. Father Tom's suggestion about the stories and John Eglinton's gloss on it regarding Turgenev were ideally timed. Instinct had impelled Moore's return to Dublin (in *Hail and Farewell* he describes this is a miraculous annunciation experienced in the Hospital Road, Chelsea: 'I heard a voice speaking within me: no whispering thought it was but a resolute voice, saying, Go to Ireland'[6]); he had obeyed and recovered his old ebullient self; his inspiration broke out of its silted channel to flow with spontaneity and ease. He had now proved that Turgenev's injunction was of worth and with *The Lake* Turgenev's great theme became Moore's great theme too.

As Moore worked at the stories for *The Untilled Field* his inspiration began to burst out of the confines of his commission. The early tales depict the pathos of the Irish peasants' existence: the bleakness, the imaginative, emotional and cultural austerity that compelled many, often whole parishes, to emigrate to America leaving their homes in ruins on the hillsides; and the indefatigable resilience of the villagers who stayed and endured, cherishing the fragile consolations offered by their religion. Patience, reverence, resilience and a sense of duty are qualities he had earlier celebrated in the life of his heroine, Esther Waters; the consolations of her life too are hard-won and fragile. In that novel Moore questions why this is so, exposing and criticising the society Esther lives in for depriving her of the opportunity to achieve the fullness of being her remarkable integrity deserves. As Moore composed the tales, engaging ever more deeply with the condition of the Irish peasantry, he again began to search for the reason why the prevailing mood *had* to be one of compassion-

[6] George Moore: *Hail and Farewell*, edited by Richard Cave (Gerrards Cross, 1976), p. 257.

ate pathos. The answer, he felt, lay in the peculiarly rigorous nature of Irish Catholicism, valuing zealous moral rectitude above sympathy and imagination and so fostering narrow-mindedness and bigotry among its priesthood. As the tales advanced priests ceased to be peripheral though powerful figures in the narratives and became the prime subject. With considerable invention Moore found ways of introducing increasingly barbed anti-clerical satire into the work without disturbing his predominantly dispassionate tone. It is the plight of the priest which becomes the occasion for the comedy. In 'Patchwork', for example, Father Maquire's moral authority is completely undermined by his parishioners' want of ready cash: he refuses to wed a young couple who cannot pay the marriage dues, but they go and hold the wedding feast and celebrate the nuptial night without benefit of clerical blessing so that he is forced to marry them for nothing for the sake of propriety. Father MacTurnan after a lifetime's work amongst a really destitute community in the West writes in halting Latin a letter to Rome, in the story of that title, making the modest proposal that the rule of celibacy be relaxed for the Irish clergy and they be encouraged to wed to improve the state of the nation:

> Ireland can be saved by her priesthood! . . . The priests live in the best houses, eat the best food, wear the best clothes; they are indeed the flower of the nation, and would produce magnificent sons and daughters. And who could bring up their children according to the teaching of our holy church as well as priests?[7]

MacTurnan becomes an embarrassment or a laughing-stock to his fellow priests (though he remains quite unconscious of the fact) and the butt of countless bar-room jokes in Dublin when the story gets known through rumour. But Moore's attitude here is complex; as with Swift, the ironies reverberate in every direction and one is left with a disturbing sense of the enormity of the social and psychological confusions intimated by the tale as an undercurrent to its humour. In the last tales this balance of sympathies is lost and the consequences of clerical insensitivity are tragic: Julia Cahill's parents are compelled to ostracise her when she refuses to agree to the marriage the priest has arranged for her, being

---

[7] George Moore: 'A Letter to Rome', *The Untilled Field*. Reprinted with an introduction by T.R. Henn (Gerrards Cross, 1976), p. 134.

incensed by the way her father, the priest and her intended husband barter for her in her presence with an exchange of livestock as if she were a mere chattel; in 'The Wild Goose' clerical interference and religious differences between husband and wife slowly stifle their passion for each other and inexorably bring about their separation; and in 'In the Clay' (later revised as 'Fugitives') a masterpiece of sculpture is destroyed by a priest's connivance because it was modelled from the nude.

Given the particular satirical turn the stories were taking, it is not surprising that only six were published in Father Tom Finlay's magazine; given the events of Moore's life at this time, it is remarkable that the anti-clerical and anti-Catholic impulse of *The Untilled Field* and *The Lake* was so scrupulously controlled. Involvement since 1899 with the literary theatre and the Gaelic revival had shown him how easily the aspirations for the political and cultural progress of Ireland shared by friends and associates like Sir Horace Plunkett, Yeats, AE and even the ardent Catholic, Edward Martyn, could be jeopardised by ill-founded accusations of blasphemy if priests on the relevant committees suspected that the consequences of any move towards progress might lessen their intimate emotional hold over their congregations. Moore learned too how readily his colleagues' political opponents could take advantage of the situation to frustrate any project they took exception to by fermenting religious unrest. Even a man as culturally sophisticated as his cousin Edward Martyn could be swayed in the most perverse directions by threats of damnation; his delicate conscience, prompted by the Confessional, could render his imagination moribund. Few of his associates, as Moore shows in *Hail and Farewell*, were willing to question the prevailing national acquiescence in this loss of an independent spirit. It was not faith he wished to call into question but the status of the Church: as Gogarty argues, 'when religion is represented as hard and austere, it is the fault of those who administer religion, and not of religion itself' (p. 96). It was this discrimination which shaped many of the narratives and controlled the tone of *The Untilled Field*.

Irish reviews of the 1903 edition were generally appreciative; only one ventured to criticize the volume on sectarian grounds, expressing shock that it should be the work of one 'himself a Catholic'. Though Catholic by birth and education, Moore's practice had long since lapsed; the review sent him, he records, 'into an uncontrollable rage'.[8] On September 24th 1903, the *Irish Times* carried a long letter from Moore publicly avowing his Protestantism. It was an understandable reaction but an impetuous one and, in the particular form the letter took, silly, for he cited as the cause of his change of faith a recent incident in which Maynooth College had decorated the walls of a room where King Edward VII and his court were to be received with draperies in the king's racing colours and with engravings of his most successful racehorses. Moore's friends, AE and Oliver St. John Gogarty, advised against linking the seriously intended avowal of his beliefs with so petty a Nationalist issue. They foresaw that it would undermine his reputation and blunt the impact of his criticism of the Irish habit of mind; and it did.

But where Moore the man lost, Moore the artist gained. The three masterpieces which followed that public declaration, *The Lake* (1905 and 1921); *Hail and Farewell* (1911–1914) and *The Brook Kerith* (1916), were each in various ways motivated by the desire to recover the esteem he lost through his flippancy. The self-defeat of the letter to the *Irish Times* ensured that the writing of *The Lake* with its depiction of how a Catholic priest came to renounce his calling should admit of no similar lapses of taste, though the temptations must have been legion. Three months before his letter was published, Moore while writing to his friend Edouard Dujardin had asserted boisterously: 'Life has no other goal but life and art has no other end but to make life possible, to help us to live'.[9] Insofar as *The Lake* is shaped by Moore's personal beliefs, the urge to didacticism (implicit in that remark to Dujardin) must have been strong; but in the published novel representation is all and dogma has no place. That Moore did have occasional difficulty in restraining the propagandist in him is evident from the latter half of *Salve*, where Moore explores the idea that no decent book has been written by a Catholic since the Reformation and the unrelieved, strident opinionating makes laborious reading. The recent failure of the letter to the *Irish Times* seems to

[8] *Hail and Farewell*. Edition cited, p. 457. The text of Moore's letter to the *Irish Times* is given in Appendix C of that edition, pp. 669–70.

[9] In a letter of June, 1903, cited in J.M. Hone: *The Life of George Moore*. 1936. p. 245.

have sharpened Moore's powers of invention and his capacity for self-criticism in composing *The Lake*. All comes back to the question of treatment and Moore did well to develop the delicacy of judgement, the carefully regulated sense of proportion and the sustained use of understatement and implication that he had experimented with in *The Untilled Field*.

The chief problem of style confronting Moore in the tales was how to deal with grey, quiet lives without seeming superior and patronising and without producing unintentional bathos by miscalculating the tone and the nature of the climaxes of the short narratives. It was not the first time that he had taken the Irish peasantry as his subject, but at least one earlier attempt had been a woeful abuse of literary decorum. *Parnell and his Island* (1887, first published in France as *Terre d'Irlande*) is a collection of rather flashy pieces of journalism expressing Moore's reactions to Ireland on returning there from Paris, his disgust at the savagery as he then deemed it of the peasants and the effeteness and destitution of the gentry in decline. Everywhere Moore boasts his cosmopolitan experience, proudly displaying his cultivated sensibility at the expense of his subjects. Inevitably the tone redounds to his own discredit, exposing his 'culture' as snobbish, superficial and insufferably cruel. It is characteristic of his want of real insight into his subject that he presents Ireland to his French and English readers through a series of character studies that are conventional stock-types of politician, priest, landlord, peasant. In none of the sketches does discrimination get the better of prejudice. The volume of essays is the more astonishing in that it followed Moore's novel, *A Drama in Muslin*, where the heroine, Alice Barton's growing understanding of the social and political situation in the country tempers her dispassionate judgements of both the landlord and the peasant classes with sympathy that ensures the characters are never lost sight of as individuals. *Parnell and his Island* proved something of a millstone in time: when Moore publicly offered his support for the Gaelic and theatrical revivals, he was often reminded forcibly of the essays in jibes questioning his sincerity. (Douglas Hyde, president of the Gaelic League, could not resist baiting Moore with the suggestion that he might serve the cause of the Gaelic revival best by reissuing the volume with the new subtitle: *Ireland Without Her Language*).

Where Moore triumphs in *The Untilled Field* is in shaping the various narratives around an undercurrent of powerful feeling which the events define by implication but which is rarely stated explicitly. The characters have little education and are incapable of subtlety of expression especially about their private emotions but the force of those emotions intimated behind their halting speech endows each of them with a vivid presence. Feeling enshrines identity; to respond to its prompting, however hesitantly, is for the characters of these tales to approach self-awareness. Consider the opening tale, 'The Exile': James Phelan idolises Catherine and she James's brother, Peter; Peter decides to train for the priesthood exiling himself from the village so that James's courtship of Catherine may prosper, but Catherine withdraws to a convent; Peter realises he has no calling and returns home; Catherine finds she has no sincere vocation and returns too; James accepts the inevitable and emigrates to America, leaving the family farm for Peter to inherit. In this summary the tale has a symmetry and an inevitability that indicate perhaps a humorous rendering would be the most feasible; but that could easily rob the characters of dignity. Comedy is not Moore's way with the story; it is the selflessness of the characters that he focusses our attention on, their respect for each other that prompts them to try to act without giving hurt. At the conclusion there is an emotional loss for one brother and an emotional gain for the other, but no sense of personal victory or defeat; there are no recriminations. Catherine arrives back in the village in time to bid James farewell:

> The signal was still up, and the train had not gone yet; at the end of the platform she saw James and Peter. She let Pat Phelan drive the cart round; she could get to them quicker by running down the steps and crossing the line. The signal went down.
> 'Pether,' she said, 'we will have time to talk presently. I must speak to James now.'
> And they walked up the platform, leaving Peter to talk to his father.
> 'Paddy Maguire is outside,' Pat said; 'I asked him to stand at the mare's head.'
> 'James,' said Catherine, 'it's bad news to hear you're going. Maybe we'll never see you again, and there is no time to be talking now, and me with so much to say.'
> 'I am going away, Catherine, but maybe I will be coming back some day. I was going to say maybe you would be coming over after me; but the land is good land, and you'll be able to make a living out of it.'

    And then they spoke of Peter, James said he was too great a scholar
for a farmer, and it was a pity he could not find out what he was fit for
— for surely he was fit for something great after all.
    And Catherine said:
    'I shall be able to make something out of Pether.'
    His emotion almost overcame him, and Catherine looked aside so
that she should not see his tears.
    'Tis no time for talking of Pether,' she said. 'You are going away,
James, but you will come back. You'll find better women than me in
America, James. I don't know what to say to you. The train will be here
in a minute. I am distracted. But one day you will be coming back, and
we'll be proud of you when you do. I'll build up the house, and then
we'll be happy. Oh! here's the train. Good-bye; you have been very
good to me. Oh, James! when will I be seeing you again?'[10]

How perfectly judged is the scruple that keeps Catherine talking
and stressing her own unworthiness when she sees how close her
confident assertion that she can make a man of Peter comes to
unmanning James. She feels compelled to speak of her gratitude
but prevaricates because she is aware how speaking of his worth
intensifies James's frustration that she cannot speak of requiting
his passion, however noble she knows him to be. Even for her to
talk of Peter hints at intimacies James will never experience. All
her efforts to calm the emotional tension between them only
aggravate their sense of the irrevocableness of their separation as
so much more than a physical fact — an awareness that ruthlessly
exposes as frail and sentimental Catherine's hopes that with time
the present experience will be simplified in their memories and its
anguish numbed. Here are three quiet lives perhaps; yet here too
three individuals have momentously shaped their whole future
selves. With fine tact Moore keeps in balance our appraisal of his
characters; his naturalism is exact yet the experience he defines is
suffused with a moral beauty. The very method of the tale evinces
Moore's wholehearted respect for common life. Henry James's
praise of Turgenev's artistry might with justice be applied to
Moore's here: 'the element of poetry in him is constant and yet
reality stares through it without the loss of a wrinkle".[11]
    The strength of 'The Exile' derives from the power of its

[10] *The Untilled Field.* Edition cited. pp. 29–30.
[11] Henry James: 'Turgenev and Tolstoy, 1897', *The House of Fiction*.
Edited by Leon Edel, 1957. p. 174.

dialogue where the characters speak directly out of their feelings rather than about them; the reader engages with the experience and is left to infer the meaning. In several stories in the collection Moore began experimenting with other techniques of understatement, ways whereby the rendering of heightened experiences could imply more than the characters involved in them could be expected to comprehend, except perhaps intuitively. The technique which most closely anticipates the method of *The Lake* involves the flexible adapting of prose-rhythms in order to suggest through a narrative told seemingly in the third-person the fluctuations of feeling that the protagonists undergo. Subjective and omniscient perspectives are subtly conflated in the reader's mind. (Moore was to develop the technique for very sophisticated effects in his autobiography, *Hail and Farewell* and his late masterpiece, *The Brook Kerith*.) A good example of this can be seen in 'The Wedding Gown', the most perfectly crafted of the stories in the volume. An elderly woman, all but in her dotage, gives her wedding dress to her great-niece to wear at a ball. It is the one remaining treasure, profoundly cherished, from old Margaret's past, which seems to be for her a kind of talisman that confirms her identity and keeps her within the bounds of sanity. At the dance young Molly feels a sudden compulsion to return home; the distorted shadows of parkland and woods in the moonlight urge her to run faster and faster; long before the image forms itself in her consciousness that she is somehow engaged in a race with Death, the prose has evoked the sensation. As she reaches the cottage, the tone changes to match the measured deliberateness with which she stirs the embers of the fire to flame and lights a candle:

> . . . and holding it high she looked about the kitchen.
> 'Auntie, are you asleep? Have the others gone to bed?'
> She approached a few steps, and then a strange curiosity came over her, and though she had always feared death she now looked curiously upon death, and she thought that she saw the likeness which her aunt had often noticed.
> 'Yes,' she said, 'she is like me. I shall be like that some day if I live long enough.'
> And then she knocked at the door of the room where her parents were sleeping.[12]

[12] *The Untilled Field*. pp. 185–6.

Dread has perversely forced Molly to race to confront what she
fears, but the experience transcends her expectations: her recognition of a common likeness and a shared mortality brings a quiet
assurance that is reflected in the simple diction and syntax and in
the matter-of-fact tone of the prose. The gift of the gown and its
consequences have taught Molly how to value generosity and how
to care: the dress is now a talisman for her too. The way of Molly's
access to adulthood is commonplace enough but it is unique for
each individual and Moore's style intimates the wonder of the
moment without recourse to a forced poeticism.

   The later stories make increasingly challenging demands on
Moore's capacity for tact. 'The Clerk's Quest', being about an
elderly, sober man's infatuation with a woman he has never seen
but whose perfume on her papers and cheques that pass through
his hands at the bank inspires his devotion, throughout runs the
risk of provoking the reader's laughter. Like 'The Exile', the
subject could be the stuff of comedy; to work the anecdote for its
pathos is to court a charge of pretentiousness. In this instance
Moore sustains a measured evenness of tone that renders the
entire story convincing even when the clerk's obsession makes
him the dupe of a variety of absurd fantasies. His visions are so
totally absorbing that they render him completely immune to the
ribald remarks of his fellow clerks, to his dismissal from the bank,
even to being spurned by the lady who returns his presents of
expensive jewellery. Deluded he may be, but the delusions foster
in him a perfect equanimity and it is that which the style, so
regular and unemotional, draws to our attention, suppressing in
us any urge to ridicule. 'The Clerk's Quest' is closely allied to *The
Lake* in its concern with sexual infatuation and hallucinatory
fantasies of possession (the final pages of the tale have a marked
resemblence to pages 115—6 of the novel) but Gogarty, unlike
Dempsey, the clerk, has his waking moods when he can sit in
judgment on the excesses of his imagination. What the tale
developed in Moore was the ability to present vividly the aber-
rations of a mind, without resorting to sensationalism. Tales like
'The Clerk's Quest' reveal Moore working to find ways of con-
veying the reader beyond the surface emotionalism of the
experiences being defined to engage with the processes of the
mind which are their cause.

   One story in *The Untilled Field* stands out as different in method from the rest. 'Almsgiving' has an articulate narrator writing subjectively about his own behaviour. Irritated by a sudden downfall of rain he refrains from giving a customary penny to a blind beggar; the ache of conscience immediately activates his reason into attempting to justify his failure in charity. With cynical logic the mind quickly finds grounds to assure him that the beggar is the one at fault in persisting to live as an object of pity: 'I asked myself why I helped him to live'.[13] Shocked by the callous drift of his thoughts, he returns on impulse and gives the blindman sixpence. They talk and the blindman tells of his reliance on regular benefactors, the narrator being one; the old man's humility provokes the narrator's cynicism again: 'It was only necessary for me to withhold my charity to give him ease . . . the world would be freed from a life that I could not feel to be of any value'.[14] He now consciously refrains from visiting that part of town till again suddenly compelled there and compelled too to question the blindman earnestly about his condition. The man's level tone intimates a complete acceptance of his lot; appreciating that fortitude and the man's strange unity of being releases in the narrator's consciousness a mood of pure joy. Like *The Lake*, this tale explores the relation Moore believes exists between conscience and instinct; private reverie alternates with impulsive actions that bring the narrator into conversation with the beggar; the donor through an access of imaginative sympathy is steadily transformed into the debtor. As the tale advances, charity and pity are redefined for the reader and purged of their self-centred motives. The blindman comes to be more responsibly known to the narrator's imagination and giving becomes a pleasure not a means of appeasing the guilt the narrator feels on account of what he initially considers his superiority. Method and meaning are beautifully integrated; but if the tale fails to satisfy at the last, it is because of Moore's handling of the conclusion. The narrator leaves the blindman and sits to contemplate the change of mood he has experienced:

> I was sitting where sparrows were building their nests, and very soon I seemed to see farther into life than I had ever seen before. 'We're here,' I said, 'for the purpose of learning what life is, and the blind

[13] *The Untilled Field.* p. 195.
[14] Ibid. pp. 196–7.

beggar has taught me a great deal, something that I could not have
learnt out of a book, a deeper truth than any book contains. . . .' And
then I ceased to think, for thinking is a folly when a soft south wind is
blowing and an instinct as soft and as gentle fills the heart.[15]

Delicacy of implication has been lost in statement and the vague-
ness of the generalisations runs the risk of trivialising the experience that is being commented on. The narrator could be judged
as indulging in smug sentimentality. To have left the narrator
aware of a new sensitivity of perception himself on his depar-
ting from the blindman, a heightening of the senses towards
details in the atmosphere and townscape that indicate the
approach of spring, would have been a more fitting conclusion
sustaining the technique of implication to the last. The final
paragraph is in fact redundant and confuses what it is designed to
clarify. It is essentially a failure in literary decorum.

Much in the story anticipates Moore's method with *The Lake*.
What 'Almsgiving' in particular highlights are the problems
involved in developing an experience of a kind which in Joyce
would be termed an epiphany towards some conscious formula-
tion of its significance. The imaginative scope of the letters Moore
devises for this purpose in *The Lake* can more readily be
appreciated in contrast with 'Almsgiving'; the technical virtuosity
is the more remarkable for its apparent effortlessness. Each letter
of Gogarty's to Father O'Grady or to Nora Glynn is an assessment
of past experiences that strives for a complete understanding but
achieves only a partial expression of the truth. Their replies
confirm and define the gap between his intention and achievement. Moore's success comes from making his technical problem
as narrator an exact analogy for his character's psychological
dilemma: how to find the language that conveys the causes why
Gogarty's castigating of Nora has unexpectedly achieved for him
the status of epiphany, illuminating, if it can be but expressed
rightly, his whole identity. Clarity of statement becomes for
Gogarty a compelling necessity of every nerve, because it is the
only proper expression of his ethical being left him by circumstance. Within the terms Moore establishes in the novel Gogarty's
moral quest is a search for an appropriate literary decorum. T.R.
Henn has described Moore's style in *The Untilled Field* as 'lean and

[15] Ibid. p. 200.

muscular, the product . . . of slow and scrupulous revision; erasing, as it were, all that does not tell'.[16] Each tale works to create an illumination in the reader's imagination as we have seen through carefully judged understatement. *The Lake* explores the processes of mind whereby judgement (in all its senses) can be exercised, paring experience to its absolute essentials. Gogarty's admission of the truth to Nora which forms the letters opening Chapters XI and XII has a forthright simplicity but it requires the whole novel to enable us to read these letters with a complete understanding of the density of implication behind each statement. To turn to *The Lake* after reading *The Untilled Field* is to delight even more richly in its technical mastery.

IV

It is most fitting that *The Lake* should be dedicated to Edouard Dujardin though for more reasons than Moore mentions in his *épître dédicatoire*. They had been friends since the 1880s when Moore used to frequent the flat shared by Dujardin, the critic Téodor de Wyzewa, and the painter Jacques-Emile Blanche during his visits to Paris. Dujardin at this time was establishing two periodicals both of which he edited — *La Revue Wagnérienne* and *La Revue Indépendente* — in which he sought to foster an interest in Wagner's operas, philosophy and theories of art and to champion the Symbolist movement as a significant development in literature of the composer's ideas. Mallarmé, that 'triste et charmant bonhomme' (p.v), who by 1905 was living at Valvins within walking distance of Dujardin's home in the forest of Fontainebleau, had established his reputation chiefly through the pages of the *Indépendente*. Moore and Dujardin had immediately recognised in each other a kindred sensibility; the *Indépendente* serialised a translation of Moore's *Confessions of a Young Man* in 1888 and when Moore expressed his dissatisfaction with this because the translator failed to catch the right satirical tone, it was Dujardin who revised it with Moore's supervision before it was issued as a book by Savine. When Moore began imitating the Symbolist methods of Huysmans with his tale *A Mere Accident*, *La*

[16] *The Untilled Field*. Edition cited. p.xi.

Revue Wagnérienne alone among English and French literary journals carried a notice showing any sympathy for his new style. While Moore rapidly outgrew many friendships, ruthlessly discarding acquaintances when they ceased to keep pace with his ever-changing literary, musical or painterly enthusiasms, his affection for Dujardin deepened over the years, perhaps because Dujardin was as volatile in temperament as himself. Both men considered conversation an art and their appetite for talk was voracious — talk with lightning transitions from the frivolous or whimsical to the serious, from anecdotes and satire about authors' personalities to considered appraisals of their artistry, from personal confession to detached generalised judgments. The wit often lay in the mode of effecting the transitions. With Moore, conversation had to be flexible and on the whole he preferred to dictate its course. Dujardin was one of the very few friends with whom Moore was content to relax at times into a receptive role as audience and not view the exchange as a battle of wits. 'To none have I given so ardent an ear as I have to Edouard Dujardin,' he remarked in his old age and admitted graciously that listening brought its recompense, for he had 'harvested most profitably' from the discourse.[17]

Dujardin's interpretations of the dramatic action of *Tannhäuser, Tristan and Isolde, The Ring* and *Parsifal* were incorporated into Moore's novels *Evelyn Innes* and *Sister Teresa* though the material was reworked into the various discussions the heroine has with her lovers about how she would perform particular roles. These two novels were conceived partly in response to what Dujardin felt was an urgent imperative for the writer of the day— to find a means of evoking through prose some of the intensity of mind-life experienced by Wagner's characters in the operas. (The novels were not particularly successful in this, since Moore's method was to evolve his narrative out of thinly disguised parallels with situations and relationships in the operas which makes for an effect of rather obvious contrivance.) By the time of Moore's return to Ireland, Dujardin's enthusiasm for literary Wagnerism had waned and his intellectual energies were now devoted to Biblical exegesis. His research, published as *La Source du Fleuve Chrétien* in 1906, examined the inconsistencies in the

[17] George Moore: *Conversations in Ebury Street*. Ebury Edition, 1936. pp. 182–3.

Gospel accounts of the crucifixion in the light of information he had gleaned about Roman political executions and primitive near-Eastern cults and rituals involving a 'hanged god'. This work not only inspired Moore with the theme for *The Brook Kerith* but also provided him with much necessary background knowledge about Roman and Jewish history and the variety of religious sects prevalent in Palestine at the time of Christ.

Moore was staying with Dujardin in the summer of 1905 while he was correcting the proofs of *The Lake* as he recounts in the dedicatory letter and while Dujardin was completing the final draft of *La Source du Fleuve Chrétien*. Moore promptly as a late correction stole the title of Dujardin's work for the book that Walter Poole is engaged in writing when he acquires Nora Glynn's assistance as his secretary. It was an appropriate theft, since Poole himself is closely modelled on Dujardin as 'a man of large appetites and fine sensibilities'.[18] This fact is less obvious from the revised edition of 1921 where many of Nora's letters describing her employer and recording his conversation have been cut leaving Poole deliberately a shadowy figure important only for the nature of his work, his scepticism and his generous interest in Gogarty. In the first edition of 1905 (the character was initially called Ralph Ellis) he emerges as something of a dilettante, erudite but suavely so, relaxed (intellectually and emotionally), quick to supply the epigram or the *bon mot* that captures the quality of a particular aesthetic experience, of unwearying enthusiasm for debate, creative in his curiosity about metaphysics and theology and totally dedicated to his writing though with a hint here of facility. The external details (Ellis/Poole as the English gentleman, owner of Beechwood Hall) are wholly imaginary but the personality and temperament as projections of what Moore considered the ideal Protestant frame of mind are a portrait of his friend. Moore never scrupled about making literary capital out of his acquaintances — his cousin Edward Martyn was the occasion for a range of such studies (as John Norton in *A Mere Accident*, for example, and as Willy Brooke in *Spring Days*) before being protrayed in his own person in *Hail and Farewell*; Lord Howard de Walden, Lady Cunard, Yeats, George Russell (AE) and Moore's brother Augustus had similarly served his turn,

[18] Ibid. p. 180

though admired friends, as with Dujardin here, usually furnished forth only minor characters but ones of some positive weight against which the protagonists are measured and found wanting.

Dujardin has, however, left his mark on the composition of *The Lake* in more ways than these. In 1886–7 Dujardin published *Les Lauriers Sont Coupés* in which he tried to realise his ambitions for a Wagnerian novel. The narrative content is slight — Daniel Prince wanders around Paris in the late afternoon and evening trying to accept the fact that his lover, an actress, has grown tired of him. His moods fluctuate through hope to misery and self-pity which Dujardin seeks to convey to the reader through recording Prince's sensory perceptions, all the numerous stimuli that are registered by his mind. For this he devised a style of terse, isolated phrases in imitation he admitted subsequently of Wagner's musical technique of *leitmotiven*. Wagner had transformed the traditional aria of opera into an experience of profound self-communing for his characters; the aria (to use Dujardin's preferred term) was now an 'interior monologue' in which the orchestral accompaniment evoked the subconscious levels of the mind, the subliminal associations, intuitions and apprehensions that control emotion and so can influence the pattern and direction of thought, represented by the character's vocal line. Dujardin's analysis of Wagner's technique is sound except for one detail and that a crucial one: he reiterates continually the idea that the *leitmotif* is 'une phrase isolée'.[19] In theory this is true; the great scenes do develop from a series of thematic phrases, but the point is they *develop* and develop symphonically. Dujardin's account suggests more what one experiences with a composition by Berg or Webern than one by Wagner. Moore comes closer the mark in viewing the operas as seamless garments of uninterrupted melody, whose brilliant improvisation organically develops, fuses, transforms, extends and counterpoints those given themes so that one is conscious not of a contrived reiteration of disjointed phrases but of a dynamic growth of melody that actualises the characters' growth in self-awareness. Dujardin believed that what he was rendering through the interior monologue that formed his novel was the activity we know as perception: 'le monologue intérieur est une succession de phrases courtes dont chacune

---

[19] See Edouard Dujardin: *Le Monologue Intérieur*. Paris, 1931. (Especially p. 55)

exprime également un mouvement d'âme'.[20] What in fact he was rendering was an anterior movement of the mind, its unconscious receptive activity prior to that selection of sense-data for conscious awareness that constitutes perception:

> Illuminé, rouge, doré, le café; les glaces étincelantes; un garçon au tablier blanc; les colonnes chargées de chapeaux et de pardessus. Y a-t-il ici quelqu'un de connaissance? Ces gens me regardent entrer; un monsieur maigre, aux favoris longs, quelle gravité! les tables sont pleines; où m'installerai-je? là-bas un vide; justement ma place habituelle; on peut avoir une place habituelle; Léa n'aurait pas de quoi se moquer.
> — Si monsieur . . .
> Le garçon. La table. Mon chapeau au porte-manteau. Retirons nos gants; it faut les jeter négligemment sur la table, à côté d l'assiette; plutôt dans la poche du pardessus; non, sur la table; ces petites choses sont de la tenue générale. Mon pardessus au porte-manteau; je m'assieds; ouf! j'étais las. Je mettrai dans la poche de mon pardessus mes gants. Illuminé, doré, rouge, avec les glaces, cet étincellement; quoi? le café où je suis. Ah! j'étais las. . . .
> Ainsi, je vais dîner; rien là de déplaisant. Voilà une assez jolie femme; ni brune ni blonde; ma foi, air choisi; elle doit être grande; c'est la femme de cet homme chauve qui me tourne le dos; sa maîtresse plutôt; elle n'a pas trop les façons d'une femme légitime; assez jolie, certes. Si elle pouvait regarder par ici; elle est presque en face de moi; comment faire? A quoi bon? Elle m'a vu. Elle est jolie; et ce monsieur paraît stupide; malheureusement je ne vois de lui que le dos; je voudrais bien connaître aussi sa figure; c'est un avoué, un notaire de province; suis-je bête! Et le consommé? La glace devant moi reflète le cadre doré; le cadre doré qui est donc derrière moi; ces enluminures sont vermillonnées, les feux de teintes écarlates; c'est le gaz tout jaune clair qui allume les murs; jaunes aussi du gaz, les nappes blanches, les glaces, les verreries.[21]

For all the patterning of language here, Dujardin does not engage imaginatively with his character Daniel Prince so as to perceive the kinds of selection his mind might encompass given his emotional upheaval. Dujardin's style is insistent but monotonous, devoid of the rhythmic variety that might suggest Prince's emotional state. Prince's mind-life is confined to the immediate

[20] Ibid. p. 55
[21] Edouard Dujardin: *Les Lauriers Son Coupés*. Edition définitive. Paris, 1924. pp. 28–9.

present; the prose lacks that density of implication, that subtext through which Moore generates narrative tension from the very opening of *The Lake*. Because Dujardin neither presents nor even intimates any of the interplay between the conscious and unconscious levels of the mind but rather presents what is normally unconscious activity in individuals as if it were his character's entire range of awareness, Daniel Prince emerges for the reader as curiously mindless and utterly devoid of stature. He is anyone and no-one.

Interior monologue more aptly defines the method of *The Lake* than *Les Lauriers Sont Coupés* for Moore can be more accurately described as exploring the nature of perception. His more sensitive appraisal than Dujardin's of Wagner's technique in its total impact in performance rather than as a theoretical scheme for composition made for a more accurate verisimilitude. Early in his career Moore had perceived how the novelist's art might be made to correspond with Wagner's:

> Wagner made the discovery . . . that an opera had much better be melody from end to end. The realistic school following on Wagner's footsteps discovered that a novel had much better be all narrative — an uninterrupted flow of narrative. Description is narrative, analysis of character is narrative, dialogue is narrative; the form is ceaselessly changing but the melody of narration is never interrupted.[22]

It was to take nearly fifteen years before Moore really followed through the implications of that inspired comment with *The Lake*. Consciousness is fluid; its movement is continuous and not by staccato jerks as Dujardin's highly unmusical prose suggests, except perhaps in moments of nervous hysteria. By envisaging perception as narrative, the narrative the mind continually tells itself shaping past and present into new relationships and seeking ever the perfect ending, Moore found an acceptable correlative for the nature and movement of consciousness. Something of the lively spontaneity of Wagner's melodic line enters the writing of *The Lake* with Moore's decision at this time in his career to compose his novels by dictation. Letters to Lady Cunard, Lord Howard de Walden and Dujardin throughout the early months of 1905 reveal that Moore drafted and redrafted the novel

---

[22] George Moore: *Confessions of a Young Man*. 1888. pp. 270–1.

repeatedly to get the right tone and density of implication. (*The Lake* was to undergo two major revisions even after its first edition.) Although he worked at it more painstakingly than at any of his previous works, there is no sense of strain in the writing. Oral composition brought both clarity of expression and an idiomatic ring to the voice of consciousness. Like Wagner's, Moore's artistry is one of disciplined improvisation. Moore lacked Dujardin's trained musical ear; his response was wholly intuitive but he grasped more fully the spirit of Wagner's art whereas Dujardin got no further than the theory and mechanics of it. Moore praised *Les Lauriers Sont Coupés* when it appeared for revealing 'the inner life of the soul . . . for the first time',[23] but that was very much to read the aim for the achievement. Characteristically Dujardin wrote no other novels; he felt no compulsion to pursue his innovations in fiction further. It was Moore who built on from Dujardin's experiment and with *The Lake* realised his friend's ambition for a Wagnerian novel.

V

Dujardin is not the only French writer whose presence can be detected within Moore's novel; Emile Zola looms there too, though in a less overt manner. Zola had known Moore since the late 1870s when they had been introduced to each other by the painter, Manet, but acquaintance had never developed into friendship, though Moore had fervently championed Zola's novels when he settled in London in 1881, had contributed introductions to two of the Rougon-Macquart cycle when they were published in translation by Vizetelly, *The Rush for the Spoil (La Curée)* and *Piping Hot! (Pot-Bouille)* in 1885–6, and had turned to Zola as his model when he himself decided on a career as a novelist. The disciple had been rewarded with an invitation to Zola's home at Medan and Moore had subsequently styled himself as 'un ricochet de Zola en Angleterre'. It was not, however, in Moore's temperament to rest easy with being any one's disciple for long. Imitating Zola's technique made Moore critical of it for

---

[23] Cited in J.M. Hone: *The Life of George Moore*. p. 134.

what he considered its inflexibility; undeniably a novel of Zola's had power of an almost obsessional intensity, but the relentlessness with which all his characters pursued a determined path to moral and physical collapse seemed to Moore to indicate that behind the fiction lay an uncompromising and 'singularly narrow vision'.[24] The essential discrepancy between them was one of psychology: Moore could not accept Zola's view of the human condition as fallen and doomed to be the victim of its appetites. With Moore's third novel, *A Drama in Muslin* of 1886, Zola's influence is to be felt only in certain effects of style for Moore's theme has become his heroine, Alice Barton's discovery of personal values that allow her to resist social and familial pressures to conform to a way of life she considers degrading. Two years later Moore's autobiography, *Confessions of a Young Man,* offered a portrait of Zola that was acid rather than adulatory in tone. The disciple was again summoned to Medan: this time to explain himself. The two men were courteous but distant and suspicious; Moore was unrepentant. Even so six years elapsed before Moore broke his ties with Zola with an article describing this last visit to the Frenchman's home that was published in *The English Illustrated Magazine*.

'My Impressions of Zola' depicts the man, his home and his art as monumentally vulgar and soulless. The timing of the article (February, 1894) is significant. Zola had visited London the previous September for the annual meeting of the Institute of Journalists; though he had declined Moore's offer of hospitality at his rooms in the Temple preferring to stay at the Savoy Hotel, he permitted Moore to accompany him and Madame Zola to Greenwich and they met again more formally at a dinner at the Authors Club. Zola had been chary of coming to England, advisedly so since his English publisher, Vizetelly, had been prosecuted in 1888 and subsequently imprisoned on the grounds that the novels were obscene. But the visit proved a triumphant turning-point in Zola's fortunes with the English reading-public. Moore's reaction to this conquest appears to have been one of undisguised chagrin — it was Henry James's response too — and the tone of the article certainly bears this out. Possible explanations of Moore's attitude are many. He prided himself on being in the vanguard of critical opinion and here was Zola whom he had

[24] George Moore: *Confessions of a Young Man*. Ebury Edition, 1937. p. 60.

championed a decade earlier for his provocative and rebellious spirit now showing evident relish at being welcomed by the English establishment. Redirected by his growing friendship with Dujardin, Moore's enthusiasm was all for literary Wagnerism. The cruel, patronising tone of the article in *The English Illustrated Magazine* is directed as much against the tardy modishness of the reading public as against the materialism and status-seeking of Zola. But there is a more serious side to these fluctuations in literary fashions. Moore's allegiance to Zola in the 1880s had occasioned a hostile press for his earliest novels; by January 1894 he had completed in *Esther Waters* what could be seen as a direct challenge to the French naturalist novel, examining one of its own particular subjects, the life of a working class girl, but conducted from very different (one might add, decidedly English) psychological and philosophical bases. One has only to compare *Esther Waters* with Zola's *L'Assommoir* or *Germinie Lacerteux* by the de Goncourts to perceive that the difference lies in the handling of the subject of instinct: Esther trusts her instincts as essentially controlling her moral being; when Germinie or Zola's Gervaise Coupeau trust to instinct, they rapidly succumb to a will-less depravity. The article attacking Zola (appearing precisely one month before the issue of the novel) can be seen as another public avowal of a change of faith on Moore's part to prevent the continued coupling of his name with Zola's, and the possibility that, given Zola's recent popular acclaim in England, *Esther Waters* would be praised by critics for its superficial Zolaesque qualities and its originality go unrecognised. Moore's move proved a sound one: few of the reviews even mentioned Zola and those that did drew what to Moore must have been gratifying distinctions.

It might be supposed that Moore's relations with Zola both as an acquaintance and as an artist were now quite over (certainly when Zola came in exile to England in 1898 to escape imprisonment for his defence of Dreyfus in *J'accuse*, Moore was not one of the circle of friends trusted by the Vizetellys with the secret of his whereabouts and invited to entertain him). But this was not in fact the case. Having been a positive presence in Moore's work, Zola now became a negative one, a force against which Moore could define his own special vision and sympathies. To appreciate how this operates in *The Lake*, we must first turn to *Esther Waters*. Moore himself admitted that this novel was consciously modelled in certain of its features on a precise literary source: Hardy's *Tess of the D'Urbervilles*. Hardy's novel was in Moore's opinion contrived in its psychology; Moore was not prepared to accept the implausibilities and significant coincidences in the plotting that Hardy offers in order to achieve his design of making Tess's private fate symbolic of the contemporary social destruction of the agrarian communities of Wessex. Moore could not accept local failures in the spirit that D.H. Lawrence could, because, as Lawrence himself put it, the whole scheme of the work 'is true in its conception'.[25] Though *Esther Waters* developed out of an adverse reaction to *Tess of the D'Urbervilles*, it contains no direct reference to its source in Hardy; there are no overt touches of satire to keep the reader conscious of precise differences between the novels so as to enhance his perception of what Moore would consider his own more accurate psychological verisimilitude. Deftly Moore parallels Hardy's plotline and disposition of main characters with scrupulous exactness, but, choosing an urban as opposed to a rural setting, he allows Esther to take exactly the opposite decision to Tess in each of her dilemmas of choice, thereby avoiding melodramatic climaxes in his narrative while creating a heroine who is not a type of victim but a woman with a sturdily resilient individuality. Though Moore took his inspiration from an existing literary source, his novel in its composition rose wholly free of its origins.

Just this same relationship exists between *The Lake* and a novel of Zola's, *La Faute de l'Abbé Mouret*, which similarly takes for its theme a young priest's awakening to his sexuality. Through excessively mortifying himself to maintain his vow of celibacy, the Abbé Mouret suffers a fever of the brain. He is taken to convalesce at a nearby estate, Le Paradou, where a vast wall encircles a ruined mansion and an exotic, overgrown garden. When his delirium ends through the care of his nurse, Albine, he has lost his memory and with it all knowledge of his vocation and his faith. An utter innocent, he begins to explore the garden with Albine; its beauty excites their senses and its lush fecundity spurs them on to seek erotic fulfilment. Shortly afterwards catching sight of his parish through a breach in the wall, Mouret recovers his memory; guilt-stricken, he returns to his church and a life of zealous

[25] D.H. Lawrence: *Phoenix: The Posthumous Papers*. Reprinted, 1961. p. 484.

repressions. Albine attempts to revive his love, but she is spurned and dies, suffocating herself with the flowers of Le Paradou. There are close analogies between the novels in the disposition of the minor characters: the influential sister, the indulgent but critical housekeeper, the fellow priest who provides a foil for the principal character defining the progress of his emotional enlightenment, the elderly, worldly and compassionate adviser (Zola's Dr. Pascal is very much the counterpart of Moore's Father O'Grady). It must be stressed, however, that the analogy is one of function rather than of moral stature. Zola's theme is the opposition between the Church as life-denying and the procreative cycles of Nature and the characters take their moral complexion simply from their allegiance to one or the other way of life. Only the Abbé experiences change but both those points of change to and from his pagan innocence are instantaneous, the transitions are not examined in psychological detail or even rendered convincing. Zola simplifies profoundly so that the implication of his novel is that his central conflict is endless being irresolvable, an effect he consciously works to create by making the middle section of his novel, the scenes in Le Paradou, an obvious retelling of the legend of Adam and Eve from the Book of Genesis, with the isolated garden, the two innocents (Albine is wild and untutored, though her whole conception defies credibility somewhat), the discovery of their sexuality and with it an awareness of shame.

The concept of the Fall is central to Zola's novel, the learning of shame; it is this which highlights the essential difference in attitude and method between his work and Moore's. Gogarty's awakening, though initially sexual, encompasses in time a total transformation of his consciousness and identity and it is significant that the myth that Moore turns to (albeit fleetingly) is that of Primavera, the embodiment of Spring, an emblematic figure quite without specific sexual reference but with connotations of a spiritual and cultural renaissance. When Moore described this new novel to his brother, Colonel Maurice Moore, this was the theme that he stressed:

> It seemed to me that men are moved to reject dogma instinctively just as the swallows are drawn by the spring tide. [Nora Glynn] represents the spring tide and her breath awakens Gogarty. He gets up and goes in search of life. The story is no more than a sun myth. The earth is frozen in dogma and the spring comes and warms it to life.[26]

[26] Cited in J.M. Hone: *The Life of George Moore*. p. 262.

The conviction underlying Moore's novel is that the mind can free itself from the burden of shame without losing its capacity either for reverence or for moral discrimination. Zola's novel makes a passionate appeal for such a liberated condition but cannot render it as a psychological possibility because he constantly confuses instinct with sexual licence. Even while Mouret and Albine are enjoying the delights of Le Paradou before they confess their love for each other, the parallel with Genesis intimates a threat of doom; sensory and sensual pleasures never find pure expression in Zola's novel. There is an important distinction to be drawn in connection with this between the two writers' handling of landscape description:

C'était le jardin qui avait voulu la faute. Pendant des semaines, il s'était prêté au lent apprentissage de leur tendresse. Puis, au dernier jour, il venait de les conduire dans l'alcôve verte. Maintenant, il était le tentateur, dont toutes les voix enseignaient l'amour. Du parterre, arrivaient des odeurs de fleurs pâmées, un long chuchotement, qui contait les noces des roses, les voluptés des violettes; et jamais les sollicitations des héliotropes n'avaient eu une ardeur plus sensuelle. Du verger, c'étaient des bouffées de fruits mûrs que le vent apportait, une senteur grasse de fécondité, la vanille des abricots, le musc des oranges. Les prairies élevaient une voix plus profonde, faite des soupirs des millions d'herbes que le soleil baisait, large plainte d'une foule innombrable en rut, qu'attendrissaient les caresses fraîches des rivières, les nudités des eaux courantes, au bord desquelles les saules rêvaient tout haut de désir. La forêt soufflait la passion géante des chênes, les chants d'orgue des hautes futaies, une musique solennelle, menant le mariage des frênes, des bouleaux, des charmes, des platanes, au fond des sanctuaires de feuillage; tandis que les buissons, les jeunes taillis, étaient pleins d'une polissonnerie adorable, d'un vacarme d'amants se pursuivant, se jetant au bord des fossés, se volant le plaisir, au milieu d'un grand froissement de branches. Et, dans cet accouplement du parc entier, les étreintes les plus rudes s'entendaient au loin, sur les roches, là où la chaleur faisait éclater les pierres gonflées de passion, où les plantes épineuses aimaient d'une façon tragique, sans que les sources voisines pussent les soulager, tout allumées elles-mêmes par l'astre qui descendait dans leur lit.

— Que disent-ils? murmura Serge, éperdu. Que veulent-ils de nous, à nous supplier ainsi?

Albine, sans parler, le serra contre elle.[27]

[27] Emile Zola: *La Faute de l'Abbé Mouret*. Volume 2. Chapter XV.

For Zola, noticeably the moment of union for Albine and Mouret is a sin: 'C'était le jardin qui avait voulu *la faute*'; and that despite the anti-Catholic fervour with which he has conducted much of his narrative. The problem he sets himself in the novel lies in his presentation of the lovers as fundamentally of a child-like innocence; Mouret is mindless of his past and Albine is a child of nature. It is their intense and shared sensitivity towards the teeming plant life of Le Paradou that excites their desires; responding to the varying moods induced in them by different regions of the parkland, they unwittingly experience the delights and frustrations of courtship; their minds remain innocent of the significance of the play of their bodies together. What moves them is natural instinct and yet, as Zola explained in his outline sketch of the novel: 'It is nature which plays the part of Satan in the Bible'.[28] For all his fancifulness, Zola cannot in imagination escape his confused fallen condition: nature is the tempter, betraying and destroying. The garden is both the agent of the tragedy and Zola's means of articulating for the reader what for his purpose must remain unconscious, subliminal impulses of the character's psyches. The central section of the novel is a massive exercise in pathetic fallacy with Zola maintaining a rhetorically charged prose through which natural description is transformed into images suggestive of the stages of erotic fulfilment. Perception implying a degree of conscious awareness on the part of the lovers operates only after they consummate their love and so lose their innocence; repeatedly (indeed rather comically in view of the insistent, heated rhetoric of the prose) they ask what their experiences in the garden *mean*. As a result, the implication of the novel is that, for Zola, perception is limited to sexual awareness and an attendant guilt; it is perception that confirms one's fallen status.

Moore takes neither so simple nor so pessimistic a viewpoint as Zola. Gogarty's innocence at first is a morally culpable state because it exacts, as Nora Glynn and the reader perceive, so many suppressions; self-awareness brings him spiritual freedom. Zola's Le Paradou, for all that we are asked to accept it as representing Nature, is a fantasy world where, though months pass by, the plants observe no natural progression in the order of their flowering; buds, blossom and fruits come into being at the dictate of Zola's poetic purpose. There is about it all too obvious a feeling of

---

[28] Cited in Joanna Richardson: *Zola*. 1978. p. 53.

contrivance. Moore's novel by contrast has a specific Mayo setting, the place of his own family home, which, though the point is
not insisted upon, is recreated with considerable geographical
accuracy, while seasonal change is observed with a naturalist's eye
for authentic details. Lough Carra is a place with which Moore is
intimately familiar and he writes about it in a way that makes it
familiar to the reader's imagination too, so that subtle changes in
Gogarty's perceptions of his surroundings can be invested with
telling significance. Lough Carra with its islands, houses for the
gentry, ruined castles and abbey, its villages and the market town
of Tinnick exists precisely in time with its folklore, legends and
history, both national and private to Gogarty and his family.
Gogarty's consciousness responds to the place on many levels.
Perception as Moore handles it has great richness and density and
this allows him gradually to realise in the closing stages of his
novel a convincing joy in living. Le Paradou is a wholly literary
conception, a bower of bliss; and perception as Zola handles it is
exclusively a matter of carnal knowledge and bitter regret.

When Zola's tragic death was reported to Moore in the autumn
of 1902, he is said to have remarked on impulse: 'That man was
the beginning of me';[29] but Moore's development occasioned
radical departures from Zola's influence in his understanding of
the nature of instinct, in the subtlety of his presentation of consciousness and in the quality of his poetic prose — differences of
attitude and method which a comparison of *The Lake* with *La
Faute de l'Abbé Mouret* makes abundantly clear. Moore never rival-
led Zola in the treatment of mass social movements in fiction, but
his maturity brought him a greater delicacy than Zola's in depict-
ing the nature of the psyche and the mind's processes of moral
regeneration.

VI

Though the dedication of *The Lake* was addressed to Dujardin on
its publication, he had not been Moore's first choice for that
honour. As happened with many of Moore's works, he proposed
dedicating it to his close friend, Lady Cunard; and she, as on

---

[29] Cited in J.M. Hone: *The Life of George Moore*. p. 144.

many other occasions, refused because the ecstatic, adulatory
terms in which Moore couched it would have been compromising
for her. His draft for a dedication to *The Lake* has not survived but
that for *Avowals* has and testifies to his tactlessness: 'For Maud, the
incarnate Spring, whom I love as the goats love the Spring'.[30]
Only *Ulick and Soracha* and the Uniform edition of *A Storyteller's
Holiday* amongst Moore's works bear explicit dedications to Lady
Cunard, though 'Madame X' to whom *Héloïse and Abélard* is dedicated is she, and Moore's letter accompanying his gift of a copy of
the novel expressed the hope that he could 'trust to [her] indiscretion'.[31] Even when Moore took great pains with his phrasing—
'I have given my mind to the perplexing question of the dedication [to *Héloïse and Abélard* in this instance] which is a subtle
commentary on the affections. The thought expressed is subtle
and the expression is subtle and I have never heard of refined
and subtle thinking provoking vulgar remarks.'[32]— Lady Cunard
was adamant, which was perhaps her wisest course.

Moore and Maud Cunard were friends of long standing. They
had met at the Savoy Hotel in 1894, when she had informed him
she thought he had 'a soul of fire' and he admitted to a predilec-
tion for her 'cold sensuality'.[33] They discovered how many cultural interests they shared: Balzac, Impressionist paintings,
Wagner's operas. The intimacy of the relationship continued
despite Maud's marriage in 1895 to Sir Bache Cunard and the
birth the following year of Maud's daughter, Nancy. But in the
summer of 1900 they appear to have quarrelled, to judge by a
lengthy gap that occurs in their published correspondence, with
Moore refusing to accompany Maud to Paris visiting picture
galleries for 'at the end of the visit I foresee much bitterness. Any
further bitterness might make me hate you and I don't want to do
that'.[34] In the spring of 1901 Moore settled in Dublin and in a
burst of Nationalist fervour he ended many of his English friendships, though he was shortly to renew them when his attitude to
the Irish renaissance became critical. As Moore recounts in his

[30] Cited in Daphne Fielding: *Emerald and Nancy: Lady Cunard and Her
Daughter*. 1968. p. 71.
[31] George Moore: *Letters to Lady Cunard 1895–1933*. Edited by Rupert
Hart-Davis. 1957. p. 111.
[32] Ibid. p. 108.
[33] Cited in Daphne Fielding: op. cit. pp. 9–10.
[34] *Letters to Lady Cunard 1895–1933*. p. 30.

autobiography, *Hail and Farewell*, he was accompanied to Dublin by a friend he calls 'Stella', Clara Christian, a painter with Impressionist sympathies, who had studied at the Slade and presumably had been introduced to Moore by Wilson, Steer or Tonks who had been her teachers there.

From Moore and Oliver St. John Gogarty's accounts of her, Clara Christian seems to have possessed considerable intelligence, wit and independence of spirit, with a commanding presence and a certain gravity of manner. In temperament and appearance she was markedly different from Lady Cunard, being tall, taller even than Moore, but slightly stooping, whereas Lady Cunard was to many of her admirers known as 'the pocket Venus'. Clara was above all quietly self-possessed, while Maud was volatile, seeming to Moore even in her old age to be 'on the crest of a wave of an exuberant youthfulness'.[35] Miss Christian acquired Tymon Lodge, a moated grange at Tallacht near Dublin (it afforded Moore the setting for Ellen Cronin's home, Brookfield, in 'The Wild Goose', the last of the tales in *The Untilled Field*); and there Moore regularly visited her until she suddenly moved to Rapallo for several months before marrying Charles Mac-Carthy, the City Architect of Dublin in January, 1905. Her breaking her relationship with Moore coincided exactly with the months during which *The Lake* was being composed. When Clara withdrew to Italy in the summer of 1904, Moore resumed his relations with Lady Cunard, staying at her country house, Nevill Holt near Market Harborough in Leicestershire, and then writing ecstatically to her from Leeds where he attended the music festival, and then from Dublin where he returned to wrestle with the closing chapters of *The Lake*. The letters address Maud as 'dearest Primavera!' and continue:

> I do not know what primavera means, or if I have spelt it sufficiently for you to recognise the word. It means Spring, doesn't it? It means joy, the joy of green leaves with the flutter of wings among the leaves. And you, dearest, mean all these things to me, for you are not, I am convinced, a mere passing woman but an incarnation of an idea. . . . In you Nature has succeeded in expressing herself and completely. You take yourself and make a poem out of your body and out your spirit. You are at once the poet and the poem, and you create yourself . . . by your intense desire of beauty and of life.[36]

[35] *Emerald and Nancy.* p. 10.
[36] *Letters to Lady Cunard 1895–1933.* pp. 31–2.

This exalted mood continues throughout the letters until the following August when Moore completed his revision of *The Lake* on the proofs, always in marked contrast with the depression he frequently suffered over the same period (which the letters also record) in subjecting himself to the great discipline the method of his novel required. Fearing he will not be able to resolve *The Lake* to his satisfaction, he frequently chides his 'dull lagging brains' and turns in preference to expressing his gratitude to Maud for her 'extraordinary kindness and sympathy'.[37] Not only does the image of Maud as Primavera reflect the myth which underlies the novel but quite specific echoes of the language of *The Lake* recur in the letters. Trying to find words to define how Nora has transformed his being, Gogarty seizes appropriately on the image with which St. Teresa describes the effect of Grace, as a fountain nourishing the garden of the soul:

> Now it occurred to him, and suddenly, that she shed light upon his life, just as a fountain sheds refreshment upon the garden — she was like a fountain! A fountain was the only simile he could find that conveyed any idea of this extraordinary woman, controlled no doubt, as the fountain, by some law, but a law hidden from him. The water seemed to burst up as it liked. The water sang a tune which could not be caught and written down in notes, but which nevertheless existed. The water was full of iridescent colours, changing every moment.[38]

In a letter dated July 13th, 1905, Moore endeavours to express how Maud has come to be for him 'the eternal idea of joy' and again he employs the image of the fountain:

> You come into a room filling the air with unpremeditated music. The best comparison I can think of is the indefinite hum of a fountain and its various colour transformations — you are as unreal as a fountain and as spiritual. The water surges compelled by a force unknown and we are cooled, refreshed, soothed, and charmed; the water falls back full of fleeting iridescent colour.[39]

It would be wrong to describe *The Lake* as an autobiographical novel but Moore does weave an amount of autobiographical

[37] Ibid. p. 41.
[38] George Moore: *The Lake*, 1905 edition. p. 261. The image is retained in the revised edition of 1921 and developed as here; only the phrasing is improved. See page 135 in this edition.
[39] *Letters to Lady Cunard 1895–1933*. p. 43.

experience into its fabric — the Mayo setting, the portrait of Dujardin as Walter Poole, and, I would argue, something of his relationship with Lady Cunard and Clara Christian into the characterisation of his heroine. To see how this operates, however, we must examine more closely some facts about the composition of the novel.

Though, as has been stated, Moore worked with greater discipline on this novel than on any of his earlier works, *The Lake* was not in its first edition the total success he had hoped for, and, interestingly for our pupose, the principal criticisms were directed against the portrayal of his heroine, who was called in that first edition not Nora Glynn but Rose Leicester. (It is not too fanciful to suppose that Rose's unusual surname, if not a covert reference to Lady Cunard, was at least inspired by the address of her country house on the borders of the shires of Leicester and Rutland.) In 1921 Moore revised the novel (this is the text reprinted here) and completely reworked the character of the heroine, stressing the change by renaming her as Nora Glynn. The other alterations are local improvements of style; no substantial change is made to the overall conception of the novel or its thematic development. The problem with the 1905 version is not that Rose is inadequately realised as a character but that her personality is incongruously out of keeping with the symbolic role she is required to perform in effecting Gogarty's restoration. Faced with creating a spirited, free-thinking woman, Moore turned for his model to the Primavera of his own life who patently had eased the bitterness of his breach with Clara Christian. Rose Leicester is not the only literary portrait by Moore of Lady Cunard; even while finishing *The Lake*, Moore was engaged on a more precise portrait of her as Elizabeth in *Memoirs Of My Dead Life*; she reappears with that pseudonym in *Hail and Farewell* and on Moore's explicit admission as the Lady Malberge in *Héloïse and Abélard*.

If one turns to the account of her as Elizabeth in *Vale*, one can appreciate why she might appear a suitable model for the heroine of *The Lake* in some respects, but why in the event this proved a serious misjudgement. Moore is describing Maud at the time of their first meeting at the Savoy Hotel:

> . . . the full, flower-like eyes, the round brow, the golden hair, a dryad by Rubens in appearance and withal, a dryad's nature. If Rubens's

dryad were to come upon a traveller's fire in a forest, she would sit by it warming her shins as long as it lasted, and then depart for lack of thought to rouse the ashes into flame, and I have often thought that Elizabeth treats the arts as the dryad the traveller's fire; she warms her shins and departs, and overtaking satyrs and fauns in mossy dells abandons herself again to her instincts. I can pick up a thread, I have heard her say, but continuity I cannot abide . . .[40]

Exuberance in Elizabeth and indeed in Rose is simply outspokenness, a lack of reticence. Lady Cunard's charm for Moore, as he records in *Ave*, lay particularly in the confidence of her 'belief that everything she did was right because she did it';[41] that confidence, that brilliance, as communicated in the fiction, carry with them unfortunately a hint of moral vulgarity, which is troubling to the reader when it is evident to him that it is essential to Moore's thematic purpose that he respect Rose. As it is, she alienates rather than attracts one's sympathy. The fault is essentially one of tone; the personality Rose's letters project is egocentric and strident, and they occasion a degree of tedium wholly absent from the 1921 version. Osbert Sitwell, reminiscing about Lady Cunard in *Great Morning*, tries especially to evoke the strange quality of her conversation; there was notably her volatile wit consisting 'in a particular and individual use of syllogism, so that it was impossible beforehand ever to tell to what conclusion any given premise might bring you'.[42] 'Tiring quickly of dullness', she developed as a hostess her own method of combating it: 'she can goad the conversation, as if it were a bull, and she a matador, and compel it to show a fiery temper'.[43] It is just this quality of urgent, at times almost frenetic, brightness that Moore reproduces in Rose's letters, as she proses on about all the new Aesthetic experiences living in London, at Walter Poole's home and later on, the continent is opening to her: visits to picture galleries, to performances of Wagner, to the homes of eminent writers. Lady Cunard's lightning transitions of subject could hold her guests spellbound and amused, for her associations, analogies and conceits drew for their comic point on a lifetime's pursuit of culture and wide, serious reading. In a young woman just entering artistic circles,

[40] *Hail and Farewell*. Edition cited. p. 605.
[41] Ibid. p. 242.
[42] Osbert Sitwell: *Great Morning*. 1948. p. 251.
[43] Ibid. p. 252.

such a manner suggests butterfly-minded pretentiousness. The inappropriate tone and manner become even more irritating in their context: addressed to a provincial clergyman in the remote West of Ireland, the letters seem thoughtlessly egocentric, patronising, even cruel — qualities quite at odds with the generosity Rose is required by the narrative to show towards Gogarty. Moore was not alone in finding Lady Cunard's company restorative; Harold Acton describes her in terms very similar to Moore's: 'Her sweet presence was a passing benediction whose influence did not pass: she offered one the chalice of her own eternal youth'.[44] Much as he wished to, Moore never succeeded in rendering the essence of Lady Cunard's personality in a novel; the bewitching charm, as he evokes it, tends to seem practised, the vivaciousness self-conscious and so neither appears as open and frank as he infers they are. In the particular instance of *The Lake*, his reproducing of Maud's conversational manner as an epistolary style is a serious failure of judgement; talk and letters require utterly distinct kinds of intimacy.

In *Ave* Moore makes a significant transition at one point in introducing 'Stella', Clara Christian, whom he is about to praise for her intelligence and tact; he draws a contrast between her and the other women he had loved who were 'like myself, capricious and impulsive', especially 'one' (patently Lady Cunard) who 'had enchanted me by her joy in life'. He pursues the distinction further: 'High spirits are delightful, but incompatible with dignity, and, deep down in my heart, I had always wished to love a chin that deflected, calm, clear, intelligent eyes, and a quiet and grave demeanour'.[45] It is Clara Christian, not Lady Cunard, who fulfils that ideal; and there could be no better description than this of the fundamental difference in temperament between the characters of Nora Glynn and Rose Leicester, in whom also high spirits are incompatible with the dignity appropriate to her function in the novel.

Moore's account of his relations with Clara Christian in *Hail and Farewell* repeatedly calls forth comparisons between her and Lady Cunard. At the time of writing *The Lake*, the breach with Clara and her subsequent marriage still rankled in Moore's mind; but

---

[44] Harold Acton: *Memoirs of an Aesthete*. Reprinted 1970. p. 390.
[45] *Hail and Farewell*. p. 242.

in June 1906, she died in childbirth. This affected Moore deeply, causing him in retrospect pangs of conscience over the ease with which he had accepted their separation, given the sudden renewal of Lady Cunard's attentions.[46] When Moore began to compose his autobiography the few friends who knew of Clara's relationship with him advised him against writing about her; but Moore persisted, wanting a complete account of his life in Ireland. The treatment required great discretion but looking closely at what Moore writes about her, one can see why he was compelled to include detailed mention of her. When Moore came to Dublin in 1901 his inspiration had got in a rut; the novel he published shortly after his arrival, *Sister Teresa*, was not a conspicuous success. His style, currently modelled on Huysmans and D'Annunzio, seemed laboured and affected. County Dublin was new to Clara; being a landscape painter, she was a great walker, ever in quest of new subjects for her canvases. She took Moore with her and, as he describes in *Hail and Farewell*, their discussion about landscape, Irish people and customs helped him discover new themes for writing. It was Clara who, amicably chiding the excessively literary analogies that littered his conversation, helped him to purge his expression of its affectations; it was Clara too who encouraged him to pursue the project for the volume of short stories that became *The Untilled Field* and who, in drawing him into the conversations she held with the country people they encountered on their walks, enabled him to find the germs for many of the tales. Most importantly of all, it was Clara who, through her discussions of how she would reproduce certain effects of light on land-masses in paint, made Moore realise the degree to which an individual's mode of perception does reveal his quintessential identity. Through Clara Christian Moore had discovered new narrative subjects, a new style and a new mode of character-portrayal.[47] The three years of their relationship in Ireland had been for him as a writer a veritable renaissance. By 1904 when they separated, *The Untilled Field* was in print and a success, *The Lake* was in process of composition and *Hail and Farewell* was planned at least in outline. Writing the history of his sensibility through that decade enabled Moore to see how deeply

---

[46] Ibid. pp. 604–5 records a conversation between Moore and his brother about "Stella's" death.
[47] See particularly *Hail and Farewell*. pp. 347—9.

he was in Clara's debt. He could not omit discussion of their relationship from *Hail and Farewell*.[48]

When Moore came to revise *The Lake* for its reissue in 1921, he in no way tampered with its structure; patently it was right in its conception. Only the handling of Rose Leicester was at fault. What was wanted was a quieter, less demonstrative woman than Rose, gifted with shrewdness of perception and tact, self-assured but in no way brazen, whose moral stature would quickly earn the reader's respect and justify Gogarty's infatuation with her. Though Moore had formerly addressed Lady Cunard as his Primavera, *Hail and Farewell* had shown him how it was Clara Christian who had more truly deserved that title for the role that she had played in his creative life. It was to Clara that Moore turned for his model for Nora Glynn. The decidedly different appearance of Nora on her first entrance into the novel establishes the new model for the heroine. When Rose first approaches Oliver Gogarty, he 'had admired a thin, freckled face, with a pretty straight nose and gray sparkling eyes. . . . God had given her a larger share of good looks than any other woman in the parish. . . . Her hair wasn't red, though there was red in it; . . . it was blonde'.[49] In changing the personality of his heroine, there was no particular need for Moore to alter details of her appearance, but Moore made the change complete. Of Nora Glynn, Gogarty remarks:

> . . . he could discover no dangerous beauty in her, merely a crumpled little face that nobody would notice were it not for the eyes and forehead. The forehead was broad and well shapen and promised an intelligence that the eyes were quick to confirm; round, gray, intelligent eyes, smiling, welcoming eyes. Her accent caressed the ear, it was a very sweet one. . . . he remarked her shining brown hair. It frizzled like a furze-bush about her tiny face, and curled over her forehead. Her white even teeth showed prettily between her lips. She was not without points, but notwithstanding these it could not be said that she deserved the adjective pretty. . . . Her independence betrayed itself in her voice: she talked to the parish priest with due respect, but her

---

[48] For a more detailed account of Moore's relationship with Clara Christian, see my article: 'George Moore's "Stella" ', *Review of English Studies*. New Series, Vol. XXVIII. Number 110, May, 1977. pp. 181–8.
[49] *The Lake*. 1905 edition. pp. 30–1.

independent mind informed every sentence, even the smallest. . . .
What impressed him . . . far more than her looks was her happy,
original mind. . . . she was happy and wore her soul in her face.[50]

Not only is the revised account more detailed, its focus is on the
power of Nora's inner radiance of being to transform her fairly
ordinary looks. Noticeably it is Clara's eyes that Moore invariably
comments on first in describing her in *Hail and Farewell* in stressing that hers was a beauty of temperament not of perfect features.
It was this quality which made her for Moore 'a refuge whither I
could run . . . sure of finding comfort and wise counsel'.[51]

The quality of joy experienced by the two heroines differs
markedly: for Rose it springs from novelty at her initiation into
cultural pursuits and encompasses degrees of elation; with Nora,
joy is a more permanent and even-tempered condition, born of a
secure sense of controlling the direction of her own life. The
words Moore chiefly employs to describe Clara Christian as
'Stella' are 'joy', 'intelligence' and repeatedly 'gravity', yet 'grave'
carries with it no intimations of earnestness or moroseness, rather
it implies an ability in Clara to make her every moment's experience reflect her calm integrity. It is just such a gravity which
Moore evokes through Gogarty's descriptions of Nora in the
novel and through the tone of her letters, making her a more
subtle and a far worthier embodiment of Gogarty's ideal than
Rose Leicester. Moore worked intensively on the text of *The Lake*
and the 1905 text proved to be a good novel. It is remarkable that
Moore could recover in later life the intensity of inspiration
necessary to re-fashion the book so as to improve the clarity of the
thematic design without in any way affecting the original structure. This was effected principally by transforming the heroine
from Rose Leicester to Nora Glynn. That transformation turned
a good novel into a great one.

[50] *The Lake*, 1921 edition. pp. 27—9. This edition pp. 18—19.
[51] *Hail and Farewell*. p. 433.

VII

Regarding the composition of *The Lake*, two facts are of interest. Until this particular novel, Moore usually worked with a reasonably firm deadline in mind; *The Lake*, however, underwent constant rewriting before he was satisfied that he had realised his aim with it. Though as early as July 10, 1903 he described the novel in a letter to Dujardin as 'coming out beautifully', he was still working at it diligently the following January when he wrote to the Baroness Franziska Ripp:

> I have only to say that I live in the new story I am writing; I write all day, seven, eight, nine hours and am falling out of health. . . . This story besets me at every moment of the day and very often at night. I shall not recover my natural self until it is finished. I expect to finish it in about a month.[52]

That hope was sanguine: on September 13, 1904, he informed Dujardin, 'The Lake is nearly finished'; later on December 12, Moore's publisher, Fisher Unwin, received news of the novel's completion but quarrels with Fisher Unwin over the publishing of a play, *Journey's End and Lovers' Meeting*, which Moore had written in collaboration with Pearl Craigie but over which she claimed sole rights, caused Moore to refrain from handing over the manuscript. While the wrangling continued, Moore extended the novel by a further 10,000 words before, in exasperation with Unwin, he offered the manuscript to Heinemann during June 1905.[53] They set it almost immediately but then as Moore informed Dujardin on July 27: 'I am still deep in *The Lake*. I no sooner saw the proofs than I experienced an irresistible need to begin it all over again'.[54] The first edition was published on November 10, 1905.[55]

[52] National Library of Ireland Ms. 21,280. Letter dated January 18, 1904.
[53] See *George Moore In Transition: Letters to T. Fisher Unwin and Lena Milman, 1894—1910*. pp. 297—304.
[54] *Letters from George Moore to Edouard Dujardin 1886–1922*. Edited by 'John Eglinton'. New York, 1929. p. 57.
[55] For bibliographical details concerning editions of *The Lake* I am indebted to Edwin Gilcher's *A Bibliography of George Moore*. Illinois, 1970. pp. 67–70.

It was customary for Moore while composing a novel to seek the help of friends to research or confirm points of detail to achieve an accurate verisimilitude and *The Lake* was no exception. Fittingly, since the novel called on much of their shared childhood experience of exploring Lough Carra, Moore turned to his brother, Colonel Maurice Moore, for assistance with *The Lake* (the Colonel was at this time resident in Moore Hall). Moore's correspondence to his brother throughout 1904 is littered with questions about village life and parish responsibilities, the precise shape of the tower of Castle Burke, folktales about the graves at Ballintubber Abbey (the Kilronan Abbey of the novel) and historical facts about the de Stantons at Castle Carra — 'you know about all these matters and could add a bit which I would be able to put into key afterwards'.[56] A cousin, Martin Blake, proved to be a storehouse of local peasant lore and legend, all of which the Colonel dutifully reported back to Moore. On July 29 Moore wrote asking for suggestions for new names for places like Ballintubber Abbey as he did not wish to use the originals: 'I shall call Ballinrobe "Tinnick".'[57]

From the first Moore appears to have had trouble in hitting the right tone for Rose Leicester's letters. While writing *Evelyn Innes* (1898) and *Sister Teresa* (1901) Moore had enlisted the help of a friend, Virginia Crawford, in drafting the scenes about convent life. Mrs. Crawford was an ardent admirer of symbolist literature and considerably influenced the tone and manner of Moore's work in the late 1890s. On October 3, 1903, Moore wrote to her with an astonishing request:

> It will be an immense help if you will write Rose's letters. Do send me her first letter, the letter in answer to the priest's invitation that she shall return to Ireland. She would probably show the priest's letter to her friend. I can imagine her coming down to breakfast and telling him she had heard from the priest. He would ask to see the letter and he would guess that the priest was in love with Rose; and he would encourage her to draw the priest into a correspondence; of course he would not do so in so many words but the tenor of the conversation would lead Rose to writing at greater length than she would have written if she had not spoken about the letter.[58]

[56] National Library of Ireland Ms. 2646. Letter dated February 15, 1904.
[57] Ibid. Letter dated July 29, 1904.
[58] National Library of Ireland Ms. 2645.

Moore then gives details about his narrative (including the plan to take Rose and her employer abroad) to help her get the tone and circumstances right. No letter survives to show whether or not Mrs. Crawford complied. One can but speculate here but the presence in Rose's letters of so much conversational chatter about Wagner, Dutch painting and German philosphy of a kind similar to that which made for some tiresome longeurs in the two earlier novels inclines one to suppose that at the least Mrs. Crawford offered some suggestions about how to characterize Rose. Interestingly Moore's friendship with Mrs. Crawford was exactly contemporary with his relationship with Lady Cunard. Both women had similar intellectual and aesthetic sympathies — sympathies which Moore himself rapidly outgrew during his years in Ireland. It is impossible to gauge the precise influence each woman had on the characterization of Rose during the various stages of the novel's composition but the very fact of their influence may account for the sense one has in reading the 1905 version that Rose's sections in the novel are in an inappropriately different style from the rest of the book. Within the symbolic pattern of *The Lake* Rose represents the new life (and so could justifiably be different in the style of her presentation) but the manner Moore actually pursues with her, in that it reflects an older abandoned style in his writing, makes Rose's letters seem utterly jaded. The difference in tone from the rest of the novel is not positive and stimulating but incongruous and intrusive. (Rose's letter printed in Appendix A will substantiate this judgment.)

Though *The Lake* met with immediate critical acclaim for its original conception, Moore's command of a new style and his 'true and searching' portrayal of Father Gogarty, all the reviewers considered Rose a failure in taste and inspiration. *The Academy* referred to her as an unfortunate touch of the 'old George Moore' and opined: 'We can take no interest in the young woman and her chatter. She and it are cheap and vulgar. . . . The contrasting vulgarity only throws up the exquisite poetry of the soul of the priest and the mournful sweetness of his country'.[59] The *Edinburgh Review* considered that the difficulty with Rose was that she was not made credible as a schoolmistress in the West of

[59] *The Academy.* November 18, 1905. pp. 1200–1.

Ireland though her mannerisms were certainly appropriate to a literary group in London.[60] *The Bookman* was more outspoken:

> It is a piece of gratuitous unpleasantness to make the object of [Gogarty's] affection (it is hardly more) a young woman who has already had one child by a nameless lover, and is at the time of the correspondence which forms the bulk of the book the mistress of another man while nominally his daughter's governess.[61]

Rose is a bore, this critic concluded, because Moore's views on art, music and conventional morality with which her letters abound in defiance of realistic characterization are already perfectly well-known to his admirers and are 'not likely to interest anyone else'.

The offending material is confined chiefly to only two of Rose's letters: the long account of her new employer Ellis, his household, tastes, his opinions (1905 version, pp. 119–131); and her description of her travels on the Continent with Ellis that constitutes Chapter IX (pp. 165–193). When Moore revised the novel for the 1921 edition he retained most of Rose's other letters and interestingly he needed to make but small emendations of style and phrasing to fit them to his conception of Nora Glynn's temperament. Only the two long descriptive letters interrupted and confused the narrative. Indeed Moore himself appears to have had misgivings about the second letter since immediately on receipt of it he has Gogarty reply with a curt note trenchantly criticising Rose's lack of taste, arrogance and immaturity: 'Your knowledge is second-hand and only just acquired'.[62] Gogarty questions the point of it all and so does the reader and that question risks undermining Gogarty's stature in the novel. It is essential that he retains the reader's respect throughout his spiritual progress. That he should persist in his relationship with Rose while being so aware of her shortcomings does challenge that respect and it says much for the power of Moore's writing in the later stages of the novel that he does recover this precarious hold on the reader's sympathy and belief.

The enthusiastic critical reception of *The Lake* ensured that almost immediately a second impression was prepared. At a per-

---

[60] *The Edinburgh Review.* April, 1906. pp. 364–70.
[61] *The Bookman.* (London) February, 1906. pp. 223.
[62] *The Lake* (1905 edition). p. 195.

sonal cost of £22, Moore insisted Heinemann should set a revised text. Chapters VII to XI (pp. 101–213), which include the two problematic letters were removed and a new long single chapter of 90 pages inserted. Moore sent his friend Edmund Gosse a complimentary copy of this new edition; the letter enclosed with it reveals that the revision was largely undertaken at Gosse's suggestion. Presumably sensing that Gogarty's stature was at risk in the middle section of the novel, Gosse had sensibly recommended Moore to develop Father O'Grady's function extending the correspondence between the two priests thereby allowing the older man's charity towards Gogarty to elicit the reader's sympathy. Moore seemed pleased (at least initially) with the result:

> My long silence must have surprised you. It was intentional; I did not want to write to you till I could send you the revised edition of *The Lake*. You see you advised me to revise the middle chapters, suggesting that the correspondence might be carried on between the two priests. That was all and that was enough. I have read the book in its altered form and should much like to know what you think of it now. Few will ever see it; no book-buyer will trouble himself to buy it, my labour has therefore been one of pure love, none the worse for that perhaps — you and half a dozen friends are my public for this book. Heinemann is shocked that such disinterestedness should survive in the twentieth century.[63]

The revision however involved more than increasing the number of O'Grady's letters. The passages of Gogarty's private musing remained virtually unchanged from the first version but Rose's letters were considerably shortened or completely altered both in tone and content. Her first three letters from London were rewritten and are virtually identical with the ones Moore retained for Nora Glynn in the 1921 edition (pp. 63; 71–2; 90 here). Moore could not quite bring himself to abandon the two travelogues though the aesthetic opinionating of the first edition was wholly cut. (The material for these accounts was rooted in personal experience culled during Moore's visit to the Continent with his cousin Edward Martyn in 1899. His brilliantly witty use of that experience in the final chapters of *Ave*, the first volume of his autobiography *Hail and Farewell*, may account for his decision to excise these letters completely from the final version of *The*

---

[63] E.H.M. Cox: *The Library of Edmund Gosse*. 1924. pp. 186–7.

Lake: good copy had at last achieved a satisfying use.) One wholly original addition to the revised 1905 text was a sixteen page account of a dinner party given by Gogarty to Father Moran, two other local clerics and an officer of the Gaelic League. (See Appendix B.)

A week after Gosse received his complimentary copy, another letter from Moore arrived asking his opinion not of the way he had developed O'Grady's role but of the new material:

> Isn't the priests' dinner first rate, who else could have introduced three new characters and all three distinct in their moral refinement, good sense and triviality? Tourguenieff could, yes he could, and Balzac. . . . who else could have written the inner life of the priest, curling and going out like vapour, always changing and always the same. What the devil is the good of good writing if nobody can tell the difference.[64]

That letter was dated Wednesday 28 November. On December 4, Moore wrote again with the urgent request: 'Write me a long letter about *The Lake*. Did you read the priests' dinner?'[65] One can only suppose that Gosse's silence was motivated by embarrassment. Undeniably the dinner episode strengthens one's sense of Gogarty's moral and imaginative superiority over his guests but their blinkered, parochial vision is so aggressively caricatured and so obviously the product of Moore's current, private anti-clerical and anti-League sympathies that it jars on the reader because it is in such marked contrast with the balanced treatment Moore extends towards Moran and Gogarty's naively bigotted parishioners elsewhere in the novel. The dinner party excites only Gogarty's exasperation which is quite out of keeping with the overriding portrayal of his temperament as generous. With the revision of 1921 Moore cut this episode completely and returning to Gosse's original suggestion about extending O'Grady's function devised the episode in which the older priest visits Gogarty's home, teases out of him unsuspectingly an admission of his true feelings for Nora and gives him Absolution (pp. 74—84). The failure of the sacrament to bring Gogarty peace causes him to explore his feelings more deeply and discover about himself what

[64] National Library of Ireland. Ms. 2134.
[65] Ibid.

he has unwittingly revealed to O'Grady so that O'Grady's visit gives a greater dramatic impetus to the middle chapters of the novel than there had been in the 1905 versions. Developing O'Grady's role allowed Moore to render more fully Gogarty's initial state of culpable innocence without making him seem in any way a fool.

Two editions of *The Lake* that appeared in 1906 need little comment: an American edition published by D. Appleton and Company that came out on February 17 exactly reproduced the text of Heinemann's first edition; and the Tauchnitz edition was substantially this text too, except for a number of minor stylistic changes. Heinemann's decision to reissue the second revised text of 1905 as a cheap edition in 1919 may have been responsible for reviving Moore's interest in the novel which led to his total revision of the text for a third English edition of 1921.

Apart from the major alterations already noted — the omission of the priests' dinner party; the modifying of all Rose's letters to conform to Moore's new conception of his heroine whom he renamed Nora Glynn and the complete focusing of the reader's attention on Gogarty's consciousness which results from this — Moore virtually rewrote the text throughout while not substantially changing the content. Redundancies were cut; a technique of implication was given greater play than formerly; the material of whole paragraphs was incorporated into a few lengthy sentences in which the original ideas were now connected by more subtle devices of syntax to achieve the flowing style that so meticulously evokes the ever-changing quality of Gogarty's consciousness. Between 1905 and 1921 Moore had produced his comic, fictionalised autobiography, *Hail and Farewell* (1911–1914), in which he defines and assesses his life as a writer by a rigorous investigation of the workings of his own mind. Moore's subject is ostensibly a history of the first years of the Irish Renaissance, but his approach is not detached or chronological but personal and impressionistic: at a deeper level the book is a portrait of himself as artist, his discovering and achieving a vocation. Virginia Woolf remarked of *Hail and Farewell* that Moore's originality lay in his devising 'a means of liquidating the capricious and volatile essence of himself and decanting it in these memoirs'.[66] Experiences, memories, patterns of association,

[66] Virginia Woolf: 'George Moore'. *Collected Essays*. 1966. Vol. 1. p. 341.

changing aesthetic and social judgments, intimate reveries and self-appraisals are effortlessly interwoven by a flexible prose style to recreate on the page the flow of Moore's consciousness. With *The Brook Kerith* (1916) he applied the same techniques of style to the portrayal of the mind-life of imagined characters in a novel. It is this *liquid* style, to use Virginia Woolf's metaphor, that Moore brought to the final revision of *The Lake*. Little is changed in terms of substance but the style, by contrast with the versions of 1905, now more accurately renders the play of consciousness as a continual movement. Having found through composing *Hail and Farewell* a versatile style that could encompass the range of states that make up consciousness, Moore did right to return to *The Lake* and apply to it his maturer craftsmanship. What *The Academy* wrote of the first edition of 1905 might with far more justification be remarked of the final version, that 'Moore has never shown himself a more finished artist in words than in this book'.[67]

[67] *The Academy*. November 18, 1905. pp. 1200—1.

APPENDIX A

Chapter IX of the first edition of 1905 comprises Rose Leicester's long account of her travels on the continent with Ralph Ellis. The chapter aroused considerable critical condemnation when the novel appeared and was either shortened or omitted from later editions. It admirably illustrates all the features of Miss Leicester which critics have found objectionable.

IX

From Miss Rose Leicester to Father Oliver Gogarty.

'HÔTEL BELVIDERE, MUNICH,
'*September 2, 19—.*

'I am glad my letters interest you; if I didn't think they did I shouldn't be able to write any more. And that would be a pity, especially now I am travelling. This journey means a great deal to me: it is a thing that may never happen again in my life, and if I don't write down my impressions they will pass away like the clouds. However intense our feelings may be at the time, a few hours obliterate a good deal, and at the end of a fortnight nearly everything but the facts are forgotten. I discovered this yesterday as I sat thinking, trying to remember something that had been said on a balcony over-looking the Rhine. That I could not recollect what Mr. Ellis had said frightened me, not because what he had said was of any importance or of any particular interest, but because my forgetfulness assured me that I had only to wait a little

241

while for everything to become dim. "Those days in Holland," I said, "at present as distinct in my mind as anyone of the pictures I admired, will fade away." I asked myself if I had forgotten our journey from London from the time we left Charing Cross till we got to Norwich, and to my great disappointment I found that very little remained. Of our journey to the coast I only remembered that I had sat at the window thinking the sunset very beautiful, saying to myself, "I shall never forget what I am thinking and feeling now." Everything grew more and more wonderful as we passed into the country, and I became entirely aware of myself. Edith was reading a novel, Mr. Ellis was turning over the pages of the evening paper, and I didn't wish my admiration of the sunset to be interrupted by any word.

'The world has seen many sunsets, but every one is wonderful to him or her whose life is at crisis. And wasn't my life at crisis? Such peaceful shadows, such hallowed lights! My mood was exalted, as well it might be, for was not my dream coming true? Was I not going abroad with Mr. Ellis and his daughter on a journey of art and literature, going to travel through many countries — Holland, Belgium, and Germany — to stop at various cities, to meet distinguished men? My head was filled with thoughts about life and the wonder of life; I should have written down my thoughts— they were worth writing down— but I neglected to do so, and they are gone for ever. I might easily have done so when we got on board the boat.

'I told you in a former letter that Mr. Ellis's descriptions of the desert were written in his tent every night before going to sleep. So I might have known that I should forget; but the experience of others teaches us nothing. I lacked courage to separate myself from my companions; a great deal of courage would have been required to have gone down into a stuffy cabin to take notes. For the evening was beautiful and calm, and I wanted to admire the eastern coast, its low sand dunes running into headlands, and the sea spreading to the horizon pale and gray, and so still that I had to compare it to the floor of a ballroom; the stars were like candles, and the moon like a great lamp. Presently a little mist gathered on the water, and no sound was heard except the churning of the paddle-wheels. I feared sea-sickness, for Edith had told me how ill she once was crossing from Calais to Dover; but there was no danger of sea-sickness, and we stood looking over the bulwarks seeing the white track of the vessel disappearing behind us. We heard the captain cry "Starboard!" to the helmsman, and the ship veered a little.

'Edith and I laid down on a bench, and Mr. Ellis came up from the cabin with rugs and tucked them about us. He was very kind. We slept a little, but my sleep was lighter than Edith's, and in a couple of hours I got up without waking her. The vessel excited my curiosity, and I wandered about vaguely interested in the sailors, trying to think, unable to do so, for my mind was tired, and refused to receive any further impressions. That was the time I should have gone down to the cabin to write; but Mr. Ellis came by, and we stood leaning over the bulwarks. There are times when he will not talk at all, and one wonders what he is thinking about. I tried to speak to him about his book, but he didn't seem in the humour to talk about it. So I went back and lay down beside Edith. She was sleeping deeply: but I couldn't sleep at all, and after awhile I got up. This time it seemed as if we were close to the land; and so numerous were the lights on our starboard bow that I thought we were passing by some town. Mr. Ellis said he thought they were the lights of a fleet of fishing-boats. He asked one of the sailors, but he couldn't make him understand, for the sailor was a Hollander. I begged Mr. Ellis, who speaks a little Dutch, to try to make him understand. I wanted to hear the strange language; for it would make me feel I was going to countries where English wasn't spoken, and where everybody thought differently from what they do in England and in Ireland.

'The conversation between Mr. Ellis and the Hollander didn't seem to progress towards information regarding the lights on the starboard bow, and during the whole of it we did not seem to get away from them. I suppose Mr. Ellis must have misunderstood the sailor, or the sailor must have misunderstood him; we must have been steaming all the while along the shore. And this might well have been the case, for Holland is only a few feet above the level of the sea. Later on we learnt — this time from an English sailor — that we were off the coast, and were steaming at half-speed on account of the mist. The fog-horn sounded continuously; the ship's course was changed many times. It appears that the navigation of this coast is very difficult. The entrance to the harbour loomed up suddenly, and we admired the way in which the vessel was steered. I am sorry I didn't take a few notes, for the scene was very impressive. All I can remember of it now is that the vessel veered many times, and that the day broke slowly. Of course the vessel veered, and of course the day broke slowly, and the dawn is silent and melancholy as a shroud; everyone knows that. But there is much else — how the light changes, and the town emerges out of shadow. One should write down one's impressions at once, as Mr. Ellis did.

'The journey from Flushing to the Hague is only a little way; and what shall I tell you about the Hague? I only remember one thing clearly — a portrait by Rubens; I half remember a portrait by Vandyke. These two portraits have been hung together, side by side no doubt with a view to enabling the visitor to see the two painters in all their qualities. Vandyke was Rubens' pupil, and at first sight Vandyke's portrait seems the better; for it is more natural, more like a photograph, and I said: "I like the Vandyke best". Mr. Ellis said: "Do you know, I think I do, too;" but as we stood looking at the pictures I saw he was beginning to regret his words, and as the thought passed through my mind he said: "We have said a very stupid thing. The reason why we preferred the Vandyke is because the smaller mind always attracts us first. Look at them. How much nobler is the Rubens! Vandyke's mind was that of a lackey. Rubens' mind was more lordly than any lord's, unless that lord were Shakespeare."

'And no sooner had he spoken than I began to realize the nobility of Rubens' mind. The women Rubens chose to paint are what are known as fat women, and therefore to many Rubens is a vulgar painter. But a loftier vision was never bestowed on man. Rubens' women are beautiful, but they are not what the man in the street regards as a pretty woman. They are his own women, and they are women — not creatures without beards or moustaches. And he praises us all the while in his own benign fashion. Painters are never more sympathetic than when they are praising women, for man's thoughts about woman are perhaps his most intimate thoughts and spring from the very depths of his nature.

'We stood looking at this picture for a long time, and we returned to it many times, and every moment I seemed to see more and more clearly that this was the type of woman that corresponded to Rubens' inward vision. Great men bring a vision into the world with them; they are not distracted by passing things like inferior men, and large, fair women, fair as roses, with pale gold hair and blue eyes and white curved hands — Rubens liked curved hands and almond nails, rose-coloured — were the symbols through which his mind found continual expression. I feel sure that if his model had been a thin, dark woman, as she must sometimes have been, he would have gradually transformed her till she corresponded in some measure with his idea: it could not be otherwise, for Rubens wasn't a photographer.

'Looking at the picture, seeing nothing but a large, fair woman, fair as a tea-rose, the superficial will say, "A gross sensualist"; but the great man always presents his work in a form which deceives the public, and underlying the voluptuous exterior there is a sadness in Rubens which only the attentive mind perceives. I tried to get Mr. Ellis to talk about this picture in the train, and he told me the picture was a portrait of Helen Froment, Rubens' second wife, a girl whom he had married late in life many years after the death of Isabelle Brandes. Mr. Ellis thinks he was drawn to her by the likeness she presents to his first wife. That was all he would say. He lapsed into silence; I couldn't get another word from him, and we were close to Amsterdam when he took out his pocket-book. After writing these verses, he handed them to me:

' "Pleine de grâce et de pâleur
Elle vit ainsi qu'une fleur,
Évoquant une fraiche odeur
Par la transparente couleur.

' "Néanmoins pour toute âme humaine,
Sa vie inconsciente et saine
Est bien l'apparence certaine
De la vie éphémère et vaine."

'You will wonder why Mr. Ellis should write French poetry instead of English. I asked him, and he told me that to write mediocre English poetry is unpardonable, whereas he who loves verse and is not a great poet may write in French, just as a nobleman may indulge in private theatricals, but should refrain from the public stage.

' "French poetry is a pretty way of passing the time in the train," he said.

' "A pretty way for you," I answered, "but not a pretty way for your companion; for I am really tired of studying drainage."

'At first he did not understand, and I added, "Look out." We were passing through flat fields intersected with many drains, not the little drains that one sees in Ireland, but great deep drains representing extraordinary industry and perseverance.

' "These drains," I said, "must have taken weeks and months to dig, and must give the farmers a great deal of trouble to keep free from weed. I should go mad if I were to live here. I like hill and dale. Just fancy walking for miles and never seeing a valley or a hilltop!'

' "Holland is a swamp," he answered; and at that moment we passed a field flat as a billiard-table with six drains in it, and this field was followed by another with six more drains. But the Dutch painters, everyone but *two*, seem to have loved their country. Everyone seems to have rejoiced in his country's platitude, topographical and domestic; so far as I remember, all the pictures we saw are about eating and drinking, especially drinking: coarse tavern revels, servant-girls dancing, and the like. Only two painters seem to have escaped the influence of their surroundings: Rembrandt and Ruysdael. Rembrandt I shall admire some other time; this time I had very little thought for anyone but Ruysdael. We saw two pictures by him in Amsterdam. One of them I shall never forget: a wild hillside, unreclaimed and unreclaimable nature; only a woodman dwells there. Some poor fellow, half man, half beast, has built himself a shieling among the rocks. The roof shows against a gray sky deeper and soberer than any Irish sky — a real Protestant sky. Ruysdael must have been a Protestant. His pictures are even Calvinistic, or perhaps I should be nearer the truth if I said he was a great pessimist attached to no particular doctrine. He reminds Mr. Ellis more of Spinoza than of Milton. I have not yet begun to read Spinoza, but I have read a little of "Paradise Lost", and it never interested me at all, whereas Ruysdael interested me. I seem to have known him in some previous existence, so clear is my conception of this moody man, whom I see wandering by himself in lonely places, in sparsely-populated districts, sometimes miles and miles away from human habitation, speaking to no one except, perhaps, a charcoal-burner, in whose hut he lies down at night. At daybreak I see him wandering away by himself, continually making drawings. But where did he find the scenes he painted? Not in Holland surely. There are no waterfalls nor mountains in Holland, nor, so far as I know, a forest; not a single rough wood did we see. He must have gone to Norway to paint.

'It appears that nothing is known about him except the dates of his birth and death. Berghem and Dujardin painted figures into his pictures, so he must have been the friend of these painters, and I can imagine his face lighting up when he saw them. I can imagine their talks; sometimes their talk was pleasant, and anecdotes were told or hinted at, but no one could have dared to speak very openly of light things in Ruysdael's presence. But what I can imagine most distinctly of all is his good-bye. When he bade them good-bye his original nature, forgotten for a time, returned to him, a sadness came into his voice. I am sure his good-bye was a sad one; I am sure it resembled an amen. "So be it, so much life is over and done with."

'I said just now that he probably went to Norway to paint. However this may be, he seems to have disliked the Dutch country as much as I do. But if I disliked the Dutch country as much as he, I love the Dutch towns as much as anyone of the painters, not excepting Van de Meer, who, I feel, must have loved them very much. I remember one street, just the street that Van de Meer's studio window should have looked out on. Edith and I used to sit there on a bench watching the pretty morning sunlight, and the little breezes lifting the foliage of the trees. It was a broad street, and, I need not say, it was level. You must remember that everything is level in Holland. The houses are low, and they have nice shutters and doorways; and what makes the street so attractive are the dog-carts. Carts drawn by dogs were always going by, and waggons drawn by oxen. Life seems more docile and quiet in Holland than elsewhere, and for this reason I like Holland, and I think I shall always remember this street. The great Professor —— lives in a little house at the end of it, with one servant, and when we went to see him I watched her peeling onions in the courtyard, and I thought of the pictures we had seen in the galleries. Professor —— is a nice old man, short and fat, and he wore a red dressing-gown. His furniture was the same as one sees in hotels — sofas and chairs covered with plush, and everywhere there were books and manuscripts. I think there were more reviews than newspapers. I don't think I ever saw so many reviews; every corner was filled with them. He and Mr. Ellis talked in French, so it was difficult for me to follow the conversation. I heard, however, the names of my good friends Jeremiah, and Hosea, and Amos. Esdras came in for a good deal of criticism, that I know, for Mr. Ellis dictated to me the Professor's views on the worthy Esdras, and these views, it appears, are most important.

'When we got out of the house he explained to me what these views were. But I have got so much else to tell you that we will omit Esdras from this letter. I might very well omit the mention of the two pictures that hung on the Professor's walls, but they interested me, so I will tell you that they were two portraits painted by Angelica Kauffmann. Now, I wonder how these two portraits of pretty women ever found their way into the Professor's house? Did the Professor ever care for pretty women, I wonder? And I suppose I shall go on wondering, for my curiosity on this point is not likely to be satisfied.

'From Amsterdam we went to Haarlem to see Hals' pictures, and we saw some six or seven, each 30 feet long by 20 feet high. Burgomasters in profile, burgomasters in full face, burgomasters in three-quarter face. There are about thirty in each picture, and that would make 180 heads, 360 hands — well, perhaps not quite so many, perhaps all the hands are not shown. I cannot tell you how many faultlessly-painted sword-hilts and scarfs these pictures contain; but faultless painting wearies one. Everything is so perfect that the pictures lack humanity. They seem a little mechanical. Mr. Ellis calls Hals the *maître d'armes* of painting, and I do not think the comparison is unappropriate. He is the undefeated *maître d'armes*, he whose wrist never slackens, over whose guard a thrust never comes. This is Mr. Ellis's picturesque way of expressing himself. I think a somewhat plainer comparison would help you to understand why I don't seem to like these pictures. I cannot admire thirty heads all a-row. Pictures of this kind reminded me too much of the inside of omnibuses. But his picture of the old women, a picture painted when he was eighty, is quite different. It is full of emotion and beauty. Hals seems to have grown tender and sentimental in his old age, or was it that he merely painted these old women to please himself, whereas he painted the burgomasters at so much a head? There is no suspicion of the omnibus in the picture of the old women. He saw them together in the alms-house; they made a group, a harmony, and he was moved by the spectacle of the poor old women, fading like flowers, having only a few years to live — old women in their last shelter, an alms-house. He was at that time as old as any of his sitters, and the picture of the old men which he began immediately after was never finished. I suppose that one morning he felt unable to paint; he grew fainter and died.

'When one has seen Hals there is nothing else to see in Haarlem. One walks about until the train comes to take one away. That I did not take a note of the weariness I experienced during one dusty afternoon is not a matter for regret. I recollect the afternoon sufficiently well — the walk along the dusty roads by little woods dusty as the roads, and the tea we had at a very uncomfortable hotel in a barren room. There seemed to be no one in the hotel except the proprietor, and he cheated us, charging two shillings for a cup of tea, which made Mr. Ellis very angry. The railways in Holland are small, or they seem small, and the miserable Dutch landscape irritated me. Hour after hour I sat looking at flat fields. Sometimes I counted the number of drains in each field. I don't know what the others did; they sat in the corner of the carriage. We had been together since early morning, and were a little tired of each other. I don't think any of us had anything to say. You can hardly believe that I had nothing to say. Well, believe it or not, as you like, but I didn't speak a word, and when I don't speak I always feel cross.

'We left Haarlem by the four o'clock train, and I felt grateful when night came and blotted the landscape out. The train seemed as if it were going to wriggle on for ever; it wriggled into and out of many a little station, and we were so hot in our first-class carriage that we got into a third. The change was a pleasant one. After a time some yokels got in, and they reminded us of the pictures we had seen. But one can't go on considering yokels for ever, and at last, unable to contain myself, I said:

' "Now, what are you thinking of, Mr. Ellis? Do you know you haven't spoken to me for two hours? Are you composing a new French poem?"

' "Well, no; not exactly. But the rhymes in the second stanza of the little poem I composed in the train coming from the Hague are all adjectival, and in French verse adjectives should rhyme as much as possible with verbs and substantives."

' "Do you think you have improved it?"

' "Yes, I think I have. I'll write out the new version."

'And with the gold pencil that always hangs on his chain he wrote:

'   "Dans sa gracieuse pâleur
Elle vit ainsi qu'une fleur,
Evoquant une fraiche odeur
Par la transparente couleur.

'   "Loin de l'Emotion charnelle
Rubens, oubliant son modèle,
Pressentit la vie éternelle
Que s'encarne un moment en elle.

'   "Sa pensée est dans cette main,
Dans sa pose et dans son dessin
Et dans ses yeux pleins du chemin
Que traverse le coeur humain.

'   "Néanmoins pour toute âme en peine
Que son calme altier rassérène,
Elle est l'image souveraine
De la vie éphémère et vaine."

'Next day we went to the cathedral, but we were so conscious of our obligation to admire and of the gravity of our visit that we experienced a sense of our unworthiness when we first saw the pictures of the Crucifixion. We wandered from one to the other a little disconsolate, shocked to find that they did not seem to us nearly as intense as we had expected. We were glad to get away from both, and we found the "Coronation of the Virgin", which, we were told, had been repainted, much more to our taste. But Mr. Ellis does not believe in the story of the repainting, and whilst we stood looking at the "Ascent of the Cross," he told us that the greatest art critic that ever lived preferred the "Ascent" to the "Descent". We wondered at his preference, and tried to find a reason for it. It could not be because the painting of the "Ascent" seemed to him better than the first. The painting is obviously the same; the pictures differ in conception rather than in execution. Whereas the "Descent" is restrained and correct in drawing even to the point of a suspicion of pedantry, the "Ascent" is tumultuous in composition, and so deliberately reckless that the scene fails to impress. The Middle Ages represented the scene on Calvary with great realism, but the realism of the Middle Ages was sincere and childlike, quite unlike the calculated realism of Rubens — one might almost say purposeful realism; and the thought came by, whispering in our ears that the explanation of the difference between the pictures is that Rubens had begun to weary of the echoes of Greece heard in Italy, and that the second picture is his first attempt to return to the primitive art of his own country, to the ages of faith, to the fifteenth century, which in the low country was the equivalent to the fourteenth century in Italy.

'I am quoting, of course, from Mr. Ellis, but I only quote so far as what he says interests me. I have not been to Italy, and know nothing of Italian art except the pictures I saw in Amsterdam, but I think I understand and feel quite clearly that Mr. Ellis is right when he says that Titian never designed a more beautiful young man than the one who slips in all the pallor and beauty of death down the white sheet into the hands of devoted women. The Renaissance made Christ beautiful. It transformed the medieval Victim into a beautiful youth who preached in Galilee, and captivated the imaginations of many holy men and women; but this Hellenization of Christ — for it is that and nothing else, the intention being to draw our attention to bodily perfection rather than to show us a suffering Redeemer — is, so says Mr. Ellis, a mistake not only from a religious point of view, but also from a dramatic. For, after all, sincerity counts for a great deal in our enjoyment, and who can say that Rubens is sincere when he is painting a crucifixion? All the while he is trying to escape from his subject; and I'm not nearly sure but he would have been a greater painter if he had never painted Helen Fromont as anything but the mother of his children, or a nymph amid a group of satyrs and fawns, the demi-animality of the vales of Thessaly. As Mr. Ellis said yesterday, supposing the gentle monk of Fiesole had been forced to depict a woodland revel, with Silenus carried by drunken with vine leaves in his hair, he would certainly have failed to convey any conceivable idea of the mythology of the woods. We shall never know whether Christ was a beautiful youth who preached about Galilee, or an emaciated ascetic. Very likely He was one and the other at different times of His life. Be this as it may, the pictures in which He is represented at Cologne carry more conviction than those of Antwerp — the bleeding, emaciated Victim is more in the spirit of Christianity. This we can say for certain, that the desire of the Cologne painters was not to escape from the subject, but to approach it and identify themselves with it.

'My dear Father Gogarty, you must forgive my simplicity of expression. You complained of it in a former letter, and I have been puzzling ever since to know what you meant. So long as I do not say anything against faith and morals, may I not express myself fully and clearly? Is it not true that the Middle Ages are always considered the ages of faith? and is it not true that the Middle Age representations of Christ are not so lovely as the Renaissance? Will you be shocked if I ask you how it is that the bleeding Victim has been better worshipped than the beautiful young man? And is it wrong for me to ask you why it is that faith goes out of the window when beauty comes in at the door?

'I am afraid you will consider this last remark unseemly, but you will forgive me nevertheless. And so that I may not offend your religious sense again, I will tell you no more about pictures. To be quite truthful, I am a little tired of pictures; we have seen too many, and I was glad to get away from Cologne and to stop at little towns on the Rhine, where there are no pictures — only parks and pleasure grounds, with walks winding through woods. In these woods one comes across temples and statues. The features of the nymphs and the fawns are weather-worn, hardly distinguishable, and I think I like satues better when the hand of man is not apparent upon the stone. We lost ourselves in one of these parks, and were very much afraid we should be captured as trespassers; but we got out without being perceived across a little wall, and an hour later we were seated on a balcony overlooking the river. A ferry-boat moved backwards and forwards in the dusk, across the slow current. There is something mysterious in a river; not in a babbling river, but in a slow-flowing river. And the Rhine reminds one of Time. How many thousand years has the Rhine flowed! Just as it flowed the day we were at Bopart it was flowing when Wotan was God, and there were nymphs in the Rhine watching the gold, the innocent gold, that Alberich stole from them and converted into money. One night we sat on a balcony drinking Rhine wine, talking of Siegfried and his joyous horn. It is worth one's while to live in Germany for the sake of the wine, and I'm sure the wine we drank that night was the same as the wine in the goblet out of which Siegfried drank forgetfulness of Brunnhilde. That dinner I shall never forget. We sat leaning over the dining-table watching the Rhine, hearing the Rhine; and when the waiter brought candles and put them upon our table we didn't get up, but we talked on about the various legends, and how they were woven together. Mr. Ellis was the talker, and his narrative was intermingled with anecdotes about the unhappy life of the great man who had woven these stories into drama, and would have written them in words if he had been Shakespeare; but, fortunately, he was not, for the world doesn't want two Shakespeares. Nature, as Mr. Ellis says, took pity upon men; and he made up this little parable on the spot: A good fairy was hiding among the flowers in a garden, probably in a lily cup; and when no one was about, she came into a room where a child was sleeping, and she said, "Thou shalt weave world-stories into dramas as beautiful as any man has ever heard." But there was a bad fairy up the chimney who heard the blessing, and, when the good fariy went away, she came down and said, "I cannot take away my sister's gifts. Thou shalt conceive great dramas, but thou shalt not have the power to write them."

'On that the bad fairy went up the chimney, thinking she had done a very clever thing. But the good fairy, who hadn't yet fallen asleep in the cup of a great lily growing by the window-sill, came into the room again, and looked sorrowfully at the cradle, for she knew not how to redeem the child from the curse that had been placed upon him. Suddenly an idea occurred to her. "I can't take off the curse that has been placed upon thee," she said. "Never shalt thou write thy dramas in words, but I will give thee music to write them with." . . . And that child was Richard Wagner.

'There was a piano in the room behind the balcony. We went to it. Mr. Ellis plays intelligently. As he puts it himself, he plays sufficiently well to give us a foretaste of the music we were on our way to hear. He played on, sketching for us the most salient things in "The Ring". There was something in that night I shall never meet again. On the morrow we hastened away. We were still far from Bayreuth. We stopped at —— to admire the cathedral, and then we started off again. This stage was the last on our journey, for we got a train at Nuremburg, and Bayreuth is but a couple of hours from Nuremburg, and about three hours from Munich. We heard "The Ring" at Bayreuth, and we shall hear it again at Munich. It will be as well done at Munich, but I feel sure it will not be the same thing. To hear Wagner you must hear him where he chose to be heard, and he knew that one could not hear the "Dusk of the Gods", for instance, amid the distractions of a city. One has to leave all things and to follow him to Bayreuth.

'The town is full of the florid architecture of the eighteenth century, pillared façades and balconies, and the old streets are paved with the original cobble-stones. Millions of feet will pass, bruised and aching, but the cobble-stones shall never pass away, and they hurt one's feet terribly. When the mid-day sun shines they burn through the leather sole. Nevertheless, I would not have these old streets torn up and paved in asphalt or wood. The cobble-stones are part of the entertainment. They remind one that one has to suffer for the Master's sake. And these streets lead from open space to open space, by red-brick palaces in which dukes once lived. Germany is full of palaces, nearly all of which are empty. One can obtain permission to walk through the rooms, but I don't think that one derives any special benefit from these walks. The pictures are bad and the furniture is clumsy. There is one thing, however, extraordinarily beautiful in Bayreuth, and, like everything else in Bayreuth, it seems an intrinsic part of an appreciation of Wagner. It is the Court theatre built for the pleasure of some landgrave, a German prince or duke. I do not know if landgraves existed in the eighteenth century. There is one in "Tannhauser". "Tannhauser" is tenth century; but if a land-grave existed in the eighteenth, I should have liked to have seen him coming to hear a performance in this beautiful theatre. Trumpeters would stand on either side on balconies to announce his arrival, and all his little court would be sitting about him in the boxes and the stalls. It would be so different from Wagner — every man would wear a sword, and the women would wear brocade and long pointed stays elaborately stitched.

'The opera I should like to see performed in this theatre would be Gluck's "Orfeo", for instance, or perhaps "Armide", for Wagner himself rearranged the overture, or did something to this opera. However, he didn't take the theatre and try to convert it to his purposes, as a lesser man would have done; he admired it, and a great man does not destroy the beautiful works of others in order to make way for his own works.

'Wagner built his theatre in the woods, someone added a restaurant — maybe it was himself who built it, for, though he wished the people to come from a distance to hear his operas, he wished them to hear in comfort, and one cannot listen in comfort without food. It is possible to spend the day by the theatre, walking in the woods, dining between the acts. An undulating country surrounds the hill-top, and when the sun strikes a distant town, the disputants forget their argument, and eyes rejoice in the effect of light. Seeing a peasant driving his plough, one ceases to discuss "The Valkyrie", and one wonders which is right — the man who drives his plough, or one's self, who has travelled to hear "The Ring", knowing it to be the greatest musical work the world has ever known. I said to Mr. Ellis a week ago as we toiled up a steep part in the woods — fir trees stood about us in solemn rows; we had reached the middle of the woods — I said: "But he wrote these things because he was a great genius, and knew nothing of our pains and woes — he stood aside, and would not know them. He wrote about love, but he never stooped to such triviality as woman's love. He knew all about it. It was all in his brain, but he never loved."

' "You are mistaken," Mr. Ellis answered. "He loved more deeply, and suffered more than any other man, and there will be just time to tell you the story before we get back to the theatre."

'And as we retraced our steps, walking hastily, for the third act of "The Valkyrie" was about to begin, Mr. Ellis told me of the woman who inspired "Tristan." I listened breathless, and when the story was finished I said:

' "Then nothing is wanting. For once Nature filled up the cup."

'Can I tell you of my expectation to hear this opera written out of the man's own flesh and blood? And when the second act was over I said to Mr. Ellis: "It is the man himself. He wrote like this not because he was less human than ourselves, but because he was more human, more capable of suffering." Mr. Ellis agreed with me in this, saying that, having experienced more intense emotions than anyone else, Wagner was able to distil a magical juice out of them, which sinks into the flesh, enters the very current of the blood, transforms, disintegrates, and produces a sort of syncope. And this is just it. One loses all power of will listening to this music, and the joy of it is an abdication of self. Yet it was written as an assertion of self; it is an extraordinary spasm of self-consciousness. I said just now that "The Ring", to be appreciated, must be heard in the condition that Wagner wished it to be heard

in at Bayreuth. But that is not so with "Tristan". One can hear it
very well in Munich — quite as well as at Bayreuth. It is a work
suited to the city, full of the emotions of the city.

'To go to Munich we had to go through Nuremburg, but the
journey through Bavaria does not bore one like the journey from
Cologne. The railway from Cologne passes through long fields,
or, I should say, stretches of country where there are no hedges,
and in these fields one sees peasants cutting corn hundreds of
yards apart. They seemed very lonely, and I thought how they
must suffer from the heat, for there is no hedge where they can lie
under. The only variation in the landscape are the pine forests.
Pines are very nice among other trees, they are a variety; but
imagine if you can the weariness of seeing mile after mile of
pine-stems, and overhead a cloudless sky. There is no underwood; nothing grows under pines, and the ground is brown,
covered with spikey things that the pine sheds. A circle of shadow
gathers round the roots of the pine at mid-day, and as the sun sets
the shadows trickle out. That is all. A rabbit is a pretty thing when
one sees one, but when one sees a thousand one gets to hate them.
So it is with pines. . . . Bavaria is quite different from the rest of
Germany. The landscape takes beautiful shapes, and the shapes
of the ground are different from anything one sees in England.
Trees climb up the hillsides in the quaintest way possible, and
there are plenty of villages at the foot of the hills. There are
villages all the way to Munich, and they seem as if they had been
built many hundred years ago. The only thing I don't like about
Bavaria is its capital town. Munich is white and ugly, and very hot.
There is a river, it is true, but not an interesting river. I prefer the
brook that flows through Bayreuth; that brook is brown and
pretty, and there are trees about it. But there are only white, ugly
buildings about the Munich river, and the colour of the water is
unpleasant. It is green, and I hate green water. I was told that
melted snow makes green water, and this may or may not be true.
Everything in Munich is unpleasant except the music. The
picture-gallery is most unpleasant. It is full of little side-galleries.
One is always popping in and out to see something, and in this
way one gets tired and loathes pictures. All picture-galleries are
too long, and I have come to the conclusion that, however beautiful the pictures may be, no gallery ought to exceed a couple of
miles.

'We came here not only to hear "Tristan", but to hear Mozart, and last night we all went to hear "The Marriage of Figaro". I knew nothing of Mozart except his religious music — that little Mass for four voices which I used to play in church and an *Agnus Dei*. Do you remember them? The first act of the "Marriage of Figaro" is the most beautiful and enchanting ever written. Dear little Cherubino! how pretty he was behind the armchair, and how exhilarating Figaro's song telling him he must go to the war and be a soldier!

'We met a young Frenchman, Emile Canton, at Bayreuth, and he has come on here with us. He, too, is an exegetist, and he is a musician. So far as my experience goes, I am beginning to think that the Bible and music are inseparable. He is quite a young man, not more than thirty — a plump, good-looking Frenchman, with clear eyes, a clear skin, and a nice moustache. He is a good talker, and he is going on to Switzerland with us. We shall see another professor there, for Mr. Ellis and M. Emile Canton are going to found a review together, and the object of our journey is to try to persuade the Swiss professor to write for the review. The conversation will be in French, and I am glad of this; I want practice, for I am determined to learn French. I want to understand Canton's ideas about Esdras and Jeremiah. It is extraordinary how real Jeremiah is to these people. He was hardly more than a name to me two months ago, and now I am beginning to feel quite interested in him. And it is well that I can take an interest in him, for if I didn't I am afraid I should hardly keep my wits. Perhaps Nature, who foresaw my destiny, endowed me with a capacity for taking an interest in almost anything. Mr Ellis said that he never knew a more appreciative person. It is well that I am appreciative, for if I were not it would be impossible for me to remain his secretary. . . .

'I had to put this letter aside — Mr. Ellis called me to do some work for him — and, coming back to it, I am astonished at the number of pages I have written, but it is too late to regret my garrulousness. Now I wish you would come out here and join us. This long letter, describing my pleasure in foreign travel, was written partly in the hopes of tempting you out of Garranard. You say that you have been longing for a holiday, and that you require one. Why not take a real holiday and come out here? You will find Mr. Ellis a very interesting man. You and he will not agree on all subjects, that is true, but I don't think that a certain difference of opinion makes any difference. You are both clever men, and clever men are always interested in each other, however different their views may be. Will you be advised by me, dear Father Gogarty? Come out here and take your holiday with us. One cannot take a holiday in one's own country: one must go abroad. I have told Mr. Ellis about you, and he is very interested, and will be delighted to see you. You have never been out of Ireland in your life, and you want to see Italy. Perhaps it would suit you as well to go straight to Rome. We shall be going there, and it will be interesting to meet in Rome.

        'Very sincerely yours,
          'ROSE LEICESTER.'

APPENDIX B

The chief addition to the revised text of the second edition of 1905 was this account of a dinner party given by Gogarty to three clerical friends and a Gaelic League official. It was omitted from the revised edition of 1921.

A moment after his thoughts went to the people who were dining with him that afternoon, Father Moran and Father Maloney. Father Maloney was bringing a friend, a priest who was staying with him, and a Gaelic League organizer was coming too.

'Have they come?' he asked, catching his breath, for he had run a good part of the way home.

'Yes, your reverence; they're all here — Father Maloney and a friend (Father Connellan, I think it is); Father Moran and a gentleman from the League, Mr. Scanlan——'

'I know. Here, take my hat.'

'Am I to bring in the dinner?'

'Yes, dish it up as quickly as you can. Do let me get past. I beg your pardon, Catherine, but you see I'm late.' Pushing the door open, he stood on the threshold looking at his guests grouped round the table, talking, turning over the books. 'Have I kept you long? I'm sorry.'

'No matter; our appetites are the better for it,' said Father Maloney; and he introduced Father Connellan, as a young man just come from Maynooth full of hope for the future of the Irish language, for the first time on the mission, appointed some months ago to a curacy near Tinnick.

Father Connellan laughed noisily at this description of himself, and Father Oliver noticed his figure, trim and athletic, and his head, round as a bullet, with fair brown hair curling about a large bony forehead; a complete contrast he was in every way to his friend Father Maloney, a tall rustic priest, dressed in old clothes, hanging shapeless and green about his gauntness; broad across, thin through the chest, long swinging arms and hard hands — a man Father Oliver instinctively liked better than the spruce curate.

Father Oliver's eyes went to his third guest, Mr. Scanlan, a spare man, tall as Father Maloney, with a long, lean face and flat bony cheeks, a country fellow, a peasant if ever there was one, in mind as well as in body, clean-shaven like the priests, and differing from the priests only in his dress. He and Father Maloney were from the same island, and Father Oliver thought they looked like the indigenous race as he turned to shake hands with Father Moran, a priest with whom the reader is already acquainted. But he only spoke a word or two with Father Moran, for the Irish (Maloney and Scanlan were speaking Irish) caught on his ear, and he had to listen, for he could understand what was said here and there, and he understood Scanlan to say that he had learned to read Irish in Mexico.

'In Mexico!'

'I was travelling in Mexico for a firm of dry-goods-men, and one day I came across a copy of the League's newspaper, *An Claideam Solus*, and it was out of that copy I learned to read Irish.'

'So you learned Irish in Mexico, of all places, Mr. Scanlan,' said Father Connellan.

'Only to read it, your reverence; of course, I always spoke it, but I might never have learned how to read it if that number of *An Claideam Solus* hadn't come to Mexico.'

'And you just felt you'd like to see the old shores again,' said Maloney.

'I did indeed, your reverence.'

'Knowing how to speak it perfectly——'

'Wasn't it his own language, Connellan?' said Maloney.

'You had no difficulty in learning to read it,' Father Connellan continued.

'Not much.'

'Let us go into dinner;' and Father Oliver threw open the door for his guests to pass through. 'Mr. Scanlan will entertain us while we are at dinner with an account of his travels in Mexico.'

The little pedantry of speech on which his tongue had slipped surprised Father Oliver, and he wondered why he had spoken like that while he helped the soup.

'So it was learning to read Irish that brought you back to us,' he said, 'and put a longing into you to hear the old tongue again, to see the shores which you could always see in memory, the quay along which the fishing-boats used to come up, and along which they still come up?'

'It was just as you are saying it, Father Oliver Gogarty.'

'And tell us,' said Father Moran, 'did you notice many improvements in the islands?'

'Sorra a difference; only this, that when I left there was only one slated roof, and that was on the church; when I returned there were two, the school-house having been slated.'

'And how did they seem, those islands — very small after America — very small?'

'Very small indeed, Father Oliver.'

'But how did they strike you?'

Scanlan looked vaguely at the priest, not knowing how to answer.

'Your friends, many of them had left the islands . . . and some were dead?'

'My father and mother were both dead.'

'And whom did you meet first?'

'A man I used to know when I was a boy; he was waiting on the quay for his wife, who had come over in the boat with myself, and he said, "Ah, then, it's you, Pat, that's looking as well as ever. America seems to have agreed with you; but you're looking no stouter." And so we fell to talking, he telling me of his wife and childers, I telling him how I had lost a heap of money.'

'And how did you spend the time? You went fishing.'

'One day we did, your reverence.'

'There must be a good deal of sadness in coming home after years. I can imagine what it would be like. . . . I dare say you didn't know which you were, glad or sorry.'

'Faith, that's the truth; for you see, Father Oliver, I was that used to travelling, and after the first few days I began to feel . . . cramped.'

'As you might on the deck of a vessel, the sea always round you.'

'It was just like that, your reverence.'

Father Oliver piled Scanlan's plate up with cod-fish, and listened to the Leaguer's tale: how one day he was on the quay watching a hooker going out; and not having anything particular to do that afternoon, he had gone to Galway in her. It was that day in Galway that he had heard for the first time of the League; and native speakers being wanted, he had offered himself. But it was difficult to get him to tell even this much of his story, and what he did tell he told so uninterestingly that Father Connellan began to grow impatient. He broke in at last:

'Mr. Scanlan is going to hold a meeting in my parish. That I'm going to support him goes without saying; but here among ourselves, frankly, I should like to be told what difference it will make to the people of this country——'

'Whether the people speak English or Irish?'

'My dear Maloney, don't interrupt. I was going to ask — perhaps you'll be able to answer the question — I've been told that the Irish will be able to produce a literature as soon as they get back their language.'

'And to be sure they will; why shouldn't they? Aren't they the sharpest witted people in the world?' said Maloney.

Connellan smiled contemptuously.

'I was going to say — well, we've heard a good deal about the dull-witted Saxon and the quick-witted Irish; I wasn't thinking of raising that question — I was going to say, since it's not proposed to discard English altogether——'

'Ireland will be a bilingual country.'

'Exactly, Maloney; and what I was going to say was, that I'm not sure that there is an instance of a bilingual nation having produced a literature.'

'Now, isn't there? How do you know that, Connellan?' said Maloney.

'How does one know anything?' retorted Connellan.

Dante's name was mentioned.

'But his Latin writings are not read,' suggested Connellan.

'Faith, I don't agree with you,' said Maloney; and the argument had reached its height when Catherine brought in three fowls. Connellan hoped that as soon as she left the room the subject whether a bilingual nation had ever produced a literature would be resumed. But everybody was so interested in his food that he abandoned hope. It seemed to him that Catherine would never leave off handing round something. Just now it was potatoes, now it was greens; and he watched Scanlan and Maloney, and thought of what they had already eaten: their share of the cod-fish, four large chops, and now they were holding out their plates and receiving wings and legs. The fowls were followed by a pie made of rice and eggs, and when it was finished Catherine brought in a dish of stewed apples and custard. There were oranges on the table. Father Maloney and Scanlan began to eat them. The tobacco-jar was passed round; and Connellan made one more attempt to speak on the bilingual question, but he was again interrupted by Catherine coming in with the hot water.

'Now they're thinking of their punch,' he said to himself; and in despair he mixed a stiff tumbler and drank it, leaning back in his chair, a contemptuous smile all the while on his thin lips; for Father Moran wanted to know from Scanlan what the Mexican churches were like. While Scanlan was hesitating, trying to remember what they were like, Father Connellan interjected:

'All the steeples have crosses; and I'm sure Maloney would like to know if you said your prayers in Irish. Now, Maloney, how would you render "There's the rub" if you were translating "Hamlet" into Irish?'

'Connellan, you're asking foolish questions, and I hope I'll never live to see the day that "Hamlet" is translated.'

'And why? You don't deny that "Hamlet" is a work of genius?'

'There are many things in Shakespeare that I wouldn't like my parishioners . . . moreover, we don't want translations.'

'Yet you'd have me agree to evening classes, boys and girls leaving their houses at night, streeling off together, and streeling home together in the dark.'

'It would be better for you if you spent your time learning Irish than listening to gossips.'

'Who says I listen to gossips? If I tell you I know that——'

'The Irish race is a pure race, and it ill becomes you, Connellan, to be libelling your parishioners, and in the presence of the laity, too,' he added, glancing at Scanlan.

'Now, will you two leave off! Faith, you make me think of two old hens pecking at each other,' Father Oliver interjected. 'Mix yourself another tumbler of punch, Connellan, and let us have your opinion on the Munster and Connaught dialects — which do you think the literary idiom?'

His face at that moment was pink all over; everything seemed to stand still, for Connellan's views regarding evening classes might bring in Rose's name. . . . His interruption, however, had come just in time: the danger seemed to have passed by; and that it might not return he was at pains to press the literary value of Munster Irish upon Father Maloney, who resented the suggestion. When all that could be said had been said, he leaned across the table pretending an interest he did not feel in Father Conellan's point that hitherto no bilingual country had produced a literature. Again Maloney fell back upon Dante. Italy was then a bilingual country.

'Moreover, the man who holds the pen is not always the original author. Now, tell us, Scanlan, do you know who wrote the folk-songs of your little island?'

Scanlan could not tell who had written the songs he had heard in boyhood. And Father Maloney's desire to attribute the best pieces to a certain fiddler in the eighteenth century amused Father Connellan. Maloney talked rapidly, and his interest in the question was so great that he let his cigar go out. Connellan twiddled his watch-chain; and his neat clothes and scrupulous cleanliness put the thought suddenly into Father Oliver's head that he was but a society priest who would sooner or later find his way to London, added to which Connellan's hysterical laugh jarred. He turned to Father Moran and began to speak to him of the roofing of Kilronan Abbey, feeling that it was wrong to put him in the way of temptation. Everybody was drinking punch; and if he were to stretch out his arm for the decanter, nothing could be done to stop him; so, despite Connellan's laughter and Moran's taciturnity, Father Oliver talked on, feeling every moment that he was coming to the end of his talk. It came to an end suddenly. It was impossible to say another word, so insistent was Connellan's voice; and Father Oliver had to listen, though by doing so he was perhaps abandoning Moran to his fate.

'Didn't you say at the League meeting that was held in your parish that you had read Greek literature, Latin literature, and German literature, and that there was no finer literature than Irish?'

'Well, I did, or something like that.'

'Now, Maloney, don't mind Mr. Scanlan; do you pay attention

to my questions. Didn't you say that the Irish language was to every Irishman a priceless possession?'

'I did — next to his holy religion.'

'Well, Maloney, if you put our holy religion above the Irish language, how is it that you reconcile your conscience to the evening classes?'

'Heaven help us! they've got back to that,' Father Oliver said to himself.

'You're libelling——'

'Never mind my parishioners; there's always danger when young men and women get together, streeling home along the roads after nightfall.'

'There's no streeling.'

'Never mind the streeling. There's danger; you'll not deny that.'

'The Irish race is a pure race.'

'The Irish speakers especially?'

'Certainly. You're not going to start libelling them?'

'Don't mind that; answer my questions. And those who want to learn Irish are to be trusted?'

'Certainly.'

'The Irish language is in itself a moral language?'

'I'd be sorry to say it wasn't.'

'And if the English were to learn Irish, they'd be as moral as the Irish? Do you hear that, Gogarty? Now, isn't it a pity that you didn't have Irish taught in your school? . . . What was her name?'

'Rose Leicester.'

'Now, if she had known Irish——'

'She couldn't have known Irish, Maloney. Doesn't her name tell you that she was of English extraction. By-the-way, Gogarty, you had to speak about her from the altar, hadn't you? I never heard the story fully. She refused to give you up the name — wasn't that it?'

'She did, and she did right, if the man—— But what's the good in talking of these things? But since her name is mentioned, I take this opportunity of saying that I've come to think differently of our responsibilities.'

'Have you had any news of her? Has any harm——'

'No, Maloney; no harm came to her, thanks to the intervention of Michael O'Grady, an Irish priest like ourselves. I'll read you the letter he wrote me;' and, going to his desk, he took out Father O'Grady's letter and read it aloud. 'I suffered a great deal in my conscience during the months in which I was in ignorance of Rose Leicester's fate. At every moment some awful thought was beside me. I assure you it was a great relief to receive that letter.'

'It was a false conscience you were suffering from, Gogarty, and I say you acted quite rightly. But some do be saying that you acted hardly with her. That was Connellan's view at the time.'

'And now it is Gogarty's own view,' Connellan chuckled.

'But does that mean it's the right one? Who was it that put that idea into his head? An Irish priest on the London mission? I'd as soon he got it from an Englishman. There's nothing I think less of than an Irishman with a bit of English polish upon him, particularly a priest — their fine accent with the Irish coming through it all the while, tearing it asunder. Your friend and adviser, Father O'Grady, has been there over forty years. How much of the Irishman is left in him by this time? Only enough for him to think that he can teach us our business. What does he know at this time of day about Ireland? I say, Gogarty, that his letter is an insult, a calumny.'

'Not a calumny, Maloney, for the facts are not disputed.'

'Yes, they are disputed, for I deny that the prostitutes in his parish are girls we have driven out of Ireland.'

'You may deny that he speaks the truth, Maloney, but it doesn't prove it's a lie. You don't know, and he does; and if what he says is true——'

'No, Gogarty, you won't stop me. I'll have my say out, and it is that the Irish priest who goes to London had better stop there.'

'Father O'Grady doesn't propose to come back.'

'So much the better. Let them mind their own business. That's what annoys me, their superior tone.'

'But you don't maintain that the Irish priest who leaves the country ceases at once to understand——'

'Yes, I *do*, Connellan, and I know them well. I've had to do with them — their literary airs and graces.'

'You don't believe in any progress, then, Maloney? You would leave the people as they are?'

'The people have the catechism and the rosary and the Irish language, which they'll have to learn, and they'll get more out of it than reading heretical literature; English literature is full of heresy. Those are my views; they don't seem enlightened to our friend here, Father Connellan. I am sorry, however, that you, Gogarty——'

'I won't deny there's some truth in what you say; there's truth in everything——'

'No, Gogarty, there's not truth in everything. Those who go to London come back with that idea. That would be Rose Leicester's view if she came back.'

Father Gogarty told how, wishing to make amends for the wrong he had done Rose Leicester, he had driven over to see the reverend mother.

At this Maloney's great square shoulders went up — up; they seemed to go to his very ears.

'I know your sister, Gogarty, and you say that she didn't believe much in the return of the prodigal?'

'Nor does my sister believe in the revival of the Irish language. She won't have it taught in her school. Even Elizabeth isn't perfect.'

'Nuns are never æsthetic.'

The phrase came strangely from Father Maloney, and everybody laughed.

'Now, what is that word in Irish?' asked Scanlan.

'The Irish have no word for it. Maloney, you must have learned that word from one of the London Irish priests.'

'Do you know, I think you're right. I think I did!' Maloney's ingenuousness amused everybody; Father Oliver hated Connellan's irritating laugh, and remembered how he had shrunk from the thought of a month's holiday on the Continent, feeling that if he went to France he would not come back the same man, unable, perhaps, to take up his work in Ireland again. But all this might be illusion, and very likely was; for why should he be different from all the other priests? Father Maloney would come back from France the same man that went there, convinced that Irish literature was the finest, and that Tuam Cathedral was in its way as good as another; if its stained glass seemed inferior, its inferiority was atoned for by the devotion of the congregation, which, after all, was the main thing in a cathedral.

'My dear Gogarty, the matter is not so simple as you seem to think. Rose Leicester——'

'Nothing is simple, Connellan; that's the worst of it. . . . We've been sitting here long enough. Would you like to come into the garden?'

Everybody said he would. Father Oliver suspected that his guests would have liked better to remain in the dining-room smoking and drinking or playing cards.

'Oh yes, Gogarty; we should like to see your flowers,' said Connellan; and, taking Gogarty's arm, he whispered: 'An excellent man, Maloney — a survival of the fifteenth century. But he was mistaken when he said that I had ventured to criticise your conduct. What I did say was that the practice of denouncing women from the altar——'

'I didn't denounce her.'

'I am sure you didn't, Gogarty, only—— Ah! here he is;' and, taking no interest whatever in the flowers, Father Maloney began to argue that the Irish race must develop along its own lines, through the language, taking up the Irish thread at the twelfth century. It was there the English had broken it. Of course, it would take a long while— perhaps centuries— for Ireland to start fully equipped with its own arts and sciences. 'I was wrong,' Connellan whispered, 'when I said the fifteenth century; I should have said the twelfth.'

Father Oliver didn't answer him, but walked on ahead picking the dead flowers, thinking that he would have given a good deal to have prevented Rose's name from being brought into the conversation. He interrupted Father Connellan's criticisms of Father Maloney, telling him that it was necessary to pick the dead flowers, otherwise the plants would not bloom again, and was glad when this odious little man ceased to follow him round the garden. While he stood lost in admiration of a little flower, 'Jack-in-the-green,' footsteps awoke him from his reverie; his guests had come, saying that it was time for them to go.

Father Connellan and Father Maloney went away on a side-car, Scanlan and Father Moran on their bicycles; and their departure he felt to be a great relief. . . . He stopped to think if it were so, and then returned to his garden. But, wearying very soon of weeding it, he stood watching the evening sky.

APPENDIX C

The following two poems, 'King and Hermit' and 'The Monk and His Pet Cat' are full translations by Kuno Meyer of the poems referred to in the text of *The Lake* on pages 94—96. To judge by Moore's account of his friendship with the Gaelic scholar which he gives in *Salve*, Chapter XIV, Meyer was in the habit of reading aloud to the novelist his translations of unusual Irish poems. As can be seen by comparing these, Meyer's published translations of the poems, with the versions Moore incorporates into his text, Moore had no scruples about plagiarising his friend's work and not ascribing his source. Minor changes have been made by Moore to achieve a more felicitous phrasing occasionally but that Meyer provided Moore with his material for this passage in the novel cannot be doubted.

KING AND HERMIT

Marvan, brother of King Gooary of Connaught in the seventh century, had renounced the life of a warrior-prince for that of a hermit. The king endeavoured to persuade his brother to return to his court, when the following colloquy took place between them.

GOOARY

Why hermit Marvan, sleepest thou not
Upon a feather quilt?
Why rather sleepest thou abroad
Upon a pitchpine floor?

MARVAN

I have a shieling in the wood,
None knows it save my God:
An ash-tree on the hither side, a hazel-bush beyond,
A huge old tree encompasses it.

Two heath-clad doorposts for support,
And a lintel of honeysuckle:
The forest around its narrowness sheds
Its mast upon fat swine.

The size of my shieling tiny, not too tiny,
Many are its familiar paths:
From its gable a sweet strain sings
A she-bird in her cloak of the ousel's hue.

The stags of Oakridge leap
Into the river of clear banks:
Thence red Roiny can be seen,
Glorious Muckraw and Moinmoy.[1]

A hiding mane of green-barked yew
Supports the sky:
Beautiful spot! the large green of an oak
Fronting the storm.

A tree of apples — great its bounty!
Like a hostel, vast!
A pretty bush, thick as a fist, of tiny hazel-nuts,
A green mass of branches.

A choice pure spring and princely water
To drink:
There spring watercresses, yew-berries,
Ivy-bushes thick as a man.

Around it tame swine lie down,
Goats, pigs,

[1] Names of well-known plains.

Wild swine, grazing deer,
A badger's brood.

A peaceful troop, a heavy host of denizens of the soil,
A-trysting at my house:
To meet them foxes come,
How delightful!

Fairest princes come to my house,
A ready gathering:
Pure water, perennial bushes,
Salmon, trout.

A bush of rowan, black sloes,
Dusky blackthorns,
Plenty of food, acorns, pure berries,
Bare flags.

A clutch of eggs, honey, delicious mast,
God has sent it:
Sweet apples, red whortleberries,
And blaeberries.

Ale with herbs, a dish of strawberries
Of good taste and colour,
Haws, berries of the juniper,
Sloes, nuts.

A cup with mead of hazel-nut, blue-bells,
Quick-growing rushes,
Dun oaklets, manes of briar,
Goodly sweet tangle.

When brilliant summer-time spreads its coloured mantle,
Sweet-tasting fragrance!
Pignuts, wild marjoram, green leeks,
Verdant pureness!

The music of the bright red-breasted men,
A lovely movement!

The strain of the thrush, familiar cuckoos
Above my house.

Swarms of bees and chafers, the little musicians of the world,
A gentle chorus:
Wild geese and ducks, shortly before summer's end,
The music of the dark torrent.

An active songster, a lively wren
From the hazel-bough,
Beautiful hooded birds, woodpeckers,
A vast multitude!

Fair white birds come, herons, seagulls,
The cuckoo sings between—
No mournful music! dun heathpoults
Out of the russet heather.

The lowing of heifers in summer,
Brightest of seasons!
Not bitter, toilsome over the fertile plain,
Delightful, smooth!

The voice of the wind against the branchy wood
Upon the deep-blue sky:
Falls of the river, the note of the swan,
Delicious music!

The bravest band make cheer to me,
Who have not been hired:
In the eyes of Christ the ever-young I am no worse off
Than thou art.

Though thou rejoicest in thy own pleasures,
Greater than any wealth;
I am grateful for what is given me
From my good Christ.

Without an hour of fighting, without the din of strife
In my house,

Grateful to the Prince who giveth every good
To me in my shieling.

GOOARY

I would give my glorious kingship
With the share of my father's heritage—
To the hour of my death I would forfeit it
To be in thy company, my Marvan.

THE MONK AND HIS PET CAT

I and my white Pangur
Have each his special art:
His mind is set on hunting mice,
Mine is upon my special craft.

I love to rest — better than any fame!—
With close study at my little book;
White Pangur does not envy me:
He loves his childish play.

When in our house we two are all alone—
A tale without tedium!
We have — sport never-ending!
Something to exercise our wit.

At times by feats of derring-do
A mouse sticks in his net,
While into my net there drops
A difficult problem of hard meaning.

He points his full shining eye
Against the fence of the wall:
I point my clear though feeble eye
Against the keenness of science.

He rejoices with quick leaps
When in his sharp claw sticks a mouse:

I too rejoice when I have grasped
A problem difficult and dearly loved.

Though we are thus at all times,
Neither hinders the other,
Each of us pleased with his own art
Amuses himself alone.

He is a master of the work
Which every day he does:
While I am at my own work
To bring difficulty to clearness.